MEETING

THE BUSINESS: JOURNAL I

Hollie Delaney

authorHOUSE®

AuthorHouse™
1663 Liberty Drive
Bloomington, IN 47403
www.authorhouse.com
Phone: 1-800-839-8640

First published by AuthorHouse   03/28/2011

ISBN: 978-1-4567-4510-3 (e)
ISBN: 978-1-4567-4511-0 (hc)
ISBN: 978-1-4567-4512-7 (sc)

Library of Congress Control Number: 2011902678

Printed in the United States of America

To Nick for all of his patience when the characters would not stop talking.

ACKNOWLEDGEMENTS

A super special thank you to Virginia who was with me from the first chapter. For her encouragement, spectacular support, editing, questions and my first introduction as an 'Author' - I owe you big time.

A serious thank you to Justin who shared his years of writing experience and hard learned lessons with me...repeatedly.

I am forever grateful to Stevie Nicks and Dave Matthews for creating music that let my imagination fly.

PROLOGUE

The Shaman sat cross-legged at the bottom of the gorge. The Aztec stood 1,200 feet above the Shaman, unseen by the Shaman, watching. The Aztec could feel the air moving gently from the heat of the desert to the south, up the gorge, traveling the face of the cliff over his body. It was the end of the longest day of the year by the Aztec's calendar.

As the sun began to touch the western horizon, he watched the Shaman at the bottom of the gorge stand; extend his arms east to west. He watched the small rocks around the Shaman rise from the floor of the gorge, circling the Shaman. The Shaman brightened as the sun continued its western drop.

The Aztec heard a rumbling begin at the mouth of the gorge - solidify to a thunder as it moved closer. The rocks swirling around the Shaman became pieces of light, adding to the Shaman's illumination of the gorge's walls. As the sun dropped further into the horizon, the light sped faster and faster around the Shaman, revealing the drawings on his body as they began to dance. The thunder became louder; the Shaman's light became brighter, circling faster, faster. The drawings on the Shaman's body lifted into the forming vortex; spinning around him in the tunnel of air and light.

The movement of the air increased, swirling up the granite face of the gorge over the bracing Aztec. The roaring became visible to the Aztec as it engulfed the Shaman. In a moment of crashing thunder; in a flash of blinding light; all was still.

The Aztec watching from the top of the gorge expected to see the Shaman dead; crushed against the granite wall of the gorge. The Shaman stood as he had, uninjured; undisturbed; his eyes closed, his arms extended. Amazing, the Aztec thought. The Shaman had swallowed the power.

The Aztec smiled, raised himself up and stepped off the cliff, settling quietly in front of the Shaman. He stared at the Shaman, his arms still stretched east to west, eyes closed, perfectly still. The pictures had returned to the Shaman's skin. This power the Aztec had not seen, even among his own kind. This power he must have. He took the Shaman. Left him dead at the bottom of the gorge.

Chapter 1

Something was different, changed. I felt it when I woke. Not good...
not bad...just different. The feeling had been with me all day. It was with
me as I stood in the cold on the sidewalk in front of my office.

My office is in one of the oldest buildings in a City of about 35,000.
Newport was founded in the early 1600s; a building being old means
something in Newport. Our address is on one of the most desirable
Avenues in the northeast. The Avenue at our end has two narrow lanes.
Parking is allowed on one side until it crosses south to the 'mansions'. Not
McMansions. Mansions built in the 1800's and early 1900's as summer
'cottages' by names like Vanderbilt, Astor and Belmont.

Our end, the north end of the Avenue, northeast side, still has the
rough marble double steps to its buildings. A remaining practicality from
the unpaved, mud, cobblestone, horse and buggy days. The only parking
for our office or any of the businesses on our block is the parallel parking
directly on the Avenue or down one of the narrow residential side streets.
We were always negotiating for a couple of the parking spaces behind the
building that belong to the residential condos above us. The price was
holding things up. The price always does.

The location of my office was intentional. A bit of a requirement for me
to actually put the business in a serious storefront. The location had been
my dream from the beginning – more than 5 years ago. Our business is real
estate. Technically all aspects - or so it says on the incorporation papers.
But all of us prefer small commercial and large residential sales.

I try to work with buyers exclusively. They are my Clients. It is what
I do best. The other Brokers in our office go where they choose. We have
been called a boutique office. Intended as a negative, under the breath

comment. I find the label a complement. We are independent and small. That is also intentional. Keep it small, tight, split commissions fairly. My Brokers get to keep eighty-five percent of their commissions when they Close, sell. The business gets fifteen percent. There are exceptions.

I have six Brokers including myself and our Administrator. She carries a Broker's License but spends her time keeping us alive. A real estate business without an administrator is like an army without logistics - pure chaos. Someone needs to manage all the paper; there is a ton of paper. Someone also needs to know who is doing what to whom. My original business plan, mostly in my head when this started, based the business on a few large transactions a year to cover overhead and as many smaller transactions as came together.

I do not put my Brokers in a do-or-die situation. The business standard for most agencies: sell a million a year or you're out. That type of pressure takes the fun out of the business. If you can't enjoy your work you shouldn't be doing it. If the business runs short, I supplement.

The Plan seems to be working. My Brokers are as happy as brokers ever get. A good year is very welcome. A normal year is always welcome. A slow year is, well, a slow year. I've had them all and been in the business long enough to know they always come and then always go.

Most people don't understand that real estate as a career requires a personality with a kink. Most successful agents play outside the corporate box to be happy. It's a mentality. Most of us have done our time inside and it drove us nuts. So we left. Frankly, I would rather be unemployed than return. Yeah, the corporate world is a steady paycheck. What it costs a good agent in sanity isn't worth it. At least it wasn't for me and apparently it wasn't for the people in my office.

I refer to the agents in my office as Brokers because they are. Each agent has a Broker's License. No Salespersons allowed. The implication of a Broker's License is independence; self-motivation. A broker can walk the agency with license in hand if they choose. Salespersons must always work under a 'Principal Broker'. To even begin the process for a Broker's License the salesman must have held a Salesman's License for a year; take additional classes, additional exams, purchase more extensive, more expensive Errors and Omission's Insurance.

I rarely look at a name on a request to join us if the Broker's License is not confirmed. If I do, it's a courtesy. I don't care if the salesperson has a twenty-year record of consistent multimillion-dollar sales. Infact, I wonder who really earned the money. Odds were that someone in their office held their hand repeatedly.

Would I be interested in the hand holder? No way. They weren't savvy enough to figure out the implications. The business isn't on their resume. That's the other thing I look for; savvy in the business. Savvy doesn't always show up in resume dollars so I have to talk to them. Not my favorite thing. I would rather be talking to a Client, my buyer.

The only person reliably in our office during the week is Mary. Mary Smyth. Yeah, that's her name. A very old friend who is our Administrator and usually the receptionist. Mary does everything that field Brokers hate; the paper. Mary does have some money of her own. Doesn't need a job. How much? I haven't a clue. She has always had money. I've never asked her about it. Mary tries to put her key in the door about 10 am, leaves when she's done. Usually about 4 or 5.

I always make a point of getting to the office on Friday afternoons for a few reasons; to make sure it's still there, that it didn't need me for anything and to talk to Mary. I do use the office at other times during the week and weekends. In, out, meet Clients, make presentations, real estate stuff; but not to discuss brokerage business, at least not for me. That was Fridays, pm. Of course, if we had a "brokerage emergency" I would get a call from Mary and come in, or not. Telephones are great, email even better.

Today was Friday, 2:30. I was on my way into the office. It was the end of February. Still winter. Not busy on the Avenue, not busy in the office. It was just me and Mary. Not odd in the winter. Not odd in the winter with snow on the ground in a "summer" City.

"Hey Mary - anything hot? Anything I need to know". She looked up as soon as she heard the door open, waited for the standard greeting. To Mary it meant I was good, no problems. She smiled, ran her fingers through her thin brown hair pulling it back from her shoulders; pretended to make a ponytail.

"Same old, same old, Vic." Mary's standard response told me we weren't filing for bankruptcy or going to court at the moment. In real estate that is a "very good thing".

Mary stood up, diary in hand, started walking through a single French door to the back rooms. "Coffee? Just made a fresh pot".

"Of course." I followed her through the first, then the second French door. All the doors inside the office were French doors. I liked them. They maximized the sunlight and opened small spaces; kept the cleaning people in business.

3

Behind the first door were three block-glassed offices; one large on the left, two smaller on the right. A center hall to an old school house door, the rear exit. The large office contained two desks separated by a hand painted Japanese screen. Dimming, but not blocking the natural light from the narrow, horizontal window high on the rear wall.

The two smaller offices created a little hall giving access through another French door to the "workroom". The rear little office had the same long window on its back wall.

The workroom, with its high rear windows, was the same size as the office space without the block glass walls. Open space containing all of the equipment we needed to run the business. Our computer stacks, wireless links, printer/fax/scanner, electrical panels, alarm systems, dark oak files and our little kitchen. A working kitchen constructed so that it was hidden behind dark oak cabinets.

Our work/meeting table is a two-hundred year old dining table, acquired at auction, refinished and topped with a piece of glass. The chairs are odd dining room chairs also bought at auction, garage sales or antique stores. Actually, except for the technology in the office, all the common furniture was acquired the same way.

When Mary was finished pouring her coffee she moved to add her raw sugar and real cream while I poured mine adding dry creamer so the coffee would stay hot. We walked through the third French door to the rear of my office.

The two walls surrounding my office were not glass, but as solid and sound-dampening as possible without eating too much space. I wasn't worried about natural light. My front wall was actually an oriel 6"x6" pane window; a fancy, large bay window, original to the building. It provided enough light and let me watch people, one of my hobbies. The access to my office from reception was, you guessed, a French door.

Mary sat in one of the two captain's chairs, my Client chairs, facing my desk. I sat at my desk.

Looking down at the old library table I used as a desk, I appraised the size of the two stacks of papers. The first, on my right, contained checks with notes attached and the Operating Account statement for the week. The second, on my left, was our agency's advertising.

"So nothing new this week?" I started our little meeting.

Mary sipped her coffee. "Not really. A visit from Karen again on Wednesday. Her third visit since the meeting in January."

"Geez, I told her no. Can't she take the hint? I've worked with her on

4

at least a sale a year for the past twenty years. The last was my last with her; one hell of a fight. So bad that I'll bring another Broker in if she appears on the horizon of one of my Clients. Split the commission down the middle. Next time she comes in let me know while she's here. I'll talk to her again." I kept my shit, rats, what an idiot, to myself. "Next".

"You know Victoria, you can't be subtle. Just tell her 'no way in hell'." Mary was not a happy camper on the subject of Karen. "Every deal I see her name on I dread."

"I understand. She costs me money. Next." For me, the subject was closed. Karen was one of those people that loves to gossip, spread rumors and generally disrupt. I was picky. My Brokers knew it. After all, they had a desk in my office. A basic rule: no office business discussed on the street. Yet I knew, no matter what conversation Karen and I finally had, a version of it would be through the community in a few hours. Shit.

"Our people need a serious reminder that license renewal this April requires 24 CEUs. You know you only have 6, right?" Mary did keep track of this stuff.

"Yeah, I know. I'm scheduled to be complete by mid-March. Send a nasty-gram or something to the others."

"You've got to take this seriously. Remember Jack. It took a year for the State to catch up with him. When he was finally asked by the Licensing Board to produce the certificates, he couldn't." Mary knew I remembered Jack. Neither of us could tolerate an agent sidestepping something so simple, yet something that would cost the license.

"I do take it seriously – like I said, nasty-gram. Next."

"The cleaning people are complaining about Mason's office again. Too many files and papers on the floor. They said that it takes too much time to move, clean and replace everything. So, we'll have to pay for it if it continues." Mary had spoken to Mason more that once to bring the issue to me. She finished her coffee, didn't refill. We were coming to the end of our meeting. Yes, Mary knew what my response would be, but I needed to say it. Assumption wasn't enough when it came to our Brokers.

Mary and I have had an off-again, on-again friendship for almost 40 years. Off meaning that she would just hop a plane and disappear for a couple of years. I would get a post card, or not. Then she would reappear and we would take up where we left off. So I guess it was friendship for about 40 years. I can't ever remember fighting with her. She is the only person I could share living space with – girls or boys. I've had my share of both. Mary was the best.

I smiled at her. "Let me see, bitch at Mason or pay the cleaning people a reasonable increase. What do you think? Ask how much of an increase they want. If it's reasonable, go ahead. I would rather have Mason thinking about the next deal than cleaning up his space. He is who he is." That was true.

Some of our people I would probably have told to straighten up or pay for the increase themselves. Not Mason. Mason considered life a negotiation. His Clients knew it. Other agents knew it. He knew we knew it. The difference between his friends and clients and the agents he dealt with? Mason's friends and clients were fascinated by him. Other agents didn't know how to deal with him. This made Mason good; very good in the commercial world.

Mary stood. "Well, unless you have anything, that's it. Ads and checks on your desk".

"I'm good. When you leave, let me know." Mary walked out of the office. We were way past niceties, knew each other too well. I wondered if I hadn't offered Mary a piece of the business, or if she hadn't taken it, would she still be here? Probably not. I keep waiting for her to get bored; hop a plane, send me a postcard. Not something I lay awake at night worrying about. Just a reality of life with Mary.

Chapter 2

I refilled my coffee, closed both of my office doors and put the mini-pile of Escrow checks in front of me with their little notes of explanation. At the bottom of the pile was Mary's weekly statement from our other checking account, our Operating Account. It told me what bills had been paid during the past week.

The only checks that I had exclusive signature control over were the Escrow checks. I've seen too many Brokers and agencies go down because of Escrow Account funny business. The Escrow Account, by definition, holds 'opm'; other people's money. It is that simple. Disbursements are well defined by law. That's it. No questions. Why someone thinks they can borrow from the funds, then replace them or not, is totally beyond me. Yes, the amount held in Escrow accounts can get seriously big, hundreds of thousands of dollars. But hey, simply writing the check gives you away. So I don't take a chance and I sleep at night.

The Operating Account is the Brokerage's money. That's the account that pays all the bills, commissions, taxes and general stuff. Mary writes and signs those. She gives me a statement once a week detailing what's been paid and a balance. If we start getting too much "slush", she sweeps it. Puts it in a money market or index account. Liquid investment if we need it. In January we talk about what we can transfer to some higher paying account for the next year – not so liquid. This system works for us. I don't have to do the "accounts". Makes me happy.

When I finished the check signing and glanced over the Operating statement it was time for the fun stuff, the advertising. I went to the second of two old lawyer's bookcases in my office. Bottom shelf, on the right, was a set of crystal wine glasses. Took one and the bottle of Australian Shiraz; returned to my desk.

Mary popped her head into my office. "Ah, getting ready for advertising. I'm leaving. Everything is locked. Don't forget to set the alarm. Call me if you have any questions." She already had her coat, boots, hat on. Mary was bugging out. I smiled at her.

"I sure will. Have a great weekend and say hi to Billy for me" Billy is her long-suffering significant other, about eight years suffering. I didn't think they would ever marry. I was sure that was just fine with her.

Yes, I keep some liquor in my office. No, I'm not a drunk, but I do like a glass of wine when the mood strikes me. At times, it is appropriate to offer more than coffee, tea, water or soda to a Client. I also keep a few good cigars and a good pack of cigarettes in my office. Again, to offer when appropriate. I poured myself a glass of the Shiraz, re-corked the bottle, returned it to its place. Began reviewing the advertising.

The only advertising the business pays for is presentation of our Agency. Individual listing advertising is up to the Brokers themselves. We provide the format and framing because the contents are required by law. I encourage the Brokers to be creative. Every once in a while someone will ask to change the format and framing. Rarely, the answer is yes. More often it is no. Again, not my call.

Rarely, but it has happened, someone is struck by the lightning of creativity and the request is great. I can't argue with inspiration.

I enjoy creating and reviewing the ads for Classical Real Estate. I view them as a presentation of our image and character to the public. Our placement cycle always contains the same ad in all of our print and serves as the face page of our website. About every three months I try to change the ad so that it presents the same message, but from a different direction.

I like to grab attention, make people think. I'm not interested in attracting people that can't think. Thinking takes too long to teach, as does reading. Yes, every once in a while I will use a "big" word. The bookcases contain, among other things, a few thesauruses, Strunk & White, a large book of Synonyms, Antonyms & Prepositions, a French to English/English to French translation, a Famous Last Words edition, a few books of famous quotes. I do have some fun. I could use the internet, and do some times, but there is pleasure in "looking it up". I never know what I will run across.

By the time I was finished with the ads the sun had set; the temperature was probably ten degrees colder than when I arrived. The sidewalk melt from earlier in the day was now frozen. I thought about a change of plans. Thought about going to the library tomorrow or taking the car instead of walking while I put on my coat, gloves and beret which I pulled over my ears. Was still thinking about taking the car when I grabbed my book bag, turned out the last of the lights, set the alarm and stepped out on to the first marble step.

I pulled the solid door firmly closed, locked it. I stepped down the second step, stood on the sidewalk to look at the office front. The two bay windows were subtly lit. I could see that the small rear security light was on. Good. I would always look back when I locked up - a little pleasure, a little satisfaction.

The library is about 3 blocks from the office. Not far to walk, but definitely much colder than when I arrived. The sidewalk's melt was indeed frozen. At least the wind was nonexistent. The streetlights on the Avenue are reproduction gaslights. The traffic was gone. I was the only one walking. If I slid on the ice the chance of being seen was minimal. The other businesses on the Avenue were closed for the evening adding only their front window lights to the low display of gaslight.

Ten minutes later I was walking up the steps to the oldest surviving lending library in the country. Although always open to the public, Redwood has never been 'free'. It is a 'membership' library. The library is supported by Proprietors who own shares, pay an annual assessment and Subscribers who pay membership fees.

When I walked in, even though the library directors had recently completed a massive structural restoration, the smell of the stacks remained. To utilize the library one must be a member. Not outrageously expensive but not cheap either if a person is living hand to mouth. The services provided to members are rather unique in this day and age. I can pick up a phone, give the librarian my name and ask them to research a word, a narrow topic or the correct format for an address. They'll hunt up the answer and call back.

The historical book collection, periodicals and newspapers relative to our area are originals, as are the maps, diaries and the paintings on the walls. Many dating to the 1600s, some earlier. Little pleasures. The library does maintain relatively current fiction and nonfiction books, periodicals and local area newspapers as well as a separate children's section, but that isn't why I visit. I visit for the wonderful world-wide selection of periodicals, newspapers and sometimes to research an old house. Unfortunately, I'm not multilingual. But I love to flip through the international fashion publications, out-of-country newspapers and of course, the quiet.

The quiet is the way I remember libraries. No talking above a whisper and if that whisper was too loud, you would be reprimanded; second loud whisper and you were escorted out of the building; no horsing around or walking loudly or you were out. Sometimes a library card would be pulled, children's parents notified. Until a few years ago all I had access to were public libraries.

I still use the public libraries to get my hands on current books for a look-see but I order them through the State computer system. Go in to pick them up as fast as I can. I rarely stay long in a public library. I don't quite know when it happened, but our area public libraries are full of kids horsing around, girls giggling on cell phones, boys playing macho and children out of control.

After a quick smile to the head librarian I moved to the periodical section which, conveniently, is located in the major reading area of the library. Furnished with a long wooden reading table that would accommodate 30 easily for dinner, my measurement factor. In the library the table provided enough room to spread many newspapers. Located strategically in this reading area were smaller groupings of old, worn leather barrel chairs whose leather was so soft it curved around your back and lower as if it was specifically made for your body. I picked out one of my favorite magazines, moved to the only empty grouping left in the area.

I always found it interesting that this area was populated, on Friday evenings, by well dressed older men. I was the only woman. That was another reason I enjoyed Friday evenings at the library. The men didn't notice that I had walked in and sat down. This was fine with me as I prefer to view and not be viewed. They were so wrapped up in their reading or discussions so quiet I couldn't hear a murmur that, when I took off my coat, I could have been without clothing. They wouldn't have looked up.

I was comfortable. Magazine open on my lap. I relaxed and started gazing around the area. In the grouping to my right was an older gentleman wearing a suit, very obviously not off the rack, grey pinstripe, classic white shirt and very dark grey silk tie, Windsor knot and pocket square. He was probably in his mid to late seventies with a full head of white hair, reading Pravda very comfortably in Russian (not the English translation). Interesting. Bet he has a history. Maybe retired CIA. Our little City is populated. I smiled to myself.

Across from me, across the large reading table were a couple of gentlemen. Early sixties, one in a well fitting blue suit with appropriate shirt and tie speaking to another wearing a dark brown sport coat over a beautifully loose knit, high neck fisherman's sweater, dark brown slacks and very high buffed loafers that reflected light the way he had his legs crossed. Sweater guy was the only non-suit-wearing man in the reading area. Very nice, maybe an independent soul, nah, but I bet they were a couple.

As I continued my inventory I noted that there were seven other men in the area; all dressed in various expensive suits, mid-sixties to early eighties, sitting in twos but not talking. Only one chair grouping remained empty. One of the interesting characteristics of Friday evenings in the reading area – no eye contact. Maybe an unwritten rule. If you didn't enter this area with the person you didn't engage either in pleasantries or greeting.

I knew some of these men were acquainted but this space was not intended to be, nor was it used as a social club. That was across the street, ironically called "The Reading Room". Again, the oldest private men's club in the country. Most of these men probably belonged, maybe even the sweater couple. Even "The Reading Room" may have moved into last century. I did know that women were still not allowed to join. Privately funded, well established, exclusive membership, no government control.

As I was flipping through my second magazine I could hear the soft rustling of men leaving and others taking their place; some moving to the large table opening newspapers, lifting chairs to the table, all the general quiet movement of Friday evening at the Library. I always moved my eyes carefully up from the publication's pictures to view the new entries and see who was leaving. Most were familiar Friday night regulars.

When I finished the fourth magazine I realized I was getting hungry, should probably call it a night before the Library closed. I had been embarrassed the few times I received the tap on the shoulder from the librarian informing me that the library would close as soon as I left. Yeah, I had been the only visitor in the building.

I stood, put on my beret, coat, gloves; picked up my bag, took my keys out. I glanced around the grouping one last time when I noticed a man looking at me; not looking down when I noticed. Shame on him. When did he come in? This I should have noticed.

Odd, he seemed to be in his early forties, way too young for the classic Friday evening readers. Knowing I'd seen him, he still didn't look back to the newspaper open on his lap. Very sharp features. Thin, hollow cheeks. Coal black eyes. Reflective black hair pulled back into a pony tail?

Sitting here on Friday night? He looked familiar. Did I know him from somewhere? Nothing came to mind.

He was well dressed but still wearing a dark grey wool coat over a suit. Too warm for the library. I turned, walked out, keys in my fingers as always. When had he come in? I didn't see him. I would have liked to have noticed him earlier, before he looked at me. You can't stare at someone in the library in the Friday night reading area. Hadn't anyone told him 'the rules'? I'd used a practiced eye glance, no body movement, never head movement. Shame on him.

I almost slipped on a hard-frozen puddle on the granite library stairs to the sidewalk. The potential pratfall brought my concentration back to getting to my car without the incident. I squeezed the keys in my fingers, didn't hear anyone leaving the library behind me. But my internal alerts were up. Not panic up, just more aware than normal. Reaching my car would be another ten minutes. This late in the evening the cold was serious.

As I turned the corner of the street to my car I took the opportunity to look around the area. All was quiet. No cars, no people. A normal February evening.

Once I was in the car I locked the doors, started the engine, kicked the heat up. All was well. Wow I was paranoid. Probably too hungry, it had been a long day. Oh well. I rarely spooked in this section of the City or, frankly, any section of the Island containing our little City; but every once in a while the alarms in my head do go off for no reason. Oh wait. I did have a reason. The guy in the library. That felt better.

By the time I reached home, all of about fifteen minutes, I had decided to do soup for dinner and maybe some crackers. Home is a condominium overlooking Sachuest Beach in the little town in the middle of the Island aptly named Middletown. The City, Newport, is on the southern end of the Island and there is another town, Portsmouth, on the north end. The length of the island is about 18 miles, running north to south in a beautiful bay, Narragansett Bay known internationally for sailing, boating and its natural beauty. Oh, and a small pocket of seasonal wealth in a struggling state.

The lights around my condo are motion sensitive and lit the area as I walked to my front door. When I walked through the front door, the lights in the entry went on as did a few lights scattered around the first and only floor of my unit. I punched in the security code to my system. The exterior lights went out. Kind of a neat system. It was installed when I asked the security people if there was a way I could have my exterior lights go on when I drove up and stay on until I punched in my code and oh, by the way, could some of the lights in the condo go on when the exterior went out? I figured they could get it to sing if I was willing to pay for it. The installation guys had laughed; told me it was no problem, more people should ask for it. My request would cost about another $150. Well, I almost dropped my teeth. Of course I told them to 'please go ahead' and left the room so I could really smile big. I wondered how much it would cost to make it cook dinner.

I hung up my coat in the entry closet, went to my dressing room and put on my "evening clothes"; sweatpants, tee shirt and sweatshirt. My little joke. The dressing room was actually a huge walk-in closet with a door connecting it to my bedroom on one side, a door to the bathroom on the other. The official floor plans called it the master bedroom suite. Creating the dressing room was a must.

I glanced at the hard-line telephone to check messages; none. Very few people have my home number. I give out my business number which is also my cell number so I can 'turn business off'. You would be surprised how many people will call at 11pm wanting to ask about a property or arrange a meeting for 7am the next morning. Not something I do as a matter of business. Of course, overseas Clients are the exception, but I'm usually expecting the call and they can't get here that fast.

When I first started in the business I was at my Clients and customers beck and call. I gave "tours" of the Island repeatedly, bought lunches, dinners and drinks, wrote contracts at midnight and talked on the phone until I had to have it removed from my ear. Not now.

About ten years into the business of real estate a friend of mine, not in real estate, was on an airplane and the guy (definitely not gentleman) sitting next to her told her he had a dinner meeting with a lady that was picking him up at their destination airport. My friend asked him how many times he had traveled to Tucumcari, New Mexico. He said he'd never been there but had called a real estate agent, talked for a few minutes and asked to see a couple of houses when he arrived. She volunteered to pick him up, show him the area and take him to dinner. He accepted her offer. My friend then asked if he was planning to move to Tucumcari. He said no; but he'd get a free tour, meal, see some nice houses and maybe get 'lucky'. He then volunteered the fact that when he travels he'd walk into a real estate office at noon or before 5, chat a bit and more often than not ended up with a free meal. She was laughing as she told me the story. I never forgot it; never will.

Chapter 3

Saturday turned out to be a nasty, snowy, rainy, stormy day. The view from my condo's library/office, on the official floor plan the second bedroom, was wonderful. Waves crashing on the beach and the rocks in front of the windows with a background roar. I love watching the water action, in the summer, the people action. I never thought I would be able to afford a location like this, but jumped in the last serious property slump when the Owner, a widower, called to list the condo with us. I made an outrageously low bid, closed on his schedule, didn't ask for inspections (my personal risk) and the office forfeited its fee. Since we didn't have to spend any time on it - bingo. He moved, we Closed, I moved in the largest snowfall of the season.

"Sea Bluff", the condominium development I live in, was built in the last decade of the 1800s as a summer residence for a family tired of living in the middle of the social scene on the south end of Bellevue Avenue in Newport. At the time Sea Bluff was built the area around it was wild, undeveloped…isolated from the city. The house itself is a shingle style construction, technically five levels, faces east, overlooking, in my opinion, the most beautiful beach and bay on the Island. Standing on my patio I look directly across the bay, over Sachuest Point to Little Compton Point on the mainland. To the north is a white sand beach and a wildlife sanctuary; to the south, the Atlantic Ocean.

I was checking my real estate email when I noticed one from some Clients I hadn't heard from in many years. Williem worked for the German delegation of the UN, managing the medical logistics section of Emergency Support. Sybille, Williem's wife, was an artist. They loved Newport, had bought some land with the intention of retiring here and building their dream house. They owned the land for about three years, found that their plan wasn't going to work so they sold it, went back to Germany and retired. I had loved working with Williem and Sybille. I was sorry to see them leave.

The email started out with the standard greetings, then said that they had told a gentleman about their experience in Newport while attending a recent cocktail party; had given him my name and the name of the Brokerage. The email made it very clear that he wasn't a friend, they had met him that night, infact couldn't remember his last name, first name was James, nor did they know where his money came from. They did remember that he seemed to have some. They were sorry about the odd referral. If I wanted to ignore any inquiries he might make, not to worry.

I responded with the standard I'm fine etc., told them I hadn't heard from him but could they describe him. Their response was a little weird. The party had been a great party and my old Clients seemed to be embarrassed that after talking about the party, neither could remember very much. What they did remember were more impressions than detail or visuals. He was about Williem's size (that would make him about 6') but not as heavy. Williem probably weighted 200-210, not fat, more athletic and for 62 years of age the last time I saw him, he was a handsome sturdy German. He was probably pushing 70 now.

Unfortunately, the back and forth emails brought me to the library the night before for absolutely no reason. I started to get a little utsy about my internal connection of the events, then realized that business comes through the office door, business call, email or a social event. Even with a referral, which I always love, the business contact is pretty direct. I sat back, looking out the windows and remembered how attractive the library guy was, how well dressed and oh yeah, how rude.

I finished my email, paid my personal bills online and decided I could go a few more days without grocery shopping, something I seriously disliked. This weekend screamed for music, movies, good books and a blanket. By Monday everything would be shoveled out, including my car, a perk of the condo. And that's what I did. I enjoyed a quiet weekend. A rare thing ten months of the year, but January and February, yeah. By August I will be praying for two days back to back of quiet and planning a midweek R&R getaway. This I always planned for the middle of September to retain my sanity to January. By mid March I will be bored to tears. I used to fight the cycle but that's the business. Accept what it is, organize for minimal burn out and don't fight the flow.

Monday morning was beautiful and frozen solid. The weekend had proved itself interesting, and cozy - good call. Snow for a few hours, drizzle, freeze hard, then more snow. Monday morning started out at 19 degrees with bright sun and winter-clear blue skies. The only thing not frozen was the ocean, although there were frozen layers of foam on the beach and rocks. The news said about a foot of snow. Serious woolies and flat snow boots with treads today. The magazines always showcase the latest boot styles for winter fashion and it is to laugh. You try wearing 3 inch spike heals and thin leather soles in this weather. I will make a serious investment in what I consider snow boots.

By the time I had motivated myself to dress and go out, very, very late morning, everything on the car and in the driveway was gone. I mean literally shoveled and hauled away. Good snow "removal". Good condo association. Wish I could say the same for the roads which always had an inch of hard packed, sanded snow, slush and ice. Drive it enough and it isn't a problem. Street parking in the City was; where else were the plows going to push the snow? I found a little space to park on a side street that had already been plowed. Park on an unplowed street and your car will get plowed in. Got to the office about five minutes before my first appointment for the day.

When the Clients were scheduled to show up I was sitting in my office with half a cup of tea and a newspaper open, waiting for them. I have mastered looking like I had been there for a while.

Mary knocked on the French door to let me know that " Victoria, Bill Goodman is here." I was a little surprised. My appointment had been with Bill and his wife Jenny. I folded the newspaper, stood up extending my hand to Bill. "Good to see you Bill. It has been a while. How's it going? Can I get you something?"

"No I'm good." Bill sat in the Client chair, not all that happy. Actually, Bill's expression ran between angry and sad and angry again. "I guess you were expecting both of us and I thought Jenny would be coming with me. Victoria, I've known you long enough to be blunt, we are splitting up and Jenny is taking the kids to live with her parents in Virginia." Bill adjusted himself in the chair waiting for my response. I think he expected me to be surprised, I wasn't. My daughter had babysat for them while she was in high school. No I wasn't surprised. I was surprised it had lasted this long. "Anyway, I need you to sell the house and find me someplace to live."

"Wow, sorry to hear this. How are the kids doing?" I started making notes to myself while I listened to Bill give me the sordid details and there were many. Pull Goodman file - 10 yrs ago?, deed expanded to common waterfront?. I know it sounds cold, but listening with ears and running lists becomes second nature if you do it enough. By the time he finished, I was ready to ask real estate questions and Bill was bouncing his leg up and down.

" What can I say Bill? You know kids pretty much survive what their parents do. I think it is built into their little systems. So you're staying here, not moving the business to Virginia?"

"As much as I would like to go with the girls, we have exactly what we want here. The new building, after three years of wiring, reconstruction, communication design and installations, is finished. My employees are great. I don't think moving is an option. Besides, Gregory likes the headquarters. You know how hard it was to talk him into Newport." Bill leased real estate. Moving real estate whose space he also leased. When I first met him I thought he had started a packaging, mailing business, like one of those franchises. He had referred to his business as 'bulk shipping'.

What is 'bulk shipping'? Bill's company leases freighters and tankers, then leases their cargo space. Big, big ships, the kind that carry cars, refrigerators, lumber, steel and oil from anywhere to anywhere on the globe. Learning about this business had been fascinating, licensing access into different ports, clearing cargo to be loaded, lots of neat stuff. Bill's partner was a South American and quite the party guy. He was the negotiator; Bill managed everything from the leasing to the ships' captains, which by the way, are also leased; clearing ports and everything else. The only hard assets in his business were the headquarters building and probably some computers even though the business probably moved five hundred million in leased cargo space a year.

"So the house goes and what do you want to live in? Lease or buy? How fast? What's your timeline?" I asked.

"Jenny's leaving the house next week, Wed I think. I want to move as soon as I can, you know, within reason. As far as I'm concerned the house can sit empty. I've bought Jenny out," and Bill produced a Quick Claim Deed in which Jenny had, infact, deeded him the house, "for one dollar and other considerations". Knowing Jenny the "other considerations" would be a sizable chunk of change. "Knew you would need this, oh here are the keys to the house and the security codes. I'll call and let you know when Jenny is gone. Just do what you need to do. Paperwork should go to the office. Just leave it with my secretary. Sometimes I don't even go home now." Bill looked down and crossed his legs.

"As for what I want - a small condo, 3 bedrooms, no maintenance. You know how bad I am with that stuff. Think I might as well buy, market's slow and it is February. Why the hell not". Bill was getting his words out as fast as he could to be done with it. He and Jenny had looked for a year before they found their house. It was one of those situations where both Bill and Jenny had insisted on some big Queen Anne Victorian with a huge porch in Newport. They told me that since they were going to live in Newport, what else could they want. After about eight months of looking, Jenny ran across the plans of the house they had built in New Jersey when they were married. Wow, thoroughly modern, open and airy, lots of windows and very clean lines. Yes it was an "ah ha" moment for more than their needs in this transaction, it was a professional "ah ha" for me. Three days later I called them, told them I was parked in front of a house they needed to see and yes, they bought it.

"Have you made any significant changes to the house? You know, taking down interior walls, adding bathrooms general big stuff." I asked.

"No", he said, " the waterfront land issue is addressed in the deed." I checked to make sure the deed had what I needed. It did - unobstructed right of way to the water.

"Bill, it looks good. I'll drop the listing package to your office, probably tomorrow afternoon with detailed directions. If you have questions, call me. I will leave the start date blank until we know Jenny has moved. I'll also leave some condos that might interest you. Price limits?" I make no assumptions.

"Try to stay under a million. It would be nice to see the water, but I won't die. Minimal neighbors if you can do it, maybe an end unit or a top floor. Stairs will cut down my gym time so don't worry about that. Victoria, do what you do, that's why I'm here." Bill stood up and reached out his hand.

"Thanks Bill. I'll do my best, you know that. Take care". Bill left. He was not a happy camper. As much as I try not to get "involved" with my Clients' personal problems I try to be sensitive to them and if I can, be sympathetic without taking a position. If I don't take this approach I have a tendency to get on the rollercoaster with everyone I see. That takes the fun out of the business. My job - sell the house for as much as I can get and find a condo for Bill to live in. Do both at the same time if possible and not hassle Bill anymore than I had to. That's it.

I closed up my desk, bundled up to go do that which I had put off on Saturday morning, shopping. Said good bye to Mary, left the office. While I was waiting for the car to warm up I noticed someone at the end of the side street I was parked on. He was just standing, perfectly straight, perfectly still, on what probably was sidewalk if it hadn't been covered in shoveled ice and snow. He was looking up the street in my direction. His face without expression. Shit was my first thought. My second thought - not the guy from the library, not just standing in 19 degree weather, that would be very weird. No way. Probably just someone waiting for a ride or a cab.

I put the car in gear and slid onto the street. When my eyes followed the headlights down the street he was gone. Just gone. The street is narrow in the summer, one way with parking on the north side and today shoveled snow. No way some car had come by that I hadn't seen. No way he had walked out of that mess without me noticing. How funny was that?

Chapter 4

As I walked through the grocery store picking out my instant menus that would hopefully last for weeks, the little weird 'standing guy' incident moved to the back of my brain. I don't like making lists to go shopping, I don't like planning to go shopping, but once I'm doing it I usually have fun and usually run a bunch of personal errands that I had also been putting off. I wandered through the store mentally creating parties I'd like to give, reading labels of imports, checking prices and watching other people. When I had finished my grocery list and couldn't think of anything else to look for I stood in line at the checkout.

I used the self-checkout when I had a few things with bar codes. Today I had many things, probably all with bar codes, but too many things to bag in my reusable bags before the very loud 'Please remove your items from the area' warning and red light flashed. The first time that had happened I was in shock, didn't move, figured my credit card had set off the credit police. The second time it happened I just dumped, jammed and squished everything I had into my bags and walked out before a clerk could turn it off. That was when I swore, never more that 6 items in the self-checkout. Since then, I have seen the same thing happen to other people and most just froze like I did. The store should install a grocery belt and bagging table in the area.

I found a line that didn't seem too bad and waited my turn. I don't mind standing in line. I get to read the headlines on the trash magazines, play with the well-contained babies and exchange pleasantries with complete strangers. It's kind of nice and every once in a while I'll run into someone I haven't seen in a while. That's kind of nice too. Chat with built-in limitations.

When I got home I started unloading the car and tried to figure out which storage files would contain the Goodman's files. Although the State says I am required to retain transaction files for 7 years, I have files that go back to my first transaction. I treat the Real Estate Licensing Board like the IRS. The files prior to leasing the office are at my condo; organized by year, then alphabetically by Client. Organized by year of transaction because of the way the State audits file retention. I could receive a letter asking to examine all of my transactions from 1993 through 1996.

Organization of completed transactions in the office is the same way. However, the office could not only get a letter but also a walk-in audit. No time there to get stuff together. The State's interest is in specific forms, so I tell my Brokers to strip their personal notes and keep them at home unless they want some State employee rifling through them. Why keep the personal notes? Incase you end up in court. Your extemporaneous notes could save your license.

By the time everything was unloaded and put away I figured I would start in 2000, recalling it was one of the last transactions completed while I was with another agency. Close. I found the files in 01. Oh well, time not only flies, it's events have a tendency to run together. Everything was there, even a copy of the original floor plans of the house along with multiple pictures of the interior. Reviewing the notes, plans and pictures always reminds me of my life in that time frame. It doesn't matter what file, what time frame, it always takes me back. Not emotionally, just remembering stuff.

I flipped on the computer and checked the clock, after 7. I went to the kitchen, poured myself a glass of wine, went to the dressing room put on my "evening clothes", took my hair down, put it in an easy pony tail low on my neck. Comfy, Bill's work was going to take some time.

When I returned to the computer it had fully loaded. Figured I would check my email before I forgot. Hadn't checked at the office. I opened the email files, did a quick scan and there it was. I didn't even see the return address, all I saw was "subject: James referral from Williem". I scanned the other emails to see if anything was urgent; decided not to open anything and get right to Bill's files. I finished my wine and poured another glass.

First up, find a place for Bill to live. He had prioritized so I went with it. There were a few out there that would do and not be far from his office. Actually one was an end unit and rather modern, three levels including a loft room over a vaulted living room ceiling, a couple of decks, 2 bedrooms on the lower level not underground but open to the condo's swimming pool and tennis courts. The whole unit had a wonderful view of Narragansett Bay. If it didn't remind him too much of his house, it could work. I hadn't thought to ask if he would have a problem with that. Oh well. I printed that condo with its pictures as well as a condo in an old stone house in the middle of the city, no water view, but more room for the girls and closer to his office. Best - it wouldn't remind him of his house. Bill's feedback would tell me where his head was at.

Do I tell him that the garden level north unit, common wall to my south unit was coming on the market? Not going to be my listing. I don't even try to list where I live. It's like, well, shitting where you sleep. I don't like to sell where I live for the same reason. I made a note for myself on the top of the package. I was going to have to sleep on that one.

Bill's listing package took forever. Between all of the forms, my cost analysis estimating how much this listing will cost me to sell; the market analysis for pricing, marketing recommendations, etc. etc. It was midnight by the time I printed out the last page. I do not share my cost to sell analysis with anyone. I find it's nice to know what my projected cost out of pocket will be before a negotiation puts me in a situation that might change my net commission.

There have been times when I have referred a listing to one of my Brokers with a caution that the listing is going to take serious money up front, or without the caution to another agency and retained a referral fee. When I have referred to another agency I have always told the Client that I was overbooked and couldn't do their property justice; give it the time it deserved. I told the other agency essentially the same thing. In a way it was the truth. I wasn't going to invest the time or the money. The Goodman's property I would take. Tomorrow over coffee I would add hand written sticky notes, the greatest invention since the microwave oven, to the pages that needed signatures when I reviewed the packages.

I needed to get something to eat and get my mind off of the business before I would even try to go to sleep, it was 11:30, or maybe some chamomile tea and bed. The email could wait for tomorrow, the world won't end.

I made the tea, did my usual walk around the house making sure my alarm was set. The alarm system wasn't a dire need but I didn't have a dog, lived alone in a condo with easy access from the gardens and a private, rather hidden entrance. The north garden condo was in the same situation but the rest of the units in the house required access through a main entrance that not only had a key lock but also required a combination linked to an alarm to enter. Why should my condo be any different? Frankly, an alarm system probably isn't going to stop someone determined to do you harm or steal your stuff, but it's going to make a lot of noise and that would at least get my attention. Yeah, the police would arrive, but a lot of damage can be done before they did. I would rather explain the body on the floor than be taken away in an ambulance. Has it ever happened to me? No, but I have a tendency to be a 'put the snow shovel and a blanket in the trunk in November so you'll never get stuck' kind of person.

When I lived in a house with a 7' stockade fence surrounding the yard, I had the privilege of watching a guy vault over the fence in one corner and vault out of the yard on the opposite corner with two rather large dogs sitting on the deck. Yes, he was running from the cops. Why? I have not a clue. But if the large mastiff hadn't let out a loud growl, would the guy have run into the house? Don't know. The next day my husband had pounded nails into the top of the stockade fence and clipped off the nail heads.

Chapter 5

I was sitting at the work table in my library the next morning reviewing the package for Bill and adding my sticky notes when my cell phone rang. "Victoria Hamilton here".

"Mrs. Hamilton, good morning," the rather polished deep voice, subtle underlying accent, on the other end replied. There were a few seconds of silence as if he expected me to respond. "My name is Johnathan Keirns. I believe my employer sent an email yesterday about my call."

"Mr. Keirns I did not have time last night to review my emails. What can I do for you?" I turned in my chair and looked out over the beach.

"I would like to make an appointment with you to discuss the purchase of a property for my employer. Could we possibly meet today?"

"Mr. Keirns, I am a little busy today, we could meet tomorrow around 1. In the meantime why don't you tell me what your employer is looking for and in what price range. I could have some sample properties ready for him to review at the meeting". My standard response to what I considered a cold call.

"Mrs. Hamilton one o'clock would be fine. My employer will not be with me tomorrow. I thought he was clear on that in his email." Mr. Keirns sounded a little irritated that I had not read the email. I was sure he hadn't forgotten what I had said.

"Mr. Keirns I haven't read the email. Could you give me his name or email address? I wouldn't want to inadvertently delete it." I always trashed my junk file after a quick glance. Everything from the office account with my name on it is a blind forward to my personal email account and is filtered again. It is possible that it could end up in one or the other account junk folders. I knew it hadn't. I knew exactly which email he was talking about. A little bird was pecking away at my stomach.

"I am sure, Mrs. Hamilton that you will find it. I will see you tomorrow." He hung up. I guess that was the end of the conversation.

I wondered if I had time to check the email as I wandered over to the computer and flipped it on. It was there, along with six new emails. I shouldn't put off reading my mail. Discipline. Discipline.

"Mrs. Hamilton,

Your name was given to me with great enthusiasm by Williem and Sybille Gottfried.

I would like to acquire a modest property in the Newport area. I do not want to exceed $10,000,000. My close friend and lawyer, Johnathan Keirns, will be in touch with you tomorrow to arrange a meeting.

I do understand that you will require a letter of credit which he will carry. I, unfortunately, will not be available to attend. Johnathan bears my complete confidence.

Sincerely,
James Fournier"

Well, that was interesting on so many levels. The email wasn't forwarded from my business account. It was a direct receipt. Where did he get my personal email address? I'm sure Williem didn't have it. Another thing I don't give out. His email address was a "do not reply". I copied it to a new email, wrote a quick non-committal note and sent it from the business account. It came back before I could return to Bill's package. He had provided the minimum amount of information I required when meeting a new Client or rather said it would be supplied at the meeting. He must seriously trust this guy Johnathan.

Being a lawyer doesn't impress me, but then very few things do. The $10,000,000 did impress me, if it wasn't a typo. I couldn't resist. I did a Google search on James Fournier. The only thing that came up was his name and the note 'Bibliophile', book collector. Hard to stay off of the web with that kind of "real" money. I had the feeling my chain was getting pulled. I'd give Williem and Sybille a call this afternoon.

I finished the package, showered and checked the thermometer before I got dressed. Still cold, cold, cold. I did decide to swap my usual black wool coat for my blood red wool, my favorite, acquired at a second hand store. It has a high collar and darted bodice that falls in four bias cut panels to my calves, fully lined. I considered this coat quite a coup for $15.00, very 60s, very vogue. The coat felt great and gave me some mental energy that I could use today. Hadn't slept well.

I stopped at the office to copy the package I was going to drop off at Bill's later in the afternoon. Mary was getting ready to go out when I walked in. "Mary did you give my personal email address to anyone recently?"

"Well hello to you too," Mary responded.

"Sorry, I'll start again. Hi Mary, how are you doing?"

"I'm doing just fine and that's better. Odd question, no I didn't. I value my butt too much to get it kicked. Who got it?" She was grinning now.

"That grin, are you super sure?"

"No I didn't give it to anyone. Hell, for as much as I'm asked for it in this office along with your home phone number I don't give that stuff out. Someone trying to sell you Viagra finally crack the code?"

"No, a potential Client. I'm probably just being paranoid. It's nothing. Where are you off to?" I didn't need to know but subject deflection was one of my talents.

"Lunch, I'm starving. Why don't you come with me? We could lose the afternoon. Ames is coming in to work on some ads. You know Ames, he'll be here all afternoon."

Come to think of it I was starving too. Right, no dinner last night, no lunch, nothing but coffee, tea and wine yesterday. No wonder I felt like crap. "You know Mary it sounds good. Not losing the afternoon, I've got a package to drop off, but lunch sounds great. I'll do my copies and meet you where?"

"Well I'm thinking chowder and Greek salad." Mary and I both knew that meant one place. A rather laid back café on the Square in the center of Newport by the Court House. On a good day we would walk and it would take 10 minutes. Today was a car day, add five to park.

"Get us a table and I'll be right down. Thanks, great idea." I walked back to copy. Now that I realized I hadn't eaten yesterday I was seriously starving. I heard the front door open about a minute after Mary had closed it.

"Victoria, rumor has it that you are actually here." Ames's voice got louder as he walked back to the workroom. "Gosh, I haven't seen you in a few weeks. How's it going?"

"Has it been that long?" I pushed the copy button turning to face him. Ames was truly a delight on the eyes. Yeah, I've got sons older than he is, but I do truly appreciate nature. Always have. Ames was what I would call a "surfer dude" with a suit. Should have probably stayed in California, but I'm glad he didn't. His sandy blonde hair and grape green eyes, not to mention that surfer body, cut a swath through this Island that leaves women and girls in cold showers. When I first saw him a few years ago, he put me in a cold shower. I didn't think he had ever sold a property to a guy, even the guy half of a couple.

"It's probably been longer. I always try to get in on Fridays when you're here but I've lost track lately." He smiled one of those big smiles full of teeth that could sell toothpaste.

"Is everything going ok?" I asked.

"Oh sure. I've been picking up some new Clients lately so I guess that's good and they are buying which is even better. Are you planning to be in this Friday?"

"You know, if it's Friday afternoon, I'm here. What's up?"

"Could I get some time with you? Not a big deal, I just want to chat about some stuff." He was now looking at the floor.

"Can it wait till Friday Ames?"

"Oh yeah, not a disaster or anything, just wanted to bounce some stuff off of you." He was looking at me again, looking at me but not smiling, a little slumped. Even I saw that he had some issues that probably should be addressed now, not in five days.

"Ames, listen. Mary said you were planning to be here most of the afternoon. I have a couple of commitments but I could be back before four. Is that ok with you?"

He looked relieved. He hadn't wanted to wait till Friday. "Sure, that would be great. I'll be here whenever you get back." He started walking to his office space.

"Great, I'll see you then." I picked up my copies, slid them into my bag and put the originals in their envelope.

I was wondering what was on Ames's mind when I stepped down the front steps, looked up. There He was. Library guy standing across the street looking at me. Hands in his coat pocket, coat unbuttoned. At least he had changed clothes to a turtleneck sweater and slacks. In this wind and cold his coat was blowing open. His face was expressionless; a little pale, the black eyes, the black hair. What the heck? He must be freezing.

It was the middle of the day, cars were passing between us. People seemed to be walking around him in the snow but not noticing him. I knew it was the guy I'd seen at the library; the guy at the end of the street and now, middle of the day on probably the coldest day of the year. I was starting to think I had a stalker. Should I tell someone? Who's going to believe me? Nothing's happened. He hadn't spoken to me or attempted contact. I didn't have any proof that it was the same guy.

I felt a rather strong bump while I stood at the bottom of the marble steps. It knocked me a little off balance, not helpful standing on ice.

"Excuse me." Gloved hands reached to steady me. "I'm so sorry. I wasn't looking…" The bumper leaned into my neck, took a long, deep breath. "Very nice perfume." He continued walking. Cold weather makes people as weird as hot weather. I returned my eyes to the space across the street. Library guy was gone. I shook my head, went to my car.

Chapter 6

I walked into the café and Mary had already ordered. There was even a glass of wine for me. If I drank it now on the empty stomach I would be flat on my ass for the rest of the day.

The café from the front doesn't look like much and infact when you walk in the front door it looks like a San Francisco bistro with a large, well stocked bar and a few booths on a rise at the rear. When one walked through a small door about half way down the bar, the space opens up dramatically to a large elliptical bar separating about thirty leather and dark hardwood booths from another twenty tables on the left by the storefront windows. The bar is a fun hangout on the weekends and at the end of the work day. Mary had picked out a booth for us so we could talk.

"Sorry it took me so long to get here. I ran into Ames and he was a little chatty. Thanks for ordering". I slid out of the coat and scarf, hung them on the hooks that separated our booth from the adjoining booth. Slid into my side. "So what's up? Not that anything has to be up for us to grab lunch."

"Hope you wanted the chowder and salad. I figured why else come here for lunch." Mary had started munching without me.

"It's great and you're right." I looked around at the other booths and what I could see of the tables. "Gosh, lawyer pickings are slim, am I that late? Court back in session already?" I pulled out my cell to check the time. "It's 1:45, I guess I am late. So what's up?"

"What can I say? Pickings were lean when I got here." We both laughed. "Hell, I'm going to have to talk to you." Mary munched her salad, took a drink of her wine, continued. "I have a couple of things I was holding

30

to Friday. But since the lawyers are back in court do you mind if we talk about them now?"

"Sure, what's happening? I didn't think lunch was a purely social invitation". Since Mary and I started working together pure social invitations were after hours and she always made it clear the occasion was not business. She kept business, as much as possible, during business hours. I did like that about her. Most people don't separate the two when they should. Going to Mary's for dinner was always relaxing and greatly anticipated on my calendar because somehow, at her parties, no one brought up the business end of real estate. If someone did bring it up, Mary would grab their arm and lead them into another room for a few minutes. When they returned the subject was gone.

I've gone to parties that, when I leave, feel like I've been working all night. I rarely return the invitation and will try to think of excuses not to attend again. There are times when I can't escape. I've tried the 'If you would like to continue this discussion I would be glad to meet you at my office' then hand them a business card approach. It usually produces a chuckle and a continuation of the subject. I then have an attack of TB (tiny bladder).

"Item number one. Vicky, its been almost six weeks since the last office dinner. We need to have one as soon as possible. When everyone is in the office it's starting to get tight. I think this is the longest we've gone without a meeting." Most agencies have a once a week office meeting followed by an office caravan, a tour of all the office's new listings. Having sat through more of these than I can count over the years it was my observation that too much Client information was shared, too much time wasted. Before it was over, the meeting would turn into a bitching session, exaggerated by everyone splitting into cliques to tour the properties.

When I decided to move into a real office and bring in more brokers, I eliminated agent attended weekly meetings. Instead, I take the office out to dinner once a month, no dates or spouses, and everyone chats, relaxes and binds into a functional office. Some find the need to let off some steam, but being in public, it is contained and usually resolved. It seems to work and I think we have fun. As for new listings, the listing broker invites the other brokers to visit the property once. If one of our Brokers can't make it, they can ask the listing broker to piggyback a showing. If not, they miss out. I feel that my Brokers are adults and are treated that way.

"Mary, wow has it been that long? I am so sorry. Of course, how about

Friday evening?" I was embarrassed as well as sorry. I pulled out my little pocket calendar and a pen from my bag. No blackberries for me.

Mary opened her blackberry. "That works for me too. How about the Pearl, back bar".

"You know, it's been so long, try to book us into the dining room and we can take the whole evening if we have to. Oh, and get double tables so we have some room. Maybe we should try scheduling the dinners for the rest of the year and see if that works. You pick the places and the times and we won't have to think about it again." The less I had to remember the better and this is important for the business.

As Mary was tapping Friday into her calendar and I was writing she couldn't let the subject die. "We said that we were going to book a year last year about this time and never did. As I recall you said you wanted to think about it. I guess you've had enough time to think about it?"

"Don't tug my chain, just do it. Next."

"Confess, you completely forgot about it. Shame, Shame. The next item is Ames."

"Yeah. He's waiting at the office for me to come back and talk. What's up?"

"It's his recent string of Clients, Vic. He hasn't said anything to me but I've been watching when he meets them at the office. Don't tell him I said anything, but I do believe that Ames is a little homophobic." Mary smiled. She liked Ames. I think that before Ames came to my office Mary may have had a multi-night stand with him. If anyone knew for sure they weren't talking. My money was on Mary's libido.

I was trying to stifle a good chuckle. "Are you politely telling me that Ames has picked up a string of gay Clients for the first time? With his looks I cannot believe this is the first time it's happened." I was laughing with tears in my eyes. With Mary I could laugh, anyone else and I would have used the TB excuse to calm down.

"You know he's not gay, right?" Mary was serious.

"Yeah, I think I know that. It's just too funny. Sorry."

"Vic, I feel sorry for the guy. Frankly, I don't think he has a clue what to do - either with the Clients or how he feels about being uncomfortable. You realize he's not only attracting guys but gay women too".

I ordered another glass of wine. I was going to have to take this seriously. I drank a half a glass of water before I continued the conversation, and I was still laughing. Ames cannot be this naïve. He's been in this business since he was 20, 13 years. "Mary, I do hope that is what he wants to talk about. He mentioned something about some Clients before I left so it probably is. I realize that you know him better than anyone in the office." Mary looked me in the eyes and the look was not funny, ha ha. "I just got the vibe when we were talking about him coming in, that's all. Anyway, please tell me, is there anything I should have in the back of my head when I talk to him?"

"Vic if I tell you this, it is you and me right? I need your word, seriously." Mary was serious. Her brown eyes were starring at me like she could see my brain working, waiting for it to process what she had just asked.

"Mary, I listen well, I don't talk. Not a word about this or anything else for that matter." I shook my head looking back at her.

"OK. At one point in his life, before he moved here, he played both sides of the fence for an extended period of time. When he decided he did prefer the gentler sex he moved across the country to get away from his friends and start over. I don't think he's thought about it since he moved here and now this." Mary did feel sorry for the guy. It takes a lot of involvement for Mary to deeply feel anything for anyone. I don't think Mary had any major trauma, I think that's just the way she is.

"That explains a lot. Thanks for telling me. I appreciate it and not a word. I promise."

"Well those were my two items. Consider Friday set up and good luck. You're not going back to the office now are you?" She didn't want us to walk in together.

"Errands, I'll be back in a while."

"See you then". Mary put on her coat, put money on the table for lunch and left. I finished my second glass of wine and realized why I never have wine in the middle of the day if I don't have to. I can drink hard liquor without a problem, but wine makes me want to curl up and go to sleep. Don't even mention beer. I sat for a few minutes thinking about what I would say to Ames and then left to drop off Bill's package.

I had not a clue what to say to Ames if that was his problem. I couldn't blow him off. He was an excellent broker and a delight in the office. I wouldn't want to lose him. I wondered if he had a girlfriend. I'm not one to push myself into someone's personal life. As long as they don't end up in jail, in a lawsuit, or it effects the way they do business, my Brokers can do whatever they want on their own time. I think it's an unwritten deal – I don't poke them, they don't poke me.

I pulled into Bill's parking lot, took the last space and pressed the button on the front door to let his office know they had a visitor. The video camera adjusted to find me. A voice from inside asked if she could help me. "Yes, I'm here to drop off some documents for Bill."

"Name please"

"Victoria Hamilton. I believe Bill is expecting the package."

"Oh, hi Victoria. Sure, I'll buzz you in". Immediately, the buzzer went off and I pushed the door open. This business is more secure than the security clearance requirements of the military. I guess it would be a real downer if someone broke in and rescheduled the cargo ships or the leasing space. A nightmare if the cargo manifests were stolen. In a prior incarnation I worked for the US industrial base on the weapons side. Actually, that's why Bill had leased this building. It had been previously occupied by one of the government's contractors and came with high security configurations and vaults. He told me he would have to goose it a bit but that it would be easier than starting from scratch. Yes, I was impressed.

Sally, with her severe navy blue suit, brown hair in a bun and one inch heels met me at the reception desk. Sally managed Bill's office and, as he had said, was the best thing he had found in Newport. I guess she did a good job. "Bill's on one of those conference calls that goes on forever. Do you need to see him?"

"Not at all. I just wanted to get this to him today. Thanks Sally." I handed the package to her and turned to the door.

"Isn't it a shame, what happened. Bill is such a nice, easy going guy." Sally's comment, in almost a whisper, followed me to the door.

"Yes it is." Did she expect me to discuss this? No way. I reached for the door, Sally buzzed me out. As much as I would rather stay and chat with Sally to avoid the office return, the topic was taboo and I had to face Ames. If I took the long way back to the office I could buy maybe 20 minutes - take the long way back at maybe 10 miles an hour and I could stall for 45 minutes. In that time maybe I would have one of those eureka moments. Right.

Ames was sitting in our reception space waiting for me when I walked in and, classically Ames, he made no assumptions. "Do you have time for me now?".

"Of course, Ames, come on in." I opened the French door to my office, took off my coat, beret, gloves, hung them on the old coat tree in the corner. "Take a seat, I'm just going to get some coffee, I'll be right back". Something had better keep me awake, no more wine mid-day if I have serious stuff scheduled. Shame on me.

When I returned he was sitting in the chair Bill had sat in. Giggling his leg as Bill had done. I wondered if there was something about the chair that caused legs to giggle. I'd have to pay more attention to the legs of the people that sat in it. Right, getting distracted. "So what's going on Ames?"

"Victoria, please understand I find talking to you about this is uncomfortable for me, but I do need some advice. For some reason, right now, all of my Clients are gay. A couple of singles and four couples and it's weirding me out. I'm not comfortable introducing them, especially the couples. One of the couples is actually married. Anyway, it's just weird across the board. Other agents showing their listings ask me if they're gay when the Clients walk into another room. I don't know if I can deal with this." He had started his little talk at a normal pace, but by the time he had gotten to the end his voice was monotone and the words came out so fast I had trouble understanding what he was saying.

"I can see that you are not comfortable with this situation Ames. First of all, were they referred to you?" Yes. Ames had a problem on many levels. But the only level I could address was the business. That was all he was discussing.

"Yes. I worked with one guy from Provincetown and he referred the first couple to me and then it kind of cannon balled." Well at least he knew how it started.

"Ames. If this had happened with anyone else, you would be happy as a clam. Serious business coming from one transaction, right? We all hope for this type of situation, right? That's what makes our business. If it were any other minority would you be having this problem?"

"No. You're right about the business side. If it were anyone else I would be more than fine about it." I was wondering at this point if Ames had been stuck in his own little panic. Hadn't thought about it.

"So why are these Clients different?"

"Well. I guess it's stuff like how do I introduce them, especially the married couple? And what do I say when the other agents ask me if they are gay, stuff like that. I know this sounds dumb Victoria." Now Ames was having trouble meeting my eyes and I thought he was starting to shiver.

"Ames, take a deep breath and try to calm down. You've got to take a step back. These are people just like any one else. They are your Clients. Just like any one else. Do you need to get yourself a coke or coffee or something?" I did need to break his rhythm. I hoped he would take the offer.

"Yeah, do you mind? I'll be right back. You sure you've got time for this?" He started to get up.

"Ames, today I've got all the time in the world. Go ahead, take the break. I'll make a few phone calls, ok?" I was glad I didn't have anything else to do this afternoon. In the order of the world this was a mini crisis, but to Ames I think it is a full blown career crisis. I walked out to the reception area and told Mary to leave when she would normally leave. Not to stay because of us. She smiled at me. Gave me a thumbs up. Gosh she was good on the up-take. She also gave me the dinner schedule for the rest of the year. "So this is confirmed?"

Mary grinned. "Now you are committed. I've already circulated it through our email. Oh and thanks". She nodded her head to the workroom. I smiled back.

I did have a couple of calls to make. Nothing important but I didn't want to be a liar. In the middle of the second call Ames came back in, coke in hand, stopped and started to go back out when I waved him in. I ended the call as soon as I could. It was purely social. I would call back tonight. Ames did look a little better.

"So where were we? Oh yeah, I was saying to treat these Clients like any other Clients. As for how to introduce the married couple, how did they sign your Representation Disclosure? Using those names would be a good start, or you could just ask. I know I've had couples come in and frankly I've messed up their names big time. They corrected me and all was well. Now I'll ask if they haven't made it clear to me. Like I said, treat them like you would any other couple. As for the other agents, how would you respond if they asked what your Clients nationality was?"

He was looking at me for a few seconds before he realized I'd asked him a question. "Ah, I would probably ask them if it made any difference. If it did, they would be breaking the nondiscrimination laws. Right?"

"Ames, what do you mean "right"? You have been in this business way to long to ask 'right?' I understand your surprise at realizing you are in this little windfall. What I'm not understanding is why this has shaken you as much as it has. You're now questioning your ability to do business and that is ridiculous. If you weren't such a good broker you wouldn't be in this office. I feel like fopping you on your head." That last little bit may have been too much, but I did want to smack him. Tell him to get a grip. Not good management 101.

"I guess I just took this too personally. Like I was sending out a message or something." Ok, I could deal with that statement. Then he blushed over what was left of his summer tan. Oh shit. This was not the venue for where this conversation was going. Ames, like the rest of my Brokers, wasn't an employee of the business, he was an independent contractor to the business. In the world of the government, personal information is personal information. I was in no position to ask the next, obvious question.

Well, I would just say it. "Ames, you know I can't ask the obvious question. It's none of my business, so if you want to continue you can and it won't leave this room. It's totally your call". There it was, I put it back in his lap.

He looked up, stopped fiddling with the coke bottle and I got the intense grape green eye stare. "Victoria, I considered us very good friends for a few years before I came here. We would have dinner together after work and chat about everything. Other people, other transactions, everything. When one of us needed an escort somewhere or wanted to go bar hopping but didn't want to go alone we'd call each other. Remember?"

I nodded. This was definitely getting odd. Yeah we did that stuff. We had a great deal actually. If one of us got lucky when we were out together, the lucky one would buy the other an odd, off the wall drink. The unlucky one would know they could leave whenever they wanted because they were leaving alone. When we introduced each other to someone it was always, 'this is my cousin Victoria' or '…my cousin Ames'. Of course Ames used the signals more than I did. Most of that time I was married, although to me, it didn't matter. Oh rats. My thoughts were wandering. "Where are you going with this Ames?"

"Vic, when I moved here I had made some decisions in my life and I wanted to start over. I'm not being clear. When I was on the West Coast I was, well, bi…ah…sexual. You know what I mean. I decided that I did like girls better, most of the time, and made a real break. There, it's out. I know how I look. I'm definitely not he-man and most definitely not macho. When I said I played both sides of the fence, I meant I played my side of the fence. It was easy for me because of the way I looked and my manner. I never had to exaggerate anything to get a date, I was just me. Couldn't you tell? I know you never said anything about it, but I just assumed you'd figured it out." He'd called me Vic. We were definitely into serious friend talk.

I'd given him the opening. He took it and ran. "Ames, I never assume anything. I saw women hitting on you constantly. A guy every once in a while. Did it enter my mind? I honestly can't say, Ames. I do not care for macho men. Don't hang with them, don't go out of my way to add them to my friends list. But that's my taste. Are you saying that you think you have these Clients because they think you're gay?"

"Well, yeah." The blush was redder and he smiled a big smile. He was embarrassed. Ames was sweet. But I don't think he had ever struck me as vehemently gay or not gay. I thought he was hot and quite good looking in his 5'11 frame. His clothes fell on that frame perfectly. It didn't matter what he wore, although I preferred his suits, he always looked great. Ames had dark blond hair that seriously streaked in the summer. The streaks were growing out now, but still looked sexy as all get-out when they spilled into his eyes.

"Ames, you did a good job for the first guy and he apparently told everyone he knew about you. Wait a minute, are all of your Clients guys?" Thank you Mary, yet again.

"No" Ames answered. "They're not." And the bell rang. Ames woke up. "Wow. They're not all guys. You're right Vic. How could I be so dumb and push my own hot buttons. Geez. Thanks a lot." He stood up and walked to the rear door of my office. "You know Vic I miss our nights out, talking and stuff. If you don't mind I'll give you a call sometime."

He stood at the door, looked back at me. I guess he wanted an answer. "Sure Ames, give a call. Have a good night." He still had a smile on his face, but no blush. Relieved. He gave me a wave, closed the French door to the workroom behind him. If he called, would I go? Of course. My relationship with Ames was friendship and nothing more. He was another person that could successfully separate boss/broker from friend. Would I have let it go further? The subject never came up so I hadn't though about it, much.

I bundled up to face the cold, told Ames I was leaving and Mary was gone so he had full lock-up duty. I did lock the front door when I went out. If you were in the back of the office you couldn't hear the front door open.

Walking in the door of the condo felt good. It was comforting to set the alarm. My barrier to the outside world. Even clicking on the computer didn't feel like a violation. Yeah, check the email before I totally shut down for the night. No more surprises. I remembered the appointment tomorrow. I hadn't thought about the appointment all afternoon. Maybe there was an email cancelling. I scanned the email, nothing urgent, nothing cancelled. Oh well. Tonight screamed hot bubble bath and so I made tea, put on some music and filled the tub.

Chapter 7

I woke to my nine am alarm. I punched the snooze button and it seemed to immediately go off again. Punched it out, dragged myself up against the pillows trying to wake up. I very rarely sleep to the alarm. I remembered almost falling asleep in the tub, dragging myself out, throwing on a tee shirt and feeling like I wouldn't make it to bed just curl up on the floor and sleep. The next thing was the alarm going off. It took another 20 minutes to focus enough to actually get out of bed. I haven't done that in a long, long time.

I put on my sweat pants, made it to the kitchen and poured myself a cup of coffee from the pot that automatically brewed at 8 in the morning, meaning the coffee had been sitting on the burner for over an hour, almost two. UCK. It would have to do.

I clicked on the computer, wrote an email to Williem to let him know that his referral had shown up and to thank him. I checked for any other new emails that might be urgent - like a cancellation - nothing. Oh well. I was going to meet this Mr. Keirns and play it by ear.

I figured I would wear one of my no bullshit suits, the dark navy blue silk. Inset sleeves, lightly fitted long jacket with a nice rear vent and a 5 bias panel skirt that swirled to mid calf. I rarely wore a blouse under a suit jacket, just a chemise. I liked the feel of the silks moving when I did. Why bunch another layer under an already lined jacket. It messes with the fit. In this weather I would have to wear tights and boots with a little higher stacked heel than normal. If this meeting turned out to be real I was dressed to be serious. If it turned into bullshit, I was dressed to end it very fast. I was not planning on killing time with this one.

I was putting my earrings in when the cell phone ran. I looked at the caller ID. It was Sybille Gottfried, Williem's wife. Gosh she was calling from somewhere in Germany. Is she calling about my email? That was fast, I just sent it.

"Hamilton here".

"Victoria, this is Sybille. I hope I'm not calling too early but saw your email and figured you were up. I trust all is going well?"

"Sybille, hi. I'm fine here. I didn't expect you to call on the email. It was just a thank you".

"Victoria." Sybille took a large breath. "At first I couldn't remember what referral you were talking about. I asked Williem and he couldn't remember. I checked my sent file and there it was so I guess we did. We don't want this to sound strange, but we both remember the party. It was given by some friends we visited for a long weekend in Sweden. But we vaguely remember this man. The email we sent the next day said his name was James so I guess it is. There is more detail in our email to you than either of us remember today. We remember the party, who was there and all of that, but our memory of this man is almost nonexistent. Anyway, we wanted to tell you before your meeting." Sybille sounded rather uncomfortable, not her usual social self. Having flitted around the UN with Williem for over twenty years, the parties, the introductions, conversations and stuff, this was definitely out of the ordinary. That Williem couldn't remember more was just weird.

"Sybille, this James is not going to be at the meeting. I am meeting with his lawyer, a Johnathan Keirns. Ring any bells?"

"No. It doesn't to me, but hold on a second. I'll ask Williem." She put her hand over the phone but I could still hear muffled talking in the background. "No, Williem doesn't recall that name at all."

"I did receive an email from this James the evening after I read your email. It introduced me to his lawyer. The next morning I received a phone call from the lawyer. By the way, the only email address you have for me is the one at the office that I sent when I opened up the new office, right?" No need to tell her the exact order of events.

"Right, the classic.com one. You know I carry one of your new cards in my purse just in case we run into someone. Hold on a second I'm looking to see if it's still there. No it's not, so I must have given it to him. I know I wouldn't have done that if our meeting at the party was just passing. I must have thought he was serious and not strange when I gave it to him." Sybille's voice was becoming more accented as she talked. She does have a delightful German accent when she is just chatting but now she was starting to hit her consonants hard and jerk her sentences.

"Victoria, I am so sorry to bother you with this. I should have looked to see if your card was gone before I called. I wouldn't have worried. Well, Williem says good luck and let us know how it works out." Her voice was back to delightful again.

"Sybille, tell Williem 'hi' for me and thank you for taking the time to call. I will be in touch." At the end of my sentence Sybille hung up. I checked my clock, it was 12:05. I had better get moving or I was going to be late.

I reached the office at 12:45, said hi to Mary and went straight to my office. Well there wasn't anyone waiting for me. Made myself some tea, this morning's coffee was not sitting well. Went back to my desk, flipped on my laptop and loaded the LSS, the Listing Service Site and organized the search for 5-10 million dollars. Sat back in my chair and flipped through my notes from yesterday.

I heard the door open and glanced through my office door to see a very tall, duck-head-in-the-doorway tall, dark man enter. My first thought was 'not my guy'. I returned to my notes. Thirty seconds later my phone buzzed. It was Mary.

"Victoria, Mr. Keirns is here to see you." I checked the small travel clock I had on my desk, 1pm exactly. Had someone else come in behind the big guy.

"I'll be right out." I was. No I hadn't missed anyone. Mr. Keirns had to be 6'4" easily. Very well tailored. I looked up until I reached his eyes. They were chocolate. His hair was in a million braids but tied tightly at the base of his neck. I held out my hand. "Mr. Keirns, I'm Mrs. Hamilton, glad you could come." He instantly reached out to take my hand.

"Mrs. Hamilton, I am pleased to meet you. Thank you for your time." He looked me directly in the eyes. His hand was surprisingly soft, his grip was firm not crushing and he released his hand in a reasonable amount of time. A gentleman's greeting. It is rare to get an appropriate greeting from a man in today's world of gender neutral fist bumping, hand slapping and occasional hugging that easily becomes way too familiar. I am truly not a snob by any means. I enjoy touching, touching good friends, relatives and especially lovers, but not at the first meeting, please. I don't think boys learn proper handshakes from their fathers anymore.

"Please do come in Mr. Keirns." I turned to walk back into my office holding the door for him. "May I take your coat?" Looking at him I noticed that there wasn't a wrinkle in his face. It moved when he spoke but nothing stayed creased, no lines, no crow's feet. It didn't look used. That was it. His skin didn't look like it had been used. Didn't he ever smile or laugh or get angry?

"Yes please." He put down his briefcase, took off a beautiful camel hair coat that already contained the gloves he had worn into the outer office and handed me his coat. Yes. It was heavy with a texture of that winter blanket that adds weight and warmth to a cold night; so long that when I put it on the top hook of the coat rack it folded on the floor.

"Mr. Keirns, would you care for tea or coffee or something more refreshing to drink?"

"No thank you Mrs. Hamilton."

I walked back to my chair, sat down. Mr. Keirns folded himself into one of my Client chairs while lifting his briefcase onto his lap. He pulled a few papers out of the briefcase, closed the briefcase, returned it to the floor. He shot his cuffs. That was cool. I noticed they were French with red ruby cufflinks. Put his hands on the papers, looked at me. All one motion, one beautiful fluid motion that certainly did not belong to such a large man. I released my breath. I smiled, couldn't help myself. I wondered if it was as good for him as it was for me.

"Mrs. Hamilton, Mr. Fournier would like to purchase a residential property in the area, off the beaten path, not too large but with the appropriate amenities. A few bedrooms, baths, a library, parlor, at least one fireplace. This property should be on a few acres. Mr. Fournier would prefer that it not be visible to the casual eye." He went right to business with impeccable colonial English. The English taught in a colonial school. Under the words he spoke there was a subtle accent, not French, Italian, German, Greek, Portuguese or Spanish, but something. English was not his first language which verified the colonial school. Where did Britain still have colonies?

"Mr. Keirns, why here? Does Mr. Fournier have business in this area, or family?" I like to know why people are looking to purchase a house when they come in. Why do they want to live here? A job transfer, relatives, something that makes them a legitimate buyer.

"Mrs. Hamilton. Mr. Fournier has a member of his family here. He would like a permanent residence that he can use in comfort when he visits. His need is that simple." Mr. Keirns was not very chatty and definitely was not going to share today. I approached the subject of Mr. Fournier's business, where he currently resided and even mentioned the party with Williem and Sybille. Nothing.

"Mr. Keirns, to view properties in the price range Mr. Fournier mentioned in his email, I will need a financial letter qualifying legitimacy in that price range as it will be requested by the owners of such properties. Do you have such a document? Also some identification for yourself?" Figured I'd cut to the chase. He hadn't said anything that told me this whole thing was fake. Infact, he hadn't said anything at all.

"Of course. I have the financial letter Mr. Fournier promised and my passport, if that will do?" He leaned over the desk with the papers he had on his lap and put them in front of me.

"Mr. Keirns, are you comfortable with a computer?" I asked.

"Of course Mrs. Hamilton." He looked a little puzzled. "Why?"

"I can set up some photos and descriptions of properties that meet your requirements if you would like. There are a few that come to mind and you can look through them while I make a copy of your passport and refresh my tea." I stood sliding the laptop to his side of my desk. He stood when I did. Habit? I showed him how to flip through the listings I pulled up. Picked up my cup, his papers and walked to the door of the workroom. "May I get you something?"

"No thank you". Mr. Keirns was getting distracted by the properties. The LSS thing was new to him. I am always glad to provide entertainment in the middle of a meeting.

I took the opportunity to glance at his passport. It was Moroccan. How interesting. It was issued about six months ago, name was the same, picture seemed to match, age said 51. That, I would not have guessed. I flipped through the stamps and in the six months since it was issued the passport reflected visits to so many countries he would have to either get a new passport or add pages. Busy boy. I copied the financial letter, walked around to Mary and asked her to verify and call me in the office. The letter had the name of a Swiss bank, no surprise there, and the name of the bank president and his phone number, both office and home. Now that was rare. Usually we had to deal with some third or fourth level bank officer and sometimes their secretary to verify. Mary would have fun with this.

I returned to my office. "Mr. Keirns, have you seen anything of interest?"

"No I haven't. Most of these properties, while large enough, can be seen casually. Mr. Fournier is a man of privacy. Do we have to increase the pricing?" He seemed a little frustrated. Emotion, that was nice.

"No I don't think we have to increase price. I do think we have to increase size." I walked over to him and turned the laptop so that I could type on it, pull up a much larger property whose price had just dropped below $10M. "How about this, although it is larger that you requested it is a very private location with about 25 acres of land. It is truly a beautiful house." I showed him my favorite property. "Does Mr. Fournier have a large family, children?"

"No. No children." He viewed the photos, read the details, viewed the photos again, read the details again. "As you said this is quite large. Would the purchase of this property bring attention to Mr. Fournier?"

An interesting question but not odd and certainly not the first time I've heard it. "Yes, it probably will. Not so much the property but the current Owner was a movie star that was having some financial issues, so I would count on it.

"There are steps we can take to keep most of the transaction private but when the deed is recorded it does become public information as do the property tax records. It would be relatively easy to set up a holding company of some type for Mr. Fournier so his name doesn't appear anywhere." Keeping something like this quiet could be a challenge around here.

While Mr. Keirns was thinking, or seemed to be thinking, the phone on my desk buzzed. "Excuse me Mr. Keirns, I do need to take this."

"Mrs. Hamilton, would you like me to leave the room?"

"No, stay if you don't mind, this will take just a minute." I walked around my desk, picked up the phone. "Yes."

"Victoria, no problem." It was Mary and that was the fastest verification ever. I had expected a few hours, this was maybe ten minutes. I returned to the chair behind my desk. This just might be real.

"Do you have the name of a local lawyer that I could work with? Someone with some flexibility?" Mr. Keirns was at the lawyer stage. "Also would you please make an appointment to view the property as soon as possible?"

I reached into my desk for the perfect lawyer's business card, handed it to Mr. Keirns. The skin on his hands also seemed unused. The joints moved and the skin moved, but when he stopped moving the wrinkles at the joints disappeared. Fifty one years without a scar or a scratch. My hands were very used. "If you don't mind Mrs. Hamilton, I would like to contact this lawyer privately. I'm sure it won't take but a few minutes."

"I'll be glad to step out." I was hoping that is what he intended. I walked out to the workroom to retrieve the tea I had made and forgotten.

I sat at the table and could see Mr. Keirns on his cell phone. I couldn't hear a thing and this was one time I wished I hadn't been so fanatical about soundproofing my office. After about 5 minutes, Mr. Keirns was still talking and listening. I guess he reached Jay Matthews, my favorite lawyer and the type of lawyer that could think and work outside of the box. He always stayed within the law, no problem there, he was just a great problem solver. His cousin and I had shared an apartment just before Mary had moved in and that is when I met Jay the first time. He had helped his cousin move out. I ran across Jay again when I was looking for a lawyer to help with the purchase of my first house. When I was dating my second husband. Jay had also helped when my second husband had adopted my children, visited my Mother when she was dying to get her things in order. Jay had actually come to her house. Since that time I had referred my most interesting Clients to him. I think playing Closing attorney bores Jay to death, so I only send him the interesting Clients and Mr. Keirns and Mr. Fournier did fit that description.

Another 10 minutes and Mr. Keirns put his phone away, sat patiently. I gave it some time before I walked back in. "Did you have any luck contacting Jay?"

"Oh yes, Mr. Matthews. He is arranging our viewing and will call here when it is complete."

My cell phone rang. I looked at the caller ID, it was Jay. This was getting interesting. I looked to Mr. Keirns, he smiled. "Jay, hi, didn't think you could get the "Girls" to respond that fast."

Jay chuckled on the other end. "Well, they did. You are booked for tomorrow afternoon at 4, which is the time Mr. Keirns requested. Is that good for you?" I could hear Jay's smile. It must be big.

"We will be there. Do I need confidentiality docs?"

"No, I'll take care of everything. Mr. Keirns has asked that I expand the privacy statement so if the girls have a problem and it's not signed I'll call you by the end of the day today. You do find interesting Clients Victoria. We'll talk soon. Good luck". Jay was still trying to contain himself.

"Thanks Jay." And I closed my phone. "Mr. Keirns, I think we are all set for tomorrow at 4. You realize that we will only have about an hour of daylight to view."

"That will not be a problem Mrs. Hamilton. We will see what we need to see. Mr. Fournier will be joining us." He stood and walked to retrieve his coat, put on his gloves and before I could move from around my desk he had his briefcase in one hand and had stretched out his other. "Thank you Mrs. Hamilton." He shook my hand and walked to my office door.

"Thank you Mr. Keirns. It has been a pleasure. I look forward to meeting Mr. Fournier. Would you like directions or would you like me to pick you up?"

"No thank you." And he was out the door.

Mary looked at me as I stood at the door a little stunned. The meeting had taken all of an hour. No wasted time, no stutters, just movement and the movement was always forward. Shows what can be done without the side bullshit. In the real estate business an initial Client meeting usually kills an afternoon, most of the conversation being niceties so no one is insulted and the Clients' life story is told. I knew what I needed to know to sell this house. Nothing more, nothing less.

"Victoria, you alright? That was fast." I think Mary was as surprised as I was.

"I'm fine Mary. That was a fast confirmation of the financial."

"One call to the home number, figured with the time difference I'd try there first. The president of the bank picked up on the second ring, confirmed everything. Said not to hesitate to call if we needed anything else for Mr. Fournier and that was it. Where did you pick these people up?" Mary was as curious as I was.

"Referred to me by some Clients I had ten years ago. So we're going to look at Ledge House tomorrow. This is a real hoot. Keirns has already talked to Jay and oh, this is as private as possible Mary. Seriously. This Mr. Fournier doesn't want anyone to know that he is buying in town. No one. Glad there wasn't anyone in the office today." I turned to go back to my office.

"That is going to be a trick. Rumor has it that one of the rags has a photographer wandering the Bird Sanctuary photographing anyone that walks the property. Good luck."

"Mary, why did you tell me that. I would rather not have known. There's nothing I can do about it. Thanks." I walked back into my office, sat down. I called Jay to let him know what Mary had just said. He told me that Mr. Keirns had mentioned the newspaper guy to him and not to worry. Oh well. It will be what it will be. I just sat at my desk. Between library guy and my new Clients this has been quite an interesting week.

I've always been fascinated by how people move through societies at completely different levels in complete ignorance of each other. Like the college girl standing in line at the store behind one of Newport's society matrons who stands behind the mother with the three children paying for her groceries with food stamps. They probably didn't speak. If I were to ask one of them who was behind them in line, they wouldn't have a clue. That is a very elementary example. But when I think about larger and larger groups everyone exists in their own little level of awareness. My mind was doing a brandy and cigar walkabout. Needed to bug out. I put on my coat, closed up my little office, said goodbye to Mary and went home.

Chapter 8

When my head wanders like that home is the best place to be. I had no sooner walked in my door and Bill called. Jenny was gone. Good I guessed. He asked if I could I find him something more modern in town? Sure, no problem. I'd known that was coming but not hard to do. He had given me what I needed, location. The classic - location, location, location. Oh yeah, and modern interior. Fortunately for Bill so many of the older big properties had been totally gutted when they were converted to condominiums. Leaving the historical shell and creating a modern New York City type interior. The difficult thing was to find original interior in this area. Well. I'd tackle Bill's problem in the morning.

I changed into my evening clothes. Today they were early evening clothes, pulled out my telescope, moved a living room chair to the windows and was watching the beach when I called Carolyn. Carolyn and I went back about 23 years. She is like my aunt or much older sister. I met her in the first real estate office I walked into but we didn't become good friends for about a year. I always picture her sitting on some very large veranda, sipping mint juleps with the most wonderful hat on, south of the Mason-Dixon line. No children, never married, extensively traveled and in the "Book". I should say "Books". There are two that matter in this area. "Newport's Book" and the "Social Register". If there is a private club in Newport, Carolyn belongs to it. The one exception was "The Reading Room". Wrong sex.

I find Carolyn fascinating. I guess we became true friends when she left real estate after a heart attack and began to develop a ghost tour for one of the old mansions on the Avenue. She asked me if I would be interested in driving around with her collecting pictures of haunted houses and graveyards in the State. We hadn't seriously spoken on the subject until that point in time. After that trip we realized we had a lot more in common than either of us had realized.

While I was checking out the beach with the telescope Carolyn had given me, thinking about the events of the past week, I realized I hadn't talked to her during that time. Usually we were on the phone almost every other day.

While I was catching her up on my side of the week, she for her side of the week, I spotted a figure standing perfectly straight, perfectly still, on a very large outcropping that overlooks the beach. I was looking north, looking at the chimneys of Ledge House when I noticed the figure on the outcropping. I tightened the focus of the telescope. Library guy was looking at Ledge House from the outcropping. I must have stopped talking in mid sentence.

"Vic are you there?" It took me a second to realize I was still on the phone.

"Yeah, I'm here. You will never believe what I'm looking at. Carolyn, it's library guy standing on the big Bird Sanctuary outcropping looking at the stacks of Ledge House." Then it hit me. Library guy is Mr. Fournier. "Carolyn, library guy is James Fournier. Well this is weird." I shivered; uttered a nervous giggle.

"So it took you this long. I'd figured it out before the end of your story. I was waiting for you to say it…you know…the punch line." Carolyn was very pleased with herself.

"Well now I've got the shakes. Shit." I was seriously laughing now. Not funny ha, ha, but nervous ha, ha. "I don't know if I can deal with this. Why didn't he just walk into the office? Why the library stuff? Why watch me get in the car? Why across from the office?"

"I don't understand. It's serious money. You've dealt with that before… Oh, I know. It's been a while since you have had the company of interesting gentlemen. The other stuff could still be just coincidence." Now Carolyn was chuckling.

"I don't consider library guy a gentleman, but he is kind of hot. Keirns yes. I'll give him that. These two together will last me a long time. Wait it's 4. I'm making a drink." I made a bloody Mary. "Ok I'm back. Carolyn, you there?" I looked out of the telescope while I was waiting for Carolyn. She either made herself a drink or took a nature break. Subtleties between us were also long gone.

"Vic I'm back. Drink and nature. You said it, I did it."

Both, she's getting fast. "Carolyn, he's gone. Oh well, that made my evening." I was not done watching library guy. Obviously he was done looking at the chimney stacks. I would have to point out that when the spring leaves were on the trees, the stacks would be almost invisible. Usually people don't even notice them when they are at their most visible. I had lived in this town for quite a few years before I had noticed them. People look to the beach when they drive in this area, not to the tangle of trees in the nature preserve.

"Vic you know you always enjoy doing business with attractive men. You've enjoyed it since I've know you. Frankly, I think we all do. To this day if an attractive man flirts at the tour I play to him. Why not? It's just for fun. Not like something would ever come of it." To say Carolyn gave a bit of a giggle would be too much, but it was her version. Her very charming version. I'd see her take over a dinner table with it, holding the table all night with her stories.

Carolyn had history and knew how to play. Play like they did in those 40s movies, then walk away. I did love to watch the other people at the table or in a group at a party. Eventually, the women would drift away and the men wouldn't notice. The men would be captivated. I guess Carolyn had a talent. A talent that couldn't be taught or copied, just natural. She did this now, in her mid seventies. Carolyn must have been deadly in her younger years.

"What I don't understand is that if this is library guy at the property tomorrow, why the hell has he been watching me for a week? Why didn't he just walk into the office and ask about finding a property? I bet it's not him." I was trying to talk myself into the practical. The guy tomorrow is somehow high profile. Library guy was just a weirdo.

"Sounds practical. But you know and I know they are the same. Don't worry, it'll work out. Hopefully you'll get a big commission and that will be that. Hey, why don't I give you a call about 5. Good excuse to break out of what's going on and if there is a problem, you can tell me. If you don't pick up I'll call the cops. Now, does that feel better?"

"You know Carolyn, that's not a bad idea. God, I feel like a little kid. I hate feeling like this. Thanks. Don't forget." I felt better. I was making way too much out of this.

"I won't. I used to call you around dinner anyway. It'll be like old times. Vic, got to go now. You'll be fine".

"Yeah, thanks. I'm sure I'll be fine. Take care." I hung up. The sun had set. No point in watching the beach, minimal moonlight. Couldn't see more than outlines. Off season there weren't any lights. Not even street lights. Tonight just a little moonlight reflecting off the surf. Always pretty. I had work to do anyway, find something for Bill.

Much to my surprise I got a good night's sleep. My last thought had been that I would never get to sleep. The next thing I knew I was waking to sunrise. The condo faces east. If the day was clear and bright, the sun made its way through my light-dampening shades, open bedroom door, on to my face.

I was having coffee, reading the paper online when the phone ran. Maybe after all this stupidity they were canceling. "Hamilton here."

"Victoria, Jay Matthews. Hope I'm not calling too early."

"No Jay, the boys cancelling?"

"Not hardly. I wanted to talk to you about my conversation with Mr. Keirns yesterday and my…ah…instructions. Got some time?" Jay sounded a bit hesitant. That's a first. He usually just said what he needed to say… come on.

"No, I'm still home. You, instructions, that's a laugh. Talk if you aren't under a gag order. Feel free." Games. Now that'll get my brain going.

"Well, Keirns introduced himself as the lawyer for someone named James Fournier who is looking for a personal residence. I guess you know this. Anyway he wanted to retain me to represent them here and this is where it gets fun. Keirns asked that I contact Cheryl for the showing today, but only if she would sign an expanded privacy statement. Then he started dictating. It was quite extensive. She can't even tell anyone she is showing it. She can't do the usual. You know, contact other potential buyers to say she is showing it etc. etc. I told him that I doubted she would sign it. He thought she might. Well, she did. Surprised the hell out of me that she didn't ask for one from the Buyers' side."

"That's interesting. Usually she fights little stuff like that. Loves the press. Oh the press guy…"

Jay interrupted me. "Wait Victoria, I'm not done. So I got the appointment. You know that. I called Keirns to tell him. He said I would have a retainer by the end of the day. Well, I got it. Direct wire transfer within the hour. A significant amount. Directly into my personal account. No strings, no nothing." I was dying to ask him how much but he continued. "An hour after that, a package arrived with the financial letter that I guess he gave to you, a copy of a contract to be used in any real estate transaction and oh, a Representation Disclosure you need to sign. I've already signed." He finally took a breath I could hear.

"Is everything they are doing legal? I mean I was thinking about this as you were talking and I can't think of anything illegal…except for the funds in your personal account. Did you give him the transfer numbers?" I was trying to find something wrong. I couldn't. With a big property it usually takes weeks to get buyers to do this stuff. Eventually, if they're serious, they do. This Mr. Keirns, except for Jay's personal account, has done everything and more in, what, five business hours. Can't blame someone for being efficient.

"No Victoria, I didn't. I'll have to write a check into the office account but it shouldn't be a problem. You've checked the financial letter, right?"

"Mary did it during my meeting with Mr. Keirns. Direct access to the bank president. No hesitation. I think he was waiting for the call. Jay, with all of this I would think that you guys don't need me. Not that I'm complaining. I could always use the business. Why did he even take time to see me?" Jay had a Broker's License and at times did practice real estate.

"Victoria, you know it's business, but I did ask that question. I was told that you specifically were to represent Mr. Fournier. I shouldn't question Mr. Fournier. Quote 'He is not a man to be taken lightly'. I almost backed out at that. But as I said, business is business and frankly my curiosity is up big time."

"Mine too. Jay, don't let this veer over the legal line ok. I mean we're good now, but who knows where this will end up. Right?"

"Don't worry, neither of us looks good in orange. We'll be fine. Hey, I've got to get to the office. If you can, let me know how it goes this afternoon."

"I will, even after work hours?"

"Sure, you've got my cell number on your phone now. Give a call." Jay hung up and I tried to remember how to save his number to my cell phone. I'm not totally technology ignorant, but if I don't do something for a while it's hit or miss a few times. I'm one of those people that just wants something to work. I don't care how it works; just make it work. As for Blackberries or Palm Pilots, my calendar is paper…both in my bag and on my desks. Every month I flip the page and write everything down. Sounds arcane, but they don't break when dropped, nor do they short out and the screen doesn't fail. Same for my address books. All paper. I've got address books going back many, many years and many career incarnations.

I called Bill to make arrangements to get the keys to his house, pick up his Listing Contract and drop off a couple of condo printouts that he might like. It's about time these properties get moving.

Chapter 9

I stopped by Jay's office to sign my side of the Representation Disclosure and was met with my side of the privacy statement. Boy, Keirns had seriously added to the statement. The statement usually said that no party involved, including agents, could disclose or discuss any part or particular of a negotiation or the resulting contract. The parties could, however, say that the property was being negotiated or would probably be going into Contract. Well, Mr. Keirns not only eliminated any and all discussion of the existence of a potential Buyer, but if a Contract was signed, any discussion of the Buyer as in even acknowledging there was one was a no-no.

The Agreement went on to say that the Listing Agent could put the property in the appropriate designations in the Listing Service Site (LSS), but if someone asked about its status the Listing Agency in total would have to deny any knowledge of the Buyer. What a hoot. Oh and the kicker; the Seller would have to sign up to the same thing. Well, Jay's problem, not mine. If this Mr. Fournier did buy a property he was going to leave a big black hole in his wake. That's a double hoot on this Island. That in and of itself would cause gossip.

I drove up the narrow winding road to Ledge House a little before four to re-acquaint myself with the property. About a half a mile up the road there was a small stone gate house on the right. It was set well back from the existing road in front of the stone wall and high rod iron security fence that marked the beginning of the main house property. I'd always thought it funny that the fence didn't surround all of the property, just the front west side.

The Gate House had been directly on the driveway when I first dared to sneak up to Ledge House. I was 16, had my first car, did it on a dare. The driveway had been dirt up to the stone wall with very deep ruts. The land was left wild by the original owners. I remember being concerned about the ruts tearing out the muffler of my 1961 MGA 1600, my first car for $600. It was already being held together with two orange juice cans… back then cans were truly cans…and hose clamps. I didn't think a third would work. I had parked the car in the overgrown brush and walked past the empty gate house and through the iron gate. The nature of the land then changed immediately to well manicured gardens and paved driveway that went another half mile to the house.

Now the dirt driveway was a paved town road up to the Gate House with driveways breaking off to attractive, secluded, new houses. The road had been moved so that the stone gate house was about 150 feet away from the road and had been restored to living condition. The Gate House, like the other properties leading up to the stone wall and iron fence had been subdivided about 15 years ago and sold.

Once I passed through the stone wall opening backed by the iron fence and gate entering the main property grounds, it was still beautiful. Well manicured, today snow-swept lawns and purposely spaced trees were interrupted with bare individual gardens all the way to Ledge House. I knew the individual gardens were three-season gardens, only dormant now at the end of the winter. The driveway was gravel so level that I wondered how they plowed snow, but it had been plowed. Actually it was dry. There were high snow mounds on either side of the driveway the closer I got to the house. Half way up to the house were serious cutting gardens set back from the driveway on the right, which would be the south side. Behind the cutting gardens were greenhouses, currently unused, and a gardener's cottage. I also knew that there was a Garden House farther down the slope from the end of the greenhouses. I couldn't see it from where I had stopped the car in front of the main house.

The main house, "Ledge House" was beautiful to me. It was what I pictured a true "Manor House" to be. I parked just to the south side of the main entry stairs, got out of the car, centering myself in front of the entry. It is a well-proportioned, textured brick and stone structure, three above ground levels that, if I remembered correctly, contained twelve bedrooms, twelve bathrooms, library, den, professional kitchen, butler's pantry, dining room and multiple undirected rooms. Most of the main rooms and many of the bedrooms had working fireplaces. The basement contained the wine cellar, billiard room and living quarters for the help. It had been a few years and a couple of owners since I had toured the house. Rumor had it that the previous Owner had added some spectacular features and done some serious upgrading. I was definitely looking forward to the tour. Seeing the houses was neck-in-neck with some of the people I meet as favorite things about this profession.

"Excuse me Mrs. Hamilton." I jumped, turned around. "Sorry to startle you. Mrs. Hamilton I would like to introduce you to Mr. Fournier. Mr. Fournier, this is Mrs. Hamilton." I automatically reached my hand out to Mr. Fournier before I looked up. When I did look up, of course it was library guy. Library guy with the most delightful smile, spectacular black eyes, wonderfully unique face. A smile that involved not only all of his face, but all of him somehow. He still looked familiar to me. Not a previous Client in any of my jobs. Certainly not an old boyfriend. Not a passing acquaintance, with those looks I definitely would have remembered.

"Mrs. Hamilton, please, James. I am so glad to meet you." He took my hand, took a deep breath when we touched and a step forward. He leaned subtly from the shoulders…leaned into me. "I am so sorry it has taken me this long".

"Excuse me. I don't believe you're late. It must be just about 4 o'clock." He stayed just outside of my personal space and continued to hold my hand. I didn't move. Couldn't move. I just looked at him. His skin had more color than I remembered from the library, a reddish coffee color. His hair, straight, shiny black, coal black, pulled back, maybe in a pony tail. I couldn't see from this how long. His eyes, oh yes his eyes, were more black than I remembered. So black that it was hard to tell the iris from the pupil. Larger than I remembered with a slight up tilt at their edges.

His face was still smiling. Very high, sharp cheek bones on either side of a strong straight nose, and his lips…wow. I needed to let go of his hand and pull back, not to embarrass, to escape. Before I could actually move, he released my hand, stepped back. His smile relaxed but didn't disappear.

"Mrs. Hamilton, of course we are on time, I don't understand." Mr. Keirns looked at Mr. Fournier, rather James, then turned to look down the driveway. A few seconds later I heard another car.

"Mr. Keirns, of course you are. James, please call me Victoria." When he pulled his hand back he had replaced a glove I hadn't seen come off. "Where did you park?" I took another step back. This was very strange. Yeah, he was attractive. My mind had already lost the coat and the shirt and well, I needed to get it together. I think Mr. Keirns was answering my question. What question?

"...... in front of the garages. We had some time to look around the grounds before you arrived. I did not think asking you to walk the grounds in the snow would be appropriate, but I see you did dress for it." I sure had; snow boots, heavy socks that were over my black corduroys tucking the pants into the boots. Oversized sweater under the long red wool coat. This time I hadn't dressed to impress. I'd dressed to work.

I looked down at their shoes. Men's wingtips on Mr. Keirns and loafers on James. Loafers, no socks with a suit. They looked new. Not a spot on them. Oh Victoria get it together, car...boots...changed before they came around the house. No socks? I smiled, looked up and saw our hosting Broker walking in our direction.

Cheryl Kingston with a bit of a startled, but pleased expression. Put that look away Cheryl, I know they're pretty. One of my favorite people, Owner of one of my favorite Brokerages. Even when I was working with one of her salesmen I called them "the girls". Actually, her brokerage is one of the finest around if one's butt was covered.

All negotiations I conducted with "the girls" was done in writing with very close attention to the details. As far as I was concerned, negotiations on the phone weren't real with anyone outside of my Brokerage until I could either put the results in an email or write it out, date, sign and deliver. It takes time but I've learned the hard way and even documenting every step of the way, a point of negotiation would be denied. With Cheryl, personally, I double documented. I was surprised when she signed Mr. Keirns's document.

I introduced Cheryl to Mr. Fournier and Mr. Keirns. James did not offer his hand nor his first name to Cheryl even after she offered it to both of the men. Throughout the tour it remained Cheryl to the men and Mr. Fournier and Mr. Keirns to Cheryl. I remained Mrs. Hamilton to Mr. Keirns and Victoria to James and as always, Vicky to Cheryl like we were old buddies. Now that was a snub. Why? Neither man had had direct contact with her that I knew of but maybe she had been their first contact in town. Hey, not my business.

The house was more beautiful than I had remembered, more comfortable. The billiard room had been moved to one of the unused rooms on the first floor. A wall had been removed expanding the formal parlor into a very large true living/family room with electronics built into the walls, very subtle architectural detail hiding the functional portions of the Bose music system and the flat, wide screen monitor. The kitchen was state of the art. Everything I remembered had been replaced. The oak floors looked newly sanded and sealed. Yeah it was grand.

Cheryl walked and talked constantly. She asked if there were questions when we walked into the next room. Agent rule 101, never ask for questions while standing in the room you just finished talking about. Buyers have the time to stop, look and think. Keep it moving, above all, keep it moving. I wondered what she would talk about when we got to the second floor. What can you say about a bedroom, much less twelve? Especially when the bedroom would probably be as vacant as the rest of the house. Sure, antique furniture could be interesting but the house was empty of anything personal. I was wondering if the current Owner had ever moved in. He had owned the house only a few months before it went back on the market.

When we walked through the doors into the indoor pool area, my cell phone rang. I realized then, that James had been walking beside me since the tour began. Mr. Keirns had been walking in front of us. "Excuse me please. Cheryl do continue, I'll be only a minute." I pulled out the phone, was it five already? "Carolyn, all is well, I'll call you later." I hung up, turned to catch up with the group and found James waiting where I had left him. I walked to the others, he followed. It was then that I realized there hadn't been any questions. No talking from my Clients for an hour and the silence continued. Through the indoor pool area, Olympic size, the hot tub, the steam room, the exercise room, all not a word.

"Would you like to see the Garden house? It's just another three bedroom, three bath house with a fireplace, kitchen and wet bar. There is also an apartment above the 8-car garage behind the house." Cheryl was not dressed for an outdoor tour. Her short skirt, bare short rather chubby legs, spike heeled boots and plunging silk blouse exposing more than was necessary, would not keep her warm under her thin leather coat.

"No thank you Cheryl. We've seen the rest of the property." Mr. Keirns was ending the tour. He quickly turned his back, led the way to the entry hall. James and I followed as did Cheryl, walking a little faster than she had during the tour, trying to catch up.

"James, do you have any questions? After all, you are the Buyer aren't you?" Cheryl reached for his arm, flashed the bleached smile. Boy, she was pushing. James stopped, turned to look at her before she made contact.

"Cheryl, I am Mr. Fournier. Yes, I am the Buyer. No. I have all of the information I require, Thank you." The irritation in James's voice was undeniable but subtle and with it came another subtle accent, English not the first language. He turned, walked to the door, opened it for Mr. Keirns,

57

myself and then stepped through, leaving Cheryl with the door. Maybe they had met. I finally got the chance to see the back of his head, hair tied with a leather strap, tucked under his coat.

Cheryl stepped through the door. Immediately started talking about the security system and the heated driveway while she walked up to our little group. So that's why the driveway was dry. It was interesting to me. No one else was impressed.

James interrupted her with a much stronger tone and heavier accent to his words. "Cheryl, we are going to talk. Do secure the house. I have what I need. We will be in touch." James turned his back to her and began speaking to Mr. Keirns. Although I was standing between them, not as close as they were to each other, I heard only slight whispers. I had not a clue what they were saying to each other. They wanted privacy. I slowly started to walk away, looking at the north wing of the house.

"Victoria, please, we are being rude." James, voice relaxed again, words without accent and when I turned to look at him, the smile had returned.

"I'm just giving you some space to talk. I realize that this property is a major commitment for anyone." I stood where I was and they both started walking to me. That, I hadn't intended. I started walking to them.

"Yes." James continued in my direction. "It is a major property. The lands are beautiful. The house is quite large. The pool was....more than I expected." He stopped talking and looked up at the house. His eyes wandered over its expanse, then returned to me. "I had not planned...this now. I do like it, the garages, the land. Do you think the lower houses could be acquired?"

"I don't understand what you are asking. Acquired with the main house?" House more than he had planned for, then, can the lower properties be acquired. Did I miss something?

"No, not with the big house, but over time." James was doing all of the talking now. Mr. Keirns was standing a few feet to his left, watching him. I guess they had finished talking.

"James, if you have the time and money, all things are possible. Probably one at a time over a space of a few years. One of Mr. Keirns's priorities had been that attention not be brought to any acquisition. Purchasing adjacent property would have to be subtle." What else could I say, it was the truth. The sun was well below the horizon now. Truly getting cold. I didn't know how much longer I could stand out here in 20 degrees. The boys didn't seem to notice.

"I don't know about you, but I'm freezing. Would you like to continue this conversation at my office?" I walked to my car, opened the door and, out of the corner of my eye saw a hand reaching over my shoulder to hold the door. I had been watching the two of them as I approached the car. James was now reaching for my door and Mr. Keirns was standing by the front entry steps, alone. James was a little too close.

I took a step back, fell into the driver's seat. 'Whoa' did come out of my mouth. I looked up. James was still holding the door with his other hand on the roof bending his head and shoulders closer. What the hell? I guess if I had to I could kick him. That would be a shame.

"Victoria." His voice was now very soft. "Jonathan will proceed with the business. I must ask if I may see you again."

I didn't see that coming. Oh yeah, it would be fun. Hell, he must be twenty years younger than I am, not that the issue had ever stopped me. No, get it together Victoria, you idiot. Don't screw this up.

"James, I do appreciate the request but it is difficult for me to see someone while I am negotiating for them. The business gets mixed up with the personal and, frankly, I never stop working. I hope you understand. It's not personal." I said it and didn't like it. I'm at the age where these kinds of requests come from older men, not younger. My brain was running in over-drive. A shiver ran through my shoulders. I took a deep breath, let it out. Tried to focus on the business at hand.

His face lost its smile. I noticed his skin, his now expressionless face, was the unused skin of Mr. Keirns. His eyes looked into me. I moved my legs into the car, reaching my hand to close the door. James did not move. He did not blink or breathe for a few moments. A shadow moved through him or that's what I thought I saw. Then it was gone and he was back.

"Are you sure?" He said as if nothing had happened. Did he think I was playing hard to get? Come on, especially after what I thought I saw.

I turned my head back over my shoulder. "I think it would be best."

"When you change your mind, I'll be waiting." He released the door, stepped back from the car and just stood, watching me. Watching me like he had in the library. Watching like he did in the snow on the side street, like he did across from the office. Just watching. No movement, no blinking, nothing.

I started the car, turned the heat to high and drove slowly past Mr. Keirns. Still watching James. I turned down the driveway. I checked the rear view mirror before passing through the gate. I expected to see them both walking around the house to the garages where their car was parked.

No. James had turned continuing to watch me. Mr. Keirns remained in front of the entry stairs. He was still watching James.

Chapter 10

I realized when I walked through my condo door that, in a good south east wind, I could spit on Ledge House. I hadn't given it thought. At least, not seriously. The house phone rang. I reached for it and stopped myself to check the incoming number. It was Carolyn. I picked up. If I didn't, she would call the cell, then call the house again. One thing about Carolyn, when she wanted to contact me she was ruthless. I did pick up the phone. "Hey Carolyn."

"So tell me, tell me all" Her voice was very excited.

"If you don't mind I have a bunch of work to do. Can I call you back later? All went well, I guess. You know first showings." I didn't want to talk and I did have another call to make.

"Sure just tell me, was it him?"

"Oh yeah, it was him. Let me call you later tonight, OK?"

"No problem honey, you know I'll be up." Carolyn would be up no matter how late I called her. Early morning contact rarely happened.

"OK." I did hang up. I wasn't ready to talk to Jay either. I poured myself a glass of wine and wandered into the dressing room. I didn't like mixing business with dating. The conversation always goes to business. An extra two or three hours of working and it burns me out,; sometimes with a hangover and odd situations. But, good God, he was beautiful. I would like to ask him why he didn't talk to me at the library. What he did for a living that made bankers snap to and who was his esthetician. I chuckled at that one. I wanted to ask how he found Newport. Keirns had said a relative. I didn't think so. Oh and were he and Mr. Keirns attached at the hip? James had said he would be waiting 'when' I changed my mind. Oh yeah, a lot of questions.

Was I losing my sense of adventure? For me one night stands were a delight. No strings, no laundry. Fun without obligation or commitment. My Father had pulled my house privileges when I was 18 for what he thought was that very reason. He had been only too glad to stand with me at the top of a church aisle for my first wedding. He had held my arm with firm determination when we started to walk. I think he knew I wanted to run, run like the wind. But I stayed seven years and three kids, then tossed my husband's ass out the door along with green garbage bags containing his clothes. I should have realized then, what I know now. I'm not a good roommate. Not a happy 'wife' and not crazy about kids. I guess there is a difference between caring for my own and liking children in general. I, frankly, don't like children. Want to stop a cocktail party? Say it, without remorse.

I finally made the phone call to Jay. When I stripped away everything but the business side of the showing I didn't have much to say, but I made the call. "Jay, it's Victoria, you wanted me to call."

"Victoria, I'm on the phone. I'll call you right back." Jay clicked off.

I made myself some soup and poured it into a huge mug designed for hot chocolate but I loved soup out of mugs rather than bowls. It stays hotter and I could take it where ever I wanted to without spilling. I parked myself in front of my living room windows watching the stars, letting my mind wander. I had finished the soup before Jay returned my call.

"Sorry Victoria but I was talking with Keirns. So how did the showing go?" Jay was fishing.

"If you were talking to Mr. Keirns you know more than I. Tell me." Of course Jay knew more than I did. I was starting to believe my involvement had very little to do with real estate.

"Well, he initially called to ask for my Escrow Account transfer numbers. If he could transfer into my personal account, why waste the time calling for the others? I asked him about that by the way." Jay paused.

"Jay it's too late at night for games. What did he say?"

"He didn't. He ignored my question and continued his end of the conversation. He told me to expect the outline of an Offer, modified for Ledge House, in my office tomorrow morning. Asked some legal questions about procedures, what is required by law in the final contract, that kind of stuff. He said he didn't anticipate I would have any questions once I reviewed the package. I tried to ask about inspections, explain wetlands, stuff like that. Keirns said and I quote 'it is of no importance'. I'm not going to argue. What do you think?" Jay was starting to sound a little excited and a little confused as he continued describing their conversation. Almost like he had taken notes but the words hadn't sunk in until he repeated them to me.

"What can I say? When I arrived at the property Mr. Fournier and Mr. Keirns had already walked themselves around the land. Cheryl did her classic house tour. They didn't ask a question. Cheryl did try to cuddle up to Mr. Fournier, was promptly put in her place and then told to go home. I guess that was the highlight of the tour. No feedback to me. I must tell you that the property was beautiful. Fully updated, billiard room moved upstairs to the first floor. The indoor pool area was grand. Live trees, stone waterfall, steam room, everything you could ask for. Oh, Mr. Fournier was duly impressed with the pool area but I don't think Cheryl heard that."

"Who put Cheryl in her place? I have to ask." Jay has had his moments with Cheryl and her Brokerage. Threats of lawsuits and the general pain in the ass stuff.

"Mr. Fournier. I was surprised. He seemed to be rather laid back until then. Actually he shut down the anger as fast as it had appeared. So you want me to come by when tomorrow?" Friday was getting busy.

"Let me see this package in the morning and I'll give you a call. Good with you?"

"Sure, have a quieter evening Jay." Jay said the same and I hung up. I then started dialing Carolyn. Just get the phone calls over with now that I've started. Mid dial and I stopped. Didn't know how much I could tell her. According to the Privacy Agreement, nothing. My gut was telling me I needed to end her interest. I was the one that started telling her about library guy. I finished dialing.

"Hey Carolyn."

"So tell me what happened. I'm listening." I told her essentially what I had planned to tell Jay. Classic first showing. No problem with the buyers. I think I was just being paranoid. No big deal. When she asked if they were going to make an offer I told her that I didn't even have feedback, didn't have any questions, so I was thinking it may have been way too much house. I tried to be as vague as I could. She seemed to be satisfied and started talking about other things. But I knew Carolyn too well. The subject would come up in a couple of days. After more pleasantries we said good night.

I crawled into bed exhausted. Closing my eyes was pure pleasure. Then I started dreaming, little short pieces of dreams. I knew I was dreaming. The more I thought about it, they were like scenes in a very disconnected play. The dreams went on all night. I was driving a truck in San Francisco, I was a guy; I was a bar owner, somewhere in the Midwest with men yelling for service; I was sitting on a horse in a long dress hearing gunshots, wondering which direction would be the safest; in a canoe, dressed in fur with beaver pelts in front of me; sitting in a chair alone in a house and someone was banging on the door and yelling. Yelling what, I didn't know. The last was the clearest. Walking in a field, beautiful clear sky and someone was walking behind me, not far behind but I couldn't see who it was. We were talking, but I couldn't understand anything. Then my alarm went off. I did not want to move. I wanted to continue that last dream. Oh well.

Chapter 11

I was driving out to Portsmouth with Bill's keys to take a good look at the house when Jay called. The package he'd received was hard copy with a storage stick to load into his computer. The package was as advertised. He didn't have any questions for Mr. Keirns. He had identified all of the normal inspections and specifically denied them. A couple of clauses on privacy that, if violated, would negate the contract. Close when the Seller wanted to. In his Escrow was sitting $200,000, transferred over night. Bottom line, offer was $9.9M, cash, 20% down, Escrow held by Jay, Buyer's lawyer. Could I come by about 11 to pick up the package and we could talk.

"Sure Jay." I said when he was finished. "Think I can call Cheryl to meet her at 12. Will we be done by then?"

"Should be. I'm just not comfortable talking about this on the cell. I don't know why, but I am. So I'll see you at 11." Jay hung up. He was having the same feeling I was having last night with Carolyn. Oh well, we're both paranoid. I called Cheryl and asked for a meeting at about 12. She asked what it was about and I told her I just needed some clarification on a few things. She said she would be available, but had an appointment to show Ledge House at 12:45. Of course she did.

Bill's house looked the same from the outside as it had when he and Jenny had bought it. A little overgrown in the front, but part of it's charm. From the street it looked like a classic Cape with salt worn cedar shingles, white shutters, small front yard with very little grass, a few holly bushes and a wonderful 4 foot stone wall set back about 3 feet from the street.

The treat to this house was that it was built on a hill that slopped to the shore of the Sakonnett River. A salt water, tidal river on the east side of the island that fed directly into the Atlantic. The slope of the hill also allowed the house to expand, in the rear, a full three levels. If you entered through the front the door, a staircase to what seemed to be a small second level was on the left; a small living room on the right with the classic fireplace. But walk down the center hall and the house exploded into one, three-story, glass-faced space the width of the of the house. The only drawback to the design was the kitchen and dining area on the lowest level. I knew there had been talk of moving the kitchen and dining area up a level. Obviously nothing had been done.

Jenny had not gone out of her way to clean the house when she left. They did have a cleaning woman at least once a week. I would have to tell Bill to have the cleaning lady come to do a complete top-to-bottom cleaning now that most of the furniture was gone. I spent some serious time checking everything, making sure things worked. Even the washer and dryer were in place. All the other appliances were built ins. No chance of loss there. Best of all, everything worked, just needed cleaning.

Interior pictures would have to wait. I exited through the rear glass doors. I knew the property would be beautiful when the grass and flowers came in; but today, no pictures. I walked, rather climbed, up the side of the hill in the melting snow. Hey, I only fell once.

When Bill and Jenny bought the house there had been a crack in a retaining wall holding the street. It was still there. The crack did look threatening. It looked as if it failed the street would fall around the house. Bill had been told by a contractor that it was a settling crack and wouldn't go any farther. I would ask Bill to refresh my mind and maybe get it looked at again. Better now than during a buyer's inspection. Gut price for the house, $675,000. Settle for $650,000.

For as many market price analysis's I'd done, gut was best. At least my gut was best. Usually the market analysis came out where I though it would. If I did a market analysis first, purely data; then visited the property - same thing. I did them now only when specifically asked for one. It would kill an afternoon and the next day the seller will tell you that his neighbor's house is on the market for some ungodly price and 'why can't his house get that much?' It doesn't matter that the neighbor's house didn't sell for the quoted price. It was only an asking price. Or, better yet, the neighbor has a heated swimming pool, a dock for a 60' cabin cruiser or seven master bedroom suites with fireplaces to his three bedrooms, one and a half baths. No, a good agent doesn't ask if they are out of their freaking minds, at least not overtly. But I must say, there have been times.

I took a few pictures of the front and sides of the house so we could get it on the market and drove directly to Jay's office. I might make it by eleven.

Jay was waiting for me in his reception room when I arrived. He was not smiling, just starring at the wall. Yeah, he was nervous. Lawyers never look like they are waiting for anyone.

"Hi Victoria, why don't we talk in my office?" Jay takes people to his conference room. Why, I don't know but he does, probably more room for paper. I think I'd been in his actual office two, three times and I've known him forever. Jay opened the door to the office and entered first. I walked through, stopped. James was sitting in one of the chairs, Mr. Keirns was on the leather cushioned bench. They both stood up. James held the chair that was obviously intended for me. It was the only one unoccupied.

"Well hi. This is unexpected." I held my hand to James. He took it, held it, ran his thumb over the back of my hand, again looking into my eyes. My stomach moved to my throat. I was hoping my knees didn't buckle.

"I thought you might have questions better answered directly." Yes, he was smiling again.

Mr. Keirns move in my direction, James released my hand. That was a little better. I took Mr. Keirns's hand. "Mr. Keirns I look forward to reviewing your package. Shall I get to work?" I moved to sit down and felt the edge of the chair at the back of my knees. James returned to his chair.

Jay handed me the package he had produced. I spread it on his desk. Everyone was so quiet. Thank heavens Jay had hit the highlights on the phone. As I flipped the pages I started to pull questions out of the air. What the hell.

"James, are you sure that you want to forgo the inspections? I have found that when the inspections are skipped there are usually regrets."

"I would expect that we will do some fine tuning. This I have been told by others who have bought property."

"Is this the first ownership for you?" He opened the door to give me more personal information.

"Yes. The first I would consider my residence. I do not believe I have had the desire until now." He answered by telling me very little.

"Are you sure about this purchase? It's a bit large for a first shot out of the box, don't you think?" Yeah, this is a big "first house". I did need to ask.

James looked at Mr. Keirns who promptly stood, walked to James and whispered in his ear. I heard some sounds but that was it. I looked at Jay and he was as bewildered as I was.

Mr. Keirns returned to his seat. James looked back at me. "No." That was it, all he said was 'no'. I couldn't help myself, I had to smile and hoped it didn't turn into real laugh. Hey, I asked the question. If his answer had been more in the vain of an explanation I would have continued explaining how hard owning a house was. But the definitive 'no' did not invite continuation. I changed the subject.

I looked up from the pages I had spread over Jay's desk. Looked at James. "I truly understand your desire for privacy and confidentially in this transaction but I do need to point out that Mr. Matthews and I can only control our side of your purchase. We cannot control others, especially the listing broker and her brokerage. Nor can we control the Seller or his people, much less the press. I need you to be clear on this."

"We do understand this Victoria." The irises in James's eyes were starting to bleed into the pupil. I looked to Mr. Keirns. He was watching James. "We understand the others who must be involved now. I will deal with any breaches."

That was an odd way to say we'll sue the bastards. But once this intended purchase is out of the bag it is a day late and a dollar short. "Fine. You have left the Closing date to Seller's choice. Would you like to put a 'not later than' date in here so your money isn't sitting in Escrow forever?"

Mr. Keirns responded to that one. "No. I do believe this Seller will Close as fast as he can. No."

"Then, if you will sign the Offer, I will be on my way." I stood to give James and Mr. Keirns room to sign and noticed that only Mr. Keirns would be signing for a corporation. Good way to go. The only thing that will show up in the town hall is a privately held corporation. No names.

James and I stepped back to allow Mr. Keirns access to the documents. James took the opportunity to ask to see me again. He took my hand with a gentle squeeze and I remembered the dream clip from last night. The last one I remembered. "You are relentless aren't you?"

"Yes. this time yes, I will be." James took a large breath, held it for a second with his eyes closed and when he released it, opened his eyes, he seemed to release a tension he held. His shoulders relaxed, his cheekbones became sharper and with that I noticed vague marks on his face, around his eyes, in the hollows of his cheeks, continuing down his neck into his collar. I saw that shadow again. James actually leaned against the wall. Did not release my hand. He had held this tension for a long time.

Chapter 12

I was fifteen minutes late for my meeting with Cheryl who was 'fake busy' in her office on the second floor of a building she leased on one of the piers jutting into Newport Harbor.

She looked up as I entered her office. "So what are these dire clarifications that needed answering face to face?" Yeah, this was the real Cheryl. Last time we had spoken face to face, maybe 5-6 years ago, I had told her that it would be a cold day in hell before she would list a certain property. Well, it had been many cold days since then and she never did list it. I had to smile.

"Cheryl, thank you so much for the showing. The property is wonderful." I closed the office door and sat down across from her. "I am here to present you with an Offer from my Client." I reached into my bag and pulled out the package, handing it to her. Well, that got her attention.

"I asked when you called if your Client was interested." She opened the large envelope, pulled out the one original copy it contained, reached for her phone. "Linda, I need some copies made."

Did she not take this confidentiality seriously? "Cheryl, I would not have copies made if I were you. They are serious about the confidentiality. You have one original, Jay has the other and I can guarantee that no other copies exist."

"Oh come on Victoria. Everyone in that price range has us sign that statement. It's no big shakes. I see it all the time." This was not good and I was trying to figure out how to stop her when Linda, her secretary, walked in.

"Linda, would you make a couple of copies please?" Cheryl handed the Contract to Linda.

I stood up to block Linda. "Cheryl, I don't know what's going on with these guys, but copies are the last thing I would do. Truly, I wouldn't want to be around if this leaks."

"Victoria, don't interfere with my office and my instructions. This is the way we do it." Linda walked around me, took the envelope, walked out.

"Cheryl, you are such an arrogant…ah…Broker." She knew what I almost said. "At least you should have read the Contract first. In a rather extensive Confidentiality Clause it says thou shall not reproduce the document."

The smile left her face. "Are you kidding me?"

"No, I'm not. You do need to read it." Cheryl left the office in a bit of a hurry. Returned with the Contract and about six pages that I had to assume were the pages that had been copied.

"Oh shit. Take these." She held the odd pages out for me to take. I did take them, but did not want to return to Jay's office with them. I sat in the chair while she read, flipped back to pages, reread sections and finally looked up. "So how do I get this to the Seller? I can't fax, I can't scan and email." She reached for the phone. I bet she was calling the West Coast.

"Hold just a second Cheryl, ok, lets talk a minute." She but the phone down and looked at me. "I think we should talk about this first. Do you have any questions? Any questions you think the Seller might have."

"Truly no conditions?"

"Right. I asked a couple of times, no conditions."

"Cash."

"Yes. You did see that Jay will hold Escrow. Close at the convenience of the Seller." Contracts didn't get much easier than this. "I would advise that when you are talking to the Seller I would refer to the Buyer as just the Buyer, no details."

"I've already talked to the Seller. I had to tell him about the showing. I called last night and talked to him and his lawyer. They though Mr. Fournier and Mr. Keirns were funny." Cheryl was giggling now. Not the brightest bulb in the refrigerator. "By the way Victoria, where the hell did you pick them up?"

"Make the call Cheryl. You don't believe anything you sign do you?" I gave up. Cheryl made the call. She didn't even ask me to leave the room.

"Hi! This is Cheryl Kingston out here in, ah, he called just now, oh, ok…" This went on for about twenty minutes, she took some notes.

Apparently the Seller's lawyer was going to fly out and be here on Monday. All I could assume was that buttons had been pushed.

By the time Cheryl hung up the phone she was pale. She excused herself saying she would be right back. I crossed my legs, leaned back in my chair and closed my eyes. She would be gone for a bit. I hadn't ever seen her shaken like this. I'd seen her mad, really mad; I'd seen her double talking her way out of lies and commitments, irritated many times, but shaken to her core…never. I do believe that Cheryl is one of those people that think they are invincible, the center around which everything revolves. Every time she had to deal with me she was irritated. Not irritated from our last encounter but irritated because I am one of the few Brokers still in the business that remembers her as a gum-popping, nasal-whining, hair-teased mall chick rental agent from North Providence working in her cousin's real estate business. Desperately trying to break into summer rentals in Newport.

Cheryl fell into owning the business when he died and I must say she's done well. She cleaned herself up as much as her taste would allow and pushed when no one was looking. By the time the agencies holding the big exclusive brands noticed her, it was too late. She took one of the brands for the State and the agency holding the other is sweating bullets. Any agent that files ethics complaints against her or her brokerage, ends up in her brokerage and withdraws the complaint. I am so glad we are small. We can stay out of the politics. Believe me, the politics of this business will eat you up and spit you out.

Cheryl returned and apologized to me for leaving. She looked a little better, but not great. "Jay had just spoken to the Seller's lawyer when I called. He will be flying out this weekend and hopes to have the property closed by next Friday. He told me to sit tight and if the Buyer wants to see the property again to let them in and leave. You can call me when you are done and I will come back and lock up. Do you have any idea what's going on? I mean seriously, do you know? Where did you find them?"

I shook my head. "I do not have a clue what is going on other than Ledge House is gone. Not too bad for us. Frankly, I'm not sure I want to know anything else. As for where they came from, they were a referral from an old Client who has since moved to Europe."

I stood to leave when Cheryl stood and handed me the Contract. "I've been told to return this to you. Let me know if I need to open the house over the weekend. Thanks". She sat back down and I left.

I knocked on Jay's office door and he told me to come on in. I looked around the office. James was gone. Mr. Keirns remained.

Mr. Keirns stood to hold my chair. "Mrs. Hamilton, James had to leave for a few days to attend to business. The house has changed some of his plans."

I handed the Contract package to Jay. "I imagine it would Mr. Keirns, considering we had spoken of three bedrooms." I held my own chair. "Mr. Keirns, please. I appreciate your efforts but standing every time I come in the room and holding my chair is just a bit much. Please relax." I sat down and Mr. Keirns sat next to me, facing me.

"Mrs. Hamilton, believe me when I tell you that I take my directions seriously and I mean no harm in my respect." What the hell could I say to that? And what directions?

"Victoria." Jay started. "I guess you know that the Seller's lawyer will be here on Monday and we hope to wrap this up by Friday. I've ordered title. I explained to Mr. Keirns that it would be best to have a title search and all it implies. Can you think of anything else?"

"Cheryl has informed me that the property is available if Mr. Fournier and Mr. Keirns would like to visit again. Other than that, I can't think of anything else. I'll give a call if I do. So, Mr. Keirns." I stood to leave. I wasn't the only one. " I must leave now. I have some office business to take care of. Please call if you would like to view the property this weekend." I shook his hand and reached across the desk to Jay. He stood. "Thank you Jay for all of your help. Call if you need me." I left, after all it was Friday afternoon and Mary was waiting. Yeah, I'm thrilled it's Friday. Good excuse to leave and flip my switch to normal stuff.

Mary was waiting for me and the office actually had people in it. No one was for me. Good.

"Hey Mary, how's it going?"

"Hey yourself. Coffee?"

"Sure, would you mind bringing it into the office?"

"No problem. Unlock the other door and I will slide in."

I needed to be in familiar surroundings. I needed to relax. The end of a very crazy, very weird week. I closed the front door to my office and unlocked the door to the workroom, hung up my coat. My desk had it's usual two piles. My cell rang. It was Jay.

"Jay I wasn't kidding about office work. What's going on?"

"Are you alright?" Jay seemed concerned.

"Yeah fine. Tired, but fine. What's wrong?"

"I can't remember stuff. You were here this afternoon, right?"

"All three of us were. I should be asking if you are all right?"

"Yeah, I was making notes about Mr. Keirns and the Contract. There was someone else here right?" His voice was starting to shake.

"Jay, yes there was. Mr. Fournier, we sold Ledge House, Closing by next Friday, you ordered title, remember?" I hoped he wasn't having a stroke or something.

"Ok. Couldn't remember his name and I remember what I'm suppose to do but no details. Not what the conversations were and definitely didn't remember the third guy, what's his name again?"

"James Fournier, and nothing else matters. I'd tell you if it did." I was trying to help. Make it easier for him.

"What did Fournier look like?"

Now this was truly getting weird. "Jay, it doesn't matter. He didn't sign anything or say very much. It's been a hell of a week for both of us I think. Why don't you call it a night, go home and have a drink."

"Do you remember everything?" He asked with a bit of hesitation. Jay is an excellent lawyer and not used to being unable to remember things. What the hell?

"Yeah, Jay I do and trust me. You remember what you need to remember. Make notes of what you do remember and call it a day."

"Yeah. Victoria if I need to, can I call you to remind me of things?" Jay was starting to sound like a little kid.

"Sure Jay, always. Have a good weekend, sleep late and all that stuff." I hung up. Mary was standing in front of the rear door.

"You sold Ledge House? When, to whom? Tell me. You don't keep these kinds of secrets." Mary was about to jump up and down with two cups of coffee in her hands.

"Mary, close the door and I'll tell you what I can." I gave her the usual highlights, the highlights for any contract.

"I haven't seen a file."

"Mary, Jay is doing everything. I need to warn you. There is an extensive Confidentially Statement with the contract. Not a word. No joke, no comments, no nothing to anyone. I would rather not talk about it to anyone. Understand?" Mary hadn't seen me this serious in a long time.

"The guy you met with on Wednesday? The guy with the bank president?" Mary remembered.

"Yeah. Now forget it. Do we have any paper remaining in the office from that meeting?" It just occurred to me that we might have something hanging around.

"A few. Want them?"

"Yeah when we're done here. Dinner at 6?"

"Why do you think everyone's here? They've been here since about two doing everything they usually do from other places." Mary seemed a little excited with everyone here. It's so rare. Our Brokers wander in and out in the course of a week, but rarely are here all at once. Actually, it's a little tight when everyone is here. If they had Clients in tow, it would be too close. I wonder if that has ever happened? I'll ask tonight.

Mary and I went over the accounts and the ads together. I think she stayed hoping I would slip on Ledge House. I told her about Bill and gave her the Listing forms out of my bag. We decided to put it in the computer Monday. It was getting late so I flipped through the ads, didn't change anything and told her to send them off on Monday. I'd do some local ads for Bill's house over the weekend. Oh, I needed to call Bill.

There was a knock on my door. "Come in."

It was Mason. "We're going to wander down. Mary, want to come with us?"

"Mary, why don't you go on. I've got a call to make and I'll be down." Noticing the clock I had better get moving. It was 5:30. Reservations at 6.

"Ok, See you at the Pearl".

Mary left and it was quiet again. I called Bill, told him I was at the house, listed the stuff that needed to be done and asked him if anything I had emailed had appealed to him. Catherine Street. He wanted to see Catherine Street, maybe tomorrow afternoon about 2. I said sure, I'd call him to confirm. Punched the 'end' button on the phone and dialed Karen, the Karen who had been repeatedly requesting to join our office; repeatedly showing up at the office trying to talk to me after I had politely said I didn't think this was the office for her. Last week I had told Mary to call me the next time she showed up. After all Mary had been telling her I wasn't available, I was out with Clients, anything she could think of for the past two months. It was my turn.

The Catherine Street condo was Karen's listing and now we would have to talk if she brought it up. Thankfully, I talked to her voice mail. Hopefully she would call me back tonight. I hung up, grabbed my coat, locked and alarmed the office and went to dinner.

Chapter 13

The Black Pearl was one of my favorites. It has been a favorite since my teens when I would get into the bar and listen to jam sessions on Sunday nights in the bar. I didn't gain access to the Captain's room until I was dating my second husband.

The Captain's room is formal and on the expensive side. Reservations only, no blue jeans or shorts allowed for women, ties required for men. The room itself is not large for a restaurant dining room and held maybe ten tables in the middle surrounded with wooden benches on three walls with two chairs on the opposite side of each table. In the summer the room could be quite full. Winter, no problem, even on a Friday night and we were early for the dating crowd.

I went to the bar to pick everyone up but they had already gone to the Captain's room. Guess I was late. I turned the corner and scanned the room. Two couples and a chatty group in the rear corner where I was headed. Nice looking office, classy looking office and as far as I was concerned, the best in the business. I did not rate best in the business in dollar amounts. To do that would be like saying Wal-Mart is the best store in the country. My rating system is reputation, credibility, honesty, repeat Clients and somewhere below that is dollars because the dollars are earned with honor. Everyone of my Brokers should be proud of that and I reinforce it as much as I can. Sounds strange in the real estate business but it is the major reason I left the box store real estate world.

"Hi everyone. Glad you could make it. Sorry I'm late." Mason stood and stepped out from the bench side of the table. My seat this time was between Mason and Nina. Every month my location was switched off.

Mason and Nina were stuck with me this month. To me, it didn't matter, I liked everyone.

The second I sat the waiter came to ask if I would like a cocktail before dinner. Of course, my problem as always, was deciding what I wanted. What I drank before dinner usually decided for me what dinner would be and my beverages for the rest of the evening. I used to mix, but not any more, not worth it. A whiskey sour, very sour. I glanced around the table. "Does anyone want another?"

"Sure." Mason spoke up. "Bourbon, rocks". For that I didn't need to ask. He would probably drink it for the rest of the evening. No one else joined him. If he paced himself and had a good dinner during the evening Mason could drink all night. Stay sober, at least on the outside. Fascinating little talent that had chagrined many an Admiral in Washington. Mason also had a talent for remembering conversations word for word, when they occurred, where they occurred and the people that were around during the conversation. I had originally met Mason when I worked for a company that produced weapons for the military many years ago. I learned a lot from him about dealing with Clients. Some of it I could use, some of it was purely Mason. I spent most of my time on the research and development side of the business and Mason's time was spent in hardware and production. Every once in a while we would cross paths. To this day my mental impression of Mason was on a horse with a cape, saber and wide brim hat. A classic southern gentleman during the Civil War. He was from southern Virginia, spoke with the classic Virginia accent and never did anything to detour my visual.

Mason showed up about eight years ago in Newport, much to my surprise. I didn't think he would ever come north of 'the line'. Said he was bored with the old business, it wasn't fun anymore. That I could understand. He quickly got a salesman's license and as soon as he could, produced a broker's license. When I decided to leave the big office I was with he had called me asking what my plans were. I told him and he was the first broker to join me. Mason has proved very successful applying his talents to this business. He has his moments. But hey, don't we all. He loves Newport.

Sitting on the other side of me was Nina, Nina Glover. Nina can tie a cherry stem with her tongue and she can do it sober. I can only do it after at least one drink. The first time she demonstrated this little talent was at one of Carolyn's larger parties. I had laughed so hard I had tears on my cheeks. Yes, Nina taught me how to do it and now it is a shared entertainment we proudly demonstrate at any good party. Still cracks me up. Nina came to me via Carolyn. Carolyn mentioned to Nina what I was planning to develop in the business and, when I finally leased the Avenue office Nina called. She is right out of the Social Register. Matches Carolyn club for club and party for party and story for story in the summer. I've stopped keeping track of her husbands. She has had three since she's been in our office. Nina doesn't change her last name because, as she puts it, 'it was getting too damn expensive to change the advertising and the business cards' or so she'd said to me when I asked if she wanted me to change her name on the office advertising. I do believe her last husband was number six. Carolyn told me that Nina was on number two when they met. Mason had better be careful. I knew they'd dated and at one point it got steamy to be around them. Now I think they are just friends. I think.

Ames sat on the other side of the table with Mary chatting up a storm. From what I could gather Ames was looking at his most profitable year yet. I guess he was feeling better about his Clients.

With our drinks came the menus. I do believe these are the only menus in town that can contain, as 'specials', ostrich or wild boar, deviled pheasant eggs, moose or what ever exotic fare the chef could find. This, of course, can lead to testing and tasting within any group eating in the Captain's room. I usually stick to the more familiar fare on this menu, but will usually taste when it's offered. Today's special was North Atlantic Eel. That was so not happening for me, but Ames went for the gold.

After our orders were given, Mary asked if I had anything to say. "Not really, I'm doing fine. How about you Nina?"

"Doing ok. It's winter in Newport. What can I say? I'm freezing, my car is taking twenty minutes to warm up." Nina took a sip of her Manhattan, yes with a cherry. "Actually, the smaller stuff is selling and I'm doing a few of those. So I'm ok. Mason, your turn."

"You know Nina, if you got rid of that diesel monster you drive you would actually be able to start you car without two batteries." Mason did truly hate Nina's diesel Mercedes. She claimed it was a classic. He claimed it provided more pollution than the city buses. I couldn't argue that one.

"Mason, you touch my car and your riding days are over." Last winter one of Nina's batteries had been taken while she was at the office. Couldn't prove it was Mason, but we knew it was. The battery showed up in her trunk a couple of days later, after the tow and acquisition of another battery.

"Nina, I would nevah…evah touch your car." Mason leaned over me, smiling at Nina. "I am doing just fine." He began but was interrupted by my cell. I was in such a hurry I forgot to put it on vibrate.

"I'm sorry Mason, can you hold it just a minute?" I reached into my bag to answer as fast as I could.

"Victoria Hamilton"

"Victoria, this is Karen. Tomorrow would be fine. I've been trying to see you again for a while. That Mary keeps telling me you're not in or you're busy and you don't answer your cell." Karen ran all of the words together as fast as she could, probably thinking I would hang up.

"Karen, good. I'll see you tomorrow. I'm with dinner companions now. Maybe we can set up another meeting for next week. Sure, I think Tues afternoon would be fine. Give a call to Mary before you come, ok?" Karen was not happy with Mary in the mix, but I had my showing. I hung up. "Ok Mason, please continue."

"You're still talking to Karen? I thought that was a dead issue." Karen wasn't one of Mason's favorites either.

"Yes it is a dead issue. She's just not listening. Guess I was too civil when I told her no the first time. I'll ramp it up this time. Does anyone know why she's looking to change offices? When I asked her in January she said she just needed a change. Didn't believe it then and I surely don't believe it now."

"Victoria," Nina offered, "I think it's a few things. You know she lost it with Frank just before the holidays don't you?"

"No, but she's lost it with him before and he just walks away."

"You should try to make it to an Association meeting every once in a while. The information flow is amazing." Nina went to the 'union' meetings in the winter for lack of anything else to do.

I waved the thought away with my hand. "Yeah, yeah."

"Well anyway, she lost it with the office packed with Clients. Word has it that Frank excused himself from his Clients, grabbed her arm, pulled her into Tracy's office and told Tracy to do something with her before he tossed her through the front window. Actually, I think that was the biggie. Later I was told that among her goals and objectives this year was getting her Broker's license."

"She had promised me that she would get her Broker's license if I would sponsor her. Why doesn't she just get it?" I asked.

"She's too cheap. The license is more expensive and the insurance is higher. Victoria, you know that if you sponsored her and she came to the office she would find a million reasons not to get it, don't you?" Mary wanted this to go away.

"Come on Mary. The license has very little to do with why she's not coming to us and you know it. Anyway, I think Mason was talking when we were interrupted. Go for it Mason." And wouldn't you know it, dinner arrived. Poor Mason. Then the wine Steward. "OK, Mason, your choice tonight." And, as always, he ordered very specifically, by year. The rule on wine at our office meetings was two bottles, one that would complement white meat or fish and one that would complement a red meat or dark fish. I gave Mason ordering honors. No one would complain. He had yet to disappoint. "So, do you want to continue?"

"I'm doing fine. Personally, I think business is good, especially for winter up here." If Mason wasn't fine, I would have known long before this.

"OK Ames, your turn."

"By the end of spring, if all goes well, I will be having my best year ever." And Ames gave the whole table a huge smile. "I certainly cannot complain about anything." I guess that answered my question.

"Mary, do you have anything to say?"

"You guys need to get those CEUs going. That's my biggie and includes you, Victoria." I nodded. The others nodded and grunted. CEUs were the bane of our existence. At least the regulatory system could roll the grandfathered date and require grandfathered agents to take classes relative to new real estate legislation or something like that. Mary was right, what could I say. "And, since we might have some extra funds soon…" Oh, Mary don't go there. "…maybe we could actually get a bathroom we don't have to share with a store. That would be heaven." Yeah, everyone agreed with that.

Ames asked. "What extra funds? Something going on I missed?"

Need to walk around this and shoot Mary in the parking lot later. "I may be falling into something in the next few weeks and I was thinking about putting some of it into the office. I'll see how it goes. No biggie." No one will ask if they think it's personal and not related to the real estate. Mary looked at me and frowned. We had not discussed the potential commission from Ledge House. I hadn't thought about the actual number.

Mary did know me. I always put money into the business when something large comes my way outside of the commission percentage that would normally stay in the business. As for stepping over the confidentiality line on this sale, if something big is happening in a real estate office, the office in general knows about it. It lifts moral, lifts the pressure to pay the bills and the owners will usually buy new pencils for everyone. But our office doesn't work that way. Hopefully the pressure isn't there to begin with and we buy our own pencils.

"So, other than everyone agreeing that it would be nice to have our own bathroom, everything's working?" They all nodded and mumbled while they continued to eat and we were good.

The evening continued. No one took Ames up on his eel tasting offers, but the desserts were shared with out question. We broke up about 9, wandering into the parking lot, saying our goodbyes for the weekend. Good dinner, good meeting. Who the heck would have believed this approach to a real estate office would work. After a lifetime of trying to fit into social concepts and corporate profiles I'd finally created something that allowed me to function. Something that does feel good. Oh heck, I guess I wouldn't shoot Mary. I was too tired and as always I'm sure Mary had a reason for bringing it up. I just didn't see it.

While I was warming up the car I called Bill to tell him we were good for tomorrow, two pm, the Catherine Street condo. He told me that the house 'to do' list I had left should be complete by the end of next week. Great, pictures. It is so nice to have a Client that doesn't argue about the necessities of selling or buying real estate. I don't mind questions, I encourage them. But a seller arguing with me about why the master bedroom should not remain grape purple with its orange carpet is beyond me. Buyers have their moments too, but I seem to be able to deal with those moments better.

Chapter 14

By the time I got home I was fighting to keep my eyes open. It had been one hell of a week. I guess a productive week and that's always good, but all I wanted to do was curl up in bed and go to sleep. I didn't even walk into the living room. Straight to bed. It felt so good drifting off in the silence.

At some point I was dreaming again. I knew I was dreaming. I was standing on the side of a street, in a crowd with a little girl on my shoulders waiting for the St. Patrick's Day Parade to start. I was wearing a Fedora, an overcoat with my only suit underneath, the one I wore to Church every Sunday. I was looking at the crowd across the street when I saw a man standing alone, looking at me without expression. I looked closer and saw red-tinted tears rolling down his cheeks. I didn't know him, but I did. It was James. The parade started.

The next flash. A room filled with the stale smells of beer, dirt, sweat. I was on trial. On trial for what? I wore a tattered, dirty brown dress with some kind of stained apron. I was barefoot, dark hair tangled, body aching. My voice screaming as I was dragged out of the building. So scared I vomited on the steps. Sick to the bottom of my soul; dragged into the street, tossed into a wagon. Whoa. I was like two people; me dreaming and me gagging. This wasn't right. Still the scene unfolded. I've got to wake up. It's a fucking dream. I started panicking. The crowd was yelling so loud, yelling at me. I looked up. In the back of the crowd was the face. The expressionless face. It was James. What?

I woke up rolling off the side of my bed; sick on my floor, cold and shaking. Oh hell.

I sat up against my headboard, still shaking. Grabbed the top blanket

82

to wrap around myself trying to warm up. Where the hell did that come from? I remembered dinner and the couple of drinks I'd had earlier. Stress, dinner and drinks. Yeah, that'll do it. Figured the only way I would warm up, stop shaking and get this super sucky dream out of my head would be the cure for all in my world; water. This late…a shower.

I set the controls as hot as I could stand; the spray as hard as it would go. I just stood. Finally, the shaking started to slow and that felt so good I began to relax, think. The dream was more detailed than the earlier one and James hadn't been in the first one, but the first one hadn't been as terrifying either. I couldn't think of any other dream that had made me physically sick. Was it rich food that made me sick and then I started dreaming? Dreams can incorporate things happening in the real world, like trying to find the bathroom in a dream when you most certainly need to wake up and go. Now that was a real possibility. My skin was pruned. I was probably as warm as I was going to get in the shower. I needed to clean up my bedroom before I tried to get back to sleep.

By the time I finished cleaning up my bedroom, the shaking was gone. I was comfortably warm in my fresh sweats topped with a chenille bath robe. The shaking was replaced by anxiety that spiked when I thought about going back to sleep. I went to the kitchen, grabbed a bottle of water. Opened the junk drawer. Took out a pack of cigarettes. Sat at the breakfast bar, lit up.

My hands started shaking again. I rarely had dreams that I remembered. Even more rare was the notorious 'scary' dream. But this one got to me even though I had figured out what happened. I could not shake the dream. I needed to tell Mary to change any future meetings at the Captain's room. Right. In my heart of hearts, I didn't think that was the problem.

When I finished the cigarette my hands were still shaking, but it was now or stay up all night. I grabbed my water. Went back to bed wearing my sweats and my robe.

I must have dropped off to sleep. The next thing I knew, the light coming into the bedroom was fading, having already passed the direct eastern rays of early and mid morning. I ran mental inventory, then body inventory. I felt fine. Had last night been a total dream? No, the rug by my bed was gone and I was hot in the sweats and bath robe. When I tried I seriously couldn't remember the details of the dream. I did know I'd had a zinger but that was pretty much all. I did remember getting sick. Oh well, it had been a stressful week, but now I felt fine. Forget about it. Move forward. Needed to meet Bill.

Chapter 15

Local real estate transactions anywhere in our country, or for that matter in any country, have their own traditions, local, unofficial area descriptions and general ways of doing things. I have found that the way things are done on the Island are quite different from the way things are done in Warwick. As the bird flies, Warwick is just on the other side of the Bay, about 15 miles away. Same State, same associations, same licensing department within the State, same rules and regulations; but things are done as a matter of everyday business a little differently.

Agents from Warwick with Clients buying on the Island will, more than likely, start the process of negotiation with an 'Offer to Purchase' almost in the form of a letter and not a full Purchase and Sale Agreement presented as an 'Offer'. Perfectly legal, but it is a step that the agents on the Island feel is a waste of time and can be rather confusing to both parties.

Usually an 'Offer to Purchase' just contains the bare bones of a full 'Purchase and Sale Agreement'. This 'Offer to Purchase' form is intended to find out if the seller of a property will entertain or counter the price being presented. The Offer also should contain a clause saying '...a complete Purchase and Sale will be executed......' so that none of the parties think the Offer is the complete ballgame representing all of the requirements and conditions of the sale.

However, a few of these little devils have been taken to court and have been held by the courts to be the full and binding Contract. Why would this be difficult? Sellers think they have sold the property. Then all of a sudden a clause shows up in the final product that is not agreeable with the seller and negotiations start all over again or everyone goes to court. Or...

Buyers think they have bought a house with every intention of adding inspections and mortgage conditions to the final product. The seller says no and pushes for a sale with the Offer to Purchase. If this happens everyone can usually kiss the deal goodbye and pray they don't end up in court.

Worse than an Offer to Purchase is the agent of a buyer who asks that the seller's agent try a verbal offer to see if a number flies before they put something on paper. That is just plain lazy. Oral discussions don't count for points no matter what is said and can only end up with hurt feelings all around...oh and they all end up in court. Yes, the basic solution to many 'little' real estate mishaps.

Traditions in local real estate extend to how areas of a city or town are referred to in local parlance. Local to the Island and especially Newport are names of areas that will never be found on a map but have, in the minds of the locals and the real estate agents, very specific boarders with very specific characteristics, house styles and histories. A buyer explaining that they would like to buy an old house on "The Point" with a 2-car garage on half an acre will be told that it doesn't exist. And frankly, it doesn't. Old house, oh yes we have plenty of those on The Point...2-car garage...not so much, unless someone bought the adjoining house, took it down and built a garage. As for half an acre, only if someone bought the surrounding three properties or more and taken the houses down.

"The Point" was developed by the seafarers of 200+ years ago. It is not odd to be able to reach from one house to the other on the second floor. A description of such a house could read "Lot size: 1500 square feet; Above Ground Living Space: 4000 square feet". And heaven forbid if someone wants to do a survey on The Point. The potential for a whole street of property lines, maybe 50, moving to the north or south would not be impossible. What property owner is going to lose a hundred feet or more of their property to stop the movement? We are truly a "meets and bounds" State – the north property line runs 30' or so to the big oak tree kind of thing for hundreds of years, back to and including the original land grants from the King of England.

The area that interested Bill was, and still is known as the "Kay-Catherine" area. They are, indeed, two street names in the area. But the "Kay-Catherine" area extends outside of these two streets by about half a mile or more in all four directions, taking a dogleg around some government subsidized housing located on some very valuable land. This whole area is located behind our office. It contains some of the most spectacular historic homes in Newport.

Not the famous mansions of Bellevue Avenue and the Gilded Age, but wonderful Victorians. Queen Annes with hipped roofs, cross gables, spindle work, patterned masonry, fabulous porches, hand worked chimney pots. Second Empire designs with cupolas, central pavilions, bracketed windows, mansard roofs with dormer windows and so much more. Walking through the "Kay-Catherine" area is, in itself, two semesters of architectural history. These houses were built by the lawyers, doctors and business owners in Newport of the 18th and19th centuries. They were lived in every day, not just a summer get-away. Most still have the "milk porches" off the kitchen for deliveries and bare toilets in the basement for the "outside" help.

When I drove up to the condominium, Bill was waiting for me, standing on the brick walkway to the main entrance. "Victoria, how are you doing on this beautiful winter day?'" He stepped toward me wearing his gloves and coat but no hat. He was warmer than I was.

"Hi Bill. How's it going? You're right, it must be pushing 30 out here. But it's not snowing and I'm happy." I gave him my usual, we're doing business smile. There are days when I get home and realize that my face hurts from that smile. "Did you see the other Agent go in?"

"Yeah. She invited me up but I told her that I would rather wait for you."

"Fine, let's go in." I started for the front door when it opened and some idiot flew out, jumping the steps and slammed right into me. He stopped, caught my shoulders before I hit the ground. Steadied me on my feet, leaned into me, took a large quick breath. He smiled. His eyes met mine.

"I am so sorry. I should pay more attention. Are you alright?" The guy from before? In front of my office? Odd.

"Yeah, sure. Slow down." He moved around me, headed across the street.

"I will. Sorry." I heard his reply as he rounded the corner. I looked back to Bill who had started to me as soon as I began to fall. I continued my walk to the front door.

"Victoria wait a second." Bill followed me. "Are you ok?" I nodded. "This is one of my favorite 'drive-by' properties around here. I didn't realize it was a condo development."

"I know what you mean. Especially during the holidays with all of the white candles in the windows. This was one of the good conversions in the 70s. The developers didn't gut the property like some of them did." I held the front door for him. One of the hand-carved, eight inch thick oak doors. The entry hall was huge. Probably thirty by forty, 20' ceiling and a large curved and carved staircase ending on the right rear of the entry. The light for the entry was a very large crystal chandelier hanging from the ceiling two stories above us.

"Bill, we are on the second floor." He was fascinated by the scroll work in the ceiling and around the two major doors that were the entries for the two first floor units.

"Only two units on the first floor?" he asked, then answered his own question, "Wow, they must be wonderful splitting, what, 7,000 square feet?"

"Pretty much. The center, rear of the first floor is the milk porch with the butler's stairs and two secondary exits for the first floor units, so that takes some of the space. I keep forgetting how much original work remains in this building." And that was true. There are times, especially if it's been six months or more since I'd seen a property that it will start blending in my head with other properties. I remember this being a great property. That did stick. But how great was a surprise.

When we reached the second floor, the memory of all three of the second floor condos came rushing back. Thank heavens. There was a condo on the west end. A center building condo, rather small and the condo with the door open framing Karen. Karen in all of her ex-fashion-model glory standing in the doorway on the east side of the building. No. I didn't farm Bill out to one of my Brokers. We had too much history. I'd thought about it but couldn't do it. Yeah, I don't like guilt. I turned to Bill.

"Bill Goodman this is Karen Taylor. Karen is the Listing Agent for the condo." I said.

"Victoria, we've already met. Come on in." Karen walked into the condo. "This Seller is leaving the area to go overseas for a few years and decided not to Lease."

The condo had ten foot ceilings and the living room at the farthest end had windows almost floor to ceiling which is where Bill went first. The floor plan was a central hall; doors on the left to bedrooms, two baths. Doors on the right to the large eat-in kitchen and a dining room that would seat ten easily. The living room took up the eastern third of the condo. Tons of windows and light. I counted eight windows in the living room; two on the north and south walls and two on either side of a glass door that led to a small deck.

When I reached the living room Bill had already stepped on to the snow-covered deck. "Wow. I can see the beach, the pond, St. Georges' spires. This is nice."

"Bill, you do need to walk through the rest of the unit before you get all wet." He was enjoying the view, but he did need to move through the unit before the snow he was standing in melted into his shoes.

"Right, I'll take off my shoes before I walk back through." He did, balancing on one shoe in the snow, took off the other shoe, then stepped into the room balancing on the socked foot removing the second shoe. He looked at Karen. "I have three questions. The first, how fast can the Owner move? Second, can I lease before we Close? Third, how many of the units in the building are rentals?"

I didn't like the first two questions. Bill was starting to negotiate. The third was one that I would have asked before we left the unit.

"Bill." I took his arm and led him to the center hall. "Lets walk through the rest of the condo and Karen will finish telling us about the necessities. You know the condo association stuff. Then we can talk." I managed to get him to the master bedroom.

"Bill." Karen followed us. "I'm sure the Seller would prorate a lease based on a sale price. What are you thinking?" Oh Karen, don't start. "Do you think you would be doing inspections? I mean the condo doesn't need one. But of course, it's up to you. Have you applied for a mortgage yet?"

I turned to face her before she entered the bedroom. "Karen I don't think those are appropriate questions to be asking Bill". I needed to shut her down before it went too far.

"Why not?" She leaned into to me pretending Bill couldn't hear her. "He obviously is in a hurry, we can put this together right now." Real estate decisions made without thought, I have learned, always end up in regret.

I turned my back to her. "Bill, lets continue touring the condo. Is that alright with you?"

"Sure Victoria, you're the boss." Bill stuck his head into the master bath, then walked back through the bedroom, past Karen to the hall. Bill continued checking out the second bath, second bedroom and third. He stepped back into the hall, looked at Karen. "So how many rental units?"

She smiled at him walking down the hall. "One I think, but I'll check. The condo restrictions for renting are rather tight. No less than a year with the rental application submitted to the condo Board for approval along with a credit check."

Bill walked into the kitchen, did the appropriate opening and closing of appliances, walked out and opened the unit door. "Well, I've seen what I need to see. Victoria, why don't I meet you at your office?"

"Sure Bill, I'll be right there." That was it as far as he was concerned and enjoyed a leisurely walk down the staircase, out the front door. I turned to Karen, stepped back into the condo, closed the door. "So, I'll give you a call as soon as I have feedback. I would appreciate an answer on leased units when I call."

"Victoria do you think he's going to make an Offer?" The only question in my head was - where have you been for the last half hour? Duh? Odds were that he was.

"Could be. I would like that answer. I'll call you later." I opened the door and left to meet Bill. Yeah I was irritated. The first exchange, well it happens. But not picking up on the rest of the conversations. They weren't even subtle. Yeah, I didn't like her for so many other reasons. Unfortunately my dislike spills.

Bill was in the waiting area of the office when I arrived. Saturday, no Mary. "Bill, sorry I completely forgot it was Saturday. The door was open?"

"Victoria, I'm here." Ames's voice came out of the rear offices.

"Thanks Ames. Bill, lets go into my office where we can talk. Let me have your coat." I opened my office door, took his coat. "Would you like some coffee or a coke?"

Bill took a seat. "No I'm good. That was a beautiful unit. The asking is still $590?"

"Sure is, hasn't changed. Yeah, it's a beautiful unit. Fees aren't bad, utilities are separate and there is parking in the rear. Don't know if you saw that out of the bedroom window." I reached into one of my file cabinets for the condo documents to this particular condominium. Each condominium development has its own set of documents. The documents contain the initial condominium plans and approvals, unit plans and approvals as well as the governing body, condo board, election criteria, fee structure and one of the biggies, second only to fee structure, the condo rules and regulations that address everything from pets to leasing.

"I noticed the parking, looked like two each unit and some guest parking." I handed Bill an extra copy of the condo docs. "Victoria, I'm sorry, I know better than to ask those questions of the Seller's Agent. If someone did that to me I would go nuts."

"Bill, that's why Greg does your negotiations." Bill laughed. "No problem. You realize from that location you can walk anywhere worth being in Newport, right?"

"Yeah, I could. You know when Greg sees this I'll never get rid of him. He could crawl home from anywhere." Bill chuckled again. "So, how do we do this?"

"Well, we need to talk about price, inspections. Are you going to take a mortgage? That stuff. Purchase price will probably determine your lease price if you want to go in that direction. Is the house that bad that you can't spend a few more weeks in it?" I was hoping he would be honest about this. I wouldn't want him living in emotional hell if that's what it was to him.

"Victoria, every time I walk in that place I see the girls. Today wouldn't be fast enough." He was being honest.

"OK, I would suggest that as soon as we get this nailed down with a move-in date, you take out renter's insurance and tell the insurance guy that it is the place you are buying. He may be able to put together a full package for you. As soon as you step in that door you will be responsible for it. You don't want to get settled in and have something happen that the technical owner refuses to fix. A water heater fails three days after you move in, it could be your tab. If you don't think of it like that the Closing could turn into a nightmare. OK?"

"Yeah, I do understand and you make a good point." Bill took out his little note pad and started writing. "As for a mortgage. I may take one later but for the Closing, I'll pay cash. It'll move faster. Still $1,000 to start, total 20% down?" Bill remembered the numbers. I shouldn't expect less from him. "Price?"

"You want this to move fast so lets go in at $550. Inspections?" I asked.

"Can we just do the utilities. You know, heating, hot water, electrical stuff?"

"Sure, we should do bugs. Most of the time it would be a condo issue but we should do it. No surprises. Bill, do you want me to be there for the inspection?" Might as well offer, I do know that Bill hates this stuff. Why make him ask.

"Wow, would you? That would be great. That reminds me, should we do one at the house - one of those Sellers' inspections?"

"Sure. Couldn't hurt and better to know it now." I'd rather just have Buyers do an inspection of his house, but he brought it up and I didn't have a valid reason not to. Any buyer would probably do their own anyway. Is it possible to have a house over-inspected? The plus for us will be Bill's inspection being attached as an addendum to the Seller's Disclosure which he will sign. To have a problem with a buyer's inspection, something totally undiscovered would have to turn up. I'll have to make sure the retaining wall crack is addressed by Bill's inspector. I made a note of that with big circles around it on the condo purchase file.

""What are you thinking about the leased units in the condo building? Two max." This, in Newport, is a serious question. Not only do lessees have a tendency not to care about noise and damage, but more than 50% leased units makes the building more of an investment building with absentee landlords rather than a residence impacting resale and mortgage rates.

"I can live with two, excluding me of course. Why don't you write it up. I'm going to the office for the rest of the day so bring it by when you're done if that works for you."

"Sure Bill. It'll take me about an hour or so." I stood when Bill did, retrieved his coat.

"Just give me a call when you're in the parking lot so I can let you in. Thanks Victoria. I appreciate it." Bill left and I went to work.

I finished the Purchase and Sale Agreement about half an hour later and didn't have an answer for Bill on leased units. I made a phone call to Karen and left a message. I then wrote an addendum stating that if there were more than two units leased, the Buyer could terminate the Purchase and Sale Agreement. That would cover Bill and we could still make the Offer.

Chapter 16

I called Bill from his parking lot. We settled into an office that would have been a joy for an electronics freak. The wall was covered with location and tracking displays. Bill had three monitors on his desk and against one wall was a huge map table for hard copy tracking. Everything was lit up like a Christmas tree. "Like it?" Bill smiled, he was proud.

"Wow. Last time I was in your office you had one display on the wall and two screens on your desk. That was what, six years ago?"

"About that. We've grown a little since then." Bill was understating the obvious. "We've leased seventeen tankers and cargos so far. It's crazy, but it's fun. We've even had one fired on in the Gulf. I guess that says we've made it." Bill was very satisfied with himself. I remembered when he was negotiating for the first cargo ship. That was one hell of a party.

"I guess you have. So want to get this over with?" I put the Purchase and Sale Agreement on his desk. "I haven't heard back from Karen so I added an Addendum to cover you if more than two units are leased."

"Great. Where do I sign? I've got the check ready to go." He took the file from me and spread the papers on the working portion of his desk.

"Bill, please read before you sign." He did need to read, at least this one time.

"I trust you. Is the lease here too?"

"Read please, make me happy. The lease needs numbers, it's there but no numbers. Bill read." He was going to read this thing. I'm sure he did trust me but he needed to read.

"OK. Want a drink before I start?"

"Sure, just point me to the kitchen and I'll get a soda while you read.

Can I get you something?" I knew this building, I worked in it many, many years ago. But polite is polite.

"Victoria, you know right where it is. Could you pour me a scotch?"

I took my time, there is nothing like having someone sitting waiting for you to read something. The walls in the kitchen were covered in old navigational maps, a good time killer.

When I returned Bill was reading the last page of the lease. "Looks fine to me. If you're happy, I'm happy." I handed the drink to him. His comment defeated the purpose of him reading it, but I'd done my best.

He signed where he was suppose to on the P&S and then signed the lease.

"Bill the lease doesn't have numbers." I said.

"Just plug them in, but call me first, ok. I'm good Victoria, don't worry. I just need this to be done. You understand, don't you?" Bill was trying to put his best face forward and now it was starting to crack.

"Sure Bill. I do understand. I'll keep you posted." I stood to gather my things. "Oh, your copy, keep it." I finished putting my coat on and made my way to the front door. Bill caught up with me, unlocked the door and I went to my car. I let it warm up a bit and was so glad I wasn't in Bill's shoes. Been there, done that and didn't even have a tee shirt. I would bet Bill was still in love with Jenny. I'd never had that illusion.

I called Karen's office to try to find her. No, she refused to own a cell phone. I had seen her sit in her office for hours, killing time, waiting for a phone call. What a waste. Life is short, get a grip. She was there.

I stepped into a Brokerage I was all too familiar with. When I left, I had promised myself that I would never be attached to a 'box store' office like that again. I'd kept my promise and it made me smile. I stopped to say hi to a couple of people I knew before I made it to Karen's desk located in a large room with a dozen desks and no illusion of privacy, much less real privacy.

"Karen, could we go to the conference room or some place more private? I have an Offer here." I hated to discuss my Clients' personal business in public. I knew with Karen it would be all over town twenty minutes after I left, but the least I could do was give it my best shot. I knew Bill wouldn't care. I would.

"Sure, I was expecting to hear from you." Karen had totally forgotten about the question Bill had asked twice and I had reminded her about once. We went to the conference room.

"Karen, did you get an answer to the leasing question?" I sat down, still wearing my coat. I didn't plan to stay that long.

"Sure. There is only one leased unit. All the rest are owner occupied. Figured I would tell you when you got here. So what's the Offer?"

I handed the package to her, walked her through the high points.

"You know, he doesn't have to do an inspection. Didn't he see that it was in good shape?"

"He did, but better to be safe than sorry. I'll be attending the inspection so we can get it done as soon as I can schedule it, obviously before he moves in under the lease. He still wants to lease." I added.

"Will he pay a commission for the lease?" Karen asked.

"I'll write up the lease." Yeah, it was already done. "We'll Close as soon as we can. I was going to let that go. We're talking a lease commission somewhere around $100, $150. No more than that." I wasn't going to ding anyone for a commission on such a small number. It would be my effort, my time.

"So what about one o'clock Monday afternoon? Is that good for you?"

"Karen." I shook my head. "We should stay focused on this deal and not mix the two things. Why don't we get through these conditions first?" Would she hold up this deal for our discussion? I had been letting Mary front for me with Karen since January and now I would pay. I just didn't want Bill to pay. I wasn't going to change my mind about her.

"I don't see why. It's not a big deal. I'll call my Seller right now and then we can talk."

"Karen, right now I am here with Bill's Offer. That is my subject. I'm not discussing anything else." I was serious.

"OK, well, I'll give you a call tomorrow and let you know what the Seller has to say." Karen remained in her chair, tapping the Offer.

The law says she has twenty-four hours to present an Offer and she was not only going to take the time, but she was going to shop it. I knew it, I knew it. Technically, that's a no, no, but who is going to complain and there is no way to prove it has been done. Never again will I show a property without a basic Confidentiality Statement signed before I walk in. I don't care what the price is, who my Client is. My mistake, my problem.

"Karen, I hope I don't hear about this Offer at a dinner party I'm attending tonight." No, I didn't have plans, but she didn't know that.

"I'll call when I've talked to the Seller." She was still tapping the Offer package. I did have to smile.

I started to go to my office and then remembered it was Saturday. I went home.

Chapter 17

I woke to my cell phone ringing, again. Telephones were starting to be the bane of my existence. The cell meant business. I needed to wake up before business, I let it go to voice mail after six rings. Who knew six rings would take so long. That was going to change too, as soon as I remembered how to do it.

I poured myself coffee and sat at the kitchen bar which allowed me to look out the window. The day was going to be beautiful. Maybe we are going to get a break in the weather after – what?...two weeks of brutal cold and snow. One day would be welcome.

I checked the voicemail once I finished the coffee. It was Ames. He insisted that I give him a call as soon as I got his message. He didn't sound bad at all so I redialed his number.

"Ames, what's going on? That was an early call."

"Morning Victoria, it wasn't that early, a little before ten. Anyway, I've gotten my hands on two tickets to the Sotheby's auction in Barrington today. Gift from a Client. Want to go?" Ames was excited.

I thought about it. Karen would call on my cell, the only number she had, so no need to stick around. It would be a great break. "Sure, I'll go. It'll be fun. I'm not looking for anything, but hey, free is free. Thanks for calling. Want me to drive?" He was providing the tickets, usually $100 to walk in the door and lunch of course, the least I could do was drive.

"Sure. Great. It starts at two, with a champagne buffet so don't eat before." This would be fun. The food at a private auction was in direct proportion to the value of the items being auctioned. Love it. Eye candy and champagne.

"Pick you up about one, ok?" Barrington wasn't that far. Drive for a complete hour in any direction in this State and you'll either be in the water or out of the State. What slows up a drive are the small roads and potholes, especially in the winter. Potholes that will tear out an axel if you're not careful. The funny thing is that if you drive into Massachusetts or Connecticut at the same time of the year, the roads change at the border. Seriously, Rhode Island is terrible.

"Sure, see you then."

I was actually excited. Even though I didn't need anything, auctions are fun and if you get there early enough you get to meet interesting people before they are upset that they paid too much for an item in the heat of battle.

When I'm seriously looking for an item I go to the "preview" parties. Usually held the day before. At most "preview" parties you can put a "reserve" price on something, like I did for the old partners' desk in my library. I didn't bother to go to the auction because I wasn't going to pay more for it. The next day I received a phone call saying it was mine, when did I want it delivered. Now it's one of my favorite pieces.

Ames and I entered the auction about twenty minutes after I picked him up. It was being held in a huge, old, stick Victorian and the main parlor was full of people. We registered for our numbers, grabbed some champagne and started walking through the house. I lost Ames on the second floor, fascinated by the jewelry displayed in one of the larger bedrooms.

The auction items were a grouping of items from all over the east coast dating from about the same era as the house, @1890. Yes, I definitely have a jewelry fetish. Don't wear a lot of it but, if it sparkles it gets my attention. Years ago I tried to stay subtle, my "classy" era, but that was long gone. Many of the pieces already had reserves on them, way over my budget. I enjoyed looking anyway. That was for me, at least fifty percent of the fun. It would be interesting to see what some of these pieces finally sold for.

I discovered a little attic room that displayed a very unique number of items. Apparently someone's great grandfather had served in the American Indian wars and brought back, as souvenirs, quite a few pieces he had acquired. I didn't want to know how he had acquired them, but they were here. One of the display cases was labeled 'braid jewelry'. It was full of what, at one time, had been beautiful feathers, bone, bead and leather pieces woven into different colored strips of hide. The colors were wonderful even though most were faded from age and dehydration. The craftsmanship sublime.

One of the pieces actually had everything woven into what seemed to be four thin, almost translucent strips. Maybe leather? Couldn't tell. From the odd originating knot the four strips were heavy with beads and what looked like bone and old feathers falling about eighteen inches. Yes, it did have a reserve, again way over my budget.

What did catch my attention was a small feather, bone and bead piece labeled 'anklet from unknown location; age unknown'. The feathers woven into the beads had been delicate and of every bright color of the rainbow. Now they were dull and misshapen with age. They looked dried out, almost about to fall apart. Yeah, there was a reserve on that too. But compared to the other reserves, I might just bid on it.

"Fascinating pieces aren't they?" I jumped a bit, hadn't heard anyone up here. A young man stood next to me with a bit of an Irish brogue. A very nice looking young gentleman actually. Hair a bit out of control but a nice suit. Vaguely familiar.

"Yes. Do you have the reserve?"

"No, unfortunately I don't." He smiled at me. "I guess the reserve isn't you."

I returned his smile. "Not quite."

I heard the bell signaling the start of the auction. "Guess it's starting."

"Yes. I believe it is." He stood away from the door to allow me to exit first but he didn't walk behind me. He didn't walk anywhere, he wasn't in the room. Another door? I hurried down three flights of stairs almost walking right into Ames.

"I grabbed us a couple of seats on the aisle towards the front, follow me." He led the way and we settled in. "So did you find anything you wanted to bid on?"

"Actually I did. Did you make it to the attic? It was full of American Indian artifacts from the wars. Maybe if something looks like it will be reasonable, I'll bid. Did you find anything?"

Ames smiled, "I found a wonderful leather smoking chair. It's worn in just the right spots. When I sat in it, I fell in love. It grabbed my butt like I'd been sitting in it forever."

I was cracking up. "Ames, I can't stand it, you are too funny. How the hell would we get it home? Do you trust my trunk?" Lucky chair. Oh, Victoria…no, no, no.

"Victoria, what are the chances that I'll actually get it? It didn't have a reserve, no one last night liked it, maybe. Anyway, you're always bragging that your Volvo trunk will swallow anything. Do you have any shock-cord in the trunk?"

"Ames, get it and we will figure it out." Shock-cord? Of course I had shock-cord in my trunk along with a huge plastic drop cloth. Who did he think he was talking to?

After about half an hour the chair came up. It was beautiful and the auction people would take credit cards. That announcement was made at the beginning of the auction. Not good for Ames. The chair came from a southern plantation house, the men's game room. Ames was sunk. There were two other people bidding against him, but Ames prevailed and for twenty-one hundred dollars, he owned the chair. Hell. But Ames was jumping up and down. I guess every once in a while we did need to treat ourselves. I'd done it with some numbered prints years ago that still hung in the living room.

About three quarters of an hour later the Indian artifacts came up. Just before the bidding started an announcement was made that there were multiple museums and some private collectors on the telephones to bid on some of the objects. I knew I was dead, but it would be interesting to watch. The numbers on some of the items reached into the five digits between the audience and the phones. The small ankle thong with the beads and dead feathers went for nine thousand.

The four-piece braid item went for thirty-five thousand . Its legend was interesting. It had been handed down through many generations of the strongest medicine men; even across tribes. That I knew was unheard of. Originating from one that is said to have met the Great Spirit and been sent back to earth. Its last Owner, some Army Captain, had taken it from a medicine man he found wandering in the southwest in 1895. Translation, this Captain mugged…killed…the Indian. I did love the legends. Usually legends came from a grain of fact. That was a story I would have loved to know.

I turned to Ames after the Indian pieces were gone and asked if he was ready to grab some food and pack up his chair. I didn't want to be loading the thing in the dark and no matter how beautiful the day had been, it would get colder. But, little surprises, when he went to pay, the auction people asked when it would be convenient for him to receive the chair. I guess he was meant to have it and they worked out a delivery time. The delivery, of course, would be at no additional cost to the buyer. There were definite benefits to the expensive auctions.

By the time we had eaten all the shrimp, lobster salad and Greek salad we could hold it was dark. We both decided we'd had a ton of fun and would have to do it again. When I stopped to drop him off in front of his condo he gave me a quick kiss on the cheek, nothing intimate, just Ames. As I drove away I remembered that I hadn't heard from Karen. Once again, I'd have to track her down when I got home.

Chapter 18

I woke up the next morning more that an hour before the alarm really feeling rested. Sunday's adventure with Ames had been very relaxing. I had remembered to shut off my cell phone before bed, set the house phone to pick up at four rings. I was tempted to set it for two. I resisted.

The cell had messages from Bill and Karen on it as well as a message from Jay.

My first return was Karen. The Seller had accepted Bill's Offer. No counter. He also asked $1,000 for the Lease. Total, not per week; no matter how many weeks it took to Close. Bill would be happy and well he should be. I told Karen I would complete the Lease, get it to her before the end of the day and pick up Bill's copy of the signed Contract. The balance of the deposit to the Seller would have to come Tuesday, along with the Lease payment. I did tell her to go ahead and deposit the $1,000 good faith check and I would call her when I had a date and time for inspections. I also gave her the name of the Closing attorney; said that a copy of the fully signed P&S would get to him before I dropped off the remainder of the money.

I called Bill, told him the good news; how much money I needed now, the specific check amounts along with the payees and said I would pick up the checks later this afternoon.

I called the inspector that Bill was using for the condominium; scheduled the inspection for Wednesday, eleven am (UCK) and got a price from him. I would write the check to the inspector and get reimbursed at the Closing. With any luck, Bill would be able to move in on Friday.

I called Jay. He was in a meeting but wanted to be interrupted when I called. "Hi Jay, so what's going on?"

"Ah, Victoria, all is just fine. I wanted to let you know that the Seller's lawyer showed up this morning with Mr. Keirns and it looks like we are a go. The Seller will be leaving everything you saw in the house. Apparently Mr. Keirns liked the billiard table, so that made him happy."

"Jay, how did you know Mr. Keirns was happy about that?" I did want to know. I'd never seen his expression truly change.

"He laughed and made a comment about he and Mr. Fournier having their own sticks". Jay was chuckling.

"I would not have pictured them playing billiards. Sounds like a good meeting. Do you need me?" I asked.

"I don't think so. Mr. Keirns asked how you were. I told him that I hadn't talked to you since Friday, that I assumed you were fine. It was a little weird. But hey, what can I say. By the way, we may close on Thursday. OK with you? Do you want to be here?"

"Of course I do. My biggest Closing in a few years, wouldn't miss it. Keep me posted Jay. Unless something comes up on my end I'll wait to hear from you. Oh, by the way, Mr. Fournier wasn't at the meeting, was he?" I asked.

"No. Keirns hasn't mentioned him. Why do you ask?"

"Just curious, I haven't figured them out yet, probably never will. Talk soon". I hung up.

Today was going to be one of those messenger days. Pick it up here, drop it off there, kind of days. Reads like a non-event on paper but every time you stop there are always the pleasantries, the courtesies that take up time and before you know it you're looking at the end of a very tiring day.

About half way between the office stop to make copies and my drive to Bill's office the cell rang. It was Mr. Keirns asking if I was well. I assured him that I was just fine and looked forward to seeing him at the Closing. That I would attend seemed to surprise him. I told him I wouldn't miss it. He remained surprised. I explained that I did not take his or Mr. Fournier's business for granted. That I appreciated they had come to me and it was my obligation to be at the transaction's conclusion. He said that I needn't worry, all would be fine. I was getting the feeling that he did not want me to attend so I explained to him that I attended all of my Clients' Closings. That is how I do business. He said that Mr. Fournier would not be returning until Friday and it had not been expected that I would attend the Closing. I told him that it was too bad that Mr. Fournier wouldn't be able to attend as it was his first residential purchase, but that I would be there and would see him then. After a few moments of silence we said goodbye and ended the call.

I couldn't think of a reason I shouldn't attend the Closing. Jay seemed fine with it and he would have certainly called me off if this was a problem. I was having trouble getting my arms around having actually sold Ledge House, much less the Buyers. Yes, I was a happy camper.

I ended up back at the office late in the afternoon. I wanted Mary to do some investigating for me and schedule some advertising for Bill's house. When I walked in the door Mary was on the phone. I pointed my finger to my office, unlocked the door and walked through to the workroom. I was craving some decent coffee and we did have that. We ordered our coffee from a little company in New Orleans that Mary had found. The blend contained chicory and when it was fresh I could close my eyes and pretend I was sitting on the porch of Café Du Monde on Decatur Street in New Orleans. If I stretched it I could smell beignets cooking. Surprisingly the pot was full and fresh this late in the day. I went to the office area to see who else was here.

"Hi Mason. Did you make the pot of coffee for a special reason?" Mason was sitting in his office area with his feet on his desk, leaning back in his chair, reading.

"Hi Victoria." Mason looked up at me with his sly smile. "Actually I did. I've got some Clients coming in from Louisiana and I though they might enjoy it. Good coffee is a rare find up here. I even brought in fresh milk. You need a cup?"

"Oh yeah if I won't short you." Setting up for Clients in our office has priority over just about everything and I wouldn't want to step on Mason's efforts.

"Sure, go ahead. I probably will need two cups out of the pot and the milk. We're going on to dinner later." Mary buzzed Mason to tell him his Clients had arrived.

I grabbed my coffee and returned to my office in a hurry. Mason would probably be followed into the workroom by his Clients. Mary was waiting. "So you needed me?"

"I wanted to bounce some stuff off of you. The money I'm expecting will probably show up sometime on Friday and I was thinking that it would be nice to have our own bathroom. What do you think about adding enough space for a conference room? Would we be getting too big?" We needed both, if the price was right.

"You're kidding? You'd do that?" Mary and I had talked extensively about this last summer when the office on our north wall had become available. I was scared to expand, chickened out. I had always planned for two more brokers but things were perking along just fine. I was truly scared to change it. I had seen too many companies in various businesses grow too fast. They figured if the customers liked their product or service, more equaled better. Frankly, it doesn't work like that. Big or little - it fails.

My ideal? Long term stability with maybe a little more demand that supply. All of us were almost in that situation. Last fall I had referred a Client to Nina and one to Ames.

"I think it's time Victoria. A small but decked-out conference room and a couple of very nice bathrooms would be great. We could do that next door and have room for two more offices if we took the whole space. Do that and stop. You worried again?"

"Yeah. It still scares me. Could you run some numbers for me?" My stomach was starting to tighten. When I bought this space I was sick as a dog. Mason kept patting me on the back telling me we'd be fine and Mary kept pushing numbers in my face showing me we would be fine. The week I Closed on the space we currently occupied, I thought I had stomach flu.

"Do you want to lease the space or buy? Don't know if we can buy but I can try to get a number out of them."

"Mary, try to lease for a year, single net, with an option to purchase at the end. Let's see if we can get a purchase price in the lease. It's a long shot but the space has been vacant for almost a year. That has got to hurt… Oh, and see if we can get the floor plans like we did for this, full up plans, OK?"

"Sure, are we quiet about this?"

"For now, yeah. By the way, I expect Ledge House to go into pending today or tomorrow at the latest and it's our co-broke. If we get any calls asking about the Buyers, we know nothing. I'm serious. I'll call everyone tomorrow morning and tell them the same thing. Oh, and don't offer my number to anyone for the next few weeks, just put them through to my voice mail." I seriously needed to remember to change my message before I walked out of the office. I made a note on the scratch pad that was always on my desk.

"That's all?" Mary stood.

"Pretty much. I'll leave some ads for my new listing on your desk. An old Client of mine in a divorce. Maybe next week I'll open it for the office. It will be easier to show next week. I guess that's it."

"Can you tell me who's buying the big house?" Mary had sat back down. I knew better than to think she'd forgotten.

"No, I can't."

"I know it's Mr. Keirns and Mr. Fournier. I made the call for the letter. Who are they?"

"Geez Mary I totally forgot. You haven't shredded that stuff? Shred it please. These guys are serious, no joke. I don't even have a file on them. My weird meter goes up every time I'm with them, so just let it go."

"OK, if you insist." Mary smiled a bit. She wasn't taking this seriously. Had she told her Significant Other?

"Mary, the Clients' insisted, not me. Got it? Did you say anything to Billy about this?"

"Only the day Mr. Keirns came in. He got a kick out of the banker."

"Rats, Mary." I stood and wanted to yell but we had Clients in the office. I could can her. I had never had that thought before about Mary. She's too smart for this. "I warned you after he left to keep it quiet. I rarely ask that stuff of you, you're usually pretty smart about this. If this gets out before Closing it will kill the deal. Significant money. You had better shut Billy up. After Closing I don't know what they will do. But I'm not talking." I was shaking my head when she walked out. I should have run the financial statement myself after Keirns left the office. A day one way or the other would not have made a difference. Actually, Jay probably would have ended up talking to the banker. If I hadn't had that confirmation I don't know if I would have sent them to Jay. Well, we were where we were.

By the time Mary stuck her head back into my office I had cooled down, working on Bill's ads.

"Victoria, I'm sorry. I'll take care of my error. I just didn't think it was that serious. My mistake. Don't worry about it." That was definitely better.

"Mary, sorry I lost my temper. I'm sure you'll take care of it. No problem. You leaving?"

"Yeah, Mason's gone with his Clients so I'll lock the front door. Bye." Mary closed my door.

I wasn't getting anywhere with the ad, so I changed my voicemail message on my cell eliminating the alternate phone numbers it contained. Well, that felt better. I locked up the office, set alarms and stood on the sidewalk looking back at the office trying to imagine the vacant office as a part of our office.

Chapter 19

Wednesday turned out to be a cloudy, cold winter day. March looked like it was coming in like a lion or rather came in like a lion. It was the third of March and felt like the third of February. Inspection day, first the condo then Bill's house. Inspectors do earn their fees in the winter. I wouldn't want to climb a roof today. The condo would be a non-event but the house was going to hurt.

Karen attended the condo inspection in spike heals, a very tight pencil skirt, tight sweater. I laughed when I first saw her. She had no intention of following the inspection. Surprisingly, she didn't say a word about the meeting I had postponed. Had she given up? No way. But she was sweet and pleasant as could be.

The Seller was moving his furniture out on Thursday so Bill could move in anytime after that. When I called Bill to tell him the inspection was fine and he could move in anytime this coming weekend, I suggested that he might want to have his cleaning lady do a once over on the condo just to start out right. I would drop a set of keys and codes off at his office after the house inspection later this afternoon. Bill was happy, happy. It's about time something went right for him.

The inspector took a lunch break after the condo inspection, before the house. I decided I would go back to the office for the hour and try to write Bill's ads. Writing ads takes inspiration, unless you use one of those ad writing computer programs that throws words together not knowing the property, but brags that its product uses as few words as possible at the reading level of a seventh grader; the level that the government's training manuals are written to. I tried an acquaintance's program a few years ago and all I had to do was answer a few basic questions about the property and push a button. Voila, there was my ad. The ad gave the information about the property that I would try to get into an ad in as few simple words as possible. The resulting ad had been dry, no flair, no feeling, just a statement. The ad was ok, but not my taste. Now when I read ads in a publication, especially real estate ads, I can see the program at work, more often than one would think.

Many years ago I ran for election to a town office. It was an experience and an education I will never forget. Nine months of pure hell. Certainly not something I would do again. No, I had lost by about a hundred votes and was emotionally burnt. I had made the consummate rooky mistake of actually being involved with the writing of and believing in my platform. The largest criticism I received through the whole election process was that my words were too big and my constituents felt that I thought they were dumb. I came out of that experience with a whole new view of the public at large. Do I dumb down my ads? No, I write what the property tells me to write.

So, I sat in my office and looked at the pictures I had taken of the house. I sat there for forty-five minutes without inspiration, then left for the house inspection. Oh well, maybe I would be inspired while the inspector did his thing.

Chat. That is what this inspector did throughout the inspection. Some of it was informative, most was gossip about what was wrong with other houses that I would know. I wondered how many cups of coffee he had finished at lunch. As it turned out the only issue he had was the retaining wall crack and suggested we bring in an engineer to look at it. Big surprise.

When I dropped the keys, codes and copies of the two inspections to Bill we ended up in a great discussion about the crack, an engineer and how much would it all cost. Not a big mystery to me but apparently it was to Bill. I suggested that we leave it to a buyer. It would be disclosed in the Seller's Disclosure form and we just would have to understand that even though a potential buyer will know about it up front, we may have to negotiate the issue at some point. The other option would be to hire an engineer for a review of the "problem" and then an estimate of cost to cure. Pick one. Finally, Bill went for the first option.

On my way home I stopped by one of my favorite Chinese Restaurants for take-out. I was starving when I left Bill's and knew I wouldn't want to heat and assemble something when I got home. I called from the car.

Most of my speed dial numbers are take-out numbers. One of the most productive evenings I had spend with my new phone a few years ago.

I only had to wait a few minutes after I arrived. Unfortunately, the few minutes was spent behind some guy demanding that his pork rice be swapped for vegetable rice as he claimed he had ordered. The guy kept trying to draw me into the conversation. No way was I touching it. When the poor girl behind the counter went to get his veggie rice, he actually asked me, hand on my arm, if I wanted a drink. I laughed, shook my head, declined…then it hit me. The guy from the condo, the Avenue? Nah…no way. A little too blue collar.

I was sitting with wine, dinner and a wonderful view of rather large waves breaking on the beach when I remembered that Ledge House was scheduled to Close the next day, early afternoon. The thought ended dinner. I was excited and scared all at the same time. I wondered if James would come back early. Shit. I realized that I missed seeing him. That started the shakes. I threw back the wine remaining in my glass. How funny was that? I was afraid to see him and scared he wouldn't be there. A high school distance crush…at my age…what a riot. Once I sorted that out, it became funny…especially when I ran to the bathroom and lost dinner.

I do love men. I admit it. I prefer their company to women. Married, single, young, old doesn't matter, it's been this way my whole life. I cannot relax around women. Even with Mary and Carolyn my radar won't shut off completely. Mary had to talk me into bringing Nina into the office. I'd told Mary to send her to Switzerland first. She thought that was funny, but I was serious. In planning the office I had never visualized women in it. When I mentioned adding two more brokers my brain was wondering which two men would I like to see in the office.

There was a time when I hid the preference. Tried to talk to women at parties. Stayed away from the men. That was a bore. Why the effort? A business client's wife had told him he couldn't talk to me anymore. Apparently, she had found my business card in his pocket.

When I was in my thirties I actually tried to develop a few girlfriends. I have no idea what they are doing now. Frankly, don't care. I gave up trying to be socially correct a few years ago. I gave up a lot of things a few years ago, like persevering when I am bored to tears; pretending I liked things when I didn't and trying to talk myself out of enjoying men because 'I'm too old'. Certain things are just not acceptable in polite society. It took a while to actually begin to live the way I wanted to live, but I'm getting there.

Chapter 20

I actually got a good night's sleep, woke up before the alarm. Good show. Before I knew it, I was walking into Jay's office actually hoping James would be there. One last look and feel of him before he disappeared into finished transactions. To that day, I could describe every male in every transaction I'd completed. I had to chuckle at myself.

Jay's receptionist, Tammy, looked up from her desk when I closed the door. "Mrs. Hamilton, Jay and Mr. Keirns are in the conference room. Why don't you go on back." No Mr. Fournier? Rats and blue meanies. I smiled.

"Fine Tammy." I said feeling a bit disappointed, no, more than a bit. Yeah, right.

Mr. Keirns and Jay stood when I walked in. The habit must be contagious. I couldn't remember Jay ever standing for me. "Hello Mr. Keirns." I said reaching for his hand. He wore another of his wonderful suits. This time navy blue tweed, vest also navy blue tweed, white shirt , tie bar with a striking ruby stone and my favorite shirt cuffs, links of course, ruby stone set in gold. His braids were still pulled back but held with blue silk. Very nice. He would have to do.

"Hi Jay." I reached for his hand. Jay, classic gray flannel and a blue tie that matched his eyes. Good job, I thought, just move the next step to French cuffs. "Am I early or are Cheryl and our fifth late?"

I moved to sit next to Mr. Keirns and yes, he held my chair. I smiled at him. I'd already given him the talk, now I would just appreciate the effort.

"Actually, Mr. Tyler, the Seller's lawyer is here. In my office talking to someone. Cheryl didn't feel she needed to attend. Can I get you something to drink Victoria?" Jay asked. Boy, on top of his game today.

"No thanks Jay, I'm good. I trust all is well with the purchase Mr. Keirns."

"It is, Mrs. Hamilton." Mr. Keirns stopped just before he started to say something else. His expression - almost like he was listening to someone. A moment later he ever so slightly nodded his head and continued. "I would like to relay Mr. Fournier's greetings and express his regret at not being able to attend this event. He did not understand its significance." He smiled and went back to the papers he'd been reading.

Jay looked at me rather puzzled. I shrugged. I glanced quickly at Mr. Keirns's ear; looked back at Jay, straightened a wisp of hair over my ear. Jay nodded and glanced at the ear on his side. Mr. Keirns was not wearing an ear bud for his phone. Ledge House was, from what I understood, James's first house. Not mine. These guys truly did confuse me.

The fourth finally joined us. Jay stood and introduced Mr. Tyler to me. Mr. Tyler walked past me, no offer of acknowledgement, to the end of the table and began to spread papers. "Mr. Tyler, why don't you take the seat next to me so we don't have to yell? We will be passing papers that you need to sign." Jay sat down. Good for you Jay. Mr. Tyler moved, he didn't have a choice. The ends of oblong conference room tables are power seats and Mr. Tyler had taken the only one left. Group dynamics, first semester. If we were going to play that game I would have laid out the place cards quite differently.

No matter the money involved, a Closing is a Closing. A Closing without a mortgage involved is easier by three quarters. The amount of paper involved with a mortgage is probably the true cause of deforestation around the world. A Closing without a mortgage involves the signing of the deed by the Seller, the biggie actually transferring the property. A financial statement identifying purchase price, prorated taxes, water and sewer fees and everything else that was to be paid at Closing for both sides; adding and subtracting monies due and monies to be paid to everyone. A government form known as a HUD, intended to disclose every penny involved to everyone involved. Did it? Sometimes, if the parties understood the basic math.

Once the lawyers were satisfied with their respective bottom lines, every one signed on that bottom line and we were done. Mr. Tyler had moved his return flight to L.A. for this evening so he couldn't get out fast enough. Jay stood to walk him to the front door but Mr. Tyler was on his phone before he left the conference room. Jay stayed.

"Mr. Keirns. The house is yours, rather Mr. Fournier's. I have some listings of staffing agencies that serve our best local families." Jay slid a piece of paper in Mr. Keirns's direction. "I'm sure Mr. Fournier will be able to fine the help he will need from any of these agencies."

Mr. Keirns glanced at the paper, then back at Jay. "Thank you very much for your efforts, but Mr. Fournier is returning with staff for the house. I do appreciate your efforts on his behalf. I'm sure we will be doing business together again." Mr. Keirns stood and shook Jay's hand. "There is no need to see me out Mr. Matthews." He then turned to me and reached for my hand. "Mrs. Hamilton, I am sure I will see you soon."

I stood, took his hand, smiled at him. "It is a small Island, I'm sure you will. Thank you." I started to slide my note pad and calculator into my bag. Mr. Keirns left and Jay asked me to stay a moment.

"Let me give this to Jane so she can record this afternoon, I'll be right back." Jay was true to his word. He returned quickly holding a bottle of Glen Fiddich. "Come into my office and we can have a drink while Jane runs her errand, then I can pay you. You don't have another appointment do you?"

"Not at all. Thanks, I could use a shot." I picked up my coat and followed Jay to his office, settled in. "We just sold Ledge House didn't we?"

Jay started laughing, "We sure did. Two weeks start to finish. I've had larger, but not easier." He poured for both of us. "Ice?" He asked.

"What? And ruin good Whiskey? No thank you."

Jay held up his glass. "To more deals like that!" I matched him and the glasses made that fine crystal ring. Jay sat down looking very satisfied. "So, tell me. Where did you find them?" Referring to Mr. Keirns and James.

I explained briefly, reminding him that he had handled both of Sybil and Williem's Closings.

"Yes, the UN couple. Interesting. Victoria, are you dating Mr. Fournier?"

I just looked at him. "Not that I know of. Why? Have you heard something?" I asked as a joke.

"Not really, but he changed when you walked into the office the other day. I mean changed. His demeanor, his personality even the way he looked. You know he is quite the businessman. Mr. Keirns almost seemed useless until you walked in. You must think I'm nuts and yes, this is my first drink of the day." Jay pushed back in his chair and put his ankle on his knee. "I mean Victoria, you must have seen what happened when he touched your hand against the wall while Mr. Keirns signed the Contract. He shimmered. Like a chill with light."

I thought for a minute. I wasn't imagining what I had seen. "Jay, I know he relaxed when Keirns signed the Contract. You remember. By the way, how are you feeling?" I also remembered our telephone conversation later that afternoon.

"Oh, I'm fine. Must have been a bug. So you didn't see it." Jay wanted an answer. "Keirns asked me if I would be willing to handle the acquisition of the subdivided properties and a few others as well. I told him I would, so I figured I'd ask you about what happened since we'll probably be doing this for a while. I like to know my players."

I was getting a little uncomfortable with this conversation but understood the context of his question. It was business, not personal. "Jay. Guys like James play with everything when they are playing with their money. Been there, done that. Not to worry. I'll probably never see him again. We'll both end up with Keirns or someone that works for Keirns." I put my glass down and stood up putting my coat on. "Jay, lets just make some money. I'll call you if I hear from them and you do the same. Deal?"

Jay stood. "Victoria, I hope you didn't think I was insulting you."

"Heck no Jay. We're way past that. Enjoy the afterglow. I'll come by tomorrow afternoon and pick up my check, ok? I've got to focus on some advertising this afternoon." Ah, good misdirection, I left.

I did need to get Bill's ads done and put his listing in the computer.

Chapter 21

I stood looking at our office entry and the vacant office next door from the sidewalk. If we did end up taking the other space our entrance was going to have to move. It would look lopsided if it didn't get moved. I walked over to look in the window glass. It looked like our office when I bought it.

"Victoria, I bet you would like these." Mary held up the keys to the vacant space.

I laughed. "Want to go in with me?"

"Sure, Ledge House is in the computer as Closed." Mary was almost giggling. "Have a check for me?"

"I'll pick it up tomorrow on my way in. Come on, lets check it out." Mary opened the door, we entered, then closed it with the click of a lock. The heat was down to about fifty so coats and hats stayed on along with our gloves. I flipped on the lights and walked towards the back. The first things that would have to go would be the industrial florescent lights. "Hey Mary, there is a bathroom back here. Not something that we would want, but the plumbing's here. We'll still have to do the windows like we did in the back of our office. I think we just flip what we have. The front door is going to have to move, which means your office is moving. You realize that, right?"

"Yeah, if we don't move the door the whole office will looked patched together. That will probably be the toughest job." Mary had already looked at the façade.

"If we do it right the first time, we won't have to touch it again. What was the bottom line on our place?" I think I had a round number in my head but Mary would have the final number.

"About thirty-five thousand including the furniture. Listen Vic, I hadn't planned on seeing you today. I'll have some serious numbers for you tomorrow. Is that alright?"

"Sure. I didn't think I'd be back today either but I have some work to do. I never did get the advertising to you." We shut down the lights and backed ourselves out of the space.

Mason and Ames were sitting by Mary's desk when we returned. They both stood up and gave a standing ovation.

"Thanks guys. I do appreciate it, but no talking remember." I said trying not to be embarrassed.

Ames stepped forward. "This came for you." He handed me a small box wrapped in sky blue silk cloth tied with a bow of the same silk. "Dropped off by an interesting looking guy, dressed to the teeth in a beautiful suit, hair in cornrows, about 6'4". Said you would know where it came from. I told him you were just next door but he said he did not want to interrupt you. So open it. Mason and I have been trying to guess."

Mary leaned over to me, "Mr. Keirns?"

"Yeah, probably. Nice thought. Let me take off my coat and grab some coffee, then I'll open it." Nice, a gift from my Clients.

I returned a few minutes later and they were still waiting with Nina added to the group. "Come on Victoria." Mason said. "You're probably a pain at Christmas too."

So I untied the bow and the silk fell away. It was a small thin leather box. I took off the lid, took in a large breath, my stomach almost passed my throat, hands started shaking. I looked up at Ames, took it out of the box. "Geez Victoria, it's the ankle tie from the auction. Whoa. I don't remember feathers on it at the auction, do you?"

Yeah there had been feathers at the auction, but they had been faded, dead, not like these bright yellows, reds and blues. Yeah, it was the same piece. It also was way too much. Way, way too much.

"I wonder if those were the people that bought some of the other artifacts Sunday. Did you see them there?" Ames was going where I was going.

"I didn't see them. They may have been one of the phone bidders. This is way too much." I was thinking that I would have to return it somehow. I didn't want to insult anyone, but it was way too much.

"Ames was telling us about the auction on Sunday. Are you saying that this was one of the Indian artifacts auctioned? Can I take a look?" Mason stepped forward with his hand out. "Don't worry Victoria, I won't break it." I let Mason have a good look and he was joined by Nina.

"I'd say the beads are gold, silver, turquoise and ivory or something, maybe polished bone. There certainly haven't been any elephants here in quite a while. There is some carving on the bone - need a magnifying glass to see it. I don't think it's strung on leather, it's too shiny for leather. Did the auctioneer say where it came from?" Nina was the office antique collector - serious stuff. Her house is full of Far-Eastern pieces.

I told her what we had heard from the auctioneer and of course she asked how much it had sold for. I wasn't going to say it, but Ames did and the silence was deafening. "Hey guys. I need to get some work done." I turned to walk back into my office when Mason stopped me, handed me the anklet.

Well, work was not going to happen now. Talk about distracted. I had sent Courvoisier to Ledge House as a thank you, but I usually don't receive gifts from Buyers.

What do you send to very wealthy Clients? It had taken a few years to figure out that there was nothing I could send in this situation that would truly measure up to the value of a property like this. My ah ha moment came when a buyer, my Client, for a large tract of land on the water smoked cigars. I sent him a box of what I researched to be a wonderful cigar. A few days later I received a handwritten note from the Buyer, yeah a 70 year old guy, saying his wife never let him "waste money" on good cigars and he appreciated the thought. So, that's the type of thing I look for when buying a gift for a high end Buyer. Since I did not have a clue how James or Keirns lived, the brandy was my fall back. I also have a Closing gift delivered. Never hand it to my Clients at a Closing. Tacky.

I finally decided that I would return the gift early next week with a note expressing sincere appreciation but I had been at the auction and knew the value of the artifact, that it was too much or something to that effect. It was beautiful, but it had to go. With that thought, I put it back in its little thin leather box and put the box in my bag. I was done for the day.

Chapter 22

I called Carolyn to tell her that Ledge House was Closed. After all it was public information at this point.

"That is great Victoria. Is that the biggest deal yet?"

"Close to it. I think the Indian Avenue property is the largest, close to fifteen million, but he was going to develop it, the McMansions. Still embarrassing. So I guess this is the largest private residence. Yeah, it feels good." I was sitting with my feet on one of my window sills, watching the moon rise, it was almost full. The wine glass was half empty. In my world I couldn't ask for more.

"So how did the Closing go? Those are never easy." Carolyn spoke from experience with a little sympathy in her voice. One of her big deals, years ago, failed at the very end because the last three antique silver settings weren't complete. It was a set of silver for thirty; twelve pieces to each place setting. Yeah, lots of silver; lots of little pieces.

Somehow the Silver had been written into the Purchase and Sale Agreement over Carolyn's massive objections. When the inventory showed up at the Closing, a few pieces couldn't be accounted for. The Trust selling the property offered to compensate the buyers, but the buyers walked out and the Agreement was cancelled. In reality she knew the buyers wanted an excuse to walk, not lose their deposit and there it was. Carolyn was pissed, pissed for weeks. The property eventually sold, but it wasn't her sale. I stopped letting buyers include personal property, anything not nailed down, in Purchase and Sale Agreements from that point on. I write up a separate list of personal property with the agreed-to price separate and apart from the property price and let the principals deal with it out side of the transaction.

I gave her a quick overview of the Closing, ending with, "Honestly, it was a non-event." She asked if I had any plans for the money along with the suggestion that I should invest it for later in my life. I didn't have any problem with that concept. Infact, over the years, I had stashed a survivable sum away for a rainy day. Carolyn is always worrying about the rainy day. So much so that she seriously limits her enjoyment of life today, which drives me nuts.

We talked about the business taking the vacant storefront next to the office which would allow me to finish my plan and the phone call ended with many cautions from her. Frankly, it was good to hear. I know I always find two sides of an issue productive when I am trying to make a serious decision.

I went into my library and turned on the computer. I was wide awake so I might as well get some work done. I moved my bag from the chair and thought about the gift. I took the gift out of my bag and put it on the desk, then fished out the silk it had been wrapped in. I really wanted to try it on. After all, the opportunity to try on something like this would probably never come again. I sat in the chair, told myself not to be ridiculous. With my luck it would break and I would spend the rest of the night hunting lost beads. I turned my back to the desk and started to enter Bill's house in the LSS. Entering took forever. I kept turning around to look at the box and touch the silk. By the time I finished the entry I couldn't resist. After all I had barely looked at it in the office. I would take a good look at it. Put it right back in the box.

I gently straightened the anklet on my desk, moved the neck of my desk light closer. It looked almost vibrant. The beads and what was obvious now as carved bone, had been cleaned and polished. The feathers were incredibly fine, perfect in shape. Their colors seemed to be even purer than they had been in the office. The leather wasn't leather at all but seemed to be very thin braided fibers. The fibers had a sheen to them. When I gently pulled on either end of the anklet the fibers seemed to give and then pull back. How truly beautiful it was. How the feathers had been restrung, I couldn't tell. I wondered if the four-tailed piece of braid jewelry looked like this close up.

The anklet seemed pretty solid and I thought I could try it on without doing damage but resisted the urge. Returned it to its little box. I started to get ready for bed when I was struck with inspiration for Bill's ads. I went back to the computer, pulled up the pictures I had taken, wrote the ads and emailed them to Mary. Wow. Now I was ready to call it a night. I was truly tired and drifted off as soon as my head hit the pillow.

Something brought me to consciousness. I woke thinking about the anklet. If it was going to bug me this much…I got up, retrieved the box, brought it back to bed with me. I was looking at the box when I realized that the desire to put it on was gone. Fine. I cuddled back into the blankets, went back to sleep.

The alarm woke me and I allowed myself to drift in and out of sleep before I finally pushed my ass out of bed and headed straight for the shower. If I didn't shower first I'd fall asleep in my coffee.

I wandered out to pour coffee before I dried my hair. It wasn't that I was tired, I was relieved. I guess I hadn't realized how stressful the past two weeks had been. The cell phone jerked me out of my haze. It was Mary.

"Good morning Victoria. I figured I'd call before it was 'Good Afternoon' and you made a stop for nothing. Jay dropped off the check a while ago so you don't have to stop on your way in this afternoon. I'm going to bank it at lunch."

"Good morning to you too Mary. Thanks for the call. That was nice of Jay."

"It was. You do plan to come in this afternoon don't you?" She asked.

"Of course. It's Friday, right?" I wasn't all that sure.

"Yeah it is. I have the numbers you wanted and the plans. I have a request from Mason. Could you come in a little earlier? He wants some time with you. He assures me that nothing's wrong."

"So Mary, is it true? No problem with Mason." I asked.

"Yeah, he's walking around here happy as a clam. Honestly, I think his Southern Clients are paying off."

"Well, tell Mason I'll be in before two, make that one thirty. Did you get my ads this morning?"

"Yeah, Victoria do you have any idea what time you sent them to me?"

"About midnight?" I had no clue.

"Try a little after three Victoria. Why do you think I waited so late to call you this morning?" Mary was starting to sound, well, like my Mother.

"That's interesting. Thanks for holding off on your call…and no I didn't have a hot date." That would be her next question.

"You sound fine so you're not sick."

"No, I am fine. See you in a few." I hung up the phone, finished my coffee, dried my hair and left for the office.

Chapter 23

Mason was walking into my office when I remembered that I had left my gift somewhere in my bed, or did I put it on my bureau?

"Victoria, wakie, wakie." Mason must have started talking.

"Sorry Mason."

"How would you like a commission on forty-million, commercial?" He asked.

"I would like it very much, what's going on?" Now he had my attention. What the hell had Mason done?

"My Louisiana Clients, from the other day, were up here to Close on the old Providence City Hotel." And, in classic Mason tradition, he reached into his suit jacket pocket, retrieved a check and handed it to me. "Don't drop it Victoria."

I was stunned. "Mason you haven't said a word. Did Mary know this was coming?"

"No, frankly I didn't think it was going to happen. There were a bunch of code violations that the owners wouldn't split with my Buyers. At one point in the Closing, the Sellers started to walk out. But, as if by Mason magic, we Closed."

I looked at the size of the check, almost fell out of my chair. Commercial commission percentages are much larger than residential. "Mason, what is this, twelve percent?" I walked to the French door, asked Mary to step in and close the door after her. Then I handed her the check. She went white.

"Yeah, twelve." Mason sat down. Mary stumbled next to him. "Victoria, this is one fucking good year."

I went to my booze stash, grabbed the Irish whiskey, poured three and took them back to my desk. "So Mason, what does the office get?" I rarely ask that question, but this deserved it.

"The usual Victoria. Providing you pick up the space next door. You need to pick it up now." Mason smiled as he sipped the drink. "I'm on a roll. Will you let me do the lease and the negotiations."

I looked at Mary, this would have been hers.

Mason saw me look at Mary and spoke up. "Mary, commissions are yours. I just have a feeling that, well, I'd like to do the deal. OK?"

"Sure Mason, no problem. That will allow me time to get the contractors lined up. Besides, the owners are a pain in the ass. I dealt with them when they had the store open. Let me get my old files and what I have started." The more Mary thought about it, the happier she was. Mary put her glass down and left to retrieve her files.

"Mason, remember. Mary doesn't get much of an opportunity to actually do real estate. Don't treat her like a secretary, ok?" Mason would, on occasion, fall back into old habits. I understood Mason and could pull him up short. Mary would cause him serious physical pain.

"Victoria, I do understand what you're telling me. I'll be good. So are you happy?" Mason finished his glass.

"I sure am. Geez Mason. Are you going to take an extended vacation. The horses will be running soon." Mason did own a few horses himself, none that he raced, but he has a real soft spot for the Big Three and loved to attend.

"I may leave for a week around each if you don't mind. I'll be done with the office way before I go. But hell Vic, I could have a good time this year." Yeah, Mason would go. His question to me was pure politeness and nothing more.

"Just remind me when you go. Let Mary know as soon as you can and get someone to cover for you ok? Have a good time Mason." I smiled at him. There was a time with Mason when he could have easily slipped out of the friend category. But the time had passed and couldn't be recalled. Mary returned with the files, handed them to Mason and started to leave. "Mary, don't we have some things to do?"

"Oh, yeah. I was going to run Mason's check down to the bank first."

"Right, go ahead. I'll be here." Mary left and Mason started to stand. "Mason, can you stay just for a few?"

"Sure Victoria, what do you need?"

"You know, I was thinking that Ames, if trained right, could be good at commercial. He looks so innocent. If he could learn from you, he would be deadly in the commercial world. What do you think?" This had been bouncing around my head for a while. Ames is one of those young men that will stay comfortable, but not push. He's not a wimp by any measure, but Mason isn't going to work forever and we would be left with a big hole. Mason is a huge talent and he should pass it on to someone.

"I'll talk to him Victoria and see how he feels about it. I don't know him that well, you do, so I'll take your word for it." Mason wasn't jumping up and down.

"See what happens Mason. It is truly your call, ok?"

"Hey, you never know." Mason was standing, "He does need a little sleight-of-hand in his life." Mason left the office.

Wow. I didn't see that check coming. I probably wouldn't have to kick my money into the expansion; not that I had any other plans for it. Maybe an early runaway to Florida. I wouldn't have to hot-bunk with my daughter, her kids and her Significant Other. Now that would be nice. I didn't mind hot-bunking with them. I just don't find it relaxing. I could lease the condo next to them. Still be close but not worry about having to get up with the kids and feel guilty having my daughter busting her butt around me. My own place? Heck, I could seriously look to get lucky.

I can't be a guest in their house. I'm mom and grandma and we all fall into our labels. When I'm by myself I can be myself which doesn't include either of those professions. I've fought it for years, only successful the past couple of years, I think.

Mary returned and brought everything she needed into my office, placing a stack on my desk. It was a big stack and each file had a note clipped to it. She sorted them into the two normal Friday piles and placed them on either side of my chair. It was fascinating. I'd never actually watched her get ready for our Friday afternoon meetings. Mary didn't say a word to me, just moved quietly around my desk, pulling certain papers out of the remaining pile, placing a few directly in front of me. Squaring off the right and left piles, she stepped back, looked at what her efforts had produced. Satisfied, Mary returned to her chair.

Mary was a truly small person. Her height brought her barely to my shoulder which made her maybe 5'2" or so. I'm 5'8" so I guess I had about six inches on her and thin. Mary had always been thin. When we lived together I watched her eat an incredible amount of food, especially when she had the munchies, and not gain an ounce. She ate everything, candy, ice cream, pasta, everything and yes, I had been jealous. Probably still was. I had fought my weight my whole life and was still fighting it, just not as hard. I would probably refuse the offer of something luscious the day I died.

Because of her size, Mary's eyes took up most of her face. Her bone structure was delicate, bird delicate. Her mouth was small, as was her nose, but her eyes would be the first item in any description of her. Large, brown eyes with lashes to match. Her hair was thin, severely straight, brown with some gray, cut to her shoulders and never really styled. She would step out of the shower, towel-dry it, run a comb through it and walk away. By the time she would enter another room in our apartment her hair would be dry.

When Mary had her notebook in her hands she broke the silence. "Ready?"

"When you are." I responded.

"I have a few notes. First, the DBR has extended the CEU deadline to August, but not the license renewal time." Well, that was a bit of a relief. The DBR is the Department of Business Regulation in Rhode Island and the issuer of real estate licenses. The layers of government and civilian regulators in our business is amazing. Between the Federal government, State government and our own little "union" I could count eleven. Yes, it is a bore.

"Good. We could all use the time. Make sure everyone knows." The agents in the State that had given up days upon days of work to meet the requirement of April 30th must be pissed.

"Next, can you think of some way that Mason would have had to give us a head's up about his potential Closing? I'm not complaining. It's just a bitch when I try to plan. Budget advertising, utilities for the rest of the year, the monthly dinners. I worry about stuff. I know you don't like to concentrate on potential income, you think it's a jinx, but shit Vic, someone has to." I knew Mary had been a bit irritated when I handed Mason's check to her. Now I know why.

"Yeah. I was thinking the same thing. I just hesitate to start having our Brokers reporting potential income. Where does it stop? I have a problem signing Escrow checks for a Closing. I start thinking about everything that could go wrong at the Closing. But I do understand what you are saying. Do you have any ideas?"

"Well, we know when our listings go into Contract, we receive the Escrow funds. Is there something we can ask that will be along the lines of depositing Escrow funds? No one seems to feel that we are invading their business when they deposit Escrow funds." Mary had a good point.

"You're right." I was interrupted by the office phone. Mary reached for the one on my desk.

"Yes, it did Close." Silence. "I have no more information." Silence. "No I cannot." Silence. "No, I cannot say. Good bye." With the old telephones I probably would have been able to hear part of the other side of the conversation. With the digital, voice activated receivers, not so much.

"What was that?" I asked.

"Press. They found us. Asked for your cell number, asked for confirmation of the sale, asked for your home address. Well, this is going to be interesting. Where were we?"

Yeah, it was. I wondered if Cheryl had kept her mouth shut. "Income projections. Let me think on it. Maybe we should just ask at the next dinner? See how everyone feels about it." It was the best I could do for the moment.

I saw the front door open and a women walked in followed by someone with a camera. "Mary, you want to get the people that just walked in the door?"

"What?" She turned to see a face trying to look in my French door. "Why don't you walk into the workroom?"

"No way. I'll wait right here." I wasn't going to run out of my office. No way in hell. Mary went to the door and pushed her way through the peepers, drawing their attention with her so that their backs were to me. I glanced to the large bay window at the front of my office and was thankful for the office sign that blocked the lower half of the window. I had hated putting a sign there. I liked watching people walk by but unfortunately it worked both ways and that bothered me. I wondered if we could replace the lower 6x6 panes with one way glass. Hadn't though of that before. Probably expensive as hell.

The voices in the outer office were getting loud. I went to see if Mason was still here. Yeah, he was. I asked him to step into the front room. Told him the voices were getting too loud.

"Sure Victoria. I'll take care of it." Mason had a twinkle in his eye and a smile on his face. Mason knew exactly what he was going to do. I followed him and kept the door to the outer office cracked.

When the news lady saw him she stopped yelling about 'right to know' and Mason started. "You're asking about old news. I have some new news." And Mason started talking about his sale in Providence. Mason could tell a story and it was certainly working for him now as he walked the news people out the front door to the sidewalk. Got his picture taken in front of our sign…good man…and continued to talk.

I walked back into my office and once again Mary was waiting for me. "You've told me about Mason before but I don't think I've ever seen him 'do his thing' as you like to say. I take back everything I ever said about him." Mary was seeing a master at work. I'd seen it many, many times. In other arenas Mason stories were legend.

"Yeah. Glad you saw that. So what else is going on?"

"Your ads for your new listing are on top, look at them first and I'll try to get them placed today. The summary numbers for the week aren't accurate. Yours are included, but Mason's aren't. Oh, in front of you are the projected numbers for the new space. Want to go over them?"

"Sure. Mary, want to co-list Bill's house. You know how much I dislike Listings. I'll deal with Bill but I'll refer the Listing to you. Would you be interested?"

"Yeah, I would. This isn't a pity referral is it?" Mary asked.

"No, not at all. It's been a while since you've been out working. If you don't use it, you lose it, right? It won't be too much will it?" It occurred to me that with the new space it might be.

"I'd love it Vic. Don't worry about time, I'll yell if it gets to be too much. So when can you get me out there?"

"We're running late this afternoon, how about tomorrow, noon?" Mary agreed and she walked me through the projected numbers on the new space. It was doable. Nice.

"Mary, lets just do it. Call our old contractor and tell him we want to mirror this office, move the front entrance and put the conference room behind the entry space some how. OK. Once he figures out how to do it arrange a meeting with the three of us. Lets just get it done. I'm tired of thinking about it." Once I realize I'm going to do something I just like it done and I'd been thinking about this since last summer.

"Great. I'm done. So get to work, look at the ad so I can get it in." Mary stood and walked out. I did what she asked and took it out to her. I'd forgotten to ask her about the one-way glass, but she was busy now. I'd email the question to her over the weekend. Not something urgent, but she would be talking with our contractor.

Chapter 24

By the time I got home the sun was down. Tomorrow started daylight savings time. The first true sign of spring coming. Other than taking Mary out to Bill's house, my weekend was blank and I would have time just to think about stuff and nonsense. Heaven.

I put on my evening clothes, made a sandwich, a drink and wandered into the living room. The moon was full; rising over the Bird Sanctuary and Ledge House, shining on the beach. This was too beautiful to pass up. I dragged one of my leather chairs and foot stools to the windows, moved a side table next to it and sat down to eat in the moonlight.

My cell phone rang. I cursed. I didn't recognize the number so I sent it to voicemail. I had no sooner done that when it rang again. Again I sent it to voicemail. Five minutes later it rang again. I turned off the phone.

When the moon had risen completely over the Sanctuary, the house phone rang. Didn't recognize the number again. But the house number was unlisted, so I answered. Phooey on me. It was some news lady calling herself Miss Katie of Channel 9 News asking for Mrs. Victoria Hamilton. I told her she had the wrong number. She wouldn't let it go. I hung up on her and changed the voicemail link to one ring. The phone rang constantly for the next fifteen minutes, then stopped.

I settled back into my chair by the window and noticed birds flying in tight circles then diving over the beach. Wow. The moon was bright. This time of the year the air was dry, cold and very, very clear. I counted eight birds diving, swirling up and down the beach. Then one at a time, the birds disappeared. I pulled the telescope into position and focused for the remaining four birds. They were hawks of some kind and it was fascinating to watch them. When the next one started to fly towards the Sanctuary I followed it. It didn't disappear into the Bird Sanctuary but circled briefly above the outcropping, 'Hanging Rock', and then started to descend to a figure below holding out its arm. I tightened my focus on the figure. The hawk landed on an outstretched arm covered in what looked like animal skins. I followed the arm back to the figure standing with his, definitely his, back to me. Black hair loose to the middle of his back. All I could see was that he was wearing brown, maybe suede, shirt with long sleeves that had fringe along their length and pants of some kind. I couldn't see any boots. He wasn't wearing a coat or hat to keep him warm, maybe he had long underwear on, it was cold out. He was working his birds. Falconry. I'd never seen the sport it up close, if this could be called close. I watched each remaining bird wait its turn by the beach, then gracefully circle to the outstretched arm. The falconer gently attached the bird's hood and moved his arm to a cage. The bird jumped off the falconer's arm, into the cage and the cage was latched. When the last bird had been caged the falconer turned on the rock and looked out to the beach, out to the ocean. He swept the horizon.

His face, from what I could see, was heavily marked, black scars or maybe a mask of some kind I thought. His features, they seemed sharp enough to reflect the moonlight in some places and hollow in others. I couldn't see all that much. He leaned down, his hair falling forward, picked up one of the cages and disappeared into the Sanctuary. Wow, what a show. Other people must have been with him. He picked up one cage. If each bird had a cage, there would have been seven other cages. I settled back against my chair marveling at how lucky I was to see that display. What a show.

When the moon moved out of my direct view, I closed down the condo for the night, retreated into my bedroom. I turned on my little television setting its timer for two hours, fished out a book I had begun more than two weeks ago and continued where I had left off. Before I knew it the TV clicked itself off. I turned it back on and the screen displayed an aerial view of Ledge House. I turned up the sound and was somewhat surprised to hear Cheryl's voice talking over the film. "This is the second time the property has been sold in the past three years."

The interview continued over still photos of the Seller of Ledge House. "Our investigative reporter stated in our previous segment that a private corporation is named as the Buyer of the property but we hear two men actually purchased Ledge House. Can you tell us about the two mysterious Buyers Cheryl?"

"Well Katie. All I can tell you is that they insisted I sign an extensive Confidentially Agreement before allowing me to show them the property. They were very, very secretive through the whole transaction."

"Well thank you Cheryl, Owner of Kingston Realty in Newport. We tried to contact Victoria Hamilton, the Broker who brought the mysterious Buyers to Ledge House," and my picture was on the screen. It looked like the picture had been taken last summer while I was walking on the beach. "But was escorted out of her office by one of her employees." And a picture of Mason was on the screen. Oh, poor Mason. "…and was refused a telephone interview by Victoria Hamilton herself, which begs the question, why all the mystery surrounding the sale of one of Rhode Island's most famous homes? We will continue to dig for the truth of this mysterious sale. This is Miss Katie Souza, Channel 9 News." And the screen cut to commercial.

Ah rats. I wondered what my Clients would do. I warned them, or at least Keirns at our first meeting. Well, at least no one had talked out of our office so we're in the clear. Not my problem. I reset the TV timer, switched to an old movie and went back to my book.

Chapter 25

I slept in the next morning. Played catch up and cleaned house the rest of the afternoon. I called Florida to talk to my daughter about an early visit which, as always, led to an almost two-hour conversation. We bounced around June, the beach would be free of tourists and the weather would be warm enough for me to enjoy.

Over the years I had visited her in various seasons. I froze in January, February, March and early April. I adored the beach in late June, July and August although it was almost too hot for me in August. Christmas was a delight. I grew up in Hawaii. My first twelve years were spent there and the holidays on the western coast of Florida reminded me of Hawaii during the holidays.

By the end of the conversation we had decided that the last week of June and the first week of July would be perfect. The huge fireworks display on the 4th took place about a hundred yards from their condo. It would be an all day party. I could get in to that. I circled the dates on my calendar and wrote "Book Flight" in red on my desk blotter. Not that I would forget.

I walked back into the kitchen to make a cup of tea and noticed that the predicted snow had started to fall, the wind had begun to blow. The snow was suppose to continue into Sunday night with temperatures dropping into the teens. Ah March, thy sting is all over my garden!

I decided to check my voicemails while I had my tea in the kitchen. I hadn't even thought about the phone calls, much less checking the voicemail all day. On the cell phone were seven messages from Miss Katie, one even threatening me with court action. Yeah, that would happen. Four from other news types. One from Jay telling me not to worry and of course, Carolyn, Mary and Mason. My home phone was full, everyone of the messages from Miss Katie.

I returned Mason's call, thanked him for intervening the day before; let him blow off steam…not even a word about the hotel sale on the TV. I thanked him again and ended the conversation. Called Mary who was way too upset. Seeing the news story then not being able to raise me on the phone had upset her. Probably completely forgetting to pick her up for Bill's house had added to the upset. I told her I was fine, so sorry about the missed arrangements and explained that I had sent all my phones to voicemail. By the end of that conversation we had rearranged visiting Bill's house and she had calmed down. I called Carolyn and she too thought something had happened to me. We chatted for a while, told her I was thinking about going to visit Florida earlier rather than later which brought on a ton of chat about her travels running the call to about an hour. Oh well Carolyn's call was fun and everyone knew I was alive.

I wandered back into the living room, thinking I would grab my book from last night, read and watch the snow. The bedroom was the only room I hadn't attacked, but I could do that tomorrow. I dug out my book and walked back into the living room.

I looked up to see James standing in the snow on my terrace. I was more than a bit surprised. He was covered with snow; no hat, no gloves, a simple cotton jacket.

I dropped the book, opened the door letting in a flurry of the blowing snow. "Get your ass in here. Good God, you must be freezing. Hurry up." Actually, he didn't look cold. He walked to the open door, shook himself to get rid of the snow and stepped into the living room. "Let me have your coat and take off, err…" I looked down seeing deerskin? What? Very thin boots that were laced up to his knees. "…your shoes, or boots or what ever they are." I closed the door behind him while he removed his jacket. I took it, threw it over my chair from last night. "Stay right here. I'll get you a blanket."

I hurried to the bedroom, pulled my comforter off the bed. By the time I returned to the living room, James had taken off his boots. I wrapped the comforter around his shoulders the best I could. His shoulders were broader than I remembered. Hmm, he seemed taller. I grabbed the jacket and boots, took them to the kitchen. "James, aren't you freezing? I'm cold just looking at you."

"No." He said from the entry of the kitchen. "I did not mean to upset you Victoria. I wanted to see you. I have been in Europe all week."

I spread his coat on the standing radiator, put the boots underneath to dry and warm up. "James, I'm not upset. I guess you surprised me more than anything." I turned to look at him and he was staring at me again. He didn't even seem wet. "Please, don't stare at me like that, it's a little unnerving. Would you like something hot to drink?"

"No." He looked down at my ankles. "Did you receive the talisman?"

"That's what you call it? Yes I did." I leaned against the breakfast bar and slid my hands into my pockets. "It was kind of you to give it to me but it's too expensive a gift. James, I was at the auction on Sunday." I was uncomfortable with this subject. "I would like to return it to you."

"Victoria." He said reaching to touch my arm. "I merely retrieved the piece and returned it to its Owner." James said this as fact, not open for discussion. "Would you mind if I set a fire?" So he was the one that changed the subject.

"Oh, no I wouldn't mind. Yes, it would be nice." So now how do I return the anklet, rather talisman? I guess I could stick it in the mail next week.

He walked with the comforter still around his shoulders into the living room. James laid the comforter on the loveseat. Walked to the fireplace. Flexed his knees so that his weight was on the balls of his feet. He opened the fire screen, leaned to the wood stack, stretched his left arm lifting one large log at a time placing each in the fireplace. I stood watching each flex of his arm, each graceful transfer of his weight from one leg to the other. When the wood was stacked to his liking he picked out a long lighting match and flicked his thumb on its sulfur head. The match blazed to life.

James waited until the match fire involved the wood, then placed the flame against one of the lower logs. A moment later the log had a flame. "How long has it been since you have had a real fire?" He didn't say fake fire but I knew he'd seen a stray piece of an instant log wrapper in the cold ashes.

"A long time." I answered. His hair hung straight and shiny down his back covering his shoulder blades. Yeah, he was a treat. Not just his body, his hair or his eyes, but the way he moved in his space. No, it wasn't just that. The way he was contained, was that it? Not really, but it was something. I'd seen each attribute before; one guy's form, another guy's gracefulness or his carriage. No, there was something else about him. I sat on the loveseat. I didn't want to fall down.

"Why? You have arranged the room so that the heat will flow to every corner. I would think you would light it every night." James backed away from the fire a few steps, bent his knees again; turned and lowered his body at the same time so that he ended up on the floor facing me on the loveseat. He seemed to settle himself. Looked comfortable enough to stay in that one spot all night. The light of the fire was reflected in his eyes, caught the height of his cheekbones and the edge of his jaw. Now I was staring.

"Thank you for the fire James. Would you mind if we talked a bit?" He looked so peaceful I hated to disturb him. But I was beyond playing games that would get me burnt and I was surprised to see him again.

"No, please say what you need to say." Interesting response.

"Your visit does surprise me. You own the house. I assume all is fine, so why are you here?"

"I am here to be with you Victoria. To share with you. To learn with you. That is why I am here."

"I don't understand. I'm older than you are by, well, take my word for it. I'm anything but naïve, James. My children have children. I admit I love to play, but the play is always honest. I outgrew games with my personal life a long time ago. Do you understand what I'm saying to you? Money, men and games. The ultimate threesome in this world." I was getting my self angry, why was that? Then it hit me. With James I could get burnt. That's why. Boy, its been a long time since that was even a possibility.

"You are not a game to me Victoria. I do understand what you are saying. I tell you that I have not been looking this long to find you and then play games, as you say." He had no expression when he said this. No insult had been taken. No anger could be seen on his face or heard in his voice. "Would you bring the talisman?"

That was the second time he'd said something like that to me. The first was at the Ledge House showing. He had apologized for taking so long. "Yeah, sure." We were back to the gift. Hoped I could find it in the bed linens. Did I dump it on the floor when I pulled the comforter off the bed? I pulled back the covers. The box was against the pillow.

I returned to the loveseat. Opened the box. Handed whatever it was to James.

He placed it on his open palm, closed his hand around it and looked up at me. "May I put this on your ankle?"

"Since it doesn't seem that you will be taking it with you tonight, I'd love to try it on." What the hell? I was still chewing on his earlier answer, rather answers. Thank heavens I had showered and put on fresh evening clothes when I had finished cleaning. I had not planned on entertaining when I dressed, just a lazy evening with my book.

James lifted my right foot. Gently pulled off its wool sock, pushed up the cuff of the leg of my sweats. Placed my foot on his ankles where they crossed. He turned my ankle so that he could better see the tattoo that was inked from my ankle bone about seven inches up my leg. Black roses on a vine. He ran his fingers oh so gently over the tattoo a number of times, then smiled and looked up at me. "You have a public tattoo. Now I am surprised. Do many people see it?"

That was an odd question, but I'd said no games. "Yes a lot of people see it. Are you asking if I hide it when I'm not wearing boots James? Is that the real question?"

Without dropping his eyes he answered. "Yes".

"I love my tattoos. They are a part of me. Hiding them would be like hiding my ears or my toes. No. I never hide them."

"You have more than one?"

"Yes."

"Do you like tattoos on men?"

"It depends on the man." That was also the truth. It's easy to tell if a tattoo is the result of trying to be cool, to fit in with friends. Those tattoos don't belong. They are almost like a label, a screaming label that says 'I'm cool. Look at all the pain I can take, I'm tough'. And make no mistake, tattoos hurt when they are inked correctly. Seeing that kind of a tattoo being paraded around pisses me off. The tattoos that belong, that seem natural on the body and it doesn't matter how many the person has, are incredibly attractive to me.

James tied the beads and feathers around my ankle but didn't respond to my answer. "Yes, that is where it belongs." The anklet felt warm, comforting, almost like it did belong. He looked up and into my eyes. "As long as you wear it, I will be with you." He looked back to my ankle. His hand moved over the anklet, rolling the beads and feathers against my skin. I inhaled as quietly as I could. James looked up at me again. For a few moments I could not release the breath.

When, finally, I did exhale, he smiled. "Do not worry about damaging the talisman. Nothing will harm it." James replaced my sock, pulled down the cuff of my pant leg and put my foot back on the floor.

He stood straight up without effort. "I believe this is enough for now. May I visit again?"

No, not enough, I thought. Nowhere near enough. I couldn't help it,

I laughed. "Yes, please visit again. If you let me know you're coming I will dress better than this."

James's smile almost broke to a laugh. "You are dressed as you are and it is fine. I am the one who dressed as I thought you would expect me to dress. I did not dress as I am." Not a clue as to what he was saying.

I retrieved his coat and the soft boots. When he leaned to put the boots on his feet, his hair fell forward, over his face. "So you were the falconer last night." He stopped his motion, looked at me. I smiled, reached to the telescope and tapped it. "You and your birds were beautiful in the moonlight."

"I did not frighten you?" He asked.

"No. Why would you?"

James opened the door, stepped into the snow, was gone. I stood for a while looking at the only four steps in the snow.

I returned to the loveseat. Covered myself with the comforter and watched the fire burn down as I fell asleep. Could be fun...could be very deep shit.

Chapter 26

The sun on my face woke me the next morning. It was strong, bright. I could see the light through my eyelids. My bedroom shouldn't be this bright in any season. I worked to get my brain moving and then I remembered last night. I reached to my ankle. Before I touched the jewelry, I felt it. I felt the feathers tickle my skin when the beads felt like they rolled. I must have tried to move my leg. I must have fallen asleep on the loveseat.

I tried to stretch my legs, but with a little movement they hit the arm of the loveseat. I had spent the whole night crunched up on the loveseat, this was going to hurt. I stretched my arm to the floor and slowly rolled myself on to it, wrapped in the comforter. Then I stretched my legs, waiting for the pain. Nothing. I sat up, leaning my back against the loveseat and opened my eyes.

The day looked beautiful. The snow had ended earlier than predicted and I could hear the drip, drip of the melt down the gutters of the building at each corner of my living room. It was warmer than predicted too. Nice for weatherman mistakes.

I pulled the comforter off of my leg, pulled up my cuff and took off my sock. The anklet was just below the center of my ankle bone, below the tattoo. The two ties stopped just above the bottom of my foot, but I couldn't see a knot. I leaned down to get a better look and I still couldn't see a knot. The two ends of the anklet where the knot had been were one piece. The hanging pieces that had been the two ends of the anklet looked like they had grown out of where the knot had been. This was either the greatest con of all times or James was much more than he appeared to be. With that thought, it rolled ever so slightly. Oh yeah, much more. Deeper shit.

I stood with the comforter, threw it on my bed, went to the kitchen to make coffee. If I wasn't careful with James I was going to get hurt. That, more than anything, scared me. I had been owned before, more than once. It was starting with the anklet. My rational for even trying it on had been that I would mail it back next week. Now I was thinking about keeping it. After all, if I'd had the money to bid on it, I would have bought it. Is that reason enough? Damn. How could just putting on the anklet have me almost crawling out of my skin. Talk about foreplay. The buzzer on the coffee pot brought me back to reality. Not thinking about it any more. Hell, I'd probably never see him again.

I called my daughter to ask if I would be miserable with the cold in Florida this week. Of course, she said I would freeze my ass off. Hey, it was worth the ask. I spent my first cup of coffee trying to think of a place I could go that would be warm this time of the year. Once I had flipped through my mental list I figured out what I really wanted. I wanted to get out of Dodge. Anticipatory run before I hurt myself. I could beat the rush, go now.

I had waited too long the last time. That had been about eight years ago after the last big fight with my third husband. By the time that run had ended I was flat broke, burnt out and divorced. I had come back to Newport. Spent a year at my old agency. Left and started my own. I swore, never again would I get involved. Didn't matter if the other person was involved. Until now, it had worked. Idiot. Why was I thinking like this? We hadn't even gone out.

My relationships were 'guy' relationships. Date, have some fun for a while, never date them again. It hadn't been a problem. I limited most of my dating to the summer people and they are out of Newport by Thanksgiving. Kind of self-limiting, at least for me. So why was he in my head?

After the second cup of coffee, I checked my calendar for the week to find holes, spare time, and I plugged them. A third meeting and he was causing this kind of panic. I had a problem. Between a Board of Directors' meeting on Monday evening and visiting Carolyn on Friday I would be busy. I was feeling better. The only day that didn't have at least one thing penciled in was today.

Even with the melt, a foot of snow had to be moved. I stood on a chair to check the west side of the building. My car was almost free. By the time I showered the nice workmen would have it clear. I could be out by one. If the roads were passable maybe I would be able to go to Little Compton.

I finished my coffee, took my butt to the shower. Little Compton was a great idea. My favorite little shops and a great place to get lobster. Sounded damn fine.

Chapter 27

I returned to the condo after dark, much later than I had planned, but the day had turned into a ton of fun and a great distraction. My favorite little stores were having winter sales, getting ready for their summer stock. I splurged and bought a beautiful Irish man's sweater to replace one that I had trashed a few years ago in an old Victorian house on the Point with a dirt floor basement. The basement had been wet, musty and moldy. It left a smell in the sweater that two trips to the cleaners couldn't get out, so the sweater had been given away.

I put on my evening clothes, turned on my computer, made a cup of tea and started listening to my voice mail when the most luscious feeling started up my right leg, passed my knee and settled like a weight at the bottom of my pelvis. I dropped the phone. The feeling moved up to my chest, my heart started beating like it was going to jump out of my body, my hands were shaking, my head was pounding. My eyes closed and I slid out of the chair, everything went dark.

When I woke I was covered in sweat, still lying on the floor. Did I need to call 911? What was I going to tell them, that I felt wonderful, because I did. My heart wasn't pounding now, my head had cleared. I wasn't shaking, everything, my legs, arms, head moved. I could think. I was fine, just a little nauseous. And wet, soaked through my clothes. I sat up and could see my sweat on the wood floor like the chalk outline of a body at a crime scene. That wasn't good, the floor would stain. I stood slowly, grabbed a rag and the floor cleaner, wiped down the outline of my body.

I went to the bathroom. Turned on the shower. Stripped off my wet sweats, socks, everything else and stood in the shower thinking about what had happened. I looked down at my ankle. The anklet was still there but my tattoo looked larger. Shit. It was larger. Now the tattoo extended over the top of my foot and up, over my calf. I rubbed my hand over the tattoo stupidly thinking I could rub it off and the feeling started again.

Damn. I sat on the shower floor before I fell. The feeling swept over me again. Shivered every inch from my scalp to the ends of my toes. This time I didn't pass out. Oh, I knew what this was. I smiled. Was almost embarrassed to admit it to myself. What the hell?...an orgasm? First in the library and just now in the shower. Not like anything else I had ever felt. But that's what it was. Either that or heart attacks weren't as advertised.

I looked to my ankle. Whatever that thing...that what...jewelry... on my ankle was, it contained magic, was magic. What had he called it last night, a talisman? Damn it, James you could have warned me that it was real. Real?...if I had been driving I'd be dead. What an idiot James. I reached down to pull it off and words were in my head that were not mine. "I am sorry. Please do not worry."

I stood up, kicked the tile. Don't worry? Shit James...I kicked the wall. Shit...I kicked the wall. Shit...I kicked the wall, pulled on the towel bar. Shit and the towel bar shattered to the shower floor. I rinsed the soap off of my body, dried with a towel, went to my dressing room to get my scissors. I put my foot on the bed looking for the best angle to cut that thing and words came again. "I am sorry. Please. Do not try to break us". And I couldn't do it. I mean, I physically couldn't cut it. It seemed loose on my ankle but the scissors wouldn't fit under the beads or where the knot had been. To get it off I would have to dig the scissors into my leg. The ultimate game was being played. Oh, we were going to have more than words...if I ever saw him again.

I returned my scissors to the drawer. Put on fresh clothes and poured myself a generous brandy. I sat in the chair by the window, pulled the telescope to me and focused on Hanging Rock. What the hell are you doing? What the hell have you done?

In my heart of hearts, ever since I was a child I had felt that humans weren't the only ones walking in this world. Science only investigates what it can understand, define. It doesn't bother with potential, brain exploding concepts. Yeah, my questions to my parents, my teachers and my ministers were not greeted with good thoughts, or actions. I remembered the one and only time my Father took me aside to try to explain that what I was saying and asking would get me put in a place for crazy people, so it would be good if I just let my thoughts and questions go. I guess I was about ten at the time. Looking at him say this it occurred to me that he felt what I felt.

But causing waves in our oh so stable Christian, military world was not acceptable. He would never admit what he knew, what he felt. We never spoke of it again. But I knew and in listening to others talk, they knew too. Was it staring me in the eye now? Daring me.

By the time I had finished the brandy and poured another my anger was pretty much gone. I looked back at the outcropping and saw James standing on it. He was looking in my direction. I tightened the focus to get a serious look. His arms were out, perpendicular, east and west, and I couldn't help but smile. What did you want? His figure shimmered out of focus for the telescope, then sharpened. He had changed. From what I could see, he had been hiding. His face seemed sharper in its angles and curves. The moonlight reflected on his cheekbones and jaw. His cheeks were dark hollows. His eyes were dark hollows with flashes of light. His neck was thinner, looked longer without its extra flesh. I could see marks on his skin that were reflected in the moonlight, but couldn't identify their detail. I watched him stand, arms out, not moving. Then I blinked and he was gone. I sat back in my chair and realized how physically and emotionally tired I was. I finished my brandy. Went to bed.

I dreamt. I was laughing, serving drinks, behind a long, unfinished wooden bar. Someone was playing piano. The place smelled of sweat and leather, dust and cheap beer. Loud, it was loud. Full of men with hats and guns wearing chaps and filthy shirts. I was hot, sweat and dirt sliding on my face. The two doors, the entrance, opened. A man walked in. I glanced up, not from here I thought. He looked at me, what was on his face? An Indian, didn't belong in here. He smiled at me. Started walking to me. I felt incredible pressure in my chest. Was pushed violently back against the bottles. Heard a bang. Glass broke. My knees buckled. I slid to the floor.

I woke with a start. Sat up. The alarm went off.

I sat in bed for a few minutes trying to remember the dream. The dream didn't upset me, not like before. The only face I could remember clearly was the Indian, his smile…it was James. I had died. I tried to remember the details of his face but couldn't push my memory that far. I just knew who it was.

Chapter 28

I called Mary while I was having coffee. Asked if I could take her out to Bill's house in Portsmouth today. Then we could stop for lunch.

"I think we should Vic. One of these days someone is going to want to see it. Are you doing ok?"

"Oh, sorry about Saturday. I'm fine. Just a very weird weekend. I'll pick you up about twelve, is that good?"

"That's fine. Mason's on the phone. I think he's talking to the owners next door. Oh and the emergency wagon was at Cheryl's office when I came to work."

"Great, I mean Mason great. Hopefully he'll get it done this week. Talk about the other stuff later. Bye." I hung up. I wondered if I could talk to Mary or Carolyn about the weekend. Actually Carolyn would probably be the best person to talk to. She's pretty open about this stuff. In the effort to fill my week I had begged a dinner invite for myself on Friday. Well, I had the topic of conversation for the evening.

On a lark I called Cheryl's office and asked for her. I was politely told that Cheryl was on vacation. The receptionist asked if I would like to leave a message for her. I politely said no thank you. I had no sooner ended that call and Jay was on the line.

"Hi Jay. What's up?"

"Did you get my message on the weekend?" He asked.

"Sure did. Thanks. I'd seen the little news ditty and was concerned. Just didn't want to interrupt your weekend."

"Thanks, I appreciate it. I received a call from Keirns Saturday afternoon. He said he thought we might be concerned but, and this is a direct quote. "Please, do not be, there is no need." If you can believe it, he sounded rather mellow. That was a first." Jay was laughing.

"That was nice of him. With Keirns I figured out of sight, out of mind. But I guess not."

"Anyway, just closing the loop. Oh how about Mason's coup? You guys are on a roll. Even if the rest of the year sucks, you won't be hurting."

"That reminds me Jay. I'm trying to pick up the vacant space next door to the office. I might need you if the price is right. Mason's dealing with it so if it works out I'll have him call you, ok?" Might as well ask.

"Sure. You know those owners are going under in Connecticut." He offered.

"Thanks Jay, I didn't know. I'll pass it on to Mason. Take care." I said.

"You too." This time Jay hung up first.

I called Mary and had her pass a note to Mason. I didn't need to talk to him, still on the phone.

The snow was seriously melting, everything was soggy. So wet that I grabbed my big rubber boots from the entry closet and put them in the car; which reminded me that I could afford to buy some real silk stockings this year and actually wear them for more than very special occasions. I made a note in my book as soon as I sat in the car. Little pleasures.

I picked up Mary on time and we drove out to Bill's house. "Victoria, you look better than I thought you would. You sounded disconnected Saturday."

"I must have had one hell of a bug over the weekend. I'm fine now, but Saturday into Sunday morning I spend between bed and the bathroom. Hope you don't get it." Well, some of it was true.

"Billy hasn't been feeling well either. Not stomach, just feeling like garbage. He's going to see the doctor this afternoon. I hope you don't mind Vic, but I put my name on the ads for this house. I didn't think you would mind. Do you?"

"I hadn't thought about it. Good I'm glad you did. I'd just have to refer the calls to you anyway." I truly hadn't thought about it. Infact, I hadn't thought about business all weekend.

We stopped in front of the house and Mary thought it was a cute cape. I took her in through the front door and the 'cute cape' became a 'WOW'. Bill had moved over the weekend in the snow. Nothing left, everything clean as a whistle. I would have to call him and tell him how good it looked. Even the windows had been cleaned. Not an easy job in this house.

Mary and I were debating on the exterior tour when her phone rang. It was Billy. His doctor had put him in the hospital saying he had had a heart attack. I put Mary in the car and took off to find Billy.

The local hospital serves our community nicely, but serious stuff ends up in Providence or Boston. It took us an hour to discover that Billy had been packed off to Providence. Mary and Billy not being married caused major confusion. Could they tell her where he was? Did it violate patient confidentiality? Finally she called his everyday doctor. Apparently Billy had had a heart attack over the weekend and then, when he was checking into the local hospital, had another one. So they packed him off to Providence. We got back in my car and drove to Providence.

We had the same problem with Providence that we had with Newport. I called Jay, explained the problem and he called someone at the Providence hospital. Twenty minutes later Mary was allowed into the Cardiac Critical Care unit and I waited in the classic hospital waiting room. I didn't think either of us would be back in Newport soon so I called Mason, last guy seen at the office, told him what had happened and asked him to lock up the office when he left.

"Sure Victoria. Is there anything else I can do?" Mason sounded solemn.

"Yeah actually there is. Could you let the others know that Mary won't be in today. You can tell them why if they ask. I'll pick up the slack tomorrow. Ok?" I was winging it. I didn't have any choice. For the foreseeable future I would be Mary. It would take a couple of days, but I had no doubt I'd be able to work out a system until she returned.

"No problem Victoria. By the way, thanks for the information on the owners next door." Mason never forgot business.

"You can thank Jay. Oh yeah, I gave Jay a head's up on the vacancy next to us so don't hesitate to call him if you need to, got it?"

"Sure, thanks. Keep me posted on Billy and I'll see you tomorrow. Bye."

I was thinking about what I had just signed myself up to when Mary walked into the waiting room. She was shattered. I knew Billy had died before she said anything. I didn't think I had ever seen Mary cry. She did for a long time. At some point a Chaplin came in and tried to comfort Mary. Mary promptly told her to 'get lost'; went back to crying.

When Mary began to wind down she started asking for help. Actual help, not philosophy but what mortuary she should call, real stuff I could actually help her with. I'd had a scene like this when my Father died. The scene had been with my Mother. The situation had been a little more complicated as the question of a respirator had come up. My Mother couldn't deal with it; completely and utterly couldn't deal.

I had never had 'the conversation' with either of my parents. I didn't have a clue what he wanted. I fell back on my Grandfather's experience, which had been pure hell, and opted out of the respirator. It had become my decision alone because I was alone. My husband at the time helped, but without siblings, it was my decision. It took me a while to get over that one.

I made the phone call for Mary so Billy wouldn't have to stay in Providence too long. One of the nurses gave us Billy's things, clothes, jewelry, stuff out of his pockets and I started driving us back to Newport.

"Mary, would you like to stay at my place for a time?"

"No. I have the animals to take care of and I just want to go home."

"Are you sure. I could stay with you if you'd like." I offered having no clue what Mary would say.

"No Vic. I'll be fine. I think I got it out of my system back there. I have a cousin I may call later. Maybe he'll come up for a while. I don't know." Mary would take her time and decide what to do. Of that, I was sure. "About the office," she started.

"Not to worry. I'll take your place for a while, ok?" We pulled up to her little house and her dogs came running out to greet her.

"I'll talk to you Victoria. Thanks for all your help." Mary walked through the gate of her yard. Disappeared into the house.

I looked at my cell phone. It was nearly seven-thirty. I hadn't realized the sun had gone down. I had missed my Board meeting. I would definitely hear about that. Not a problem if I had called earlier, but no-shows are frowned upon. Should I trust Mason to close down the office? Yeah, I would trust him, he was a big boy. That reminded me I had to hang on the phone tonight…that I should move my car or Mary would think I was spying on her. My brain was running a mile a minute. I guess I was a bit upset. Upset for Mary.

I didn't know Billy that well but he had stabilized Mary and she had been happy. Billy was an artist that didn't draw sailboats or lighthouses. Rare in this area. He was also quite active in the Island's art colony. So much so that he would send tickets to gallery openings my way, if he though I might enjoy the artist. Billy painted what moved him in that particular moment: moonrises, sunsets, animals, flowers and portraits of people he found interesting – or people that paid enough. He was very fond of nudes, male or female, it didn't matter to Billy. Mary's nudes stayed in their house. I don't know if she wouldn't let him sell them or he just didn't want to part with them.

From what Mary had told me, Billy kept their house, their animals, cooked and grew all of their vegetables which Mary shared when a particular crop was good. I did, at times, wonder what Mary brought to the party. As I think of it now, probably just herself.

By the time I got home I had a ripping headache. I hadn't eaten all day. I allowed myself a treat…a peanut butter and jelly sandwich for dinner along with a glass of wine. I ate in my bed with the TV on. I couldn't ask for more. Yum. When I had finished 'dinner' I made the phone calls. Every one was sorry, offered to help, etc., etc. What could I say. Mary should hear this, not me.

In the middle of an old movie I felt movement against my ankle. I hadn't thought about the anklet since Mary and I had entered Bill's house. It moved again. The movement was almost a tickle. Without thinking, I reached under the bed covers; put my hand around the jewelry, pressed it against my ankle. It was warm. The whole area was warm, comfortable. It moved in my hand and I said out loud, "I'm fine. Everything is fine." Now I was sounding a little nuts to myself. Oh well. I laughed, then relaxed. Went back to watching my movie. My hand stayed on my ankle.

I woke to my alarm and the TV spouting today's weather. No dreams. That was nice. I had slept a full eight hours, maybe more. I must have been seriously tired. I remembered the office. Mary wouldn't be there. I should be. Forgot to change my alarm. I showered, dressed and was in my car in record time. I hadn't even had coffee.

The office was open when I got there. Thank heavens. When I walked through the door, Ames was sitting in Mary's chair.

"I knew you wouldn't get in early Vicky. Good morning." Ames smiled up at me. Gave me a salute with his right hand.

"Geez Ames, thank you so much. I really appreciate the thought." I smelled coffee. "You made coffee?"

"Sure. Why don't you get a cup and then I have a couple of ideas I'd like to bounce off of you, ok." It wasn't a question. It was more a statement with those horrible two letters at the end.

"Sure. I just need to clear the office voicemail first." I walked back to the workroom.

"Already done."

I thanked him again. Cleared my cell voicemail while I poured coffee, walked back to Ames. Cell messages. Jay, Mary, Mary and Bill, not bad. "So Ames, what's happening?"

"Well, you know, I know and everyone else knows that you will not be in this office before 11am. Right now it's ten thirty and I'm surprised you got here this early. To solve that little problem and take some pressure off of Mary I have a Client that is looking for a job. He managed a real estate office on Long Island before he and his partner decided to move here. I could call him.

"Second. Did you sic Mason on me to do commercial? Third. The funeral for Billy is Thursday morning. Fourth…"

"Whoa Ames. Slow down, one at a time. As for someone taking Mary's slot…I don't know. Who is it? Do you have his resume? I don't know how long Mary is going to be out, you know she does a lot more than open the office and answer phones. Me disappearing would have less impact on this business than Mary being gone for a few weeks." What could I say? He was trying to help but adding people, even temporary people, to this office well, I'm picky.

"It would just be until Mary comes back. You know, open the office, do the phones, you know, the dumb stuff." Ames apparently didn't know how intentional this office was. Actually, he had no reason to know. The only person besides myself who would understand would be Mary. What the hell was I going to do?

"Let me give it some thought, ok? Yes, I did sic Mason on you. I thought you might enjoy commercial and Mason is going to make the horse racing rounds starting in May. Someone needs to cover commercial for him." I should have talked to Ames before Mason got to him.

"It's not the commercial that bothers me, it's Mason. He's ok in little doses but he is an arrogant s.o.b. I don't know how you can stand him Victoria."

"Yeah, Ames, he is. That's what makes him good in his little niche. His Clients love him. To them he can do no wrong. I don't' know what else to say. If you don't want to do it, that's fine, I'll call him off. This isn't a do or die situation. Not to worry about that Ames."

"Please do call him off. I need to do my CEUs, so maybe I'll concentrate on commercial and see if I like it. But if I do I'll work myself into that side of the business, ok?"

"Sounds good to me. And I am sorry about Mason, Ames. I should have talked to you first. As for Billy's funeral, we'll shut the office down Thursday. I think that is the easiest. People can go, or not, whatever they want to do. You had a fourth?" I was smiling now.

"I did but…Oh, right. Apparently Cheryl had a nervous breakdown in her office yesterday. Thought you might be interested. I was there when it happened."

"Mary said something about the emergency wagon yesterday morning. What happened? You were there?"

"Oh yeah. I was presenting an Offer to Julie when Cheryl started screaming something like 'you're a monster, I knew it' over and over again. Charles, you know that big guy in her office, ran up the stairs and a bunch of people followed him. Cheryl just kept screaming and screaming. I guess someone called 911 because about fifteen minutes later a bunch of EMTs ran up the stairs. Victoria, she was still screaming. Anyway, I could hear the EMTs trying to calm her down and they weren't having any luck. Finally they must have drugged her because she stopped. They brought her down on a stretcher and left. Funny thing was, everyone just went back to work as if nothing had happened. Anyway, my Contract got signed." Ames was shaking his head.

"Now, that is one hell of a story. Yesterday was a weird day wasn't it? I'll take Mary's chair now if you want to go make some money." What could I say to that. Not a whole lot.

I returned Jay's call and he told me a smaller version of Ames' story.

"So Victoria, do you think her little problem had something to do with our friends?"

"I don't know Jay. I guess all things are possible. By the way, thanks for your help with Mary's Billy. He did pass away you know. Thank heavens she got in to see him in time." When in doubt, change the subject.

"Glad I could help and I'm sorry to hear it didn't go well. I enjoy Mary, a bit of a free thinker." I hadn't known Jay knew her.

"Oh, on that subject. Would you know someone that could do some basic office stuff until Mary get's back? You know. Someone that might be good in our office." Might as well ask. Ames was right about us needing some help. I wasn't going to be in there at ten, at least not day after day.

"Not off hand, but I'll keep my eyes open. Talk soon." And Jay beat me to the hang up again. He was getting fast. Yes. It could have been a very specific one of our friends. That thought, well, I didn't know how it sat with me. Cheryl had been warned, probably more than once. Drugs? That too. It also could have been just out and out stress. Not unusual in our business. Although our usual release of choice was drinking, missing appointments, not an out and out freak show. Time for the next call.

"Hi Mary, it's Vicky. How are you doing?"

"Hi Vicky. I'm doing alright. Billy's funeral is Thursday, 10am. His side of the family is serious, old school French Catholic so you know what that means. He'll be laid out Wednesday night at the Funeral Home. I got it down to one night, two hours. It was the best I could do. His kids'll be in town tonight. Did you even know he had kids?" Mary sounded beaten up, tired.

"I think you may have mentioned it once or twice. Did you call your cousin. Is he coming up to stay with you?" Mary sounded like she needed a buffer of some kind with Billy's kids.

"Yeah. He landed in Providence a few minutes ago. Shit Vicky, all these people coming up to stare at a body and look at me like I should be non-functional. I don't know how long I'm going to be able to do this. Billy and I had our own little world, you know. No one ever stayed with us. Billy always got them hotel rooms. He kept them out, but they'll be in here this week. Oh that reminds me. Can you stop by and pick up the nudes? Maybe keep them at your place until they leave? I don't think his family will enjoy them." She gave a hoarse chuckle.

"Oh yeah Mary. They probably should be out of there. All right if I pick them up later this afternoon? I have a rather large place to fill here for a bit."

"So when did you roll in this morning?" Mary did know me too well.

"Ames told me it was ten thirty while he was trying to get me to hire one of his Clients as a temp for a while."

"Maybe you should do that. I've been doing some thinking and I may have to make some changes." Mary sounded hesitant. Here it comes. "Don't worry, I'm not leaving. I was just thinking that I might want to get back out in the field more, that's all. Oh Vicky, don't think I'm going to hop a plane. No. Infact, I can't wait for things to get back to normal. No, No. Not going back to my nomadic life style." That was a bit of a relief. Way too many people had been telling me not to worry lately. That, in and of itself, was enough to make me worry. "Have you heard anything from Mason about next door?"

"No. Actually he was my next call."

"Keep me posted. I've lined up our contractor, tentatively for next

Monday so keep Monday free." Now Mary was starting to sound better. The ultimate change of subject.

"It's going on my calendar as we speak. I'll keep you posted Mary and see you this afternoon. I'll call before I come." I started to move the phone away from my ear when I heard Mary yelling.

"Don't hang up yet Vicky. Please. Take your cell phone off of direct voicemail. People will need to get to you, including me. Now you can hang up. See you later." Mary hung up and the office phone rang. I had to stop and think about what to say when I picked it up. It had been a long time.

"Victoria, it's Mason. You finally got in. It's only 12:15. Not bad." Oh yeah Mason, you'll pay.

"I'll have you know I've been here since 10:30. I have a witness."

"Oh that is early. How's $22,000 for the space next door sound?"

"Not bad. That's fifteen less than asking, isn't it?" Not bad at all.

"So, you'll sign if they sign first?" Mason asked.

"Yeah. Let me make sure the money is in Operating but bring it over when you can. I'll be here 'till about four." I needed to call Mary and make sure we had at least a deposit available. And didn't I need to write a check to Mason for his commission?

I called Mary. Asked her about the account. Felt like an idiot. I should know what the balance is. After all, Mary gives me the numbers every Friday. Then I remembered. Last Friday's numbers weren't as good as they were today. Ok, that's better.

All the craziness in Mary's life and she knew exactly what we had. Mason's check was in the safe with mine, already to go. We did have plenty of money in Operating to write the deposit, but she would have to move some money to Close. I promised I would let her know. Told her that Jay would handle the Closing. Mary actually did sound happy about the office next door and would call the contractor to confirm Monday.

Mason showed up about an hour later. He passed Ames leaving the office with some Clients, which brought to mind the talk I would have to have with Mason. They passed each other and didn't say a word. Damn. Had I screwed up my office?

I signed both original copies of the Contract. Close in twenty days, nice. I gave Mason the deposit check as well as his commission check. "Thanks Victoria. Nice number isn't it."

"Oh yeah, nice number. Can we talk for a minute?" I asked.

"I was about to ask you the same thing." He sat down. "Ames?"

"Yeah, Ames. You know it's not going to work."

"I knew it wasn't going to work. We are too different. Not a problem with you is it?"

"Not at all. I gave it a try. You guys didn't even say 'hi' a minute ago. Can you fix that?" I didn't want to do it even though I'd created it.

"No problem. Consider it done. Ames talk to you?" Mason asked.

"Yeah. He said, essentially, the same thing you did."

"Good. I'll take care of it. Having fun playing Mary?"

"No. I think I'm going to try to find a temp or something. It's just going to be hard to find someone in this area who's, you know, who we can trust. Doesn't come with established loyalties." Mason would understand that.

"How about my daughter? She wants to move to Newport, not a kid and you can trust her."

"Could she do it? And Mason, she wouldn't be treated like your daughter. Be warned." Now this had possibilities.

"Think of her as Mary south. Her name is Georgette. Good sense of humor, good work ethic. Her degree is in European lit and she's been teaching for the past twenty years. She is sick of it."

"How do I talk to her Mason? And how much would I have to pay her?"

"The first question I can help you with. The second, you'll have to talk to her about that and anything else you'd want her to do." Mason said. "I'll tell you what – I'll have her give you a call. She's talking about visiting for a few weeks anyway."

"Mason, I didn't ask but would you be ok with her sitting in this chair? No problem with that?"

"I'd rather her sitting there than you. It's not your talent and a waste of your time. Never was, never will be." Yeah, I've known him too long.

"Sure. Give her a call – we'll talk. Thanks Mason." I was getting a little excited. Not too much, but I truly am not an administrator. Hell, I'm bored the minute a Contract is signed.

I tried calling Bill twice. Each time the office phone rang looking for Nina and I had to abort my calls. But we did, finally, connect. He sounded great. He had moved in over the weekend. Laughed about being willing to move if there had been three feet of snow on the ground just to get out of the Portsmouth house. I told him the house looked great on Monday but I would be going out in the next couple of days to finish pictures. He was fine with that. Asked that I keep him posted on the condo Closing.

By the time we got off of the phone it was four. I told Mason I had to go out to Mary's and asked him to lock up.

As I pulled up to Mary's I met her returning home after a jog with four mixed breed dogs. Tongues hanging out, trotting behind her in order of leg length. I had to laugh. The littlest guy was a corgi-something small mix. He was one pooped pooch. "Mary, I wish you could see what I can see."

"Oh. I've seen it. It is a riot. Figured we could all use a bit of fresh air." Mary continued walking through her front gate with the parade. "Vic, come on in and meet my cousin Kevin. He just arrived from Philly. Got some time for tea?"

"Sure. It would be nice." Mary sounded better than I thought she would. Maybe it was the run, or her cousin arriving, or both. She held the house door for her dogs and for me. I was fifth in line.

"Why don't you get cleaned up and I'll make tea. Do you think your cousin will want some?" I knew where everything was and started walking to the kitchen.

"You know you could ask me." A man with a clerical collar walked from the dining room. "Hi, I'm Kevin. You must be Victoria."

Mary yelled from a back room. "Oh Victoria, that's my cousin. I figured he'd know his own name."

I laughed. "Yeah, Mary, but can he spell it?" Kevin laughed and extended his hand. Kevin was about five foot nine or ten. Not that much taller than I was. "So, would you like tea?" I was looking at his collar.

"Sure. It's Episcopal. No guilt." Oh, this guy is funny, Mary.

"It was nice of you to come up for Mary. I think she needed some family around." I had no clue what to say around him especially about Mary. The clergy in general make me uncomfortable. I believe I make them uncomfortable. My history with the clergy wasn't the best and it didn't take long for them to know it. I was hoping Mary's shower would be short. I wondered who Mary had truly taken the nudes down for. "It's a shame about Billy."

"It is. I figured I would come up to give Mary backup for the rest of the week. I guess his kids said something about wanting to see his art. That they might want to take some home with them. I don't think Mary is up for what I know is going to happen. Apparently they had an art dealer call her this morning wanting to go through the house and appraise the art. Can you believe that?"

I wasn't all that surprised from what I'd heard about them. "What did she say?"

"I believe it was along the lines of 'go to hell'."

"I'm right here guys. Why don't we take the tea into the living room?" Mary was standing at the door. "Anyway, yes. That is exactly what I said."

When we had settled in the living room I noticed the stack of canvasses, actually two stacks, against the far wall. "So you want me to take those?" I asked.

"Yeah. The nudes are there along with a couple of others I found in the studio. There is one there for you Vic. I don't think it's quite finished, not Billy's style but I though you might like it." Mary walked over to the stacks, dug down a few canvases and pulled out a rather small one. "It seems to be a pen and ink of somewhere in the southwest with two Indians. I didn't know Billy did pen and inks. The Indians are done but the deep background is vague." Mary turned the picture so I could see it. "I guess it qualifies as a nude. Not bad though. Actually, if you decide you don't want it, I'd be glad to take it."

I wanted to say shit out loud but instead bit my tongue, unconsciously reached for my ankle. It tickled. I stood up to pretend a closer look. It was James and a women embracing while they stood. He was covering her body with his arms and legs. Almost like they both knew they were being drawn, or in today's world, photographed. James seemed leaner than I had pictured under his clothes. The muscles in his legs, butt, back and arms were well defined. Some kind of tattooing covered his body. Something in his hair. The two sets of tattoos that I could pick out seemed to be incredibly detailed. The canvas looked like one big etching. Not an easy undertaking. "Mary, Billy wasn't working on this when he became ill was he?"

"No, it was laid to dry. Probably something he did a few weeks ago, but it is beautiful now that I look at it again. I know he intended for you to have it. You're the only one we know who hangs American Indian Art."

I did. I had two numbered prints and an original painting of a Shaman in the living room. They are, infact, the only pieces of art hung in the condo. "I think it's a wonderful piece. Plains Indians maybe. Did Billy spend time out there?"

"Yes. I think a few years. But hey, Billy had a whole life before I met him. Anyway, it's yours Vic. Think of Billy when you look at it." I reached over to Mary and hugged her.

"I will. I should get the rest of the stash in the car. I've got to babysit tonight." It was getting late. "If the paintings stay in the car until later tonight, they won't crack in the cold or something will they?"

"Actually Vicky, the acrylics might. Could you try to get them home?"

"Sure, let's get moving."

Between the three of us we got them in the car in record time. Nine pieces including the pen and ink. We said our glad to meet yous and our goodbyes. Told Mary I'd call her tomorrow and got home as fast as I could.

Four trips to unload the car; threw on my jeans, a sweatshirt and arrived at my granddaughter's house about five minutes late. The babysitting was a nice change of pace and ate up the evening. She loved the anklet. When she asked how I got it on, I told her it was magic. She was happy, it was the truth. We painted, played with dolls and both fell asleep while I was reading. Her parents woke me up about eleven.

It took everything I had to drive home. Didn't notice the note in my front door until it fell to the ground. In very neat handwriting it said 'I have missed you. May I visit tomorrow?' It was signed James. I locked up the condo thinking about calling Jay for Keirns's number. Wondered if I seriously wanted the number, what would happen if I didn't call. Wondered if it would all go away. Wondered if that was really what I wanted.

When I got into bed I reached to my ankle without thinking. Stopped. Slid my hand under my other pillow.

Chapter 29

Again, I woke to my alarm. I had forgotten the reset, wondered why no one had called to bug me about being late again. A repeat of yesterday and I walked in the office door at 10:15. I was getting better.

"Hi Victoria." Mary was sitting in her chair.

"What are you doing here?"

"What am I suppose to do? Sit home and stare at the kids going through what is left of Billy's art. No way in hell. Kevin will take care of it. I would rather be here. Coffee's made."

"Geez Mary. It's great to see you here. Thank you for coming in." I went to get my coffee. Little surprises. Nina, Mason and Ames were sitting in the workroom. A bigger surprise. There was money on the table. They were laughing. It was good to see Mason and Ames laughing. I guess Mason did take care of it.

"So I won. Told you guys she'd get better with practice." Mary walked through my doorway, took the four $20s off the table.

"So, when did you guys think I would get here?" Mary probably started the bets.

"I had eleven." Nina said. "Mason had one and Ames didn't think you would get here at all."

"Thanks guys. I'm so glad you all have such faith in me." I poured my coffee and sat with them at the table. Mary joined us. "So what's going on?"

"We wanted to talk about the new office and maybe some suggestions for a couple of new brokers." Ames said.

"Well, go for it." And we did for the rest of the morning. Mary pulled out the plans we had for the current office. The open space plans for the new section was already on the table. Ames sketched out the conference room and double bathrooms. Nina sketched out the new entrance and Mason did the two new office areas. Mary was happy with it. I couldn't find anything wrong with it. I told them we'd go with it. I remembered to ask Mary about the one-way glass for the Bay window in my office, told her we would have to match it with the Bay in the new office if we could get it.

The subject then turned to potential new brokers. That prompted the discussion of a full time receptionist/assistant that would help Mary. Mary talked about doing more field work while keeping some of the management that she was doing now. If Mary was going to do field real estate would we only want one new broker? Major discussions started and we all decided to talk again on the subject. Mason said his daughter was planning to come up this week so she and I would be able to talk face to face. Great. This whole expansion thing had a life of its own. My ankle buzzed like a little electrical shock, then tickled. I remembered I needed to call Jay, didn't I?

Jay was kind enough to give me Keirns's cell number. It was almost two. I swallowed hard. Made the call.

"Keirns here."

"Mr. Keirns, this is Mrs. Hamilton. I received a note from James last night and would like to get a message to him. Could you possibly help?"

"You can tell him yourself Mrs. Hamilton."

I waited for him to put James on the phone. I waited two or three minutes thinking yes, no, yes, no, figuring he had gone to find James. I heard a very deep exhalation into the phone. "He didn't explain, did he?"

"Explain what?"

"Ok. Put your hand on your talisman, say what you will." Keirns sounded what? Exasperated?

"It's a talisman. What do you mean?" James had said it, I hadn't listened. I started to unzip my boot.

"Yes, Mrs. Hamilton. It has given you link. Are you somewhere alone?"

"Yes, I'm in my office. Wait. What happened Sunday isn't going to happen again, is it?" How would he know what happened to me Sunday?

"No. I can guarantee it will not."

Keirns did know. I was embarrassed. Had it been his words in my head? Were my issues with Johnathan Keirns, not James?

"Mr. Keirns, why don't you just tell him tonight is fine?" Pass a message, how hard can it be?

"I'm not with James, he is not here. I cannot contact him now. Please just do what I ask. He will explain tonight."

I completed the unzip, slid my hand inside my cotton sock to hold the anklet. I said quietly, "This evening would be fine." The anklet moved, tickled. My stomach rolled, definitely didn't tickle.

"Did it move?"

"Yes."

"Good. We'll see you this evening, Mrs. Hamilton." He hung up.

'We'll see you'. What did he mean 'we'. I wanted to talk with James. I wanted to try to understand what was going on. Keirns was just going to have to hear it. Not my problem.

I refilled my coffee; wondered if James did look like the pen and ink Billy had done. Why had Billy penned it? Why had Sunday happened? What about my tattoo? Why couldn't I get the anklet off? I had way too many questions. OK, tonight. Should I ask Mary to join me. No. She's burying Billy. Ames, two on two? Nah, probably too personal for Ames. I'd have to tell him where I lived.

Mary gave her standard two knocks on my office door. "Got a minute?"

"Sure, my time is yours if you want it."

Mary sat in her usual chair. "I wanted to tell you that I don't expect you to do the wake thing tonight or the church tomorrow. I know how you feel about that stuff. Hell, I feel the same way, but I'm the pig, I'm committed." She laughed at the old joke that she loved. So many opportunities to use it. And I had to admit, the joke is funny. What's the difference between eggs and ham? The chicken is involved, the pig is committed. Even as I thought of it I had to laugh out loud.

"Thank you Mary, I am going to take a pass tonight but I will be there for you tomorrow. I figure Billy knows how I feel."

"Yeah, you're right. If you're going tomorrow would you come with me and Kevin? I would appreciate it. You know they are going to stick him in the ground. He wanted to be cremated but never wrote it down. His kids didn't believe me when I told them. They said that I'm a pagan and cremation is a mortal sin and all that bull. Anyway, I would really like it if you would come with me. We'll pick you up around 9:45."

"Sure Mary, no problem. Good effort this morning. Thanks for setting it up." Subject change, one of my best things.

"Actually, Ames started it. He asked to see the plans when he came in. Yeah, it worked out better than I thought it would. Now we don't have to do it." I could tell by her eyes that her mental subject hadn't changed.

"Mary, if you want to bug out go ahead. I'll stay around for a while."

"No, I figured I'd go to the funeral home from here. Kevin's picking me up at five. We'll grab some dinner, then wander down. It's six to eight. Hopefully it will fly by. We'll pick you up about a quarter to ten tomorrow." Mary stood, started walking to the door. She was cutting it close, but I guessed they wouldn't start without her.

"Sure. I have a few things I can do here then I'll bug out. Are you planning to come in on Friday?"

She turned back to me. "Of course, I'll be here. It'll be Friday, we need to do Friday, right?" Mary wanted normal desperately.

"Sure, Friday. Maybe we can get out to Bill's house."

"Sure, sounds good." I was left alone. I glanced at my calendar and was reminded of dinner at Carolyn's Friday. I had forgotten.

I checked all of my electronic message sources; returned emails and phone calls for the rest of the afternoon. One interesting call was from Jay saying that Cheryl had been admitted to our local crazy ward for ten days of evaluation. She is claiming that James had appeared to her. That he was a monster trying to kill her. I told Jay that we all had our stress limits and it seemed that Cheryl had found hers. "She's not one of my favorite people, but I feel bad for her." Jay asked if I thought there was any truth to what she was saying. That question I wouldn't have expected from Jay. I laughed, asked him what he thought. He laughed, told me to take care of Mary and hung up. Oh, this was fun.

When I got home I realized that I had scattered Billy's paintings all over the place when I ran out to babysit. I changed clothes and decided to stand each against the wall around the living room. Billy truly had talent. I put the pen and ink in the bedroom. I thought about dinner but the minute I did, knew it wasn't going to happen. I checked the clock, reset my alarm.

I poured a glass of wine, sat in the kitchen. What the hell was I going to say to either one of them tonight? By all right and reason, James should be off playing with some chippie right now, not coming to see me. Hell, he could be doing both. I felt a little better with that thought, it took some pressure off of me.

I wandered out to the loveseat thinking, waiting.

Chapter 30

Minutes later James appeared a few steps away from the garden door standing in wet snow. Keirns was a bit behind him. I opened the door, smiled at James when he entered. He had one thin braid in his hair holding the four piece braid jewelry from the auction. I held the door for Keirns, ah Mr. Keirns. He walked to the door frame, stopped. I was watching James walk to the fireplace and hadn't noticed.

"May I come in Mrs. Hamilton?"

"Yes, of course." Keirns was not wearing his standard uniform, the tailored dark suit, shirt with French cuffs, the beautiful cufflinks. Infact, when I looked down he wasn't even wearing shoes. But that wasn't the show stopper. The show stopper was, well, where to start. The cream linen vest, every inch embroidered and embellished with various trinkets of gold and silver, beads of crystal and pearls and small carved ivory animals. The vest partially covered his very dark, hairless chest. Without closures on the vest, when he moved I could see his nipples. The vest reached the top of his waist where it met the very wide, very long red silk scarf whose width began below his ribs to the top of his hips, tied on his right side; or the heavy ecru colored linen pants that pleated from the scarf, loosely over his thighs to the middle of his calves ending in a small loose cuff. No shirt, no shoes, his hair was still braided, but not pulled back, not secured, so that the individual braids fell over his shoulders, over his chest to the top of the silk scarf. Did he dress down or dress up? I guess, at probably more than 6'4", he would make a statement either way.

I looked to James, almost embarrassed. He, on the other hand, had been watching me, smiling. "Victoria, may I set a fire?"

"Yes, please." James...James was wearing the soft, maybe deerskin shirt and pants that he had worn when I watched him with the birds. What he had worn on Sunday, when I was so angry. The long fringe of the arms and legs, each set with beads, moved with him; with the rhythm of him when he reached for the logs, when he placed them in the hearth, one by one. The deerskin he wore was so soft that I could see his shoulders, muscles move under the shirt, his thighs flex under the pants.

Mr. Keirns brought my attention back to the reality of the moment. "Mrs. Hamilton, why don't we sit."

"Of course. Mr. Keirns but please, call me Victoria. I would be more comfortable if you called me Victoria."

Keirns turned, look at James, James returned his look. A moment later Keirns turned his eyes back to me. "I would be pleased to call you Victoria. Please call me Johnathan. I believe we need to relax a bit."

I walked to the loveseat, surprised that Johnathan had followed me, intending to sit next to me when there were two very comfortable chairs opposite the loveseat.

"Would either of you care for a drink or some tea?"

"No thank you Victoria." Johnathan was still standing in front of the loveseat. I heard James flash the sulfur on the match stick, heard the log flame. The room had become incredibly quiet. We both were still standing when James stood, bent his legs as he had done before, turned to the loveseat and was sitting on the floor in front of me. I had forgotten to sit, so Jonathan was, of course, still standing, watching James.

James settled in at my feet. "May I put my hand on your leg Victoria? I only intend communication, nothing more." I looked down at him. Thought about the request. He waited. What the hell. I nodded. His hand moved to my leg, added a bid of pressure so that I would sit. Oh, right, I was still standing. Dumb, distracted.

Of course, when I sat, Johnathan sat. A little closer than I thought was necessary. We sat this way; still, quiet, James watching my eyes, mine watching his, Johnathan watching James, the crackling of the fire, for what had to be more than ten minutes.

Someone had to start, my home so it was me. "James we need to talk." I started, still looking at his eyes. "I feel, well, that this is out of...no... this may be going in a direction that you didn't intend and that I may not want." In my head I had not been quite so polite. But looking down at him, his eyes looking up at me, his hand on my leg, the other words would not come out. I blinked, started to look away. James didn't move. Then he started to talk.

"Victoria, I cannot hide from you. When I am with you, it takes too much concentration, too much energy. I cannot function around you. That is why I brought Johnathan tonight.

"I have thought for many years how I would do this. Talk to you. Show you my reality. I have often wondered what I would do when I finally found you in time...before your wheel turned again. In all of my imaginings I could not get past the thought of finally standing next to you. Touching your hand. Now I am here." James stopped talking. Dropped his head. Withdrew his hand. Almost seemed to disappear. Johnathan leaned to him putting the weight of his hand on James's shoulder.

After a few moments James seemed to answer an unasked question with the movement of his head; looked back up at me, returned his hand to my leg. Johnathan removed his hand from James's shoulder, leaned back into the loveseat.

"I have not been frightened in a long time Victoria. I am frightened now. Frightened of you. That you will run. That you will be repulsed, be horrified. Many have been. That you are more open than I anticipated gives me hope. That the talisman has accepted you as if it had never been separated from you, gives me hope." James again stopped, closed his eyes, dropped his head.

The talisman was real? Contained true magic? I realized in that moment he would take a breath only to talk. The thought, the link of the two thoughts, made me shiver. My shiver seemed to bring James back.

"I must tell you first that I have accepted what I am, what I have become. My nature is as it is. May I be myself with you?" It was truly a question spoken very, very carefully. I was so out of my ... what?...depth, reality, no...no word for it.

I reached down, touched the side of his face without thinking. "Please, I would prefer it James." He put his hand over mine, smiled.

James stood in one motion. Looked at Johnathan. Closed his eyes. The shimmer I had seen briefly in Jay's office, on the rock through the telescope, started again. This time it took on more colors than a rainbow, second by second became more violent releasing static...no...energy...no not the word...power, pressure into the room. When I thought it would consume James, consume me, the massive shimmer blended into a gray mist over his skin.

I saw the shadowed outlines of a great snow owl, a large wolf with a huge ruff. A snake followed, maybe being chased by a large eagle, a bear... shit. Everything moved across his body, settled on his skin...in his skin?

The mist began to fade. I took a very deep, much needed breath. My heart beat a little faster. A flush rolled down my body. This I had not expected. Maybe in a movie – not in my living room.

When the mist cleared James stood in front of me. Perfectly still. Arms held out, east and west. His features were much sharper. His skin pale under a reddish brown. His eyes were infinitely deeper, blacker than before, only broken by what looked to me to be flashes of pure white light in the black irises. His cheekbones were much higher, sharper than they'd been a moment before, almost like a layer of tissue was gone. Those cheekbones dropped to the deep hollows of his cheeks giving way to a broad, strong jaw. His eyes closed.

His nose was Roman. There was no other way to describe it, pointing to perfectly formed deep red lips fed from the hollows of his cheeks. His hair remained long, straight, as black as his eyes, shiny, reflecting the flames of the fire. The four lengths of braid jewelry seemed to move in his hair. His neck seemed longer without the extra layer of flesh. His shoulders were wider but not bulkier, his shirt hung much looser. A layer of tissue was definitely missing from all of his body.

I could see the waist of his pants sitting on the bones of his hips, stretched only against the length of him. That alone would have received my attention when he stood at the garden door. He remained standing perfectly still, not breathing, almost as if he was on display. He knew, expected me to be staring at him.

His tattoos, from where I was sitting, looked to be superimposed over one another. The background of one side of his face and neck was the head, the face of the owl I had seen move in the mist. The other side of his face and neck seemed to be the face, the head of the wolf. Over these tattoos were very dark, small, black-clawed paw prints on one side of his face small black snakes ready to strike on the other. The darker tattoos curved with the arch of each eye; the figures growing larger as the line of each ran the circle of its cheek, over his jaw, neck and shoulder disappearing under his shirt.

There were tattoos of animals on what I could see of his arms, the tops of his hands, his palms and fingers. I could see, on the top of his left foot, the incredibly detailed head of a snake whose body disappeared around his ankle and up under the leg of his pants. The tattoos, all of them, were black, a sharper black, a lighter black. James was a pen and ink drawing. It took me quite a few minutes to take in all of James. When I had seen all that I could comprehend, James opened his eyes.

There was more. I knew in my heart of hearts this was not all of him. He was still holding back. If we were going to do this tonight, let's be done with it. I was so far out of my reality already, more wouldn't matter. "James. Everything. Everything that you are. Now." No reaction. Then, in less than the blink of an eye, James moved to me. Johnathan was between us. I curled into my corner of the loveseat. The talisman was moving, hot. My head was swimming.

When I opened my eyes I saw that Johnathan had pushed James across the room against the wall. James's eyes were wild. His whites were red. The flashes of light had overtaken the black, looking at me. His teeth had locked into Johnathan's bloody shoulder. Immediately, James calmed. Closed his eyes. Released the shoulder, allowed blood to flow. He slid down the wall. Johnathan leaned over him. Blocked my view. They seemed to talk. The blood from Johnathan's shoulder appeared at the back of his pants where the red sash ended. Whoa!

After a few minutes of silence broken only by the burning logs Johnathan stood, turned, looked at me. His eyes were red where they had been white. In the black of his irises were the smaller bolts of light I had seen in James. I could see the light from across the room. Blood was now beginning to stain the ecru of his thigh. James had done some damage.

By the time Johnathan returned to his seat next to me, the red had gone from his eyes, but not the light. The blood on his pants had stopped advancing. James remained on the floor against the wall. His head was on his bent knees held by his arms.

My reaction? I wanted to laugh. A lifetime of thought and speculation had just played out in front of me. No panic. No terror. Surprise, oh yes. Maybe the other would come later. I didn't know. My thoughts had stopped. I had only one desire.

The desire was to go to James, touch him. Tell him that I had been surprised at the last, not frightened. I knew that if he had intended harm to me it would be done. I started to stand.

"Don't Victoria. James will join us in time. You are not frightened?"

"No. My heart is a little excited. I feel a little light headed. But no, I'm not frightened. Actually, somewhere, I think I expected something... Is James alright?"

"He released a great deal of energy, power, and emotion at the same time. Emotion he has kept to himself for years. When he is truly himself, I will leave. You and he can talk for a while. You will be safe. I assure you."

"I am going to get something to drink. I need a bit of a break. Can I, oh, I suppose not. Do you need anything for your shoulder?" I smiled at Johnathan.

"No I'm fine. I'll feed the fire." He stood, smiled at me.

In the kitchen I figured I needed something a little stiffer than wine. I poured myself a short scotch, took a healthy sip and a deep breath. I guess that last little bit had taken me by surprise. I had already guessed there was magic, powerful magic from somewhere. When they had moved, I knew what they were. Yeah, I was ok. I didn't have a clue where this was going. Questions? A million and none at the same time. Something told me to run out the front door. Right, that would definitely fix everything. I would ask honest questions if anything relevant came to mind. But I needed to listen, observe, assess tonight - see where the pick-up-sticks fell. That was probably the best I could do.

I returned to the living room. James was standing by the fireplace – his back to the room. I didn't think the last part had gone as he had intended. He had lost control. I knew this, I felt it. Johnathan was still sitting on the loveseat. I put my drink on the floor. Stood next to James.

"May I touch your arm?"

He looked at me, smiled. I put my hand on his arm. Touching him felt good, comforting. James turned to me. Put his free hand on my shoulder, leaned down…hesitated…put his lips on mine. I shivered, closed my eyes. I knew I was in trouble. I didn't care. I don't think I was capable of caring. The flood of emotion I felt was too much.

James took a step back. "Are you ready for words Victoria?" I released his arm, walked back to the loveseat, picked up my drink, sat down. There were things I wanted to do but talking wasn't one of them. This was my tacky thought. I kept it to myself. James had recovered…I wasn't hiding in the bedroom…we probably should talk.

"James may I leave now?" Johnathan asked standing.

"Yes, Jonathan. Thank you for your help."

Jonathan turned to me. "Thank you Victoria, for still being here, for your patience." He opened the garden door, stepped through, quietly closed the door, was gone.

James checked the fire, returned to the floor in front of me. He looked up, into my eyes, put his hand on my ankle. "I expected many things to happen tonight, but this was not one of them. I show myself to you completely. I lost control. Yet we are sitting here. You are letting me touch you." He shook his head, smiled.

"I don't know what you expected from me James. You scare me, but not in the way you think." OK Victoria, I thought, the truth. "James, you are beautiful."

I traced his face with my fingers starting at the edge of his eyes, over his jaw and down his neck. His skin was warm, soft. I could not feel the ink under his skin like I could feel when I touched my tattoos. Unused was, again, the only word I could think of. Even with that under layer gone. I ran my fingers over his hair, moving it behind his ears. When I looked back into his eyes a red tear was rolling down his cheek. I wiped it with my finger. Looked at it. James took my hand placing the finger in his mouth. He ran his tongue over my finger, tasting his tear. I shivered. My heart pounded again, my head buzzed.

"James...I don't think you want to go there tonight." He took my finger from his mouth, kissed it, put my hand on my lap.

"Victoria. I have not explained myself in many years. The last was Johnathan. Please continue your patience. I am the.....I was the Shaman of my family, when I was taken. I had power when I was born. I collected power as I grew. As I gained the spirits you see on my skin, my power, my magic became great. I was considered a Shaman of great magic when I was taken." He spoke without expression, without inflection as though he was reading from a very boring scientific paper.

"When I woke, I could see like never before, feel all things. I understood what I had thought was not possible to understand. I stayed in the desert until I could begin to know what I had become. What had happened. When I returned to our...my people, my village, my family was dead. My wife was dead. All that I knew was dead. Destroyed by the one who tried to destroy me. My anger controlled me. Owned me for a very long time.

"I learned years later that taking a being of power had never been done. Was never to be done. Adding energy to energy is the only thing we truly fear. I was told that the one who had made me was destroyed by others. I am the first, the only. My power stills grows." James stopped, became quiet.

"Why here with me, why show me?" I couldn't resist.

He lowered his head, closed his eyes, became still. "Do you truly want that answer tonight?" His head remained lowered, his eyes remained closed. Good point, but James began to speak again. Slowly, deliberately. "Your soul is my soul."

Not the expected answer. His hand returned to my leg. His head lifted. His eyes opened, returned to mine. When he said it, I had no questions.

All of the things that had happened in the past two weeks clicked into place. The clicks started working backwards. The odd pieces of my life started falling into place.

James moved closer to my legs. Tightened his arm around the one he had been holding, leaned against me. I relaxed against the back of the loveseat with my hand in his hair. No thoughts. I was blank. I don't know how long we stayed in that position. Neither of us spoke. I knew what I needed to know for now. James had said and done what he had needed to do.

I must have dozed. James moving brought my brain back into the living room. He was standing over me. "I must leave now. May I return later today?"

"I will be with a friend who lost her partner earlier this week. I should be back here early in the evening. Then, yes." James had taken, honestly, irrecoverable risk. It was my turn.

"Ah, yes Billy. I was sorry that he had to leave. That is why you have his wonderful art around your room?"

"You knew Billy?" Now that was a bit of a surprise.

"Yes. We will talk later." James leaned down, both hands on the back of the loveseat. "May I kiss you?"

"That would be nice." He leaned to my lips. His lips open slightly, adding a bit of pressure to their touch. He held the kiss for a few moments. Stood. Left by the garden door. I went to bed, crashed.

Chapter 31

I woke to my alarm thinking about Billy and James. Didn't give thought to other events. I took a quick shower, dressed; a black wool skirt, heavy black tights, plain black leather boots, a blue silk blouse, black silk vest with matching blue detail. I did get the chance to eat some yogurt and have a cup of coffee before Mary arrived. She stepped inside while I put on my black coat, gloves and beret.

"How are you doing?" I asked.

"I'm doing good, fine actually. It's almost over. Kevin went with the kids this morning to close the coffin. I guess there is a ritual for that. The funeral guy told Kevin that some very well dressed man showed up this morning, very early, before dawn, asking if he could say good-bye to Billy. The funeral guy let him in, waited about ten minutes, then let him out. Hurry up Vic. Anyway he asked Kevin if it had been alright and should he tell the rest of the family. Kevin told him it was fine and that telling the rest of the family would just upset them. Is that weird or what?"

"Weird Mary, but like you said, Billy had a whole life before you." Mary held the door open while I checked the mirror one last time. "Ok, ready." I assumed Mary wanted me to go to the cemetery, hence the beret. I could pull it down over my ears if it was too cold.

By the time we got to the church, parked and started up about thirty steps to the front doors, some men were starting to close them. I wondered, if we had been five minutes later, would we have been allowed in? The three of us were led to the front pew. The front pew had a four foot fence that separated us from the crossing, the Priests, altar boys and provided a kneeler. So much for thinking I would be able to enjoy the art of the church from the back during the service. I did notice quickly that the altar was elaborate and its examination would kill some time.

Billy's coffin was in front of us covered in a lavender blanket of roses. I could smell the roses in the air. The perfume reminded me of a short-lived lavender rose bush I had in the back yard of my old house.

I had given up faking different religions years ago. So when the kneeling and standing started, I stayed where I was. Put me in the front of a church at your own peril. It wasn't long before Mary joined me. In the middle of something the priest was saying, while he was burning incense around the coffin swinging a little ball, Mary leaned over to me. "Thank you."

"Thank you for what?" I whispered back.

"I don't like faking it either but didn't have the nerve until you didn't kneel. Are you going to take communion?"

"No." I didn't say hell no. I'd made my point. So there we sat. I did enjoy the soloist. She had a beautiful voice. Organ music rarely did anything for me, but I do admit that some of the most beautiful music composed was sponsored by the Catholic church.

The priest held up the service telling us directly, in full voice, that it would be alright with Jesus if we took communion. Mary turned red. I shook my head. He asked if we were sure, that Billy would want it, pressing the issue. I finally spoke up. "We understand what you are saying, but no thank you." The priest blessed us anyway and returned to his altar. I bet he thought he would burst into flames. Why? Because obviously, we hadn't and someone had to. The people in our pew walked out the far side and around to the front.

Finally, the priest and the altar boys walked into the central aisle with their incense, followed by the coffin; each pew emptied behind. There was a log jam at the stairs outside the front doors. It seemed that one of the legs of the dolly carrying Billy's coffin wouldn't collapse the way it was suppose to and one of the funeral guys, in his good suit, was under the dolly with a pair of pliers when we walked out. Now I know what funeral guys dream of when they have bad dreams.

Kevin directed Mary, then me, to one of the limos. Mary objected as strongly as she could, but in the end we sat with Billy's sons and one daughter for the ride out to the graveyard.

"You know Mary, you were expected this morning. Didn't you want to say your last goodbye to Billy before his coffin was closed..." Billy's daughter intentionally hesitated. "...forever?" Oh rats. It was starting out to be the longest nine mile trip on the Island.

"Darlene, I said goodbye to Billy in the hospital. I didn't need to talk to an empty shell." Good for you Mary.

"Well the least you could have done was take communion. I mean the priest was kind enough to invite you and your friend personally." Darlene was going to keep pushing.

"We've had this conversation before Darlene. Drop it."

Before Darlene could say anything else one of Billy's boys started commenting on the service. How nice it was; how Billy would have liked it. He managed to talk us to the middle of the Island.

We walked to the graveside, stood on the plywood boards covered with Astroturf that hid the fact we were standing on mounds of frozen mud next to a eight foot deep hole in the ground lined in concrete. The flowers from the church were displayed so that the rest of the area looked like a sea of flowers. When the priest started the committal prayers the wind came up. It was cold. I pulled the beret over my ears, tightened the wool scarf, huddled in the coat. We stood there for about thirty minutes. When it was over, everyone ran back to the limos, the cars and headed to Mary's house to warm up, drink, eat and talk about Billy. The best part of a funeral, probably the best remembrance, is the 'after party'.

By the time we arrived, there must have been at least twenty cars parked along the road. We could hear the talking and laughter from the yard. I always heard great stories about the deceased. Those were the stories that stayed with me a long time.

Mary was greeted, hugged, kissed by Mason, Ames and Nina immediately. Told not to do or worry about a thing. As fast as they had rushed the door they returned to what I guessed were their assigned jobs. Mason played bartender. Ames and Nina passed around trays of food from the kitchen. I wandered to the kitchen to see who was playing cook.

A woman about my height with short blonde hair and a chef's apron seemed to have total control of the kitchen; answering to various dings and buzzers from the appliances. She was wearing ear buds and singing to music that I hoped she was hearing from her walkman. Catching me out of the corner of her eye, she removed the ear buds.

"Hi, I'm Georgette. I'm with Mason."

"Oh, Mason's daughter?"

"Someone had to do it. Can I help you?"

"Well not today. I'm Victoria Hamilton. Mason said we should talk next week, that infact, you might be able to help me." I walked closer to her to shake her hand.

"Oh, hi. Yes, we should. Mason told me I had the kitchen today, so this is where I'll be." Georgette was happy as a clam to be in the kitchen.

"I am impressed. You look like a pro."

"My hobby, cooking. Give me a kitchen, stock it with my list and I'm happy." She plugged in the ear buds and was back to doing her thing.

Well, Mason, good for you.

I wandered back into the main room, retrieved a screwdriver, the drink not the tool, from Mason and played social meet and greet. Before long the room was so crowded I could hardly move much less track Mary. I worked my way back to the bedroom. Knocked on the door. The smell around the door was sweet.

"Mary it's Vicky. Can I come in?"

"Sure Vic, only you right?"

I opened the door. "Yeah, just little old me."

Mary was lying on the bed, smoking some weed.

"Mind if I join you?" I laid on the bed next to her. She offered me a hit, I took it.

"It's the last of our stash. I've been saving it for today, feels good. One of Billy's many pleasures he shared with me. His kids took most of his stuff but can't seem to find that beautiful seven point turquoise star he wore. Darlene accused me of hiding it from her, but hell, I don't have it." Mary offered me another. I refused. Any more and I would end up asleep. One hit and I was pulling a buzz. Either I was out of practice or Billy had some good stuff. "I brought it back from the hospital and put it in his box on the bureau. Maybe one of her brothers has it. Was it like this when your second died?"

"No. But then I had hidden a few things and let the kids have at it. Between all the tools and books, they couldn't take enough to make me happy. I had already passed his Mother's and sister's things to his kids. My kids had minimal attachments, so it wasn't a problem."

"I'm worried that Billy's upset with me for allowing him to be buried, but I just couldn't fight with them anymore. I cannot get the visual out of my head. Do you think it will ever go away?"

Whoa. Uck. "Mary, I don't know what to say to that. My experience has been that something visual stuck in my head usually fades, but my visuals, well, haven't ever been like that. Frankly they're usually other topics." I laughed.

"Yeah, I understand what you're saying. Until now mine have been hot sex too." We both laughed. Mary leaned over to me, put her arm on my stomach.

"You know Mason came over last night after the wake with his daughter, Georgette, and they told me not to worry, everything would be under control at the reception. Did you know he was at the wake?"

"I didn't know Mason was that close to Billy." I didn't.

"He wasn't that I know of. I think he came for me. You know Mason can be sweet when he wants to be Vic."

"Mary, I've known Mason for many years and yes, he can. When the rubber meets the road you can count on him. It was very nice of both of them. Have you had a chance to talk much with Georgette?"

"We talked for about an hour last night. I like her." Mary had finished the joint, was starting to drift.

"Mary, I'm going to cover you with the blanket. Catch a nap, ok?"

"Yeah. Thanks Vic."

I returned to the living room. The crowd was starting to thin. I was thinking about leaving. Yeah, it was time. I needed a ride. I looked around for a familiar face; a face that already knew where I lived. A face that looked about ready to leave. Those requirements did narrow my options.

"Victoria, ready to go home?" It was Kevin.

"I think so." Kevin could qualify, he'd be getting on a plane soon. "Could I talk you into giving me a ride? It doesn't look like anyone else is leaving. Mary's sleeping in the bedroom."

"I figured that's where she was. I don't think anyone will bother her. Grab your coat and I'll tell Mason."

I met Kevin at the door and we left. Kevin drove rather slowly, then started talking.

"So I guess Mary told you about the early morning visitor at the funeral home?"

"Yeah, she did."

"What I didn't tell her was that the funeral director said that when he returned to the room Billy was in after letting the visitor out, there was a heavy smell of burning brush, ash on the deceased's chest and on top of the ash a white feather. The funeral director said he cleaned up the ash and moved the feather inside Billy's jacket so no one would see it when they came. He asked me if Billy was an American Indian. You seemed to know something about the pen and ink yesterday, so I though I'd ask you."

"Kevin, I don't have a clue about Billy's heritage. I would think Mary would know. Did you ask her?" Kevin shook his head. "I thought his ancestry was French. It was nice of you and the funeral director not to freak out though. People in this area take their Christianity seriously… oh Kevin I'm sorry… I'm sure Billy would appreciate his friend's actions." What could I say. The ultimate misspoken phrase.

"Yeah, no harm done." Kevin pulled into the condo's driveway. "I'll probably be leaving in the next couple of days. Keep an eye on Mary?" Kevin handed me a piece of paper. "Here's my number if you think I should make a return visit. Don't hesitate to call me if Mary needs me."

"Believe me I will. Kevin, thanks for coming up. It was good for Mary. Take care." I closed the car door, went into my refuge. It felt good to be home.

Chapter 32

By the time I had changed clothes my thoughts were drifting to last night, to James. If I didn't know better I would have put what I had seen into the category of some very fine LSD. There hadn't been any acid. What I had seen had been real. Holy smoke.

Did I want to go for the ride or keep my life the way it was? My life, all in all, wasn't bad. I guess my biggest fear wasn't really the magic. It was the fear I always had. Letting down my guard. Truly letting anyone in. What he was didn't scare me. I'd always known there were other beings; magic that wasn't seen everyday. After all we were, us humans, magic. We just don't like thinking of our existence, of the universe itself as 'magic'. The established churches aren't too fond of the magic idea either.

That I would ever truly see others; be allowed to interact with them. Well, that answer was easy – no, never. I was just me. I wondered if James would show up tonight looking as he had left last night. Would he seem to me as beautiful or was there so much energy last night that I had been confused. Was that what he truly looked like? Maybe he would have second thoughts and not visit. Ah, interesting thought.

My brain continued to review events while I heated some soup and wandered around Billy's paintings while I ate. It was easy to see the paintings that were Mary. The remaining five were of three men and two women I didn't know. I remembered the pen and ink and added it to the others.

I hadn't looked at it the way a pen and ink needed to be viewed; with patience. I started seeing more. A vague owl flying, a large cat curled behind the couple, a fire burning next to a blanket on the ground. The man was definitely the James I'd seen last night, wearing the braid jewelry, his tattoos. The woman wearing a talisman with a vine tattoo rising from the top of her foot, wrapping her entire leg until it disappeared behind James's leg. Yikes. I looked to my ankle, to the garden door. James was waiting, had been for a while, watching me.

I opened the garden door, soup cup still in my hand. "Hi James, are you alone tonight?"

"Yes." He was wearing loose jeans that buttoned, a dark blue sweater, the soft boots. His eyes were black with small flashes of light. He was covered with tattoos. He hadn't hidden from me tonight. I wanted to touch him. Rats.

"I am glad to see that you are yourself tonight, that you didn't feel you had to hide from me."

"I was hoping you would accept me after a day to think. May I…"

"Yes, please light the fire. You are getting me hooked on a wood fire in the evenings." I went to clean up the kitchen, put the cup in the dishwasher. I steered clear of the wine. When I returned to the living room James was walking around Billy's paintings, the fire was blazing. I noticed the laced footwear, no real sole. Made of, maybe, the deer skin of his other clothes. They were laced with leather strips from ankle to knee.

"Billy was a wonderful artist." I joined him. "You said that you knew him."

"Yes, I do know him. I know the soul that became Billy. His soul brought many of the spirits to me." James was standing in front of the pen and ink. "It is as I remember it."

"James, can we start there? Can we talk? Will you explain Billy to me, why you were at the funeral home this morning?" I turned, walked back to the loveseat in front of the fire. James turned, followed me, sat on the floor next to me. Looked at me. I smiled. He put his hand on my leg. Much better.

"Billy's soul is the soul of the Shaman that called many of the spirits to me. We have recognized each other at every turn of the wheel for him. When I learned that he was to be put into the ground I released him from his old body. I went to the cemetery today to make sure he was free. He was. Others were not. I released them." He spoke these words as simple truths. No more, no less.

A few moments passed before I spoke. "You speak of the turn of the wheel. Isn't that from Eastern Religion?"

"It is a truth. I understood when I died and woke. My wheel no longer

174

turns. I am here." He held my leg closer, running his hand over the extent of my tattoo sending shivers up and down my body.

"James, I cannot think when you do that." My truth.

He stopped, still looking up to me. "Does my touch hurt you?"

"No. Just the opposite. I am frightened of me, of what I want. I don't know if I can allow myself your touch for just one night. I thought you would go on about your life after the house closed. Then you came to mine. I thought you would go away after that, but you left the anklet. Until last night I thought you were playing little games. You either trust me more than I can imagine or after you have played you'll clear my memory like you did to Jay, to the Gottfrieds. Leave me with a hole in my heart you cannot erase." Figured I'd take a shot at what I thought had happened and make an assumption that his reason from last night was true. Nothing to loose. "I have been broken too many times. If I allow it to happen again, you could be my final break."

I was embarrassed and relieved to have said it when I finished. For me, it needed to be said, whether or not a relationship was intended. I looked to the fire, stood to walk away. James was in front of me, blocking me.

He put his hands on my shoulders, "Victoria. Coming here was for you. The house was more than I expected, but it allowed me to bring others. When Williem spoke of his time here, I saw you. In your old office, the one he knew." Again, he spoke each sentence as simply fact.

"Johnathan tried to stop me. Wanted me to wait until I was sure it was you. My compromise was to send him to speak with you. To touch you. Through him I knew it was you. For as long as I have had this nature - seeing you at the house, touching your hand was the hardest thing. When Johnathan signed for the house I thought, finally. I almost lost control. That would not have been good. Johnathan said you saw me, felt me. He wanted to alter your memory then. He did alter the lawyer. I would not allow him to interact with you in such a way. Touching you now I am doing all that I can to control myself. I am willing to wait as long as you would like. No, Victoria. I will never break you." I had more answers than questions.

Tears started to fill my eyes. I was losing control. I do not cry, didn't when my parents died, didn't when my son was ill, didn't when I was hurt, didn't when I broke. I was not a crier. Emotion in my world was swallowed. This, I would swallow. My eyes dried, that I managed. But my heart, that I couldn't slow. James pulled me to him, held me. I felt the animals on his skin move, they moved over me, through me. I was comforted like I had never been. "I will heal you Victoria, not break you."

James put his hand under my chin, lifted my face to his, kissed me. This time, I let it go where it would. He breathed into me. My tongue tasted his. His hands moved over my back, mine over his. I felt the movement of his skin, the animals, under my hands. We held this until I thought I would faint. Damn.

I broke the kiss. "That, that is the problem. You can invade me, you are capable of owning me. Just with your touch, with your kiss, with the talisman. You could own me, control me." Finally, I said what was really bothering me. I didn't have a choice.

"No Victoria. What you think you feel from me is not one way. I feel from you the same things. I feel what you feel. You control me. Sunday, you have wanted to talk about Sunday. Yes?"

I pulled myself from him, returned to the loveseat. "Yes, Sunday."

James sat on the floor, unlaced the right boot, removed it. Lifted the leg of his pants. On his ankle was the twin of the talisman I wore. It was grown together. The beads, the feathers, were the same. "Come down to the floor." He said. I did. "Put your hand around the talisman, roll it against my skin." I hesitated.

James put my hand on the talisman, pressed my hand and the talisman against his skin, moved it as he had moved mine. He closed his eyes. His head fell back. I started to feel warmth against my ankle. Sunday's feeling started. I pulled my hand away. The feeling faded. James gathered himself, opened his eyes.

"Sunday. I was trying to feel if the talisman were linked. They were linked tighter than when we were together. I was surprised. I could talk to you, you were talking to me. You can do the same. You only need to learn as I need to learn. That is all." He moved my hand from the talisman. Placed it on his thigh. It was going to take some time to get my head around his words.

"Thank you for explaining. Can you fix the towel bar in my bathroom?" I smiled at him.

"No. But I will have it repaired."

"No, I'm kidding. I do have a couple of questions. If you do not want to answer, just tell me, ok?" Maybe we have had enough truth tonight.

"Ask, please." He put his hand over mine on his thigh. I could feel his energy, like electricity, flow from his hand, through mine into his body. It was a nice feeling, a connection.

"I have seen you out during the day. Is the myth of vampires and daylight truly a myth?"

"I am other. Vampire is a word of the commercial world. No more, no less. It says nothing of us. Some that know us call us Asra-pa. That we are. I die at first light. For all that my kind has been given, we are humbled every day at dawn. We are reminded where all things start and end." He smiled. "The sun does not cause us to catch fire or burn, nor are we stopped by running water, so-called holy water or incantations of a priest or any holy man. It is nothing." James stopped talking for a minute. Took a long hard look at me. "Do you want me to continue?"

"Yes." It would be good to know something of his natures if I was going to be around him, yeah if. The other, I thought, would be a piece at a time.

"We do feed on blood. We do not kill to exist. One cannot drink a human to death. It would take many. After we feed, we heal the bites, erase the time. The person goes on about his life. There are times when we allow ourselves to be known. We have always been here alongside your kind. There are very few of us. What else can I tell you?" James thought for a moment. "To make another, to stop their wheel from turning, is rare. I have done it out of necessity and gratitude four times. They are now a part of me. They have free will and do what they please. But they are a part of me." Again he stopped speaking. He took my hand from his thigh, pulled me to him so that my head was on his chest, pulled his leg out from under my body. Wrapped both of his legs around me. I moved my arms around his chest to his back. His arms around my shoulders, hands resting on my back. I relaxed into him. "Thank you Victoria. My love is only for you." I closed my eyes, fell asleep.

I woke sliding slowly off of James to the floor. "I must go now. May I visit tomorrow?"

"I have to work tomorrow. Rather this afternoon and I have a dinner commitment with a good friend tonight. I am free Saturday. We could talk then."

"I will return on Saturday. I will think of you." He leaned to the floor. Kissed me as if he would swallow me. I shuddered. He lifted me to his body. Held me tightly. So tightly that I felt that I would pass through him. James put me down, was gone. I don't think he bothered with the nicety of the door. If he did, I didn't see it.

I moved into the bedroom, cuddled into my pillows. I didn't know how much more foreplay I could stand. I may just have to jump him and be done with it. If it had been any other guy I was attracted to like this, I would have jumped his bones a long time ago. I would be bored now. He would be gone.

I could see the very beginnings of sunrise through the bedroom door. I felt a tickle from the feathers then an electrical buzz at my ankle. James was gone. I was a bit sad to know that as fact. He told me what happens. For the first time I understood what I had been feeling.

Chapter 33

I allowed myself sleep until noon. It was a wonderful, deep sleep. I took my time with the coffee, watching the waves roll on to the beach. It was a beautifully clear day and I noticed, most of the snow was gone. If Saturday was like this, walking on the beach was going to happen. Spring might seriously be coming.

I checked the cell voice mail. Mary had left a message suggesting that we might get in a look at Bill's house. She was going to show it tomorrow. With that message I figured I should get my butt into the office.

I was getting good. I walked through the office door at two minutes after two. "Hi Mary. You're showing Bill's house tomorrow?"

"Sure am. Is today a great day Victoria? I'll meet you in your office." Mary had a big happy smile on her face. She had always been a person of the moment. It was working for her now. Most would be curled up in a bed full of tranquilizers.

"I'll meet you there." I wandered to the workroom, poured coffee and, as usual, Mary beat me with her stack of papers.

"Mary, you look great." I said. She did look great, her worry lines and the black rings under her eyes were gone.

"Vic, after I passed out yesterday I dreamt about Billy. We were walking the dogs and laughing and I was so relieved he wasn't mad at me. Then last night I had another dream. He told me that he had to go. That he loved me. That all would be fine. There was a man with him that time. The man from his drawing with the tattoos. Billy said he was a very old friend, that I should thank him for what he did. Then I woke up. Wow, blew me away. I felt so good. Billy didn't hurt anymore. Weird, right? Do you know anyone that looks like the guy in Billy's pen and ink Victoria?"

I was thinking about what to say and I felt the electrical buzz hit my ankle, the feathers tickled. James was awake, my first thought. The feathers and beads moved, tickled again. I reached down, touched it, smiled. No boots. Just stockings and low heels. It was kind of nice knowing he was there. It was terrifying that it comforted me. "I'll have to think about it Mary. The odds of me knowing someone like that. Someone that Billy would know is what, a bazillion to one. Anyway what's happening?"

"Well, our super friend Karen wants to schedule a meeting with you and asks that you call her."

"Mary, it's so nice to have you back. Ok I will." I made a note to call the Closing lawyer before I called Karen. "Next."

"There aren't any Escrow checks today, but Ames has two Closings scheduled before the end of March and Nina has one. I asked them for basic info so we could plan. No one's objected yet. You need to tell me too, right?" Another issue solved.

"Right. What do you think of talking with Georgette about coming in to take the reception/assistant duties off your shoulders?"

"I've been thinking about that. I'll have an outline of the position description for you on Monday. Remember, we're meeting with the contractor for next door. You skipped ahead on my list. Should I give Georgette a call for later next week?" Mary asked.

"Sure, why not. Are you going to take one of the new Broker's desks?"

"Yeah, I am. I'll put together a 'job description' for myself so we can talk about them together. Figured might as well. Mason wants the new window office, so I'll take his old space – ok?" I was wondering why I even came in and laughed.

"Sure, sounds great. Anything else?"

"The Operating Account is looking good. I put $100k in liquid and left the remainder because of the office Closing, the contractor and other stuff. It's on the only sheet on your desk. No ads this week. Everything has been placed until the end of the month. So, want to go out to Bill's?" Mary was standing.

"Sure, let's do it." I stood, grabbed my coat, planner and we were out.

I drove and Mary told me that Mason, Georgette and Ames stayed late last night to clean the house. Mason actually told the kids it was time to go. Darlene told Mason that she couldn't be asked to leave her father's house. Mary said she had a real nice time telling Darlene that the house was hers, that she had paid cash for it and owned it outright. Billy had been staying with her. Mary's eyes were twinkling. I wondered how much interface she had actually had with Billy's kids. Obviously more than I had thought.

Mary loved Bill's house which is nice when you're trying to sell it. You don't have to fake enthusiasm. Mary chose to walk the property. I declined until I remembered my rubber boots in the car. I explained the crack in the retaining wall and the decision Bill and I had come to…let a buyer hire the engineer, at least for now. She agreed. We talked about the area. I pointed out the houses whose owners I knew and Mary took interior pictures. We were climbing the stairs to the master suite when she noticed my tattoo, then the talisman.

"What happened to that little tattoo you had?"

I had forgotten that it was bigger, much bigger than last fall. I hadn't even noticed it when I put on the stockings. I hesitated, reached down, touched it. "I had it extended when the boots came out. Did it on a lark."

"Jesus Vic. Now it looks like Billy's art. And the anklet. Where is the tie to the anklet?"

"It's there, it just ties small." I continued up the stairs.

"OK Vic, if you don't want to tell me now." Mary did know when to back off, but forget, never. She continued taking pictures of the interior and we were done quickly.

"Let me know how the showing goes tomorrow so I can tell Bill. Oh, when do you want me to return Billy's art? "

"I was thinking that I would come by and pick it up after the showing tomorrow. Somewhere around noon?"

"I'm going beach walking tomorrow, so I'll wait for you. Call if your plans change ok."

"Great, wish me luck." Mary closed the car door, returned to the office. I drove to Carolyn's.

Chapter 34

Carolyn's home would be considered in the "Kay-Catherine" area of Newport, just around the corner from the office. No off-street parking so I pulled up just behind her car. The car, unintentionally, is the same color as her house. She finally named it "Rose Cottage" after trying every relevant house name she could think of; bouncing each name off of every friend she could think of.

Actually "Rose Cottage" is a cottage in almost every sense of the word. It was built in 1920; as cute as a button, but much smaller than the surrounding properties. The wooden picket fence has a rose arbor at its gate overgrown with roses that continue on either side of the path to the front door.

To me the best feature of her home is the inglenook. With the fireplace lit, surrounded with antique horse brasses, the inglenook is the best place to sit in her house.

The house itself is three bedrooms; one very small, one very large and a guest bedroom. The living room with the inglenook, a secretaries' den, a very nice dining room and a long, narrow kitchen with a breakfast area. The kitchen, dining room and breakfast area overlook a very formal garden. Every flower is cutting quality with an incredible variety of roses. In the summer her house is filled with very large rose bouquets containing colors that blend, surprise and entice the eyes and the nose. Her gardening is so far beyond me that, at times, it was depressing when I had a garden for comparison.

Having dinner at Carolyn's house was a treat for me. Her family's history is on her walls, in her furniture, her silver and china, every candlestick and even her beds. I have never known Carolyn to buy a piece of furniture. She still sleeps on a feather bed with outrageously soft linens.

There is a rhythm to dinner at Carolyn's house. It begins with drinks and hors d'oeuvres in the living room. Good conversation with our ritual exchange of books and magazines, some gossip. When she makes second drinks, if one of us remembers, dinner will go in the oven and is ready to eat after the second drink, if we drink slowly. The third with dinner in the breakfast area and the talk starts to get deeper; usually on a subject broached during drinks in the living room. If we decide to watch a movie, dessert is taken in her bedroom, on her bed. That is where her TV, tape and DVD systems are set up along with the laptop computer she finally acquired last year. Carolyn lives in her bedroom.

If she is having problems with her computer, I'll play with it for a while. One of these days Carolyn is going to realize that I have faked the installation, setup and maintenance of her laptop, but until then she'll continue to do fine.

Tonight's first drink went along as usual. The second brought up the subject of Ledge House; who bought it, where did they come from, why did they want it? Semi-normal curiosity producing the answers that I had given her before with some embellishments. The subject of Cheryl's breakdown came up. Newport is small if one is as plugged in as Carolyn. I danced around that too. I told her that she probably knew more than I did.

Dinner was general chat about her recently deceased beau. His family was in Philadelphia and Carolyn had been told that there would be a memorial service. With that information we spent most of dinner designing a trip. The last time we had traveled together we had gone to a family auction of the estate of one of her relatives on Long Island. Short of visiting her spot in the family plot, uck, I had a good time. I think it had been much more stressful for her than she let on, although we did come away with a nice haul of antique jewelry. Of course Carolyn bid and negotiated for me, family only, but it was a treat.

The Philly trip would be a train ride. Carolyn would pack a nice basket of food and drinks. The trip would take a few hours to say the least. She was also going to try to find us someone to hot bunk with. If that didn't work, we would again share a hotel room.

She was, indeed, having a problem with her laptop. So after dinner we moved upstairs. For a lady who had trouble using a digital phone she was doing great on her computer. Carolyn was actually starting to troubleshoot her own problems, but that sometimes led to pushing the wrong button.

I discovered she had disabled her firewall causing her system to send up security warnings the minute it was turned on. Once I found that, the problems went away. Again, from my point of view, finding the problem was pure luck.

I was climbing off of her bed when Carolyn noticed the expansion of my tattoo and the anklet.

"Vicky when did you do that, the larger tattoo? You didn't have it the last time you were here. Geez, you went for it this time." She had gone with me when I had the original done, was very familiar with its original size. "If you had it done the day after you were here, it should still be healing. But the anklet is cute. Let me see it." Thank heavens it was under the stockings so her view would be a little blurred.

I moved my leg up the bed. "Cute isn't it."

"Yeah, it is. Are those feathers?" Carolyn started to run her hand over it and jerked back. "Oh, did you feel that?"

"Feel what?" It had been a bit of a shock. Apparently touching the talisman was limited to its owners.

"Vicky, it's moving, ever so slightly, but it's moving. Victoria, it's bloody magic. Where did you get it? It has a spell or something attached to it." Carolyn was a bit sensitive to "other" things. She had told me a story about a black nanny her Mother had employed. The Nanny had spent time practicing voodoo around Carolyn. Had told Carolyn she was a witch. It was a great story. I had asked her if she had practiced. She told me that she stayed as far away from 'that' stuff as she could.

If I had thought she would be that sensitive I would had gone home, changed clothes, been late. It just hadn't occurred to me. "Vicky, seriously, where did you get it? How did you put it on? It's all one piece." She scooted farther to her side of the bed. Carolyn was spooked. Hmmm, talk is easy, reality, well apparently to Carolyn, is another story.

"I went to an auction and picked it up a few weeks ago." I said.

"So you put it over that tattoo when it was healing? Vicky it moved. Where did you get it?" Carolyn was getting irritated.

"The auction. Come on. It didn't move on its own, the stockings moved. I think we've both had a bit much tonight. I have to drive, so I think I'm going to bug out." What else could I say?

"Yeah, maybe. You know you can stay here if you can't drive."

"No, I'm ok to drive. If not will you bail me out?" Actually, I'd crashed in her bed before, had been stiff for a week after, way to soft. "Stay where

you are. I'll lock on my way out. Great dinner sweetie. Thanks so much."
I slid off of her bed.

"Thanks for the computer help." Carolyn seemed to be on the verge of nodding for the night. The talisman hadn't bothered her that much.

I walked down her stairs slowly. One drink too many. Found my coat, locked her door on the way out. I was sitting in the car when the talisman started moving. It was rolling a good inch up and down my ankle. Enough so that it was pulling the stocking. I reached down, touched it. After a few more rolls it stopped and the feathers tickled my ankle.

It was a beautiful night. Clear, chilly but not arctic cold. When I drove by the beach I could hear the surf run on the sand. No tourists. No other cars on the road. No snow. I couldn't ask for much more. By the time I got home it was close to midnight. With the drinks and a great dinner bed was the only option.

Chapter 35

I dreamt again. This time there was no scene set, no lead up. I was just there. I didn't realize I was dreaming. I was just there. I could feel people around me. I could see them but couldn't understand why they were not helping me. I was on my back, on the grass. A man was over me. No...not a man. Something. A horrible thing. A crazy thing. A crazed face. Insane, light flashing eyes.

I couldn't understand why no one was helping me. My family, my friends were starting to run away. I was screaming. It was tearing me apart with its hands, its claws. I was screaming for help. Where was my love, my warrior? It wasn't words; just flashes. Visual, sensory, emotions overlapping, terror flooding my head. I felt the long cuts on my body, their fire. I could feel the thing inside of me, breaking me. I could see it watching me; enjoying everything. It was killing me.

I continued to scream. The thing smiled. There would be no help, no saving. I saw it bare its teeth and felt my throat rip. Heard the scream stop. I was frozen. My eyes closed. It struck at my breast. It struck at the inside of my thigh, my stomach. The black came. The fire left.

I woke in the sweat soaked tee shirt I'd worn to bed. Soaked into the sheets, into my blankets. There wasn't a pillow on my bed. I sat up shaking, cold, hurting. I was terrified. I turned on the light fixed to the wall next to my bed. Realized I was alone. Nothing in the room but the terror. I could still feel the dream; see the dream. I reached for the TV controller, turned it on. Maybe this would relieve me of the dream. Anything to make its reality go away. No luck. I relived the dream over and over again as real as the first time.

I had no idea when I'd woken nor how long I had sat wet, cold, aching in my bed. I could see the beginnings of daylight around the doorway into my room. I felt the feathers at my ankle move, felt a flood of regret, sorrow, the snap of electricity. James was dead. The snap of the talisman brought me back to reality.

I swung my feet to the floor, stepped on pieces of glass. I focused. Saw the bedside clock smashed to the floor. The bottle of water against the far wall open, flat. The books that were on my nightstand torn, all over the floor. The nightstand itself in pieces. One leg here, one leg there, its wood top in pieces. My room was a mess. I was a mess.

Tears started. I just wanted to let go, freak out, escape. Escape the dream. The images it had left in my head. The talisman. James. Everything. I felt helpless. Totally and completely helpless.

I picked up the face of my clock. It had stopped at 5:45. The cable box read 6:20. I shook the glass out my slippers. Walked to the bathroom. Turned the shower on. I knew this feeling. It had come before. The first time when I was much younger. If I didn't fight it, I was going to slide into serious depression, swirl around that drain, eventually be sucked in.

The last time it had happened was a few years after I'd married number two. I had finally fought out of the swirl by taking control, control of everything. Was I losing control now? Is that what this was all about? Was that what the dream was trying to tell me?

I stepped into the shower, relief, water therapy. I just stood there. I stopped thinking. Didn't move for who knows how long. The shaking finally stopped. I scrubbed from top to bottom, twice. Almost forgot to put conditioner in my hair. Without the conditioner and a few other things I would have Janis Joplin hair big time. Change, I needed some change, then control.

I did the conditioner, nothing else. Put on a pair of very old baggy jeans; the oldest shirt I could find. A blue, embroidered work shirt from my protest days. The shirt must be at least forty years old. It felt good. I walked back into my bedroom. It was a mess that I would have to clean up, but I would do that later. I needed coffee, badly.

I walked into the kitchen, realized that I was barefoot. Tile is much cooler to the touch that hardwoods. I laughed, looked down at my feet. The vine covered the top of my foot, wound under my toes. It was bleeding. I looked behind where I stood. There were bloody footprints from one foot back into the dressing room. I unbuttoned my jeans, dropped them. Blood was smeared down my leg. The tattoo had circled around my leg, over my knee, ending at mid thigh. It was oozing from the new areas. I took my pants off. The one leg was sticky with blood, the talisman was soaked. I hadn't noticed. I needed to get a grip on myself.

I put a bunch of paper towels under the tap, cleaned off the bottom of my foot, returned to the shower. I rinsed my leg and the talisman with the hand sprayer until the water ran clean. I let it air-dry while I looked around the bathroom. My towels were bloody. The foot prints led back to the bed. At this point all I could do was shake my head. I wrapped toilet paper around the length of my leg, stuck it between my toes. The oozing had pretty much stopped, just a few spots. I put on a pair of socks and picked my way back to the kitchen. I made coffee, put the jeans in the washer. I sat in the kitchen watching the breakers crash on rocks.

I decided I would get the blood off the floor, wait for Mary, then walk the beach. Maybe book a flight…get the hell out of here for a while.

I finished the floor in the bedroom. Realized the bed was stained.

Not only with sweat from the dream, but with blood. It was strip it now, try to save the blankets and linens or lose them. I stripped the bed. Thank heavens for the mattress cover. Treated every stain I could find. Put the jeans in the dryer. Started the process of washing everything.

It occurred to me that if Mary had to come all the way into the living room, she would see the mess. I moved all of Billy's canvases into the entry. I then began to peal the toilet paper off my leg. Some of the pieces had dried to the tattoo and my skin, but easily pealed off with water. The tattoo seemed healed. That was fast. It hadn't even scabbed over. I spread the leg with half a tube of triple antibiotic, one of the great medical inventions, put my jeans back on. The talisman looked untouched.

Maybe space. Maybe a beach warmer than here would let me sort my head. I knew the beach I wanted. Didn't care if I had to wear a jacket. Wondered if I could pull it off. The beach sans grandkids. I definitely did not need grandkids right now.

I poured a fresh cup of coffee, went to the library. Flipped on the computer, checked flight availability, Providence, 3:30. Clicked, booked. Hotel far enough down the beach away from grandkids, clicked, booked. Car in Tampa, click, booked.

I searched for Plains Indians and myths. The results weren't what I was looking for on this pass. I went back to the auction house site. Found what the appraisers had called 'Four Piece Braid Jewelry – male – Age: unknown – Tribe: unknown – Myths surrounding piece extensive, click here. "Estimated value: $22,000 Sold at auction: $35,000'. The page that revealed itself were the myths told by the Army Captain to his children.

Supposedly from the man he 'bought' the piece from. What caught my attention was the warning he was given when he passed the piece around the Fort. Among stories of a dead Shaman, the Great Spirit and revenge was the following: '....Two Indian Scouts in the employ of the U.S. Army wouldn't touch the piece, told him to throw it away. 'Give it back to the maker Spirit or it would be retrieved.' Not long after the incident, the scouts deserted, never to be seen again. The Army mounted a search for the Scouts. The search was not successful.'

Apparently the Captain had lived a long life. Telling stories of his adventures and his collection. He had many children and died a peaceful death in his sleep. Asshole. I was starting to calm. Running. I was running from what, dreams? James? Running started to seem pointless. Did I think he couldn't find me if he wanted to? Get a grip.

Tickets cancelled. I was already in too far. That I couldn't deny. Worst case. I had to think about what exactly, personally, worst case would be. I got bored? No loss. It wouldn't be the first time I walked away. Could be one last hurrah, hell of an adventure, a hoot. Not worst case. I go with it, let it flow, let myself fall, was left high and dry with nothing but pain. Yep. For me that was worst case. I had only one event like that. 38 years ago. Never let it happen again...until now. Now had potential.

Philip still hurt, probably would for the rest of my life. Just that thought and the hole opened. Philip had left. Fuck.

I was pulled out of my head by the doorbell. It had to be Mary. Fake it.

"Sorry I'm late Vic. I should have called, sorry."

"No problem. I was playing in the computer, totally lost track of time. How'd the showing go?"

Mary stepped into the entry and realized that I had all the canvases against the wall. "I guess it went ok. They thought that the main kitchen on the lowest level was a bit funny and would be a bitch to move. They also were of the opinion that the retaining wall was about to fail. I'm thinking that Bill may want to get the engineer out. Could you ask him about it?"

"Sure. He won't be surprised. I'll take the canvases out. You're in work clothes."

"That would be great. This is the only suit I've got right now." Mary followed me out to her car to unlock it. "I'm going to drop off the canvases at home and take off to the Mall. Want to come?"

"Not really. I was waiting for you, then I'm off to the beach." There was a light buzz to my ankle and the talisman tickled. James was up.

"I can see that. Letting it go native?" She was laughing.

I didn't know what she was talking about at first, then it occurred to me. "Oh, my hair. I've declared today a sixties day. Let my freak flag fly."

Mary was having quite a laugh. "No kidding. Geez, I think I've seen that shirt before. What? Thirty years ago?"

"You're close Mary." She laughed again, shaking her head.

"Thanks Vic, I'll see you Monday. Remember Contractor at one."

"I'll remember. Have fun." Mary backed out of the driveway and was gone.

I was walking back to the door when I heard clopping on the road. How neat. Someone was riding. It was such a beautiful day. The clopping got closer. I turned in the doorway hoping to see the horse go by. It didn't. The horse came down the driveway. James was riding. Shit, I'd just felt the talisman.

The horse was beautiful, very large, very strong. James sat straight on the animal, hair loose, a sweater, blue jeans and his soft, skin boots laced over the jeans. No saddle, a very heavy blanket, maybe two, no bit, simple leather reins. All I could think was what beautiful animals, both of them. I smiled for the first time since I'd gotten home last night. James was on the ground, in front of me, holding my shoulders, looking into my eyes before I could see how he got there. "Victoria, what happened?"

"Oh, my hair. I didn't blow dry after I showered. Thought I'd get to it before you came."

"No, your hair is wonderful. What happened to you?"

I was going to tell him. "Horse, what's with the horse?" That's what came out.

"I wanted to take you riding."

"Why don't you take your friend to the garden side. He'll be less visible there. I'll meet you at the door." He was himself. He had ridden here without hiding. I was surprised. I closed the front door. By the time I reached the garden door, James was waiting. "Do you need to secure him?"

"No, he will not leave me." James walked into the living room, looked around, focused on the open bedroom door. He walked to the door, stood in the doorway. "Victoria, are you alright?" He asked again.

"Now, I'm better than I was a few hours ago. I had the most horrible dream." And the dream came back to me. My heart started pounding and the terror started building with the shaking. "God. I can't shake it, can't get it out of my head." I lifted the leg of my jeans to show him my foot. "This time it was bleeding. The tattoo now stops in the middle of my thigh." He was just looking at me. "Say something James or I'm going to freak out. Take it off my ankle, stop this." I was starting to lose it.

"Victoria." He started to walk to me. I stepped back. "Victoria, let us leave. You will need a sweater." He looked at my feet. "You will need some shoes. Where are they?" I didn't move. The only thoughts in my head were the dream. "Stay where you are." Like I could move. James went through the bedroom to the dressing room. I could hear drawers open and close. He was saying something I couldn't understand. He returned with one of my old but serviceable heavy sweaters, socks and sneakers that had seen better days. James put the sweater over my head. That started me moving. I put on the shoes and socks.

"James, I have to clean up this mess. I have the bed stuff soaking in the kitchen, a load in. I need to get this cleaned up now."

"No. I have asked my friends to come, clean this for you. It will be fine."

"How much will it cost? I can do this." It was the only thought outside of the dream.

"They are my friends. Do not worry. They are glad to help. Let us go." He took my arm, started walking me to the garden door.

"I need to lock up."

"No. Your home will be safe." He opened the door for me and waited. "Please, Victoria. Please. You will feel better. We can talk. We will ride."

I stepped out into the garden. "Why the horse?" I asked again. "Oh, you already told me." I was a little better than I was this morning, but not much. I wasn't opening my mouth again until I could form a reasonable thought.

"I am going to lift you, swing you over the neck of the horse. Swing your right leg over the horse, hold his mane. He will not move, you will not hurt him. Do you understand me Victoria?"

I thought for a second, figured out what he was going to do. Good luck I thought, but said, "OK". And he did exactly what he said he was going to do, no effort. I though I wouldn't be able to balance on the horse with the strength he had used. I did.

"Victoria, I am going to mount behind you. You will not fall. The horse will not move. Do you understand me?"

Again I thought about it. Stay where I was, don't move. James was going to sit behind me. "OK." Before I knew he'd moved, he was behind me, reached around my waist. Pulled me back against his chest with his right hand, took the reins with his left. He squeezed the horse with his thighs, the horse started to circle around to the driveway. James squeezed his thighs against the horse at the beginning of the driveway. The horse stopped to let a car come in.

The car parked next to mine and two women started to get out. James moved the horse to the car, smiled at them and spoke in some language that was totally beyond me. Both women were in their mid thirties. Resembled each other. Probably sisters and not ugly by any way, shape or form. When they were finished talking, James turned the horse with his legs and we started up the driveway.

We trotted down the hill to the beginning of the beach, but took the road as if we were headed to Ledge House. The cars that passed us slowed around the horse. The horse didn't once spook. Now that was amazing. We passed the street that would lead to Ledge House and took a parallel dirt road. The horse started to move faster up the road to the top of the hill. James was holding me against him with both arms now. No reins. At the top of the hill the horse picked up speed. We passed the quarry and kept going. The faster we rode, the tighter James held me, the better I felt. We rode the crest of the hill down to Green End Avenue.

James slowed, crossed the road entering another dirt road, almost pathway, picking up speed. I couldn't recall this open land other than the "Greenway" that had finally been connected by acquisition and lease from about Green End Avenue in Middletown to maybe Quaker Hill in Portsmouth. The speed and steadiness of the horse and rider was amazing. I saw the golf course through trees on my right and knew approximately where we were on the Island.

Another twenty minutes of riding and we began to slow; then circled a field on the east side of Quaker Hill. I could see the Sakonnet River from where we stopped. It was my only clue as to where we were.

James leaned to my ear. "Feel better?"

I laughed. "Yes, much better. That was a thrill. It was spectacular."

"Would you like to get down and talk a while?"

"Yes, I would." James was down again before I realized he had moved.

"Bring your right leg around the horse and slide down. I will catch you. The horse will not move." I did what he said, didn't have to think about it. He pulled the blankets off the horse, laid them in the field. The horse started walking away. Before I could say anything James spoke. "The horse is fine. He will walk for a while and return. He is safe Victoria. Please, sit with me." I walked to the blanket. Sat with James, facing him. He put his hands on my knees. "Tonight we will talk about the dream, it is too fresh now. I would like to hear about your life. Tell me about it."

I was trying to be solemn, firm, serious but it wasn't going to happen, yet again. My panic had faded. I wanted to talk about the dream, the talisman, what was happening to me. But that wasn't going to happen now either. "What do you mean, my life?"

"Ok, tell me about your office, the people in it, start there."

I could do that and get another question answered. He thought he was going to get around some tense subjects. I'd tell him about everyone, especially Mary. I told him about Mason which led to when I'd worked with Mason before. Told him about Ames and started laughing when I told him our dating deal. There he had a question.

"Have you had sex with Ames?" Whoa, that was blunt.

"No. We're close friends."

"Would you?"

"I don't know. The subject hasn't come up, why?"

"Just interested." His eyes hadn't moved from mine. That question would force most eyes to wander. "So tell me about Mary, Billy's partner." Change of subject.

I told him how Mary and I had met. He smiled broadly at the narc story. I told him what our relationship had been over the years. Then I asked him. "What do I tell my friends when they ask about the talisman and the growth of the tattoo? Most I can talk around, but Mary and another friend are not going to let it go. Last night Carolyn touched it. It shocked her, then moved. She is definitely not going to let that go."

"Oh yes, your friend last night. The talisman was threatened. I thought you were threatened. I realized the touch was your friend. Carolyn contains her own power. The talisman felt it. I felt it. If she touches it again nothing will happen. It will know her. Someday, I would like to meet her."

"Who is in Billy's pen and ink? Why did he draw it. It's not his style."

"It is more his style than his friends or family know." James smiled. "Billy and I had been talking one evening. He was glad that I found you. We talked about very old times. Told stories. It was a very good evening. Shared times with his amulet. I added power to it. When I did we both saw that day. I did not know he had been sitting on the hill. I often think about that day, your touch. I believe I had forgotten the visual of the Plains. Billy inked it for us. For you and me a few days later. When he showed it to me he told me that he would give it to us when the time was right. I believe you ended up with the drawing much sooner than he had intended." James closed his eyes for some time. "We should return. I believe your home is clean."

"I hate to sound like a wimp. I don't know that I'm ready to go back there." When I thought about the bedroom my stomach started to jump.

"Your home is clean. I will light a fire. You will have some wine. It will be as if your experience never happened. I promise." He stood. The horse returned to James. "The ride home will be chilly. I will mount first."

He put the blankets on the horse, ground side up, took two steps. On the second step he was high enough to swing his leg over the horse. When James had settled himself, he reached down to me with his left arm. "Victoria, take my arm. I will lift you up to me. Swing your right leg over the horse. All in one motion. Do you understand?"

Funny, I could see the movement. I must be feeling better. I took his arm, he lifted. I swung my leg over the horse and I was sitting behind James. "Move as close to me as you can. Put your arms around me. Hold tight. We will ride." I did what he asked. It felt great. I held him as tight as he had held me. We started with a slow trot, moved to a slow gallop; then increased. Just before we reached the golf course, the sun set. With the horse still at a full gallop, James let go of my arms. Lifted his arms east to west and screamed at the top of his lungs as loud and as long as his one breath allowed. I wondered if anyone had heard him. He brought his arms down; returned them to my arms around his middle. I felt his joy.

When we came to the end of the quarry he stopped. "Do you mind if I put the horse up? He could use a rubdown and some food. Johnathan will give us a ride to your home."

"No problem." I'd do just about anything to delay my return. Clean wasn't my real problem. I knew what the condo felt like.

James turned the horse to Ledge House. When we crossed over the property line more than one owl started hooting, a coyote howled…then another. We rode to where the garages had been three weeks before. The eight doors were now multiple open spaces. The roof had been extended another five or so feet. All I could see were shadows. I could only guess at the modifications.

We rode to the other side of the structure where there were some subtle lights hidden under half of the eves. I realized at least the back side of the garage structure had become a multiple stall horse barn. I couldn't count the stall doors. Only two reflected light.

194

A man met us as we rode up to the only open stall door. I noticed that the land, beginning about fifty feet from the barn, had been cleared of underbrush. Only a few of the wild trees and large stone outcroppings remained. I could pick up the outline of the Wildlife Sanctuary fence with its signs.

James was again off the horse before I realized he had moved. I slid to him, then to the ground. He walked up to the man, spoke to him in, what, German?

"Hello Victoria. Did you have a good ride? I know James did. I heard him." I jumped at the unexpected voice.

"Hi Johnathan. Yes, it was great on such a beautiful afternoon." So someone had heard him. I had to give Johnathan a smile.

James took my hand. We walked to one of the two cars parked at the edge of the driveway that curved around the house to the garages. He and Johnathan were talking loud enough so that I head them as we walked, continued talking when we sat in the back of the car. James was telling him about the ride, the pluses and minuses of the trail and the ride back. They both laughed when James was told he was heard. James asked if my home was complete and the language changed to the Slavic tones. The closer we got to the condo the more dread I felt.

When the car parked in front of my condo, I didn't want to go back in. It wasn't just the dream but what the dream had left in the condo. The vibes. The terror. If I had been by myself, I probably would have gotten on that plane and told Mary to sell it. If James's arrival had been fifteen minutes later, I would have been gone. I hadn't realized it then, but now; yeah. I would have been gone. James squeezed my hand, got out of the car with Johnathan. Johnathan opened the front door. They both entered.

I didn't see any lights go on. Neither had asked me to go in on the first pass. Good for them. I wasn't running to the door.

I began to wonder what was taking so long. I stepped out of the car, leaned against it. I started to see the lights go on...no not lights. It was a soft glow that first illuminated my bedroom, then the dressing room, the bath, the entry. The glow seemed to get brighter as it appeared to be spreading to the other rooms. I was tempted to walk around the building, to look in the east windows. A few minutes later the glow started to fade. Then it was gone. I watched the front door open. Johnathan emerged, told me that if I was ready to go in, "...your home is fine."

"I will. Just give me a second. If you and James would like to leave, that would be ok. This is my problem. Not yours."

Johnathan went back into the condo. I was thinking about actually taking a step when the two of them stepped out, started walking to me.

"Victoria. Your home is fine. It has been thoroughly cleaned." James was earnest, his head slightly tilted.

I stepped back from him without thinking. I saw a look pass over his face. He took a step forward, recovering some of the space I had taken. "Victoria. I am going in with you. Please, do not do this."

"Do what? You weren't here this morning. I was. I was the pig. You were just the chicken."

His eyebrows lifted. His eyes questioned. "I do not understand what you are saying."

"This morning I was committed. You were just involved, James. The dream was mine. You came later." James shook his head, that look still on his face. No clue. "You know, ham and eggs for breakfast. The pig is committed, the chicken is just involved."

It took a second, then it dawned on both of them. The laughter was probably heard at Ledge House. "Victoria, trust me, if only for this moment. If you are still upset after walking into your house, we will leave."

I couldn't argue with that. I walked to the door. Opened it. Stepped in. James followed me. Johnathan stayed by the car.

The entry area was fine. Hmm. I walked into the living room. Talk about physically clean. The floors, the windows. They had cleaned the freaking windows. I took a deep breath, blew it out. There was a smell of brush, but not. Under that smell was a smell, an ion smell like the air after it has been treated with an industrial air cleaner. Better yet, the room felt good. Nothing crazy.

I looked toward the bedroom door. Walked slowly to peak in. The bedroom looked as if nothing had happened. The bedside table had been repaired. My books were in place. The floor was clean. The bed made and blankets returned to their places. I stepped in. The space felt warm, comforting. The smell. Not unpleasant. I walked through to the dressing room. The bathroom. Neither room had ever been this clean. The towel bar had been replaced.

I walked out. Headed to the kitchen. "Victoria. Is it ok? How do you feel?" I looked at James and broke a smile that felt too big for my face.

"I feel like it never happened James. Thank you so much. Thank your cleaning people for me. Are you sure I can't pay them?"

"No. You can not. I am glad you are pleased. That I will tell them. You will stay. You will not leave me?"

"What do you mean 'leave you'?"

"You were going to leave everything when I arrived. You were still thinking about it when you stayed outside just now." He had my eyes again. He had been truly worried.

I looked down at my newly decorated foot and realized that the talisman was moving, the feathers were tickling, each amulet rolling. It had been moving all day. Where had I been that I hadn't felt it?

I looked back to him. "James. I don't know that I could truly leave you, but that is a problem I must deal with, come to grips with. Not you."

"You were going to run."

"Yes. I was heading to that answer. Where did the dream come from? I've never had a dream like that."

"Let me set a fire and if you will allow, I will look at it. You will not leave me tonight?" James walked to the fireplace, I sat on the loveseat. I watch him move as he built the fire.

"No, not tonight. What do you mean 'look at it'?"

"I need to see, feel what you saw, felt, to help, if I can. I will control it. For you it will be like flipping through the pictures in a book. The pictures will mean nothing to you." He lit the match, touched it to a log, turned to sit in front of me. I thought about what he had said. Heard the car start, move in the driveway. I needed to understand the dream or I wouldn't be able to let it go. "Do you trust me Victoria?"

Here goes. I didn't think he wanted to 'hurt' me. I wasn't all that sure if our definition of 'hurt' was the same. Wasn't sure his reason for being here was what he had said...hell, I didn't understand what he had said. I was hooked; that I didn't like. Much longer and I wouldn't be capable of either. That I didn't understand. I didn't understand any of what was happening; what I felt. I either let go of my concerns or shut down and run like hell. James had not moved.

"Victoria. I meant what I said. You are my soul. To cause you pain would be to return to my pain."

"You can get inside of my head?"

"No. You are screaming your thoughts. They are nothing but open emotions. Please." He unfolded his legs to a V. "Can you sit on the floor with me? We need to touch. The more we touch, the more control I will have. Victoria, like when we rode out this afternoon."

There was no way to rationalize what I was about to do. No logic. I sat between his legs. He pulled me as close as he could. Wrapped his arms around me. Put his head on my shoulder leaning against the side of my face. James adjusted himself so that we had full contact from where my feet reached his calves, up our legs, his crotch against my butt; his stomach, waist and chest followed my spine to my shoulders where his neck rested over my shoulder and head to head. His arms followed my arms wrapping myself around my ribs; his fingers tucking to his lower chest. God, it felt good.

"Victoria, just close you eyes. Do not fight what you feel. I will not hurt you. See what you see. It cannot hurt you. Do you understand me?"

"I think I do. Give it a try."

"Good." James went still, pulling me with him. I could feel a soft touch. A touch on the wrong side of my skin. The one touch was everywhere. I didn't think I could relax more, but I did. The pressure of the touch started to move without loosing contact. The pictures started.

The first was clear. It was where I had entered the dream, but it was just a picture. I was looking up at the horror. The next two were faster, the next faster still. I lost tract of the pictures after that. James was right. It was like thumbing a book or a deck of cards.

It didn't take long before the cards stopped leaving only black space. The black became flashes of light. I felt a soft comfort join the touch. That feeling was joined by a feeling I could only relate to as coming home after being homesick when you're a kid at camp. We stayed that way. Just stayed. The feelings continued. The light show continued.

Time passed before an open space began to define itself almost as another dream. Ground, brownish with tuffs of wild grass; hills, blue sky. I felt sun warmth. I felt touching. I felt, then saw my arms wrapped around his neck. His head buried in my neck. His arms wrapped around me, lifting me. I had a leg wrapped around the top of his. He had a leg wrapped around mine. We were standing. There were no clothes, just sun, just each other; what I knew...I felt. It was me. It was James in Billy's picture. I felt complete: my heart, my soul. There was nothing else.

James spoke soft words into my ear, brought me back. "I want you to know what I remember of that day. I only saw, remembered us. Billy gave back to me our home." He relaxed his hold. I held his arms. I would not release him. "I saw your dream. I felt your terror. Until now I have only been able to imagine what occurred after I died. When I found you it was done. Long done. The dream you had was your death after mine." James was quiet, still for a few moments. "Understand Victoria. This has already happened. Your wheel has turned many times. Do you understand what I am telling you?"

"I have had other dreams."

"Other dreams?"

"Yes. But you were in them, at the very end. I realize that what I have been seeing, dreaming, is the end of very specific lives. Why now, why those?" As soon as I said it, I knew. "You were in those lives weren't you? That's why you apologized for being late, for taking so long when we met." My brain was doing another one of those click, click, clicks. Things falling into place. Oh. "I understand. James, I need to get a drink. Do you mind?" Realizing that I'd played in this world before had given me comfort. Understanding that I'd play again, maybe fit in next time, had always given me hope. The overwhelming sense of the 'something missing' that had caused so much friction in my life was real, true...sitting here. Yeah, I did want a drink.

"No. Unfortunately, you will have to let me go to do that." I had forgotten my grip on his arms.

I started talking as I stood, moved to the kitchen. "I don't know if you realize the revelation you just gave me." James was following me into the kitchen. "That what I've known my whole life to be true, is true. I don't know how to explain it. But for me, the reality needs a drink to digest." He sat at the breakfast bar, watching me.

"Your family is a Christian family?"

"Yes, very. My father knew something, I'm sure. But it was never said, never discussed. We were the classic American military family with church on Sundays, choir practice on Wednesdays and Saturdays for me, and on and on."

"Do your parents remain in this life? Do you have brothers and sisters?" Now James was asking questions.

"No and no. I have three children, but two live in other places. Only one here – they have their own lives."

"You are not a part of your children's lives?"

"Sometimes...no...I'm not. Not in the way you're asking." I sat next to him at the breakfast bar. My brain kept telling me I wasn't nuts after all. Relief. I wasn't thinking about his questions...or my answers.

"You were married?"

"Yes."

"Did he leave this life?"

"No. The second did. No to the third. James, my life has been filled with starts and stops. It took a long time for me to realize that this world doesn't fit me, this life. Hey, maybe it's me that doesn't fit. Either way I'm finally in a situation where I can pop in and out as I please. Sorry…I'm whining. Why are we on this boring subject anyway?" I stood, walked to the doorway, drink in hand.

James moved to the doorway before I noticed. Arms out, legs in the corners, blocking me. "Victoria. I want to be with you in your world! I want you to be with me in mine. That is why I asked." I stopped moving. I looked at him.

All I wanted to do was touch him. My unreasonable attraction to him, my desire for him was becoming unmanageable. With his arms and legs blocking the doorway I could see the waist of his jeans hanging on his hips, his navel, the beginning of his ribs. I could see the drawings on his skin. I had to close my eyes, try to compose myself. I was trembling. If I didn't sit I was going to fall. I moved back to the main counter. Put my drink on it, my back against it. Slid to the floor. I opened my eyes. Watched him moving to me. My grin turned into a laugh. "Victoria are you alright?" A very funny question.

"Oh yeah, I'm fine." By the time I answered he was on his knees in front of me. I reached out. Allowed my hands to move under his sweater. Pulled him closer so that I could touch all of the skin on his back, run my hands from his shoulders to the waist of his pants. Oh my he felt so good. Unexplainably good.

Was this, what I wanted, even possible? I didn't care. What I was doing was just fine. James started to lean into me. "No. Please. Stay right there." He leaned back. Closed his eyes. A shudder moved through his body.

With all the layers of ink, James was perfectly smooth. There was no hair. When my hands started to move around his waist, he lifted his arms for me. My hands moved slowly to his stomach. I could feel every inch of his skin. The more I touched, the faster my heart beat. My hands moved from his stomach over his ribs, over his hard nipples to his shoulders. He moaned.

I brought my hands down from his shoulders. Stopped over his breasts. I could feel his nipples pushing against the palm of my hands. He whispered my name. I moved down his arms as far as I could reach under the sweater. I brought my hands back over his arms, under his arms, down each side to his waist. I moved them along the top of his jeans to his back. Pulled him to me so that I could lay my head against his stomach; the wonderful skin, the wonderful movement of the art. The animals, the tattoos were moving against my cheek. Odd. James was so warm, so quiet, so peaceful.

I felt his hands move around my head, press me closer. I heard a heartbeat. Oh yes. Right here. Here I could stay.

James moved his hands, reaching for his sweater. Don't move, my only thought. He pulled his sweater over his head, let it drop to the floor. I looked up. Every inch of his body was covered with the art. "May I come down with you?" I pulled at his hips. He stayed on his knees. Slowly moved closer. Put his hands to either side of my jaw. Leaned to a kiss.

I tasted his lips, his tongue, his teeth, their very sharp extensions. I tasted every inch of his mouth. I wanted to swallow him. He tasted me; my lips, my tongue, my teeth and sucked me into him. His lips, his tongue moved down my jaw, my neck as far as the sweater, my shirt would let him. I did not want to break this.

James moved his mouth around my neck. Stopped at its pulse. He licked at the pulse, hesitated, moved back to my mouth. The kiss became urgent. He put his hand behind my head. Stopped me from moving. Pressed me harder against his mouth. I took a stuttered inhalation. James took my exhalation into his lungs. I let go of him. Pulled my sweater over my head. Allowed it to drop to the floor next to his. Moved my hands to unbutton my shirt.

James lifted my chin to look at him. I continued to unbutton my shirt. "Victoria." Oh God, he's going to stop. "Victoria, now?"

I finished unbuttoning my shirt. Damn shirt. "Yes James, now." Finally, I had control, my decision had been made without conscious thought. I went with it.

I kissed his stomach. Ran my tongue over those wonderful pictures to the top of his jeans. I reached for the first button. Released it with one hand. My other low on his back, holding him to me. Experience. I licked under the open button. Released the next, licked. His hand came to my head. His fingers spread in my hair, slowly sliding to my back.

I reached for the third button. He was pushing against it. I carefully slid the button free. Kissed him. Moved my tongue over the tip of him, around him. Freed the fourth button. Kissed him. Licked more of him, around him. Released the fifth. Kissed him. Circled the ridge of him with my tongue. His hands gripped my back, I licked him, sucked him, kissed. Released the sixth.

James bent his head to my ear. "Please. Allow me to release the remaining buttons. I will not survive twelve." Chicken. I smiled. Licked the exposed length of him. Released my hold. I popped my two snaps, dropped my zipper. Waited for him to move so I could get out of my pants. James stood quickly, discarded his.

Standing above me he was wonderful. Smooth, hard, etched. Looking down at me his hair fell over his nipples, his ribs, bracketing my view. I saw a straight line of etchings, from his testicles to his forehead. He bent to the cuffs of my pants, pulled the jeans off, slid me down the cabinet to lie flat on the floor. He started to lie down next to me.

"No James." I reached pulling him over me.

"Victoria?" Again, he was questioning.

"Now James, Now." I'd had my foreplay. I knew he'd had his. James moved himself between my legs, holding himself above me on his hands, looking into my eyes. I pulled is face to mine, held it so those eyes now became my view. I licked his lips. Pulled him even closer. Lifted my legs. Secured my heals at the top of his legs, below the rise of his ass. Pulled my heels up, pressured him into me without resistance.

No fumbling; no hands adjusting. I was not new to him. James did not feel new to me. I gasped, he moaned. James slowly moved himself into me. A bit in a bit out. He teased the way I had teased with his buttons. He pulled back from my mouth. Held himself up, over me. My hands at his back. He could move, watch me, watch himself. I could watch every inch of him. Watch the muscles move in his stomach, his chest, his arms. I could watch his face, his eyes. I could feel him inside me, every movement, every thrust, every withdrawal, his length, his width.

James tapped the end of me. I shuddered the little ache. My eyes closed. I dragged my nails down his back. My feet moved to the floor. Enough. I lifted to meet his thrust. Dropped my hips. Raised them sharply. Pulled him down to me. "Victoria. Slow down."

"No. This time. The first time. Together." I arched my back. Squeezed him inside of me with all my strength. Held him for a moment. Released him. James entered faster. His arms, his hands moved to my back lowering himself to me. Held me against his chest, his stomach. Our movements faster.

I felt myself there, at the top of the wave, balancing. I balanced until I couldn't balance anymore. "Now." I whispered. Let myself slide. Let my body grab him, try to hold him. His grip on me tightened, his rhythm lost with the last thrust. I felt his release. James shuddered. I shuddered. Started to spasm again from the bottom of the wave.

James pushed again. We crashed again. James shimmered. I felt his animals lift. Wow! My eyes opened. I watched as they danced across the two of us. Another shudder took my breath. I couldn't feel where I stopped, James began. He seemed to melt into me. Another shimmer took me with him.

James lifted his head, opened eyes full of light; the whites red. He smiled, lowered his head to my neck. His lips resting against my pounding pulse.

Slowly my head, my heart gave up the pounding. My muscles began to relax. James, without movement, covered me. My back was cooling against the tile. I was beginning to cool down. I turned to his face, his hair across my cheek.

"James, the tile is cold. I need to move." He lifted his head to look at me. His eyes were still full of light, full of blood. He had not fallen out of me. Unusual. His hands lifted his chest up. Began slowly to withdraw. Stopped. He flexed his elbows bending to kiss.

The kiss pulled my breath into his lungs. He held it, gave it back. Took it again. Returned the breath to me. Each was a rush pushing into my brain, spread to my toes, then back up, out to him. He held himself over me, completed his withdrawal. Leaned back to his knees. He was still hard. Very hard. Odd. My eyes focused on his. "Are you ok?"

"I am fine." I looked down then back up to his eyes. He smiled. "My heart has slowed. I will soften."

"Could you have…ah…continued?" I had to ask. What woman wouldn't. I sat up. Reached for my shirt and underwear tangled in my jeans. Fabulous, wonderful, amazing, completely unexpected sex leaving way too many questions. For me now came the awkward moment.

"Yes. Another time, yes. Victoria. I did not think of this tonight. I was not prepared for this." He stopped moving, talking…hesitated.

I stood. Reacquired my panties, slid them on. Started with my jeans. "Out with it James. It was good…but." …want to have coffee sometime? I didn't say it. Damn. I didn't want to mess this up. For the first time in years I was willing to let him stay. Most men like to initiate sex, feel threatened when the woman initiates. I hoped he wasn't one of them…holy moley. I actually cared.

"No Victoria." His eyes were wide, surprised. "I would have moved to you in the old library. I have not wanted to scare you. Upset you." The light in his eyes was back to flashing in his irises. The blood was gone. He was soft, still inviting.

I was thinking about touching him when I noticed his skin. It was going gray. The spirits were sharper against the pale gray skin especially around his eyes. Actually, as I watched the skin around his eyes it darkened to deep gray rings under the tattoos. He was starting to look truly gaunt.

I moved closer to him. "James you are really starting to look ill." I reached out to touch his cheek.

"Victoria, I am fine. I cannot remember when I felt this good. Maybe in the field with you." He sounded great. "I did not expect this. I have not… fed in a few days. Do not let it concern you." James reached to me. Closed the distance. Held me against him. Held me tight. Kissed me. His skin was cool. I relaxed. Hadn't realized I was tense. "I will have to leave soon. I do need to feed before sunrise."

I laughed, shook my head. Moved out of his embrace and walked to the counter for my drink. Now that was a new line. The first guy in years I hadn't wanted to toss so I could get some sleep. The drink's ice was completely melted. The screwdriver was room temperature. How long had we been occupied? I took my drink to the living room. The fire was ash.

"Victoria. I have no choice." James followed me, stood in front of me. Watched me. "You have a history in this life...please do not apply it to my intentions. Maybe you will let me see some of your life tomorrow."

"James. Thank you for yesterday, last night, this morning. Thank you for just now. If I see you tomorrow, maybe." Shit, why did I say that? Training, like Pavlov's dogs. "Sure, tomorrow." I forced a smile, kissed his cheek, walked to the garden door, opened it.

I watched James move slowly to the door. Put arms around me. "I am sorry that I have to leave now. Someday I will not." He kissed me, was gone.

I finished my drink, more for the orange juice that the vodka. Went to the shower, turned it on. Why the hell did I feel like this? I didn't want to say what I said. It was reflex. Over forty years of training doesn't go away in one night, one week or one month. The shower felt great. 'Feeling wonderful' did have a new standard now. At that I had to laugh out loud. Freaking great sex. With that thought I felt his touch.

The cleaning people had left two white feathers on the pillows. I guess less fattening than chocolates. I didn't even remember my head touching the pillow.

Chapter 36

The house phone woke me. I did not want to move. It went to voicemail. "Vic, it's Mary. You have to call me back when you get up. I'll be home all day." It wasn't a panic call back request. Who knew what time it was. I rolled over, held my big pillow, went back to sleep.

I was slowly coming to the surface when the phone rang again. "Vic, it's Mary again. It's the middle of the afternoon. Give me a call." Ok, now I should get up. Legs to the floor, socks and slippers on, sweat bottoms on, sweatshirt on. Ok, good. I glanced at the clock on the VCR. Well, two isn't bad, certainly not the middle of the afternoon.

I wandered to the kitchen. Looked at the floor from last night. I stepped over it, nothing wrong with it, just didn't want to step on it. Made coffee, realized I was starving. I hadn't eaten yesterday. Made eggs while the coffee dripped. Sat at the bar next to the phone. Ok Mary, now you can tell me what's so important on the second, no third, blue sky day. Could the snow be over for the season?

"Hey Mary. What's up?"

"Finally got your butt out of bed. If I hear right you're eating too."

"Yeah, got up starving. What's so hot that you couldn't call me on the cell?"

"I've tried on the cell since yesterday, you didn't call back." Mary laughed. "Get lucky yesterday? That's the only thing that separates you from your cell. Most of the time anyway." Mary started laughing again. Once I had answered the phone during sex, had a conversation with her. The only reason I hung up? The 'gentleman' I was with said something along the line of 'Victoria, put the damn phone down!' Mary had laughed for a year every time we had talked on the cell. Where the hell was my cell phone anyway? Did I have it yesterday? No.

If she only knew. A guy that could come two, or was it three times, without a break. She would love that. I laughed again. "You wish. I wish. It's somewhere here. I'll find it. So tell me."

"Did you see the horse when I left yesterday?"

"Yeah, when it passed the driveway. Why?"

"It was the guy in Billy's pen and ink. I swear Vic, it was the same guy, with the tattoos and long black hair. No joke."

"No. You're kidding Mary, right? I didn't see him. It was just a guy riding a horse. You have Billy on your brain, that's all."

"He didn't turn into the driveway?"

"Oh, Mary I would have noticed that, come on."

"Could have sworn I saw him turn in. Maybe it was the house next door, but I don't think so."

"Mary, believe me. I would have been on the phone to you. Was your shopping venture successful yesterday?" Subject change.

"You should have come. I would have waited for you to change. Yeah it was. A couple of suits and blouses and some matching slacks. No shoes. But I can find those around here. Want to come out for dinner tonight?"

"Another night yeah, but I enjoyed the great outdoors yesterday and I've got to do laundry and stuff today. Sorry."

"Have you hung the canvas yet?"

"Billy's? Not yet. I can't decide whether to put it in the living room or bedroom. I do like it. The detail is fine…and no, you can't have it back." In case she was having thoughts.

"Wasn't thinking that. Just the guy on the horse, it was the first thing I thought of, that's all. Oh well. See you tomorrow."

"I'll be there. Mary are you doing alright?"

"Oh yeah, I'm doing much better than I thought I would be. No problem."

"You would tell me if you seriously needed company tonight, right?"

"Oh, Vic, sure. No problem. I'll see you tomorrow and find your cell, please."

"Right."

I finished my coffee and eggs; started the cell hunt. Thank heavens it was a short hunt. Next to the computer in the library. The cleaning people must have put it there. Geez, I've got to call Bill and tell him how the

206

showing went. Needed to check on his Closing. Stuff I had planned to do yesterday morning. Called Bill.

"You know I thought about getting an engineer in the other day. Sure. I'll call one of the guys on your list. And by the way, the condo, I love it. Thanks." Bill still sounded happy. Maybe he had wanted out of the marriage too. I glanced at the book I keep for work, notes, conversations, things I need to do. Friday's list had included a call to Karen.

She didn't have a cell so I took a shot at the office. She picked up. "Karen, Hi, this is Victoria Hamilton."

"Hi Victoria. Can we meet this week? I mean he didn't have any issues with the inspection and that was the only condition in the Contract. How about Tuesday? Monday I'm busy."

"So am I. Could we do it on Wednesday about three? I'll check to see if we have a Closing date tomorrow. I'll be more comfortable meeting if we have a Closing date."

"Well, I guess Wednesday is ok."

"Hey, I'm putting the meeting in my calendar, 2:30 or 3:00?" That should leave time for the talk with Georgette.

"Good. That would be good. 2:30. See you then."

I poured another cup of coffee and began to think about the layout of the office. I was going to make some changes. It was my office. I started to sketch. If Mary was going to do our management, she would need more privacy than Mason's old office would give her. Our reception room, the room she was in now, was more private than one would think. Very rarely do Clients, other agents or our Brokers linger in the area. Even in the summer when we are busy, people only passed through. The back offices were more likely to have people staying in one spot for any length of time.

Maybe the thing to do would be to move the workroom to the back of the new offices; convert the current workroom into Mary's office. I'll seriously have to look at the plans tomorrow. Do we need two bathrooms. Did we decide that? I didn't have notes on the meeting. Shit.

When I stood to put my dishes away, the talisman gave off a little buzz, moved, tickled my leg. James was up. I checked the time on the computer, 3:45. He was up late today too. Not just me. What makes the talisman move? Did his move when I thought about him? Did he feed on the Island? Do people truly not remember the event? I would. So many questions. I wondered if he would even come over after my paranoia last night. Victoria, that was really stupid to push him and then get weird. No.

It wasn't. It was just me. I was surprised that I had wanted him to stay. Great lay, but it wasn't that. It was something else. Oh well.

I turned on the computer. First time since when? Thursday? Getting sloppy. Checked my email. An old friend was making a stop in Newport for a few days before going on to Europe. Great. There was a problem with my one and only management property – uck. The basement had flooded in the melt. I'd have to go see it. The owner had a little apartment in the basement for when he was here and that was about once a year.

An email from a couple that I couldn't immediately place. They were coming to Newport the end of May, early June. Wanted to look for a summer condo. Could not remember them. I reached for one of the four membership listings I had for each 'thing' I belonged to. The listings are usually my first hunt for names I couldn't place. The couple was in the third book, the listings for the Order. Still couldn't place them. Carolyn would know who they were. The talisman tickled again. Surprise!

My head knew James was at the garden door. Said he would return today. That he actually showed, hmm. He looked much better than he had when he left.

I smiled. Opened the door. James reached for me, pulled me to him and I was on the receiving end of one of those swallow you down kisses. I stumbled back. "Wow."

"Are we alright?" He was concerned about 'we'. Hell, I was surprised he was here.

"Yes, we are fine. More than fine." I pulled him to me, returned the favor. That definitely felt good. I stepped back into the room. "I just need to finish up some work I was doing. Make yourself, well, at home. Oh and please, make fire." James laughed. He smiled at me often, but actually laugh, not so much. I had heard Johnathan laugh at the car, but I've never seen him laugh. I returned to the library.

I still couldn't remember the email couple. I needed to know before I answered them. I called Carolyn.

"Hi, Carolyn. Can I ask you a question?"

"Sure, what's going on?"

"I've got an email from a couple in the Order. For the life of me I can't put faces to them. They've written like they know me. Winn and Chrissy Wilson. What event do I know them from?"

The phone was quiet for a moment. James joined me in the library, scanning my books. "You know who they are. We sat with them at the funeral in the Castle a few years ago. You loved her jewelry. Remember? You also admired her hat. The Canadians."

"Oh, right, I remember. You're right. The jewelry was like looking in the Winston store window in New York. Thanks. Now I can answer." A phone call with Carolyn is always more than one subject.

"They would be great in Newport. She's a royal you know. They could be Sandcastle Club material. New blood for the summer. Hey, are you alone?"

"No, why?" James was leaning over my shoulder, reading the screen.

"Who? The giver of the anklet?"

How did she know that? "Carolyn, how did you know I wasn't alone. That's weird. Are you getting weird on me?"

"No, I just know he's there. Say hi to him for me. I'll hang up now." And she did. That had to be the fastest Carolyn call ever.

I turned to James. His head was on my shoulder. "She knew you were here."

"Yes. She felt me. She just doesn't know she did. So, this is where you work when you are not in the office. Nice. Your selection of books is interesting. The religious and metaphysical subjects surprise me."

"James. I need to reply to these people then I'll be done. I can't concentrate with you on my shoulder. There's a chair over there."

"Too bad." He tilted my chair back. Ran his hands over my sweatshirt. Held my breasts, leaned down, kissed me. Sent a charge to my toes. Whoa.

"If I get this done now, I can turn it off." If he continued the email wouldn't get done until tomorrow. He allowed the chair to return to its original position. Stood at the window watching the beach.

"You have a limited amount of time."

I returned the email in two paragraphs. If they answered, I'd ask them to give me details of what they wanted. Doing that now, well, I had other priorities.

I clicked off the computer. James was in front of me, hand reaching for my sweatshirt. He hesitated. Looked to my eyes. No words. I smiled. He continued the movement. The sweatshirt and tee were on the floor.

His eyes found my second tattoo. A small vine of peonies next to my left nipple. One hand on my right breast. The other moved a finger over the tattoo, the nipple of the left breast before he took both into his mouth. His touch started the shivers. His tongue, his teeth moving over the nipple turned them into shaking. That kind of stimulation from my breast, that

209

intense, was completely new to me. What was he doing? I was about to lose control.

I broke his rhythm. pulled his tee shirt up to his arms. When he moved back to pull it over his head I slid out of the chair to the floor. James smiled. Lifted me to the edge of the chair securing fingers under the elastic of the pants dropping them before my skin touched the seat. He was on his knees. One hell of a move. His kissing of the inside of my thigh turned my laugh into a gasp, returned the shaking.

James slid his hands under my ass, tilted, licked. The shaking became spasms. My hands went to his hair, his head. My breath became an effort. Second time is usually slower. I was lost, completely - totally lost. "Geez, James, slow down."

He lifted his head. Eyes light. Whites red. "No. This time is mine." He put my hips down, feet on the floor. Stretched his arms, his hands up to my shoulders. James pulled himself slowly up my body. Entered when he reached my mouth. Kissed. Continued the climb until he could go no further, until he tapped the end of me. I grabbed his ass, held tight. I needed a moment, just a moment to catch my breath. When did he lose his pants?

James moved his arms under my shoulders. Pulled me up, out of the chair. My legs wrapped his waist. He lifted. Let me slide his length. I had no breath to release. My arms circled his neck. His hands balanced my ass. He could move me any way he wanted. He did.

James touched places inside of me I didn't know were there. I started sucking, biting his shoulder; something to relieve the building pressure. I moved my hands. Realized I could let go of his neck without interrupting his movements. I could even lean back. Bend, suck his nipple. James moaned louder; moved faster. Gripped me tighter.

"James. Bedroom. Please. I'm going to come."

"Good." He whispered. I crashed. He slowed to feel me grab every inch of him; pull him farther into me. I grabbed his neck. He took in a full breath. Found my mouth; breathed for me. I was going under.

We were in the bedroom before I knew we were moving again. My shoulders, the top of my back were the only things touching the bed. James's hands were on my breasts. I could felt him bend with every thrust; every withdrawal. Was he bending or was my body giving? His eyes were on mine. Pressure building again. The shimmer started slowly. Built. I barely saw the outline of his body. Just his eyes. Felt him inside of me. Felt my point of no return. James lifted me off the bed. Held me against him. Pulled me into the shimmer. My pressure released. I screamed. He screamed his release. I felt it as if I were in his body. Felt his spirits move in my skin. I knew them: the owl, the hawks, a bear, a snake, so many. They joined our release.

I wasn't in my bedroom, in my body. "Let go Victoria." James whispered. I did. We were free, flying, still releasing. I let go of his neck. Felt air on my arms; on my body. James's arms stretched along mine. "Straighten your legs." I released his waist. Didn't fall. My legs stretched to his calves. He was still inside of me; the feeling still rolling through me.

We flew. We turned. Swooped. Never separating. Felt a pull. I was with him in the bedroom, the way we were. My shoulders on the bed, my legs around him, his eyes; red, light. His body thrusting. With his last push the feeling returned. Peaked. Drifted away.

James withdrew. His body slid to the floor. Sat next to my legs, my feet on the floor. I slid off the bed next to him. He started laughing. I started laughing. Couldn't move. My body wasn't working. James turned to look at me. The red fading from his eyes. The light remained. "Victoria, you are truly my love. I can only fly with the missing half of my soul. Did you enjoy?"

"Very much. You were with me. James, you were there." He gave me the most gentle kiss. Stood. Walked to my office; returned with our clothes. I chuckled. "How are you going to get that into your pants?" He remained, well, hard. Yeah, I was smooth.

"Like this." In less time than a blink he was soft. He wasn't circumcised, of course not. Hard he was fully tattooed. Soft he was fully tattooed. I would have to ask how that was done. Not now. Not soon. But sometime. James laughed at my reaction. He had been watching my stare. Had stopped sliding his pants over his hips. I looked away. "Do not be embarrassed Victoria. I am pleased you enjoy my body as I enjoy yours." That helped. I knew I was screaming red but I had to ask the question.

"I know this is probably a personal question, but how do you do that?" My eyes stayed on the floor. If I looked at him...

James lifted my chin so that I was looking into his eyes. "My dear Victoria. Between us there are no questions so personal they can not be asked." He kissed my lips. Straightened. "I slow my heart. No circulation. No erection."

"I have felt your heart beat. I don't think you were hard."

"It's more in the order of heart beating, desire, erection, pleasure, stop heart, lose erection." He was very matter of fact in his tone. No big deal. I was glad of that.

"Thanks. I understand." I put on my sweatshirt.

"Let us move to the large room. I will feed the fire. We can talk." He moved easily. Still shaking, I followed. I sat on the loveseat, he sat on the floor, arm around my leg.

"Victoria. I left you early because I truly did need to feed before sunrise. I need time to feed. Before this morning I could go many days without feeding. It was not a problem. To have sex, to use the energy, I will be required to feed more often. It is my nature. If I do not feed more often it is possible that one day I will not wake. The only reason we could have sex was my need, my desire for you." James thought for a minute. "You overrode my desire to wake. With anyone else I would have stopped. I would have left. Years ago I began to go without release. To channel the energy, the spirits elsewhere…to find you. Am I clear?" Again, just fact.

"Yes, you are more than clear. I was a jerk this morning." Rats. Should I stop talking here or totally embarrass myself? "James. I'm not sure how to say this but If you had been someone else I wouldn't have been able to get you out the door fast enough." Couldn't be any more truthful than that.

"May I see some of your life?"

I thought about that. Did I want him peering into my knickers? Into my life? "Are you sure you want to know about it?"

"I will do it the way I saw your dream. I will only see the pictures. I will not invade your feelings. It will help me…" James again thought about what he would say. "…understand you better. Where you have been to come to now. To be who you are in this life."

"James. No one knows all of my life. Some know pieces. If all the pieces were put together it would still contain decade gaps. I like it like that. You are asking for a lot." Too early for a drink.

"Victoria. I do not relate well to my own family. To people I have lived with since their birth. I do not see as others do. I do not experience as others do. My request is to be able to understand your reference points. So that I may be able to communicate with you. What I see stays with me. I do not share us." My insides started to shake.

"Do I have to live through it again? Once was too much James. What if you see something you don't like?" He hesitated. I took a breath, then another. If I had walked into my life a week ago, I would have walked out. James was still here.

"I will move very fast. No. Your life is yours Victoria." James moved his hand over the talisman. "Nothing will surprise me Victoria. We are here, now. Before is only reference. It is only coming to now."

"Ok. Someday you will share with me?" I wasn't jumping up and down about it. There were things I wasn't sure I wanted him to see.

I sat in front of James. "Victoria. At the time you will be able to look I will share." An answer to my question that I would have to think about.

James adjusted us. We touched even more. I have no idea where he found the space. He took me to the stillness. I felt the touching inside of me. More than before. The pictures started flipping quickly. Faster. Until the pictures were a deck of cards being shuffled.

James slowed at points, then moved before I could see the picture; figure out what had caught his attention. It didn't take as long as I thought it would. The very last he slowed on.

The last wasn't from me. The pictures were his. His feelings, his views. The first meeting at the house. The pain he was feeling. His horrible homesickness before his first touch of my hand. The cure. The joy. The security. In Jay's office when Johnathan signed the Contract. His overwhelming desire to just let it all go, release his control.

Honestly, I didn't believe I was capable of that kind of depth. I truly did not believe it was in me to live with that kind of pain. I couldn't honestly understand it. Why did he leave me with it?

"Thank you." His touch withdrew from the inside of me. James did not talk about what he had seen. He spoke of last night. "You wanted me to stay with you last night Victoria. I truly did need to feed. I am also afraid. Afraid that if I die in your bed. I grow cold. You will leave. You will run from me." His frankness surprised me.

"James, I don't think I'll freak out. The only way to know what will happen is to stay. When you are comfortable enough to stay, stay. No matter what happens in my bed, I know it is you. You will be back. Is there anything I need to change in here for you to be more comfortable?" He laughed.

"You mean coffin, dirt, lightproof room, remove mirrors? No. Your home is fine." James stood, added more wood to the fire. "The cord is almost gone. I will have wood added to the stack outside."

"I can order more. Not a problem." I offered.

"Victoria, please, stop."

"Stop what?" I had not a clue.

"You wanted to pay the women that cleaned. I tell you that I will stock your cord wood. You say you will order more. I tell you these things will be done. They should not be your concern. Your concerns, your actions are of other things. There are others in this world whose concerns are of cleaning and providing wood; as yours are of other things." James returned to the floor wrapping his arm tighter around my leg looking up at me.

"James, explain please. These are things I have done for myself most of my life. I don't understand." I really… "Are you talking karma?"

He thought for a moment. Straightened himself so that he was watching me. "The way you understand the word, yes. But I would add to your understanding one thing."

"Please."

"A being doing the karma, relieving their burden, is a great thing, Victoria. Allowing the karma to be done is, in itself, the elimination of karma also. The being allowing the karma to be eliminated is also allowing a burden of their own to be eliminated. Do you understand? Am I being clear?"

It took a second. "I do. It makes perfect sense. How did I miss that after all these years?"

"Many, many times we are so concerned about ourselves. Our own burdens. We forget the burdens of others."

"Thank you James. I understand the immediate point you are making, but it goes much further. I'll have to give it some thought." I was shaking my head, laughing to myself. So simple. "Please. Do what needs to be done."

"You understand. Reading your life helped me to understand what you were saying." Then almost to himself. "Much easier."

"I would like to ask if we have made love like this before?"

"No. Not like this. Victoria, did you enter me, feel what I felt? Feel my spirits move across your skin?"

"Yes. Did you enter me?"

"Yes."

"Has this ever happened to you?" I was curious.

"No…some I could surround with the spirits. But no, nothing this complete. I will have to give this thought. I could fly myself. I have never brought anyone with me. We slipped into the heavens. I am curious only as to why this has happened with you. What is it about you that allowed us to do such an amazing thing. Did it make you uncomfortable, fearful?"

"No, it was amazing. I would be interested in what you learn. Another question if you don't mind? Am I boring you with these questions James?"

214

"No. It is good that you ask rather than make assumptions."

"Did you go into the City to feed after you left this morning?"

He looked down. I think he was debating the subject, not the specific question. His eyes looked back to me. "No. People at the house will allow me to feed from them. Would it have bothered you if I had?"

I needed to give him more than a one word answer. "James. I was purely curious. Like asking me if I use chop sticks when I eat Chinese food. I understand the implications of that part of you. Yes. I use chop sticks. No it doesn't bother me in the least." James stood in front of me, leaned down, kissed me.

Still standing over me he moved his mouth close to my ear. "Would it bother you if, someday, I asked to feed from you?"

I thought for a moment. He didn't move. "No. I don't think so. Ask sometime, we'll see." It was the best I could do. Thoughts of the last fight with my third started seeping into my head.

"Victoria, those thoughts are so hateful. I cannot help but know them. He was a very sad man. Let the things he said to you go free so that they can return to him." James kissed me again, took the thoughts from me.

"What did you just do?" I asked.

"Moved the thoughts to the back of your mind. That is all." James gently pulled me to my feet. "Victoria, before I leave, may I share your bed?"

Then I could fall asleep with his smell? Oh yeah. "James, let me set the alarm on my phone. Yes, I'll meet you in the bedroom." Nice.

By the time I walked into the bedroom he was lying on the bed. Clothes gone. Eyes with light watching me. Lips with a slight smile. His heart beating. I lost my sweats as fast as I could. His arms moved around me as I lay down. Pulled me to him. On our sides, face to face. The softest kisses. The slowest touches. I allowed myself to feel his body as I touched him, kissed him; combed his hair with my fingers, looked deeply into his eyes. His caresses were gentle, loving, not missing an inch of me. We were both craving when he lifted my top leg, entered me, pushed my breath out as a gasp.

James moved slowly. I moved slowly. Our eyes stayed together, locked on each other. He rolled me to my back. Moved a little faster. I matched his movement. The pressures started to build in both of us. I ran my hands down his back. Pressed him to me ever so slightly. James's movement increased. His touch remained gentle. I did not think that the crest of our release would be as high. But when it broke over both of us, it was total, complete. Everything I had emptied into him. Everything he had emptied in to me. His eyes flashed so brightly that I saw those little black dots.

James moved his head to my ear. "Victoria. I love you." He slid off of me. Out of me. Held me against him. No breath. No heartbeat. I started to fall asleep. When I was in that completely relaxed limbo, James leaned over me. "I must leave now. May I return tomorrow?"

Without opening my eyes I held his arms around me. "Yes." I was asleep before he left the bed.

Chapter 37

I woke with the sound of the cell phone. I reached to the nightstand, answered the phone. When it rang in my ear I realized the ringing was its alarm not a call. It took a minute to remember why I had set the cell. My simple, analog, travel alarm clock had been demolished. Well, at least I set something. I rolled over, smelling James on the linens. How nice. These sheets won't get changed for a while. I was rested, awake, but had quite the time tearing myself away from where his body had lain last night.

Finally, the reason for the alarm came to mind. Office design, contractor, in early. Rats. I rolled out of bed. Realized I hadn't made coffee. Dragged myself to the kitchen. Made the 'get it together nectar', checked voice mail and email while it brewed. The tenants of the management property had called again. I wrote a note to stop by this afternoon.

Mary was quite surprised to see me at 11am. I was surprised to see everyone in the office.

"Mary, can you get me both sets of drawings? I want to look at them again. Also the sketches from last week if you have them." Might as well see everything.

"Victoria, they're in the break room. Everyone wanted to look at them before the contractor came."

What? "Mary, you and I will speak to the contractor. Do they think they are in on the meeting?" I hoped not.

"Well, we thought…." Mary started.

"No Mary. Why don't you come into my office with everything. I'm just going to grab coffee." I did not remember inviting everyone to our little meeting. Probably, just a misunderstanding. I retrieved my coffee, returned to my desk. Mary came in soon after.

217

"Did I leave an impression that all were invited to this meeting?" I asked Mary after she had settled in her chair.

"Well, yeah Victoria after you said we'd go with the ideas they suggested last week. And then Mason and I talked about it over the weekend."

Now I understood. Classic Mason. He was cashing in on the full 15% of his commission that stayed with the office. I'd offered to take less given the amount. Mason had said take the full fifteen percent. I should have known. Well. If push came to shove, I'd write a check for an additional five percent. Now I'd have to talk to Mason, power hungry bastard. I must have smiled at that thought.

"What's funny Vic?"

"Nothing. Wait here a minute Mary. I'll be right back." I went out to the others. Explained that there must have been a misunderstanding about the meeting; revoked the imagined invitation as nicely as I could. Mason grumbled as expected. Nina said she had come in early for nothing. Ames didn't say a word. I returned to my office.

"Mary." I said. "I own 95% of this little operation. You own 5%. We provide legitimacy and structure around the others' businesses. That is it. Nothing more. Remember that. Now, let's look at the redesign concepts again."

We moved everything off of my desk and spread out every piece of paper we had on the two plans. I explained to her what I had been thinking. She hadn't thought about my concerns until I brought them up, but agreed that privacy in Mason's old space could be a problem.

We started measuring. Between the architects ruler we retrieved from the workroom and measuring with our feet, we worked out some possibilities. The heavy glass block we had used around the office to allow light in was also pretty good at insulating sound. If we cut the existing workroom space in half, used the wall construction that my office had for a three-quarter wall topped with the glass block for the office/bathroom wall; beefed up the existing wall to the other offices. We could create a relatively secure office for Mary. Moving the workroom to the other side, behind the conference room would still leave room for two more broker offices; Mason's and a broker to be named later. It could work. I was satisfied. Mary was satisfied.

Mary and I then discussed the job descriptions she had developed. She saw herself with the financials but gradually moving the advertising to Georgette, if she worked out. As long as Mary held the financials, I was good.

"So you think we should pick up Georgette? I have some concerns."

"Vic, what are your concerns? We'll have the only PhD as a receptionist...ever. I don't think I'll have to spend too much time teaching her the telephones."

"Mary. You know as well as I do that one person, even a receptionist, can break a real estate office. I've seen it happen. I just don't want another person peering into the knickers of the business. What's her relationship with Mason like? Do you know?"

"From what I've seen, it's good but not too close. Not weird close." She thought about it a little longer. "I understand what you're getting at. Individual broker's confidentiality. I've got it. I don't know. But it doesn't matter who we bring in, until tried we won't know about them either."

Mary had a point. Maybe I'm just a little paranoid with Mason. I've known him too long not to understand that Mason, above all, is a gunner for Mason. Mason needs to be the center, the top banana, the highest earner. I understood this when he asked to come with me.

"You're probably right Mary. Let's see how Wednesday goes. Do you want to sit in?" I most definitely would have to talk to Mason before Wednesday.

"If you want me. I assume anyone in the receptionist slot you want to bring in as an independent contractor, right?"

"Yeah, why don't you plan on sitting in. Thirty days enough time to pull a salesman's license?" I asked.

"If she can start classes next Tuesday, yeah. I don't think another set starts until June. Do you think a receptionist needs to have a license?"

"She will if she's going pick up what you do. Even playing receptionist you hunt info on our listings. Unlicensed, she wouldn't be able to do that. Not the way you do." I gave it another moment's thought. "No, anyone will have to be licensed. We're not going to get caught in that little legal trap."

I watched an unlicensed receptionist give a State regulator a detailed description of a property including the status of a swimming pool. She was fine until she started talking about the actual condition of the property, its beach sand foundation, the condition of the pool equipment. She didn't get prosecuted but the agency paid an $8,000 fine. Fifteen years ago that was big bucks. No, we're not going there.

"Vic, I want to grab a sandwich across the street before the contractor gets here. Can I bring anything back for you?"

"No, I'm good. Mary, you realize that anything we discuss stays here.

That's what makes this whole thing work, right?" I had to say it. I didn't care what relationship was developing between her and Mason, but I had to reconfirm.

"Right Vic. I know that. I'll be right back."

I phoned the Closing lawyer for Bill's condo. Closing next Tuesday. Then called Karen and confirmed our meeting 2:30 Wednesday. I started to go see if Mason was still here when I felt the talisman send its little shock, then tickle my leg. James was up.

Mason was on his phone. I waved at him, walked back to my office. Ten minutes later he came in.

"What's up Victoria?" He sat down.

"Mason. I have this feeling that a little power struggle is starting between you and me. Is it?"

"Not that I know of Victoria." He looked through me as he spoke. Oh Mason, don't do this.

"Are you having second thoughts about the 5% you left in the office? It is a chunk of change, but I'm sure you know that."

"Maybe a little, but I'll get over it." Mason leaned back in the chair, putting his ankle on his knee. Mason had a 'tell'. That thing people do that gives them away when they're playing cards or just out and out lying. I'd seen him do it more than once when he sidestepped the Admirals in Washington. He was doing it now.

"Mason, are you still happy here? Is something going on?"

""No. Nothing like that. I just haven't been away in over a year. I think I need a break. That's all. You know me Victoria. I have delusions of grandeur when I don't get away. When I'm tired. It's been too long."

"Wow, it's been that long? Can you do something before the first of May? If it were me I wouldn't last that long. It'd seem like an eternity."

"I was thinking of just doing some wandering for a month and end up at the race. Would that be too long Victoria?" Now that we were getting to the bottom of this, Mason uncrossed his leg, sat up straight in his chair. Ha.

"Mason, if something happens I can always cover for you. Remember, you taught me how to 'fake it'. Worst case, hop a plane back. No big deal."

"Thanks Victoria. I appreciate it." Mason left my office.

Geez, I was thinking I was going to lose Mason in a big brawl. As I thought about it, I should have seen it, the beginning of burnout. How had I missed Mason's 'no vacation'? Ames had gone to the West Coast for two weeks around Christmas and Nina had spent the holidays in Europe some place. Mary and Billy had gone to Aspen skiing in January for a few weeks with the dogs. I smiled at the thought. That had resulted in some funny pictures. I went to Florida in the fall, second trip last year. But Mason hadn't gone anywhere.

I wondered, as we get a little bigger, if I will be able to be as aware of my Brokers as I am now. Or would my business concept for this office start breaking down. I know there is a 'critical mass' somewhere. I just would rather not find it.

Mary tapped on the door and my cell rang simultaneously. I waved her in, the contractor followed. I checked the caller ID for the cell.

"Hi Bill. I called to tell you that we have a Closing next Tuesday. 1:00 good for you?" I asked.

"Great Victoria. That will be great. The engineer said he would have something back to me in writing. Estimates and all by Friday. I didn't expect response that fast. Your name is golden in his office. I was getting the runaround until I mentioned your name. Anyway, we're cooking."

"You called Frank. Yeah, we get along pretty well. I look forward to seeing his thoughts. Oh, and I'll get the numbers to you mid-week by email if you don't mind." Oh Frank. Frank and I had quite the exciting couple of months a few years ago. When it ended he was so worried someone would find out about it – worried that I would talk. I do get fast service when I call him. What the hell.

"Victoria, you remember Joe." Mary said.

"Sure do remember Joe. We're sitting in your work." Joe and I shook hands before he took the second chair. Joe was a classic contractor for this area. Small, about 5'5'; graying brown hair; heavily tanned skin; maybe 67-68 years old and many, many children, five or six. Uncounted grandchildren. "I'm sure Mary talked to you about what we want to do. I wanted to walk you through our ideas, get your thoughts and get an estimate. Sound good?"

"Sure Mrs. Hamilton. So you're adding the space next door?" More confirmation than question.

Before Mary and I started sharing our thoughts, Joe took a hard look at the plans we had. When he looked up, the fun began. We talked. He talked. Yes this was possible. No, he would do it like this. It was fun and before we knew it, both sets of drawings were marked up and we had a plan. Joe took the drawings to his 'guy' to draw out the final and would get it back to us with some numbers in 'a couple of days'.

Joe had a 'guy' for everything. The final work was good. Permits always pulled. Inspections on time - never kicked back. Couldn't argue. I was feeling better about the space addition.

I started to make notes about the day's events before I went to investigate the flooded basement when Carolyn called.

"How are you doing Carolyn?" Rare for her to call me in the middle of the day.

"Vicky, I just got the strangest phone call from that weird guy that does the cemetery ghost tours. He asked me if I had the names of the real buyers of Ledge House. Of course I said no. Then he asked if, since I was friends with you, I could get them for him." Carolyn was talking fast, obviously upset.

"Slow down Carolyn. That Kenny guy?"

"Yeah, that guy."

"Carolyn, he's a joke. He probably wants to use the names in his little tour. Don't worry about it. Is that all he said?"

"He said that if I didn't do what he asked everyone I knew would rot in hell." Carolyn was verging on hysterical. Unfortunately, I chuckled.

"Honey. If he was serious about this he would be calling me. He hasn't. If he calls you again, just hang up the phone. Everyone's fine. Don't worry about it, ok?" I wasn't sure that was going to work. Once Carolyn is upset, it takes a while for her to calm down. "Do you need me to come by?"

"Could you?" Yeah. I needed to put this to bed.

"Sure. I've got to check out a flooded basement then I'll stop by. We'll have a drink. That good with you?"

"Could you stay for dinner?" Knew she would ask.

"I can't tonight. I've got some work to do before tomorrow. Let me get going so I can get to your house. OK?"

"OK. I'll see you soon."

I stood outside my little management property. Actually not so little. Close to 4,000 square feet, three apartments, next to an old graveyard about three blocks from the remnants of the first Quaker Meeting House. The house had originally been much smaller. Built by a carpenter that made coffins for everyone in the area a little more than 130 years ago. Over the years he had added the upper two floors. More recently, maybe fifty years ago, a poured concrete basement and all of the modern necessities had been added.

I returned to the car, retrieved my faithful pink rubber boots and set out to investigate. It was flooded. About 2 feet flooded. I moved slowly through the water to the cistern that remained. The water was going nowhere. The Owner's little apartment could be lost. I'd never received keys to the apartment. I'd never had a need for them. The Owner was not going to be a happy camper.

I was surprised that when I entered the utility area the gas heating systems - there were four - and the water heaters were safe on their cinder blocks. As poured, the basement slanted slightly to the cistern and saved the utilities.

I stood in the side yard and tried to track down the property's plumber. Three calls and all I could do was leave voicemail. Oh well. I left a note in the door of the first floor apartment to let them know I had been by.

When Carolyn opened her door I asked to use her computer before I noticed how pale she was. "Carolyn. What happened? Did he call again?"

"Two more times. I let them go to the machine so you could hear them." She went to play the messages for me.

"Why don't you make me a screwdriver and I'll listen." She didn't need to hear the messages again. Who knows how many times she'd played them already. I pushed the flashing light.

"Carolyn, I know you have the names. Give me a call." He left a number. "Cheryl isn't doing too well, that could be you." The second message was essentially the same. Kenny has been on this Island his whole life. I knew his brother, nice guy, but Kenny was always a little strange. His latest thing, the past few years, was that he was a vampire and the only one qualified to do cemetery tours. If it wasn't upsetting Carolyn as much as it was, I'd have been laughing. I deleted the calls as she returned with drinks.

"Thanks. He's finally gone over the edge Carolyn. If you weren't so upset we'd both be laughing."

"Vicky, I can't take another call." She probably couldn't. Carolyn was probably as close to an Aunt as I would ever have. I needed to stop this.

"Carolyn, how about if I disconnect the machine. When the phone rings, if you don't recognize the number, punch the speak button twice real fast. That will disconnect the call. Do you think that would work for you?" She thought for a minute.

"Well...." The phone rang again. I thought about picking it up, maybe I could deflect.

I picked it up. "Hello".

"Carolyn?"

"No. Is this you Kenny?"

"Who is this?" Yea, it was Kenny.

"Kenny, this is Mrs. Hamilton. You should have called me to get this information. Good God, have some class."

"Well, then give me the names of the guys who bought Ledge House. I know you have them. Victoria, it is for the good people of the Island."

"Why do you need their names?"

"I can't send them away without their names. You know what they are. I know you do." Kenny was getting a little angry.

"Yeah, I do. They are people with the money to enjoy a beautiful property Kenny."

"They're monsters. You probably got them to buy it."

"Are you saying I'm a monster Kenny?" What the hell.

"You must be. You brought them here." I probably shouldn't have started this, but I'd rather he bugged me than Carolyn.

"Get a grip Kenny." I hung up the phone. My cell rang. "Hamilton here."

"Don't you ever hang up on me or I will send you away too. Better, I'll kill you all." I punched the end button. Kenny was going over the deep end.

"Well Carolyn. He'll probably start bugging me now. You may be in the clear."

"Thank you. I don't know what I would have done if you hadn't come over." Carolyn took a good big swallow of her drink.

"Can I quickly use your computer?" I started walking to the stairs.

"Sure, why?" Carolyn followed me.

"Just need to send a quick email to the owner of the flooded basement. Have you been in yours recently?"

"The wench did laundry yesterday. She would have told me if there was water." 'The wench' is Carolyn's pet name for her cleaning lady. Carolyn loves her cleaning lady. I wondered what she calls me when I'm not around.

"Good. It'll just take a minute." I swung my legs onto her bed without thinking and started accessing my email accounts.

"Vicky, what is going on?" Carolyn was looking at the tattoo. "How far up does that thing go?" She reached for the hem of my skirt, pulled it up. "Victoria." My full name. "It's all the way up your leg." Carolyn touched it. "It's got magic in it." She looked at me, shocked. "What are you into?" I continued to type while I thought.

224

"Carolyn, we can talk about it another time, ok. It's not anything bad. I promise you. I would tell you if I had a problem. I always do. In the meantime, just trust me. I will tell you." I clicked send. "I'm still going to disconnect your machine before I leave." I picked up her phone. "Press like this." I pressed talk twice. "That will disconnect the call."

"Yeah, sure. Give me a call tomorrow ok?"

I leaned over to kiss her cheek. "Will do. Call me if you need me." I went downstairs, disconnected the machine. Locked her door on the way out. I did not have a clue what I was going to tell her about the tattoo.

I was driving home when it occurred to me that I was starving. I was going to have to eat earlier in the day. The thought of cooking and eating with James in the house bothered me. Odd.

I pulled into my favorite Italian place. Ordered an antipasto to go and a glass of wine while I waited. No matter what I ordered to take out from this restaurant it took twenty five minutes. The Chinese place took ten to fifteen, the Steak House was twenty. To me cooking in general was a pain in the ass. Take-out, well, I figured I had at least nine personal chefs in the area. My cell rang. Should have turned it off while I was waiting. I checked the number and sent it to my voice mail. Kenny.

I changed clothes, took the salad to the library and had a working dinner. The plumber called and would go check the basement tomorrow. I told him to go ahead, pump it, everything was open, which reminded me to call the first floor guy to tell him I had left the basement access open intentionally. In real estate it was never just one phone call.

I finished my notes. Realized I would have to set the cell alarm again. Forgot to pick up a travel alarm. Checked my email, answered a couple including the Wilson's from the Order. Actually looked at the calendar on my desk. I hadn't flipped the month, still February. I flipped to March and matched it with the one in my bag. Board meeting Tuesday, five pm; Committee meeting Thursday, noon. Now, if I could remember to match the bag calendar with the one on my desk at work, I would be in good shape.

It was time to listen to Kenny's message, put it off as long as I could. Actually it was Kenny's number but not him on the message.

"Mrs. Hamilton, this is Father William. Kenny has asked me to contact you. He seems very concerned that you have provided a home to some unsavory spirits whose current names you will not divulge. Would you be so kind as to return this call." He left his number. What the hell?

Kenny had made those calls in a church? The cell rang before I could save the message. I answered the call. The message wasn't going anywhere.

"Mrs. Hamilton. This is Father William. Did you get my message?"

"Just now. Why are you calling me?"

"Kenny seems concerned about your recent sale and…"

I interrupted him. "Listen Father, I don't know how well you know Kenny but he's a little off the wall on this. He's harassing an elderly woman. Actually threatening her. I told him and I will tell you" He interrupted me.

"Mrs. Hamilton I find Kenny to be a reputable soul and I do believe he…"

I interrupted him. "What church are you with Father?"

"I am a fully ordained priest of the Church of Heavenly Cleansing Mrs. Hamilton. Recognized by the Federal Government. I assure you that my credentials are impeccable. If you would just give me the names of the residents of the house I will be able to do my job."

Oh, this was good. It doesn't get much better. I was writing as he was talking. "Listen Father Willy, you and Kenny are absurd." I clicked the end button noticing the sun was just about set. Looked at the time. James was running rather late. Well, I know what that's like. As soon as I had the thought the talisman moved.

James was standing at the garden door, with the horse. He wasn't hiding. That was becoming important to me. The minute I saw him I wanted to pull him in, strip him and have my way with him. No, that wasn't going to happen. "Would you like to ride?" He stepped in for a kiss.

"At night, fun. I need to grab some warm stuff. Come on in. I'll be just a minute." I moved as fast as I could, grabbed anything I could find to put on. Long sleeved tees, heavy sweater, tights under dead of winter sweat pants, two pairs of socks, heavy hiking shoes, scarf and beret. That should do it. I tied my hair back. Returned to the living room in probably three minutes.

"Victoria. You are wearing your closet." James was laughing. "I don't know if I can lift you to the horse."

I looked at him for a second. "Nice, you look lovely too. I do believe you have an advantage. It's chilly out here." Probably about 40-45 I guessed, hoping for the high side.

"You should ride behind me. Is that alright?"

"Sure, like before." This time he was on the horse before I had registered

226

movement. His arm reached down to me. I hoped I could do this again. He pulled me up with a little swing that stopped when my left leg touched the side of the horse. I dropped into place. That's how he did it. James felt my leg touch the horse. I settled in behind him, my arms around his stomach. We started to move.

James stopped, held my arms and pulled me closer, tighter to him. "Much better. I love to feel you against me when we ride." I hadn't realized there was a breath between us, but he did move us tighter. Geez, he felt so good.

James walked the horse up the gravel driveway and on to the road, a little faster than before. He held the reins with one hand, guided the horse with his legs. As soon as we were off paved road he released the reins and we picked up speed. At the top of the quarry we moved east along the property line of Ledge House picking up one of the Sanctuary trails and rode the trail north.

We passed the clearings that contained the Sanctuary's various buildings and barns. Lights were on and cars were parked in the visitor's lot. James didn't seem concerned that we would be seen. When the Sanctuary's property ended we started moving on property lines. We wove around fences like he had ridden this a hundred times.

"Victoria. We will be doing some small jumps, just hold on." The horse started to speed up. Sure enough, we started jumping some of the lower fences. The first two caught me by surprise. I forced myself to relax, move with James and the horse. It was fun. I guess I was paying more attention this time. It occurred to me that it was like a motorcycle. If I was the rider I needed to relax into the movement, not stiffen. This was much more fun. From the side of the rise we were on, I could follow where we were. Many times I knew whose property lines we were riding.

We reached Green End Avenue, walked across the asphalt, entered another path I'd never noticed. Picked up speed to what I though was as fast as the horse could go. I was wrong. As soon as the trees cleared, the horse moved faster. Frankly, I was thrilled. The air was cold but the number of stars, I couldn't get over the number of stars. The people in their houses were oblivious to the beauty of the early spring night sky.

James slowed as we approached the top of Quaker Hill, where we had stopped before. My arms were free. James was off the horse waiting for me to slide down before I had realized we had stopped. I slid, he caught me. Removed the blankets from the horse, laid them on the ground. Removed the reins from the horse, began rubbing him down with a third blanket.

There was a third blanket? When he was satisfied he released the horse to wander.

"The sky is beautiful tonight, the air is clear, you are with me. Are you cold Victoria?"

"I'm good. It's not summer, but worth every second."

James sat in front of me, faced me. He slid his legs under mine, around my back. I held him with my knees at his hips, my feet at his back. He put his arms around my shoulders, hands moving against my back. My hands moved around his chest to his back. His eyes were nothing but black and light; more light that the stars in the sky. James started to talk.

"I am going to have to travel for the next few days Victoria. I must visit one of our labs to hear their progress. The lab is in Europe. It is an obligation I must perform. Please do not fault me for leaving." He was looking into my eyes. Looking at my face, So serious, so intense.

"James." I smiled at him. "I was wondering when you would have to go back to work. Did you think I thought you did nothing before you came here? That I though you sat in your little world playing with yourself?" Oh tacky. "Sorry, didn't mean it to sound so crass."

He laughed. His shoulders dropped. He relaxed. "I did not know what you would think."

"You flipped through my head, you didn't figure that out?" I was a bit surprised.

"Victoria, I did exactly what I said I would do. I saw your life. Nothing more. I saw your reactions to events but have no idea what your feelings were. How can I put this?" He thought for a moment. "I saw pictures, heard words. I have none of your real emotions to what I saw. All I know is what was said. Not what was truly felt. What you thought. Like a very bad play. Think of Shakespeare without emotion to the words spoken."

"Really? I know what you told me, but honestly I thought you had it all."

"No, not your emotions or the emotions of the other people as you saw them. That forever is yours unless you allow me. So, I ask again, are you concerned that I will be gone?"

Learn, learn, learn. That is all I can do. "No James, I'm not concerned unless you are. But now I'm curious. What is your business?" I had to ask. It's the first time it had come up. "I am very interested."

"You are...interested?" He stopped speaking for a moment. "This particular trip will involve review of some research we have funded."

"More bait. You have given me more bait. What's the research, who's

228

doing it? You own a lab? What kind of lab? Now you have to tell all." I started to laugh.

"More?" He asked. From the look on his face he was surprised I'd asked.

"Hasn't anyone else you've been with asked, been interested?"

"Been with?" Was he stalling?

"You haven't been in an isolation chamber for I don't know how many years James. You've have relationships before this...spent time with women, men." I shrugged my shoulders. "No one has asked, been interested." Naïve I am not.

"Victoria, you surprise me. I have been waiting for the question of other relationships. You have made a very large assumption and do not seem to be bothered by your assumption. In all my years this truly is a first. Thank you.

"No. No one has been interested beyond asking to accompany me. Can they shop while I am in the boring meetings." He leaned to me placing a wonderfully soft kiss at my neck; laying his head on my shoulder. I tightened my hold on him. Held him. If I hadn't been touching him, I would have though he was gone for those few minutes.

James pressed tighter against my neck. Licked its pulse, kissed. "Are you cold?" He looked, sounded almost drugged. I wondered if he'd bitten me. Was that what he was like after he'd fed?

"I'm a bit chilly, but good. You know I'm not going to let the topic of your business go, right?"

"Yes. I am glad to share it with you." He was brightening, coming back to himself as he spoke. "I just do not want you to get too cold. We will start back. I will make a fire." James started to pull his legs out from under mine. I pulled him back, gave him a hard kiss, let him go.

The horse returned, uncalled. James returned the blankets to his back, ground side up. Returned the reins. "I would love to have you in front of me on the way back Victoria. You will be warmer behind me." He was on the horse reaching for me. Third time and I hadn't flipped over the other side of the horse. The thought was too funny to hold. James turned to me while he was pulling me closer.

"I'm laughing because I am amazed that I haven't flipped off the other side of your horse in three mounts. This is a surprise to me." James smiled. We were moving at speed on the Greenway path; walked across the road, slower on the trail to the quarry. James continued to my condo with the horse.

He took the horse around to the garden door. I did my slide. "Victoria, do you have a very large pot?"

A big pot. Me? Oh, water for the horse. "Let me see if I have something big enough." A bit of digging. Yes, there it was in its own cabinet. A huge stainless steel 'steamer' pot. I used it once a year for a little party that included steamers, lobsters and anything else that sound like it would be good in the pot. A party? Hadn't used the pot since I'd moved from the house. "I think I've got one that will do. I've got to fill it in the bathroom. Just a second." It fit in the tub but I had to use the shower head to fill it.

"Tepid water, not cold." James walked into the bathroom, checked the water temperature, made an adjustment. "Water this time of the year is too cold for him. I rubbed him down with the blankets. He'll be fine."

"If you want to wrap the reins over the door latch go ahead. The cliff is not animal friendly."

"He will stay where I put him." James took the pot out, returned with his arms full of logs. Started to lay the fire.

I went to remove some of my layers; maybe even run a brush through my hair. I got to the tights. Felt an extra pair of hands sliding inside the tights, around to the tops of my legs. One hand worked its way between my legs; the other moved under my breasts, bending me back. His clothes gone. His heart was beating wildly. I could feel him against me, hard, ready. Geez. All James had to do was touch me. I was way past ready.

I turned. James relaxed his hold, moved his free hand into the tights. Facing him. Eyes red. The black overshadowed by light. More light than I'd seen. I pulled off my two tees and the sweater, tossing them somewhere. I reached to remove the tights. James leaned to my ear. "Let me do it." He dropped to his knees. Eased the tights lower; kissing, licking every inch of the way. When his tongue replaced his hand, his fingers, I had to grab his shoulders to steady.

James tapped one leg, I lifted my foot. "James slow just a bit." He moved my legs farther apart. I felt his tongue enter me. "James."

"Go." James tightened his hold. "Go."

"I'll fall." He said nothing. Moved to the sweet spot. Secured his hold. Sucked harder. I had no choice. He sucked long, hard. My whole body wanted to give way, let go. Drop. I held on. A deep moan left my throat. I slid slowly through his arms until I was on my knees, his arms under my arms. He laid us on the floor. Held me. Gave me time to recover.

"Our bodies are all illusion Victoria. Let go when we make love. You are holding back. I will not let you be hurt." He kissed me. Moved to my neck with his tongue, kissed my pulse. I reached circling my fingers around him, he was wet. James had come with me. Enjoyed his efforts. I hadn't touched him. I gave him a light squeeze. He sucked sharply on my nipple. We began again as if never before.

Explorations, kisses, nibbles, small bites. I was sitting on him, he was inside of me. "Victoria. Look at your thigh." What? I looked. Stopped moving. My tattoo didn't. The tattoos on the left side of his body, the animals, the spirits were sliding over, under, around the vine of roses on my right leg. I could feel them moving, almost playing around the vine, the roses. My only thought: 'that's interesting'. I laughed.

James pulled me down to him. Rolled me to my back. Thrust into me, withdrew, thrust harder. "Ride with me Victoria." The release was there. I felt him come with me. He slowed, stopped, kissed me like he would swallow me.

A thrust, withdrawal not complete. A thrust and it was there again as strong as the first. I felt him as strong as the first but he didn't slow. Didn't stop. For both of us, wave after wave. My heart was going to burst. How long could I continue without it bursting?

James slowed. Slowed to a stop. Too much. I had to move. I started laughing, pushed him off of me. Rolled to my side. Grabbed the wall. Balanced slowly, stood. Staggered to the bathroom. My knees started to give. James had his arms under my shoulders. Slowed my drop. I leaned my head over the toilet, lost dinner. I was laughing, throwing up, laughing. James wet a towel, lifted my hair and wiped the wet towel over my body.

I was still laughing when I pulled my head out of the toilet. Way too sexy. Every time I started to move I started to laugh my body shook, I gagged. Finally, I took in the biggest breath I could, held it, let it out slowly. My body calmed down.

James wet the towel again, handed it to me. I wiped my face, my neck. When I got to my breast, its tattoo had wrapped my nipple, started to my shoulder. I looked to my thigh. The vine had made a last twist around the top of my thigh. Had moved into parts of me too tender for tattoo. I looked at James, shook my head, smiled. "Now. We really need to talk." He didn't return the smile. Turned, walked out, returned with our clothes. I brushed my teeth. Splashed my face with water. When I looked into the mirror, James was behind me. He had no idea what I was going to say… or do. His expression started edging to panic.

I turned to him, put my hand to his jaw. "James, you look as though your last horse was just shot out from under you." I shook my head. "You look…worried. Don't be. We just need to talk." I went to my toes, gave him a kiss. Better. He relaxed a little. We dressed in silence, returned to the living room. At some point he had added logs to the fire. When did he do that?

"Do you want a drink Victoria?"

"Not after that. I'm fine." He was, what, pacing in front of the fireplace. "James, what the hell, calm down. You weren't this tense when you showed yourself to me."

"Victoria. I am sorry. I am so sorry."

"About what?" I started to sit on the loveseat…no - not the loveseat. I sat on the floor. That stopped him. He sat next to me, tentatively put his hand on my leg. I put my hand over his, squeezing, holding, intertwining his fingers.

"I am so sorry Victoria."

"James stop saying that. Just tell me, come out and tell me."

He thought for a moment. "Your spirits are returning to you. They have also found you. I had hoped maybe some months, maybe years from now they would. That we would have talked about the possibility. That we would have talked about other things. Many other things before they began to return." He'd said it.

"Well, that's certainly interesting. I have so many questions on top of so many questions. But I have one that is probably the most trivial, but to me rather urgent at the moment. Do you think they will stay where they are? Will I be able to keep them covered?"

He finally turned to look directly at me. "Victoria. I believe I understand your concern." He thought for a moment. "They are beautiful Victoria." Again, thoughts.

"Victoria. The spirits, my spirits, have taken the space on my body that is good for them, comfortable. In the beginning, the space they took seemed to be the largest unoccupied space until the space was covered. To promise that you will always be able to cover them with clothing, I cannot do that."

"I agree they are beautiful. They are truly spirits. Amazing. Together while we made love, was beautiful. I felt so close to you." I shook myself. "But James, I don't think the population of the Island will think they are beautiful."

James nodded, squeezed my hand. "Like me, no. I would not think so. That is why I cover. I did not think the soul you carry would recognize me as quickly as it has. That it would rise to greet me as it has done. It has been

232

looking as I have. You have been looking as I have. That, I did not know. Victoria, it has been more than 700 years since we have touched."

"What?" Holy shit. "You have been as you are for 700 years?" Talk about old fart and I was feeling bad that I had maybe 17 years on him.

"Asra-pa. Yes. I lost track of the time at first. I lost interest. I visited countries without seasons. Johnathan keeps track of these things. He keeps journals - the house is filled, you will see. He figures from the stories I have told him, I was about 200 when I made him. He knows precisely the time he was made." He leaned in and kissed me. "I will think about this while I am away." I had many answers. Still had a ton of questions. I had a piece of the truth as James knew it.

"Will I be able to feel you wake, feel you sleep, will the talisman move at all when you are gone?" I had to ask. I was beginning to enjoy a tickle at random times, the buzz shock when he woke. Couldn't help it.

For the first time since we had been talking he smiled a great smile. I could see all of his teeth. "Magic…power does not travel in a straight line like radio waves or light. Magic goes to magic. We are all beings. Magic. You know all existence is magic, power, energy. We are finally connected as we should be Victoria."

I did. The concept got me thrown out of teaching Sunday school when I was 17. I nodded. "James it is so nice, so comfortable to be able to…I'm not sure how to say this…to be myself with you. Not to have to edit." I stopped, had to smile. "My turn, not as dramatic, but you have allowed me to begin to think again. Explore again. Realize things again. For that, allowing me comfort in myself again, I will always thank you." It was true. It had been a very long time since I'd allowed myself to been this mentally free.

"Victoria. For you, anything within my power is yours. It always has been." James leaned in to kiss me, he held me, started moving to me.

"James, the bedroom. Falling asleep with you, waking to your smell. Please, the bedroom if there is time." He stood. Looked to the window, the horizon. Reached his hand to me, pulled me to my feet. We went to the bedroom. The most gentle touching, kissing. The most tender of intimacies.

"I love you Victoria." He was gone. Soon after, the talisman told me he was truly gone.

Chapter 38

No alarms. I woke when my body wanted to wake. I lazed in bed. My nose in the woody smell that was James. Almost like the smell that was in the condo when I returned. My thoughts started drifting to things I didn't want to think about. Not right now. Just allow me this, I thought. Told the paranoia, the doubt, I'd give it time later.

The cell phone brought me back to the day. I looked at the number. Didn't recognize it. Let it go to voicemail, but caught the time,12:30.

I felt fine. Actually, as soon as I had stopped getting sick last night, no, this morning, I felt fine. I stood in front of the mirror in the dressing room, something a woman my age rarely does, and took a good look at the tattoos, no...the spirits. They were beautiful. They looked like Billy's work. The peonies had extended about half an inch from my nipple, circling it clockwise up to my collarbone. If I had the nerve and could have been sure the work would have been this good, I might have had it done years ago.

Yeah, Carolyn would freak out. Mary, actually Mary might even think they were cool. The extension on my thigh looked like it extended inside of me. Wait until my doctor sees that in a couple of months. I smiled at that thought. Hey, healed, no infection, she probably would have a good story to tell other doctors. My foot. The roses now went over my toes, all five of them, the length of my foot and started to curl around my leg in the opposite direction. The tattoos, no...the spirits had made me sick last night, not the sex.

Coffee and eggs again. In the library. I checked the cell voice mail while I ate. The call was from crazy Kenny's number. The message. "If you will not listen to reason we will try another way to talk to you." I didn't erase it, might need it. I called Mary to check the office.

"Everything is fine here Vic. I was going to call you. The Seller of the next door space wondered if we would like to Close earlier; like Friday. What do you think?"

"Could you call the contractor. If he can start sooner than we planned, sometime next week, sure. I don't want to pay taxes and fees on something I can't start using. I'll call Jay and see if he's good. Anything else?"

"No, that's it. I'll hunt Joe on his cell. Give me a call, let me know." Mary hung up. I called Jay. Asked the question.

"Sure. No problem Friday. Hey, I was about to give you a ring. Keirns just transferred some money, about half a million, into my Operating Account. Got any idea why, because I sure as hell don't know." Jay was so laid back it was scary.

"Not a clue Jay. None of the houses on Ledge House Road have come up."

"Victoria. I'm sitting here watching my account and another 500 from another bank just showed up. You know this is funny as hell. I'm wondering if I should have them transfer into their own account. You know, keep their money separate." Jay was thinking out loud.

"That might not be a bad idea Jay. When you talk to Keirns you might want to suggest it. I'd keep it separate from mine."

"You're right. Actually, I'll set it up and tell him the new numbers."

"So I'll see you Friday. What time Jay?"

"Can we make it eleven? Is that too early for you?" My reputation for 'not before 1:00' precedes me.

"Sure. I'll be there." I hung up and called Mary back.

"How's eleven, Friday?" I asked.

"Joe says he can start next Thurs. I told him to put us on the schedule. Plans will be here this Thursday afternoon with the estimate." Mary was excited again.

"What do you think the number will be?" I asked.

"Within ten percent of my estimate. If you don't believe me we could put some cash on the table. Oh, he can do the one way glass on both bays. A little more expensive, but Vic I think you'll be happy. Twelve dollars a pane."

"Ouch. Wait. Ok. Not that bad when I think about it. Great. I'll see you tomorrow. By the way, I'm getting some press calls on the cell so I'm letting them go to the voice mail again. Not shutting it off. Call if you need me. Bye." Well, this is fun.

I started running a list of Brokers that might fit us. Searched their sales in the little program that links with the Listing Service Site. The access is only to Principle Brokers; brokers responsible for offices. Nice little perk. No one talks about it; but it does come in handy at times. Any member licensee can look up their own stuff. But cross checking is not allowed to non-principal brokers or salesmen.

I felt James wake, then the tickle. I reached to the talisman, pressed it to my leg. "Good morning James." I had not a clue that he could hear me. I wondered where he was. The cell rang. Crazy Kenny.

I was cruising through the new listings for today in another part of the system when I noticed the condo next door was up for sale. Tina had it. $700,000. A little high, but I wanted to get a look at it. I wasn't going to buy it, no way. Honestly, I wasn't going to try to show it to any of my Clients - too close to me. My rule, not in my neighborhood if I could help it. By law, if it fit someone's needs I had to include it in any package I gave them and if they wanted to see it, I had to show it. If they wanted to buy it, well, I did my best.

I called Tina, an old friend and a Broker with an agency in Little Compton. We exchanged pleasantries. I asked if I could 'piggyback' a showing; arrive a little early or after a showing to take a quick look. She was having an open house Saturday. I told her I'd come by. She had no idea I lived next door. Few people knew where I lived.

Cell again. Crazy Kenny again. The clock told me to shower; Board Meeting in an hour and a half. Remember to replace the travel clock.

On my way to the shower I saw some workmen outside the garden door. I stood watching them for a minute then opened the door. I watched one stacking firewood in the cord holder. The other placing a short, beautifully carved, deep water trough on newly laid slate against the south side of the patio. Nice James. They looked at me. Started to explain in broken English. "Mr. Fournier, Mr. Keirns." I nodded my head yes, smiled.

"Thank you." I stepped out to grab the empty pot but they wouldn't let me. One of them wiped his boots and brought it in for me. Again, I said thank you. They waived their hands to me. They were done and left. Well, at least I wouldn't have to drag the pot out every time we went riding. I wondered if there would be a problem with the neighbors. I quickly checked for horse poop in the grass, found none. No harm, no foul?

Some Board Meetings go on forever. This one was scheduled for an hour and rarely went over. I'd been on the Board for about ten years. It ran late maybe three or four times. The late runs had been because of some financial issues we needed to formally address. No power struggles, no gossip, just business. It was a pleasure. I picked up dinner, a turkey club and a travel clock on the way home.

I started to fall asleep about ten. James's smell was still in the bed. How nice. As I was nodding I felt the talisman tickle then the buzz. He was gone. I checked the clock - he was seven hours ahead of me?

The new travel alarm clock worked. I find it amazing when I replace something I've had for years and not have to go through a learning curve. The new travel clock I could set in my sleep. Even better, turn off in my sleep. Trust, even mechanical, is an odd thing.

I walked into the office at 12:55. Mary was chatting with Georgette but excused herself and accompanied me to my office.

"What's up Mary?" She handed me a piece of scribbled, lined paper. The edges burnt, hand drawn crosses in its corners with red ink.

"I found this. Shoved through the mail slot, this morning." Mary was not a happy camper. The message was written in blue ballpoint ink.

Mrs. Hamilton,

We need the names to complete our calling. We've talked to Cheryl Kingston. Fire purifies!!!!

Our Love In The Lord,
Father William

"Shit Mary. This is verging on the absurd. Keep Georgette busy, I'm going to try to track Jay." I didn't want this event to involve more people, but I also didn't want the office burnt down.

"You know about this Father William, Vicky? What's going on?" Again, more people involved…now Mary.

"Mary, I just need to talk to Jay. I'll explain later." Mary didn't like that response from me. What could I do without the day sliding late? I don't like to sit waiting for appointments with people not involved in emergencies. Last time I looked there were very few real estate emergencies.

Third number for Jay and he picked up. The background sounded like a café. I explained what had been going on beginning with Carolyn, ending with the note. "Can this be stopped without involving more people Jay? Do you know if Cheryl is out of the hospital, did they go to the hospital to talk to her?"

"She's out, back at work. Can these guys track you to your home?" I hadn't though of the possibility. Truthfully, I hadn't given the whole thing much thought.

"I'm unlisted Jay. They would have to follow me. Do you think they're that serious?" How dumb. I just couldn't bring myself to think they were that serious.

"Victoria, let me get back to the office and make a couple of calls. Can I get you on your cell?"

"Jay, if you can, call me at the office. My cell ringer is off."

"Because of these guys?"

"Well, yeah...just call the office. I'll be here." I've killed my ringer before. Sellers upset with a Client, advertising sales people on speed dial, newspapers; guys I had told I didn't want to see anymore. Jay didn't have a clue how many times I'd killed it.

"Mary, Georgette hi, sorry about the distraction. Let's get this show on the road." They followed me back into the office. Mary handed me another copy of the job descriptions. I will miss her being a thought ahead of me. My copy was on my desk at home.

"Georgette, glad we finally got some time together and I've got to ask, why something like this? Why not go to one of the Colleges nearby? Salve, Roger Williams, URI would be glad to have you."

"Honestly, Victoria I'm sick of teaching. It's that simple. I need a full change. Place, people, job – the whole thing. Every time I visit Dad, rather Mason, up here," Georgette smiled, "I don't want to go home. It's been going on since Mason came up so it's not new." Mason's been here for, what, almost ten years. Georgette continued. "I held out until I could leave with retirement. I passed that last August and took a light load last semester. Only one PhD. Candidate this semester. I can monitor him from here. He'll be on his own in May."

"Has Mary talked to you about how the office works?" If I didn't have to, I didn't want to have to try to explain it.

"Yes, she has. That and Mason talks about it all the time, so I think I've got a feel for your thoughts." That's interesting. "Mary also told me that I would need to get licensed as soon as possible. That won't be a problem. Although I haven't taken an objective exam since my SATs." With that comment, she laughed.

"I know the feeling. A professor pulled my exam in a law class when I requested a fourth 'comp book'. Told me he'd give me an A if I would just stop writing." We both laughed. It was true. 'Comp' books are those little black and white checkered composition books you can buy at the store. Law professors love those little books for exams. The class was "Law of Negotiable Papers, Estates and Real Property". Funny, I can't even remember the three essay questions now.

"Georgette, I have two concerns. The first is that after a week you are going to be bored out of your skull and second, it will be impossible not to talk to Mason about what's going on in the office." The phone on my desk rang. Mary picked it up.

"It's Jay, for you." She held the phone out to me.

"Excuse me." I said to Mary and Georgette. "I need to take this in the workroom. I'll be right back."

"Jay, I'll be right with you." A second later I picked up in privacy. "I'm here Jay."

"Victoria, long story short. These guys were picked up trying to set fire to a revival tent in Portsmouth last fall. The cops agree that they are nuts. If you drop the note with Lt. Barnard he'll see if they can pick up the fingerprints on the note. I assumed you and Mary have held it, at least that's what I told him. They already have Kenny and the Father's prints. So if it's not too smudgy, they'll pick them up and call you."

This was going to become a big deal, rats. "Will do Jay. I'll have Mary drop it by the station. Are we going to have to go to Court?"

"Let's see what happens Victoria. They maybe nuts enough to admit writing it. Who knows. They admitted to the tent fire. I'll keep you posted. Talk soon." Jay hung up. I returned to my office.

"So Georgette, going to get bored with us?" I said sitting down.

"With everything going on around here, I wouldn't think so. And as for your other concern, well, what can I say. Mason's going to ask, you know that. He always asks me about my teaching and I've never said anything but 'it's fine'. Mason and I have lines, we always have. It's probably why we can spend time together. The only way you will know is to give it a try."

"You're right. Has Mary explained the independent contractor thing and pay?"

"She has. I bill, you pay. We'll have a Contract."

"Mary, do you have any questions or comments?" I asked.

"I've told Georgette that a class starts Tuesday night for ten nights. Exam right after. She said she had planned to be up here for three weeks anyway, so not a problem. She's willing to work with me during the day for a few hours —of course we'll pay her for her time."

239

"Good. You realize that I'm the high maintenance person in this office. Right?" Might as well say it, we're getting to the bottom line.

"You admit it?" Georgette said.

"Of course. I'm very aware of how I work, what I like. Why deny it. You need to be comfortable with it Georgette."

Georgette leaned toward me. "You know Victoria, it could be fun." She leaned back.

Bingo. It could work. No bullshit. It was hard to believe Georgette was Mason's daughter. Guess he hadn't been around much when she was growing up. I hadn't been around my kids either.

"OK. I think Karen just walked in Mary. I'm good. Hope it works, Georgette." I stood, reached across the desk to shake her hand. "Mary does details, but then you know that. Mary, give me a second, I need to take a break before Karen."

I was about to call Mary to tell her I was ready for Karen when I felt a tickle on my ankle, no buzz. The talisman was rolling, moving. I reached down, held it against my ankle. "Thinking about you too." I spoke in a whisper. Nice. I hadn't felt him wake. Probably slept through it. I called Mary.

Mary knew the game played here. Formal, official, something Karen would understand. Would Georgette pick up on this stuff?

Mary opened the door for Karen. "Wow you must be busy. New agent?" Karen walked through door carrying a stack of papers. This stuff was why she wouldn't fit; the instant question about my previous meeting. Try to work it into the conversation if you felt it was competition, but not right off the bat. Subtle she wasn't. Picky, picky Victoria.

I gave no response to her comment. "Karen, sorry I kept you waiting. I hate to do that." Karen; a suit, hair and makeup seriously done, jewelry everywhere, four-inch heels, the whole show. She placed the huge stack of paper...no...LSS printouts on my desk before she made her self comfortable.

"The last time we talked Victoria, I got the feeling that you didn't understand how many properties I've sold. So I figured I'd bring them so you could see what I've done."

I looked at the stack, looked at her. Did she think I hadn't looked before we met the first time. "I'm aware of your lifetime sales Karen. I was aware of them the first time we spoke."

"Well I was at the office five years before you. I was there when George left." George was my first Broker. "You know that was a big deal." What? George leaving?

"I'm aware Karen. Listen, I was serious during our last meeting. This office is different. Much different than any of the offices around here. I honestly don't think it would be your cup of tea. Why leave a place that works for you? Seriously." I needed to be patient.

"Victoria, I know we've had our little disagreements, but that was years ago. It wasn't a big deal. I'm just looking for something new. You know what I can bring to this place. No one else can bring what I can."

I was torn between reaching across the desk, popping her in the nose and asking her what she could bring that we didn't already have. So tempting. My history with Karen was one of the few things that could still light me off and my Bic was out. The talisman began to roll, tickle. I reached down, gave it a pat. I didn't know if it just felt me or James had felt the beginnings of anger. "Karen I appreciate your persistence and I take it as a complement that you would like to move to my office. Thank you. But, frankly, it will not work for you. It's not the place for you. If you feel you need to move, there are a couple of offices in town of the caliber you are in now. Cheryl has picked up a few agents from your current office. Why don't you talk to her?" Yeah, I knew about the actual fist fight they had gotten into a few years ago. At a showing with Clients no less.

Karen stood, all 5'10" of her plus heels; smoothed her skirt, straightened her jacket. She was not happy. "You know Victoria, this place is going to go to hell if I have anything to do with it. I will shut you and your Brokers out of this town. You think we're Closing next Tuesday? We'll just see about that." Loud words. I glanced at my door, Mary was there. I stood.

"Good luck Karen, I do hope you find a home." She looked into my eyes. When I held hers she threw the stack of papers at me. Waited for me to do something. I did nothing. She literally stormed out of the office. I was waiting for the rain behind her.

Mary held the door to my office open. Karen was gone. With the personalities in this business, someone could write a book. "Holy crap." Mary stepped in. Georgette was behind her, smiling. "Think she'll want to talk again?" Mary gave a little chuckle. "What are all the papers?" She reached down. "Listing printouts, no, sale printouts - check the dates Vic."

"I know. Want to ask why she's not here?"

Georgette took a step in to help Mary pick up. "No, not really."

241

"Hey guys, I'll pick the stuff up. Don't bother. Georgette, can you give me some time with Mary?"

"Oh, no problem." Georgette closed the door on her way out.

"Mary, please, just sit down if you would. I'll tell you about the note." I told her what had happened yesterday in as few words as I could find. I explained that Jay had asked us to drop the note to Lt. Branard this afternoon. I then asked her to do it and call it a day.

"Vicky, you know I don't like playing with cops." I'd forgotten. No, not forgotten, just slipped my mind.

"Mary. Sorry. I wasn't thinking. No problem. I'll zip down, then call it a day."

"We'll clean up here. I'm assuming you have no need for this. Could you stop by tomorrow and sign Georgette's Contract and the form for the class?"

"Right. Sure. I have a Committee Meeting at noon so I'll come by after. Thanks Mary. I appreciate it."

"No problem." Mary laughed. "I thought you were going to punch her."

"Who, me, never. I'm more the knife in the heart type. See you tomorrow." I told Georgette that I looked forward to working with her and headed to the police station.

Lt. Branard was a nice little treat for the eyes. A little too workout happy for me, but still a nice surprise. We exchanged pleasantries. I gave him the note in an envelope. I asked him to let Jay know what was going on. I did not have the history with the police that Mary did, but I could think of other places to be right now. It had turned out that the badge Mary had flipped out when we first met had been real. She had taken it from a cop during a drug bust she had escaped. Not hard stuff, just some smoke. The incident had prompted her return to Newport and our roommate meeting. I don't think that had been her only brush with the men of law enforcement, but it was the only one I knew about.

I broke down and decided to do a little grocery shopping before going home. It had been three, maybe four weeks since the last venture. Standing in line the idea struck me. The weather was so nice that I'd go home, put on something warm and head to the beach. With that thought, my patience with the line ended. The light at the register started blinking. I was next in line. My stuff was on the belt so bailing was not an option. The older gentleman in front of me was having trouble meeting his tab. He was counting change, $3.00 short. What's the big deal?

242

I dug out my wallet, handed the girl at the register three one's. The poor man was mortified counting the change to pay his bill. He must have been 90 or more. I asked him if he was ok; could he get home with all the groceries. He told me that his wife was waiting in their car and he was just fine. If I would give him my address he would send me the money. I asked him to please allow me to do this. Returning the money wasn't necessary. He waived at me when he left the store, a smile on his face. It wasn't the first time I'd done something like that. I was sure it wouldn't be the last. It was automatic, no thought. Now, I understood what James had said.

The beach was chilly but beautiful. Worth leaving my kitchen full of bags and not hanging up my clothes to get there before the temperature dropped. My cell rang. I dug it out of a layer of pockets thinking it would probably be one of the funny boys. It was Mary.

"Victoria. You have to come to the office. Hurry. There's a fire."

"A fire. Is everyone alright?" I was moving as fast as I could back to the car. "Fire Department?"

"Yeah, they just got here. We're ok. Oh, just get here. Cops just pulled up. Got to go." Mary disconnected.

I had to park in the library parking lot. The trucks, rescue wagons and cops had the street blocked. What the hell?

"Victoria, over here!" Mary yelled.

I walked in her direction, lifting the yellow tape. "Wait Please. Have to stay on the other side of the tape." An officer met me halfway to Mary.

"I think it might be my offices burning." Although the fire looked out, no flames, a little smoke. He took a good look at me. Sweats, beat up sneakers, my old 'bag lady' jacket as my kids called it. Screaming orange jacket, obviously men's and a red beret over my ears. I looked like I owned the property. Oh yeah.

"Please. You have to move back." The officer started lightly pushing me back.

"Officer, it's my property. Mary" I yelled.

"Officer, I think she does own the property. Mrs. Hamilton is that you?" Lt. Branard. I didn't know if he was serious or not.

"Yes, it is me Lt. Branard. I need to get to my Manager. She was here when it happened." Whatever it was that happened. The entry was scorched. It looked like the majority of the fire had happened on the marble steps and sidewalk. Someone had thrown something at the door was my guess. There were what looked like brown beer bottle shards all over the area.

"Mary, are you and Georgette alright?" I saw Ames walking to us. "Was Ames in the office?"

"We're fine. Ames was walking across the street to the office when it happened. He's alright too. Georgette and I were getting coffee in the back when we heard what sounded like bottles hit the door and your window. When we came to the front all we saw were flames. We went out the back door. I guess the alarmed door was a good idea. I called 911 and they already had the alarm. The fire department and emergency wagon were pulling up by the time we walked around the building." I bet I was at least the fourth person she had told the story to. "Don't worry Vic, the insurance is paid." I did have to laugh at that.

"Mary, I have no doubt. Didn't enter my mind."

"The young man over there," Lt. Barnard gestured to Ames, "says he saw the whole thing. A car parked against the curb. Guy driving had a collar, you know clerical collar. The other guy threw two lit bottles at the building. Then they drove off."

"In the middle of the afternoon? You have got to be kidding me. Ames, could you identify them again?" I looked over Mary's shoulder.

"Maybe. I did get the car plates. It was an old caddy, green with flames painted on the side and a big cross on the hood. All red." Ames was smiling.

"Am I in a bad movie?" I asked no one in particular. Ames started laughing, then Mary and Georgette behind Ames. I hadn't seen her. One of the firemen was trying the door latch. The door opened, no problem. He looked in, careful not to step in, then pushed at the door frame and ran his hand along it, pushing and pulling. He walked in, around to my office bending below the bay window, where, on the outside there was scorch. A few minutes later he came out, walking to us.

"Lieutenant. I don't think the fire did much damage to the building itself. Wood this old is hard to burn. I think it'll be ok. I'll go with the ladies to check the alarm, if that's ok with you?" The emergency wagon drove down the street. The firehouse was less than a block away.

"Go on back to the firehouse. I'll check the alarms." The Lieutenant said. He started walking to our front door with the four of us following. We stood in front of our code box. "Go ahead. Wait, is everything closed?" I walked to the back door, opened it then slammed it shut. "Ok. Activate the panel." Mary automatically stepped up to do the job. "Ok, open the front door." Ames opened the front door. The alarm gave a long shriek. The Lieutenant spoke into his shoulder. Told someone at the other end it was a test and gave our address. "Ok, shut it off." Mary punched in the code. Silence. "I think you are good to go. Give a call to your alarm company to have them check it out tomorrow. Mrs. Hamilton, I'll stay in touch with you and Jay. Your friends just escalated their little letter." Lt. Branard left.

"I'm going home. Whoever stays, make sure the front door is shut tight, ok. I'll see you tomorrow." I left the three of them talking.

It had to be somewhere around nine. Too cold for the beach. I went home, took a quick shower, made soup. The talisman ticked, then buzzed me. James was gone. I flipped on the local news, channel 9, my favorite - most laughs.

Sure enough our little weenie roast made the local news. 'Fire on Bellevue Avenue in Newport'. You would think that a major historic block had burnt to the ground. Crazy Kenny and his friend's face flashed on the screen. Apparently they hadn't been found, but had been seen going over The Pell Bridge, more commonly know on the Island as "The Bridge". A span that linked the Island with another little Island in the Bay and then linked with another bridge to the mainland. One of three connecting the Island to the mainland. How could anyone miss the car that Ames had described. Actually, they would have been over the bridges before the fire trucks had arrived. Hell, they could have been in Connecticut before I had gotten to the office.

I checked the travel alarm. Set the TV timer, rolled over, took a big whiff of James, slept.

Chapter 39

I woke to the sound of pounding rain. Thank heavens it wasn't snow. This time of the year it was a 50-50 shot. The closer we got to April the less likely it would be snow, but we've had snow in the middle of April, on Easter day. Even though some of the bigger nurseries were starting to sell plants, the only thing worth buying and trying to plant was pansies. I know the desire to get outside this time of year and had, at my previous house, given into a major planting effort at the beginning of April one year. Lost everything. A hard freeze and snow on Easter. I'm nervous planting my patio planters in May. The investment now is much smaller but I would hate to see everything die the week after I'd planted.

I sat in the library drinking my first cup of coffee, waiting for the computer to load when the cell rang. At least Mary waited for me to get coffee.

"Did I wake you up Vic?"

"No, actually just sat down with coffee thinking about calling you. Do you need me in before my meeting at noon or can I just stop by after as planned?"

"Call before you stop by after the meeting. Your favorite news lady is sitting across the street waiting for you. That's why I called. She's apparently talked to the bombers. She wants to get your take on what they are saying about the buyers of Ledge House. I told her I was just the dumb receptionist and didn't know anything, which kind of was the truth."

"Good for you Mary. Right now you know pretty much what I know."

"Vicky, I truly doubt that, but I'm patient."

"So, alarm company coming? Oh, did you call the insurance guy?"

"Alarm company I called last night and they are here as we speak. Insurance guy will be by this afternoon. You know Vic, we're moving the door anyway. Why don't I just get a check made out to us. I think it would be a waste of time to repair it now. What do you think?"

"I agree with you. How bad does it look?"

"Well, the paint looks like the burnt skin of a marshmallow under your window, the door isn't that bad, more scorched. The question is can you live with it for a couple of weeks?"

Yeah, can I live with it? "I'm going to have to drive by. Can you give Joe a call. He's going to have to do my window. It's staying where it is. We're going to use the door. Maybe if those things were done now, we could leave the door frame and the side stuff for later." The thought of walking into an office that looked trashy from the outside turned my stomach. First impressions are real estate musts. "Mary, after my meeting I'll come to the back door and give you a call. I'll be able to check out the front with any luck. How does that sound.?"

"Go for it Vic. If something happens, give a call." Mary hung up and my cell started ringing in my ear. Familiar number.

"Hey Jay. Thanks for the Lieutenant's name." I wondered if he had heard about last night.

"So are you supplying the marshmallows?" Yeah, he'd heard.

"Like I said, thanks for the contact. He showed up last night. It was quite a show. Have you driven by the office today?"

"Of course. Love the news van. The damage isn't that bad Vicky. You know, Father whoever went to Channel 9 last night. They're going to do an interview by phone, live at six." Jay spoke the last part as if he were advertising the news segment. I laughed. "Well Vic, it was a fire." This channel always had some fire as its bait story. One of the big jokes in the area. "Anyway, I'm sure you'll take care of the damage. The real reason I'm calling: got an email from Keirns this morning. It contains a list of donations to be made with some of the money he's wired. A biggie to the Land Trust, actually two biggies. The same amount to the Wildlife Sanctuary. Smaller to the new golf course off Wapping and then some smaller donations to the gun club, the FPO, The Glen, you know places like that. I bet if I mapped the donations, I could run a path down, pretty much the center of the Island. Victoria, do I have to pull my plat maps or can you tell me why?"

Sometimes Jay was too savvy for his own good. "That's interesting. Does he say anything else?"

"Oh, yeah, he requested that I set up an account for them, of course, 'if you wouldn't mind'. So polite." He was baiting me to tell him more.

"Jay, are they taking too much of your time? You know, eating into the other parts of your practice?"

"No. All in all, very low maintenance. I certainly can't complain about the pay. I guess I'm just curious. So what's going on Vicky?"

"Jay, I have not a clue. My end has been pretty quiet except for the nut balls and I told you about that. But, interesting I must say. Hey, I've got to bug for a Committee Meeting. I'll let you know when I know something. OK?" Now I seriously was starting to run late.

"Talk soon Vic." I shut down the computer and headed to the shower.

The Committee is a subdivision of the Board of Directors that I belonged to. Our job was to set up and organize the fundraisers for our non-profit. I usually sat and listened this time of the year. The event that was being planned is a charity golf tournament. I know nothing to speak of about golf, so I usually nodded sagely on the subject. The office usually bought some holes and, if I could, I'd go help with the dinner. As with the Board meeting, the Committee meetings were pretty fast. Most of the members were there on their lunch hours so they ate while they talked. Less formal, but usually productive.

It was still raining when I drove by the office. Our façade wasn't as bad as I'd imagined. If the door was scraped and painted along with my window, I could live with it, I think. The news van was still across the street. I could see the people inside. No one noticed me. I had to park about three blocks from the office on a small street that would allow me to walk to our back door without being seen. I called before I left the car. Mary had the door open when I walked up, a bit damp.

"Love your shoes." I was wearing my big, pink, life saving rain boots from the car. A few years ago I'd found myself standing on the main waterfront street in Newport, talking to some Clients before a showing. The rain was a frog choker in the middle of the summer, but hey, I looked good. Summer slacks, blouse, jacket and heels. The water was running over my ankles draining into the Bay. After the showing we went to lunch in an air conditioned restaurant. I froze. The next day I went to a farm store in Portsmouth and bought the boots. As winters require snow gear, I have developed my summer gear – blanket for the beach, rain boots, Helly Hanson made for sailing in bad weather, 2 umbrellas (one for Clients) and bottled water. You just never know.

"Well, made it around the newsies, I think. Front's not too bad." I gingerly stepped into the office. Mary handed me a towel.

"I think the rain has washed some of the carbon away, thank heavens. Georgette and I had to clean our shoes after we walked in. Good call, hardwood floors, not carpeting. It wiped right up." Mary followed me into the workroom for coffee. "Georgette's Contract is on your desk. The alarm system is fine. No fixes needed. You just missed the insurance adjuster. He thought it was a mess, especially in the Historic District. He talked about $6,000 to restore the façade."

"Mary, you just made my day. You're not kidding are you?" I asked while thinking it was a shame they hadn't hit the façade on the new space.

"Vicky, I don't kid about money. Actually, that's about the only thing I don't kid about. Let's see, what else…oh, Joe's going to stop by on his way to work tomorrow. I think he's the only guy in the State that hadn't heard about the fire. Anyway I'll be here for him. I guess that's it. Oh, the Sellers from next door called to see if we still planned on Closing Friday, what with the fire and all. I told them we would be there." We both heard a commotion at the front door. Ames and someone talking then the door slammed.

"Everything alright out there Ames?" I yelled from my office.

Ames opened the French door. "Yeah. Just the news people. That broad is going to poke someone's eye out with her umbrella. See Victoria, it's not too bad."

The front door opened with stronger words at a higher pitch. Nina pushed her head around Ames. "Anybody got a gun. She is going to drive me nuts. Hey, I'm surprised. The fire damage isn't bad. From the news I was expecting the façade gone."

"From what I saw last night, it should have been the whole block." I said.

"You know Vicky, Karen's not too happy with you. Listening to her, I was wondering if you'd physically drop kicked her out of a negotiation yesterday." I guess Nina had gone to the Preservation Society dance last night.

"Hot date Nina?" I asked.

"Is there anything else and he's a good dancer. Did you really kick her out of a negotiation?" I was laughing. Mary was trying not to.

"Come on Nina, you know me better than that. I would have called Ames to do the dirty work." We laughed. "You know she wants to come to the office. I politely told her no in January. She wouldn't stop calling, stopping by to see me, so we had our second meeting yesterday. I said it a little stronger, that's all."

"I figured, but I had to ask. What's with news lady wanting the names of the Ledge House buyers so bad. What have they got to do with the fire?"

"Nina, watch the news at 6 on channel 9 tonight. It should be interesting. And to answer your question, nothing, but not according to the fire bugs. Anyway, watch it, should be fun."

"So you're not going to tell me?"

"Nina, the only link between the Buyers and the fire is in the heads of the 'nuts'. Nothing else. Now go, go, go. I've got stuff to do." Everyone left the office. The talisman tickled, then buzzed. James was gone. Hmmm. Location move? Kind of weird, knowing he's died. Didn't know how much I liked knowing that.

I clicked my computer on to finish what I had started this morning. The Wilson's sent me all the information I had asked for – very nice. Bill's Closing numbers for next Tuesday - those I printed to review tonight. Also, print for the file and forward to Bill. Email from Johnathan.

"Dear Victoria,

James will be making an unplanned visit. His return has been postponed, probably one day. I believe he will return Saturday, mid afternoon. He is well.

Sincerely,
Johnathan

Well, I appreciated the information. Actually, it was nice of Johnathan to let me know about the delay, also to let me know James was alright. Probably just business to him.

I finished looking at the new listings; moved my attention to Georgette's Contract. Could Georgette have handled the fire? Mary would have still handled it. Would Georgette keep her mouth shut with the press, or anybody else the way Mary has? I tried to think back to when we started here in the office. Mary and I had learned stuff together. Learned to work with each other at the same time. What made us work, the office work, is the way our friendship has worked for so many years. I don't know if that could be taught. My guess would be no. Mary wanted to grow. I wouldn't stop her. Guess I'll have to suck it up.

I read the contract. I signed both copies. Said goodbye to Mary, went home. Tonight I needed a drink.

I reached the condo; poured a drink and was ready for the local news at six. I didn't move for the whole story. What a fucking mess. These guys needed to be locked up. Kenny sounded out and out nuts. Father William, the name of the church wasn't mentioned, sounded rational until you listened to the words he was saying.

" Two demons have purchased Ledge House. They have brought their animal familiars with them to do their bidding. They must be eliminated for the sake of all our souls. They must be burned out. Mrs. Hamilton refused to tell us the names the demons are using. Until we have their names, we cannot rid our lovely Island of these creatures from hell."

The news lady, Miss Katie, announced that an interview at Ledge House would follow when the news returned. Surprise.

When the show returned, the cameras were at the gates of Ledge House, in the rain. She introduced the property manager employed by the new owners. A youngish looking man stood at the open gate holding a dark gray umbrella. He wore a gray suit, tie, businessman's short hair, looked like an end of the day beard growth. He was smiling at Miss Katie and into the camera. He spoke, what, perfect American. Just enough slang, just the right amount of 'big' words. He was the perfect American, his name appropriately ethnic, Charon. I had to smile. He did look somewhat familiar to me but I bet he was familiar to a lot of people…Geez, he was good.

Charon pointed out that the owners were a delightful family that valued their privacy. The animals were horses and some birds. He couldn't understand what all the fuss was about. He expressed apologies to me for the damage. He felt bad for the two gentlemen and suggested that some professional help would probably be useful. Then, in the rain, he invited the news crew to see the horses and any of the other animals they would like.

Miss Katie asked if she could speak with the owners. Charon simply said that it would not be possible. He invited her again to view and photograph the animals. This time using hand gestures with his verbal invitation. Miss Katie was frustrated, no story. She declined.

What did I see in this story? James and Johnathan had done this before. What was happening with these two nut cases, had happened before. Touché! I couldn't stop laughing.

My cell was ringing, it was Jay. "So, you saw the show?"

"Oh, I sure did. Frankly Jay, it was very good. What can I say?"

"I told you Mr. Fournier wasn't stupid. But this, I must say, was very good."

"What do you mean Mr. Fournier?"

"It's his show. You do realize that don't you Vicky? His money, his business, it's all his. Mr. Keirns may take care of the details, but they are definitely not equal partners. No way. The show belongs, lock, stock and barrel to Fournier." Jay needed to stop thinking about these transactions, these people in such detail. I was tempted to tell him to do what he was asked to do, collect his fees and, frankly, forget about the people. I didn't. Jay's a big boy.

"Interesting, you had mentioned that before. Well, hopefully, after that it will go away. It's a pain." Tickle, buzz, James was gone. Definitely change of location. "Anyway, I'm going to soak in a hot bath. I guess I'll see you tomorrow at 1:00. You didn't forget did you Jay?"

"Of course not. See you then." He hung up. I went to soak in the tub.

The bubbles smelled great. I relaxed, letting my brain wander to the concept of having walked the earth for 746 years, give or take. Getting my arms around the implications, was well, damn near impossible.

The physical experience, what James had witnessed, was one thing. The perceptions, understandings, the learning, they were a whole other ball game. I would no sooner grasp one concept, wonder what James thought about it then another would pop into my brain. Me, in my short life was still coming to realizations, understandings about things that had happened when I was five; much less what I found to be true in the last, what, four weeks. I did give a thank you to that intelligence for the privilege of knowing that, infact, I hadn't been crazy for most of my life.

I woke to a bright, clear sun Friday. I was actually excited about the Closing on the storefront. I didn't have a shred of dread about it. Mary wouldn't have to buy me a Manhattan before the Closing. The Closing for the current office had almost sent me off the deep end with the burden and pressure of having to support the cost. I had just moved into the condo and couldn't shake the feeling of too many changes, too many undertakings in a year. Mary had subtly steered me to one of my favorite bars next to Jay's office. I almost had to crawl to the Closing. The rest of that day is a blur. It wouldn't happen today.

Had I asked Mary to come with me? I couldn't remember, but better late than never. I gave her a call.

"Mary did I ask you to come with me today, to the Closing I mean?"

"You did, right after you signed the Purchase and Sale Agreement. You don't remember?"

"No, honestly I don't. Good. How are things this morning?"

"Joe came. Said he'd have a guy over to work on your window, then the door, starting Monday. He agreed that it would have to been done anyway to blend the two storefronts, so no big deal. Do we have to make a stop before the Closing?"

"I woke up excited. No, I'm good with it. Hey, I'm thinking about inviting Sam, Samuel Condon to join us? Give it some thought, but only between you and me. We'll talk later about it - I do plan to take you to lunch after the Closing. You don't have anything planned for later, do you?"

"Georgette will be here for the phones, walk-ins. You know, hold down the fort, so no I don't. Can I bring the Friday stuff with me?"

"Is she ready for that Mary? Sure bring everything, we can lose the afternoon. I'll pick you up at about 12:45. So is she ready?"

"Not a problem. I gave it to her most of yesterday. She allowed me to do accounts, end of the month coming you know. Advertising, general stuff. She was great. No problems. This is going to go smoother that you thought it would. I'll see you later."

"See you later Mary."

I started to worry; but heck, I trusted Mary. When I start to interfere in the day to day stuff, well, the office gets messed up. I let it go.

Mary was waiting for me when I stopped by to pick her up. Jay was waiting for us, with the owners of the store front when we got to his office. Happy Buyers, happy Sellers, cash, another heavenly Closing. All I could think was my time will come for the Closing from hell. Oh well, it will come when it comes. Jay handed me a copy of Johnathan's email and a copy of the trail he had verified buried in a few other papers. I handed everything to Mary, not seeing them.

After we ordered lunch, Mary pulled them out of her file. "So what's this?" Mary handed the email and the map to me. I knew Mary hadn't had time to look at either.

"Jay just being funny, that's all." I folded the papers, slid them into my bag. Changed the subject. "So what do you think of Sam?"

"Seriously, Vic what's with the map?"

"Mary, let it go. It has nothing to do with the Closing. It's a little ditty Jay's playing with that he though I would think was funny. That's all. So what do you think of Sam?" Actually, it was true. It had absolutely nothing to do with me, almost. It was a map of the trail on the east side of the Greenway James had taken on the second ride, the night before he left.

"So again you're not going to tell me?"

"Mary, ask Jay. Please ask Jay. Now tell me what you think of Sam."

"He could be good. Cuts a nice line." Mary laughed. "Seriously Vic, I know him a little. Seems quiet most of the time, polite. I've never had any dealings with him though."

"I have. Kind of like Ames with a serious edge. Good negotiator. Values his Clients. He's stuck in one of the wholesale agencies. Lots of office time required, rules and regulations, you know. I bet if he were let loose, he could be quite productive and interesting. I don't think he's married. I think I'd like to talk to him. I've never wanted to approach someone - you know stealing agents is illegal. But he could call me. Think Ames would ask him for a beer?"

"I think he might. Vic, we all know a new broker is purely your call. Give it a shot." Mary was right.

"Do you remember if he was on anyone's list?"

"I have the lists with me. I figured we should look at the names." She pulled a file out of her briefcase and flipped through the papers. "Yeah, he's there. Take a guess who suggested him. Go ahead, guess."

"Obviously not Ames. I wouldn't think Mason would have noticed him – Nina? You're kidding?" Oh rats. I was laughing. "Has she done anything with him? I mean real estate?" I was still laughing.

"Not that I know of. Oh, Nina gets around. God, she must have twenty or more years on him at least. This is just too funny." We were both laughing.

"I'll talk to Nina. Just too good. I love it." Lunch arrived.

My supper, favorite bar/restaurant is really a cigar bar in the lower level of what used to be a gambling, whorehouse a century ago in Newport. It was frequented by the upper crust of Newport's "Gilded Age", when the mansions were built, when Newport was the frontline of America's society pages. The first floor was a piano bar and larger restaurant. Food was fine, but I went for the atmosphere. That I loved. Subtle lighting, intimate seating so you could have a good conversation with someone and not be overheard. If you didn't want to be seen, that was easy too.

Mary and I moved to standard Friday talk. Ames had three Closings next week totaling close to a million - good for him. Nina had one, for over a million – nice. Mason was going on a month vacation at the end of next week, returning after the Derby. I was glad to see that. Of course, Mason could be avoiding our construction. He disliked that kind of disruption almost as much as I did. I returned Mary to the office about 4:30, picked up one of the two copies of the plans Joe had brought earlier, went home to work.

I used the removable sticky stuff to put the plan on the wall of the library. It's easier for me to pick out problems with plans if I can look at it over time, a glance here, a hard look there, just easier. I called Nina, congratulated her on the sale and asked about Sam. "Nina, I was looking at the proposed brokers you guys listed for me and Sam caught my eye. Do you think he might be open to talking to me?"

Nina sounded excited. "Victoria, you just made my day. I think it would make his year. He's getting frustrated with all the office stuff where he is now. Apparently the franchise is talking about blazers for it agents. He's not into the steak knife or Caribbean trip games." A not so subtle reference to a Mamet play about real estate. One of my favorites. The first year we had the storefront on Bellevue I gave everyone a copy of the DVD.

"Well, one star for him. What else can you tell me about him?" I asked.

"He spent time in the corporate world and it drove him crazy. He got into real estate thinking it would free him of the office stuff. He got his Brokers License last year thinking it would give him a little more freedom and mobility. It didn't. Did you know that each Purchase and Sale Agreement is reviewed by the Office Manager before it can go to a Client? Even a dumb Offer. Anyway, when I tell him he should give you a call, he'll call. Oh yeah, Vic. He's a great lover." We were cracking up.

"Nina, you are way too much. You know if you ever said anything like that in front of Mason he'd fall over in a dead faint, right?"

"Oh yeah. Our consummate little southern gentleman. I've been tempted." In the office Nina was the consummate lady.

"Haven't we all. Tell Sam to give me a call.""

"Hey, Sam. Victoria Hamilton wants you to call her." I heard laughing in the background. "Victoria, give him five and he'll call. He needs to shower."

"Nina, I'm dying here." I could barely talk I was laughing so hard. "Tell him to make it ten. I've got to stop laughing." I hung up and walked out onto the patio. I couldn't stop laughing.

True to the conversation Sam called me in ten minutes. Should have told Nina twenty. I couldn't talk to him with a straight face. Wondered if I ever could again. "Sam, I'd like to talk to you about making a change in your agency situation. Would you be interested?" Not easy to say without laughing.

"Victoria, I would love to talk to you. I would have called you sooner but you didn't give the impression you wanted to add anyone. What's good for you?"

"How about the cigar bar, Sunday around one?"

"Sure. Do you want me to bring a resume or anything?"

"If you have one fine, but don't write one for me, ok."

"Sure, I've got one up to the real estate. I'll bring that. See you Sunday at one." We hung up. I chuckled my way into the computer.

Bill had emailed me the report on his retaining wall crack. Bottom line, probably stable. To upgrade and modernize the wall so that it wouldn't crack again the estimate was $5,000. Not as expensive as I thought it would be. I emailed Bill telling him to let it lie, don't fix it. We'll supply the engineer's take on the crack, along with the estimate in the Disclosure Package. I copied the full email with my response to Mary.

I walked myself through Bill's Closing Statement, running my own calculations. It looked good. I sent that to Bill. Every once in a while the numbers from the lawyers contained an error. Wrong taxes, credits and/or debits incorrect and it was embarrassing for me to find it at the Closing. Especially if it was on my Client's side of the calculations. One time the identification of a property had been wrong. According to all the paperwork the Buyer was buying the house next door to the actual house they were buying. The Closing was put off for a week to straighten out the paperwork. Go to find out the wrong house had been transferred in the last three sales. Yeah, it can happen.

The talisman tickled, then moved on my ankle. No buzz. I reached down, held it against my ankle. "I miss you." I said. It moved, tickled and moved again. A feeling of comfort, warmth moved into my leg, just enough, to make me smile. When the feeling faded, I went to bed. No buzz. Wherever James was, the sun hadn't come up.

Chapter 40

I woke to a wonderfully warm, sunny Saturday. Either the gods were playing a nasty trick on us or winter was gone. I took a café chair out to the patio for morning coffee. A delight of spring, the first patio coffee. The open house next door started at eleven, ended at one. I didn't want to be the neighbor everyone from the open house talked to; so I had about twenty minutes to enjoy before Tina would show up. I would move the car to the visitors parking section and walk in through the front door. When I was done I'd go down to the beach for a walk until one.

I was the last sale in this condo association. I'd used my maiden name to purchase. Everything I personally held, the real estate, my car, my personal accounts, are held my maiden name. Actually, my legal name was my maiden name; except on my Broker's License. Probably because of the previous license transfer and Jay's kindness. If one dug hard enough there is a document that says I chose to keep my married name for business purposes. I remember signing it years ago. When Tina pulled the owners' names for the condos she would see Victoria Thorne. Good by me. I would sign into the open house with Hamilton.

The condo was a mirror image of mine, decorating was different. Much darker, more Victorian, many more pictures on the walls. The library space was still being used as a second bedroom and its door was still up. The kitchen was a little more professional than mine. Serious cook top, serious double wall ovens and bread warmer, but, all in all a mirror image.

I watched the other people walking through the condo while I was there. None of them appealed to me as new neighbors. The existing Owner was a widow that came to the Island from Florida for July and August only. Frankly, having real neighbors didn't appeal to me. I wondered what they would say about James's horse. I thanked Tina when the open house ended, went on to the beach.

For as beautiful a day as it was, the beach was pretty empty. A few surfers at the west end, a couple of people walking their dogs. When the season opens animals are not allowed on the beach. I had bitched about that ordinance.

I was about half way down the beach, in my own world, when a horse pulled up beside me. I didn't have to look to know who it was. His arm came down, I held on. James pulled me up side saddle, in front of him. I swung my leg over the horse's neck. He turned my head to the side, moved his face around me for a swallow you down kiss. He wasn't hiding. I just wanted to hold him. He pulled me back, touching all. "Ride?" His only words.

"Yes, please." I held his one arm around me as tight as I could. Complete. I hadn't realized I wasn't while he was gone. James navigated us carefully down the beach, cutting over the dune path, through the parking lot before we reached the surfers. Without hesitation we moved up the dirt road parallel to Ledge House, picked up speed across the crest of the hill past the quarry. James trotted us across Green End Avenue, pushing the horse as fast as he would go to the field by Quaker Hill. Not a word was spoken.

I slid off the horse but wasn't allowed to touch the ground. Instead, my legs went around his waist. The kiss that started when I slid off the horse, didn't stop. My heart sped up. His matched mine beat for beat. With one hand James put the blankets on the ground; removed the reins from the horse, laid me on the blankets covering my body with his. When he moved to kiss my neck, I held his face, looked into his eyes, red, so much light. "I missed you James. I didn't realize how much."

"Too long." He whispered. I could not touch him enough. When my hands went under his sweater it felt like I'd never touched him. I wanted to be at the condo. I wanted to kiss him from head to toe. James reached between us; unbuttoned his jeans, unbuttoned mine. His were gone in the blink of an eye. By the time mine were to my knees I didn't care if anyone saw us. I truly didn't care. As James slipped into me he screamed, I moaned. I almost couldn't move. The delight of that feeling spread over my body like a rush of water. He was holding back for me, holding back to be gentle. He shook with every movement. I just shook.

"James. I can't stand it. More of you, faster." He didn't hesitate, took me at my word. The next thrust hit the end of me, the next faster - harder.

My jeans were gone. I wrapped my legs around him hard enough to lift off the ground with his thrusts. The release hit me. I had no warning, no words. His last thrust felt like it would never end. Then release, so warm.

James bit into the shoulder of my sweatshirt, not me. His mouth moved to my pulse, kissed. Thrust again. The orgasm was there, again. He released again. I released again. A shimmer. James sunk into my body as if I had no skin; looked out of my eyes. His heart was mine, his body was mine. The back on the blanket was his. "I am home" echoed in my head. Comfort echoed in my body. A shudder. James was back in his body.

I don't know how long we remained as we were. His arms around my back, his mouth against my neck. My arms around his back, my legs wrapped around his waist. Not long enough. When James lifted his head, looked into my eyes, the sun was on the west horizon.

"Victoria. I did not think the hole in my soul could ever be as bad as it was when we were separated. Leaving you was harder. Being away from you was the most painful thing. I went to your home, saw you on the beach. I did not care who saw me, cared about nothing but getting to you. I do not know if your neighbors truly saw me."

"James I didn't realize how empty I was until you were next to me on the beach." It was the truth. I put my hands on either side of his beautiful face, pulled him to me, kissed his mouth, kissed the hollows that were his cheeks, kissed his light-filled eyes, his forehead, his nose, his mouth… again.

I felt his heart slow. James rolled to his back. "We should return before you chill." I sat up, looked at James watching the sky. Realized that I was probably locked into his ride, wherever it went. Was he locked into mine? I didn't know. "Victoria. Is something wrong?"

"I'm fine James. Just fine." He handed my jeans to me. Took my hand, pulled me up. The north breeze hit, I shivered, pulled them up. James was dressed before I could get one last look. Rats. The horse walked over a little hill to James.

"Where does he go when he wanders?" I asked.

James was returning the blankets to the back of the horse. "There is a fresh creek at the bottom of the rise and some good trees. Nice space. Sometimes the farmer's horses and cows are there. He enjoys their company." James was on the horse, arm down for me.

"Behind you?" Being surprised half way up, well, that was asking for trouble.

"Yes. You will be warmer." He lifted and, yet, once again, I settled behind him. He pulled me closer, lifted his sweater over my hands, arms. "Please, Victoria. Touch me while we ride back. I want to feel your skin on mine." I spread my fingers, ran my hands over his stomach, his chest. He held my arms over his sweater, held me tight to his skin. I laid my head against his back, closed my eyes. I could feel his muscles move with the horse. His back radiated heat, I could feel ever so subtle movement under his skin. I didn't remember the heat.

James stopped at the edge of the quarry where a small trail broke into the Ledge House property. "Do you now have neighbors?"

"No. She's not back. She put the condo on the market, no problem now." We continued to the condo, took the horse to my garden door. I slid off, started to walk back around to the front of the building.

"Victoria, where are you going?" Right, the door had been open the last time, the first time he brought us back on the horse.

"James, the garden doors are locked. I need to go in the front, disarm my alarm. I locked when I went to the beach." I looked at him. Did he think I locked it to keep him out? I walked as fast as I could around to the front. Set a record for disarming the alarm; opened the garden door. "James I didn't lock it to keep you out. You don't think that do you? Get your butt in here." I looked to the trough. He'd filled it from the garden spigot. He was carrying the blankets. "I could warm the blankets in the dryer if they can take it. Your horse should get some pleasure out of hauling us."

"They are woven cotton, not too much heat. May I…"

"Fire please James." I tossed the blankets into the dryer, cotton. Didn't know it had a setting for cotton. By the time I returned he was lighting the match. It bothered me that he would even let the thought enter his brain, that I set the locks for him. "Follow me. I want to show you how to disarm the alarms."

I pulled the keys from my pocket, removing the extra from the ring. I handed it to him. He smiled. That's better. I gave him the alarm lesson with the codes. I wrote the codes down, handed them to him. "Come in at your pleasure." For all of the reassurances he had given me, I could give him this.

We settled in the living room. The fire felt good. I joined him on the floor this time; his hands on my thighs. "I do believe you are the only one, other than me, who has the alarm codes. I always figured the firemen could hack their way in. If there was a break-in, well, something would be open. I usually set the alarm at night, except for the nights you have been here."

"Victoria, thank you. I do not recall you locking when we rode. Are you locking because of what happened?"

"Yes. You know about it, the fire, the note?"

"Yes. Is your office ok? Was anyone hurt?"

It was a sincere question. He knew the answer but he wanted me to tell him. So, in as few words as possible, I told him.

"You realize that they know nothing of us."

"I know Kenny, the fake Father was a joke so I figured they knew nothing. Has this happened before?"

"Yes. Someone does what they did or they are sensitive to us. Either way, you could still get hurt. You know you could have contacted me. I am surprised the talisman did not transfer your emotions. You have Johnathan's number, yet you did not call."

"James, I knew they were a joke. The last thing I would do is harass you about nothing. Your friend Charon did a wonderful job with the local news lady. Right out of central casting. He even looked familiar to me."

James thought for a moment. "Charon does manage the property. He has taken care of my home, wherever I am, for years. Charon is also our face…to the public when we need it. Yes, he is quite good." James smiled. "His American is done to perfection; as well as his French, Spanish, Greek, Russian, English, Chinese dialects, many others. He is also good at looking human. Could you tell he is Asra-pa? He is so much better than we are…at adapting." James seemed to be enjoying just talking. "There were four of us at the house. Now there are six. It is, to my surprise, getting crowded."

"What do you mean? There are twelve bedrooms and the two apartments."

"I have my room and an office together. Johnathan has his room and office. Charon has his bedroom and office. Charles has his. George has his. The rest of the family have their own families. Two young children. It pretty much eats up the house, the apartments. The couple I returned with are a part of my family. I will need to find a place for them. Would you mind if I bought the condo next to you rather than have strangers living there?" Wow, James had never been this open.

"James, you've never talked to me like this. About yourself, your family. What happened while you were gone?" I had to ask.

"Am I assuming too much? That you would be interested. That you would want to know these things?"

"Not at all. It's part of you. Anything that is a part of you I want to know. It's important to me." It was. I realized it was when I said it.

"Would it bother you? They are very interesting. He is a veterinarian as is his wife." He laughed. "They were in jail. I needed to get them out. That is why I was late returning. In Tibet, a Chinese jail. I had to get to them before they ended up in China. It would have been much harder to retrieve them from a Chinese prison. If they were next door we would not have to be concerned about the horse. They would also be there for you if you ever needed help and I could not get to you."

"James, my only concern…this will sound strange to you. I am not a 'neighbor' type person. I say hi to my neighbors, but that's about it. I don't like friends living next door to me. It takes too much work. Don't take this wrong, but another concern would be ah…how can I say this…"

"Victoria." He cut in. "I will say it for you. Will they report you to me. Will they tell me what you do?"

"Yes." I moved my eyes from his.

"Look at me. I understand what you are saying very well." He put his hands to my face, rose to his knees. "Anytime I want to, anytime you want to, we can know what each other is doing. I have never invaded you when we were not together. You have never invaded me. All you need to do is hold your hands over the talisman. Hold it to your skin, concentrate. Johnathan told you how, you talked to me. I have shown this to you. What do we need others for? I admit I was tempted when you did not call Johnathan after the fire. I did not. If you want to talk to me, you will. If I want to say something to you, I do. Do you understand this?"

Until James said it, I hadn't given it much thought. "Yeah. I guess I do." I took a moment to think. "James, you are going to have to be patient with me. The metaphysics as reality is new to me." I gave him a good smile. I felt a little stupid. My lack of knowing this little piece of trivia was my fault. Thinking about the magic lead to thinking about James, where this is headed, does it even matter?

"Victoria. Let me bring you to Ledge House tomorrow. The family is with me at their choice, not mine. You need to at least see the house, how it works. I have wanted you to come, but Johnathan thought you should be more comfortable with me first." James leaned in, kissed me.

"Now please. Tell me about your business. I saw plans on your wall." Subject change. Was I going to Ledge House? I didn't know either. Shit. I needed some time. I bought the time with an answer to his last question.

"When it looked like you were going to Close Ledge House I started thinking about the empty space next to the Agency. When you Closed, we offered on the office space. It closed Friday, yesterday. The plan combines the spaces; gives us a conference room, two more office spaces and our own bathroom." That was it in a nutshell.

"You have not mentioned any of this, why?"

"Honestly, I didn't think it would be interesting conversation. It is what it is."

James looked down, thinking, composing his response. "Victoria as you said to me, I am interested in how your life works, what you do. When I was gone I wondered what you were doing, where you were, who you were talking to, what was being said. I have never been in your office. I do not know who your friends are. You told me who was in your office, their names. The only one I know anything about is Billy's Mary. Why are they in your office? Why do you own the business? What do you do when you are not working? These things are becoming very important to me. Is it because you still think I am 'playing with toys'?"

Deadly question. I stood, looked down at him. It was late enough, no one would be at the office. "OK James. Grab the drawing. I'm taking you to the office. No one will be there now. Come on." James had the plan in his hands before I finished grabbing my bag and car keys. "Will your horse be alright?"

"Follow me to the house. It will take a few extra minutes." I was walking to the car, James was already up the driveway. It took us all of ten minutes to return the horse.

As we were driving to the office, alone on the road, James started asking questions about the area, the buildings we were passing. He started with the large stone structure, spires, beautiful grounds not far from the condo. I explained that it was a private secondary school and church which produced more questions. I realized that he hadn't explored the Island. Johnathan had said he had family here when I'd asked at our first meeting. Obviously, James had never been here. "This is new to you?"

"It is."

"Johnathan said you had family here." James was staring at me.

"I do." Dumb Victoria. Don't ask unless you're ready for the answer.

This time of night I parked in front of the office.

The first thing James did was examine the damage from the fire. "This should not have happened Victoria. I am truly sorry." He ran his hands over the doorframe and window damage. I unlocked the office door.

"Looks a little different...closer." He straightened.

"I was not sure you had seen me. Charon taking your scent, your energy, distracted you." Oh yeah, he had my attention. The guy that bumped into me? James just smiled walking up the steps while I disarmed the alarm, flipped on the lights, thought about what he had said so easily. I opened the French door to my office. "So Mary is here?" He was checking out her desk.

"What? Taking my scent?" His eyes looked up from the desk.

"Yes. I was not going to wait for another turn of your wheel Victoria. Charon stayed with you. This is Mary's place?" James spoke as if I should have expected a bodyguard, no big deal. Was it a big deal to me? I'd have to think about it.

"For now. We've hired someone to take some of the day-to-day work so she can do more field real estate." I walked into my office. James followed, sat in my chair momentarily. He felt the wood of the desk. Walked over to the lawyer's bookcases, checked out the Client's chairs. We walked back to the workroom. He again checked out everything in the room. I took him through the workroom French door into the office space.

James walked into every office, sat in every chair. Touched things that the desk's owners would touch. I told him who sat where when they were in the office. Mason would have had a fit. James ran his hand over the glass block walls. I opened the French door back into Mary's area. He stood at the doorway, looking back into the office space, turned back to Mary's space.

"Victoria, during the day the light must be interesting. No fluorescents, no carpeting. Did a designer do this?"

"No. I had it designed a couple of years before I had the opportunity to do it. The light was a big deal to me, as was the industrial carpet in most offices. I'd rather sand and varnish every few years than clean carpets every 6 months. I think the wood floors are warmer, just like the incandescent."

James smiled at me. "I have seen the hardwoods but never the incandescent as the sole lighting in this type of office. Are you doing the same thing next door?"

I set the alarms, locked the door. We stood on the sidewalk between the two spaces. "Let me grab a flashlight. You have the plan." He pulled the plan out of his pocket and I walked him through what we were doing. "With any luck it will look as though the space has always been one, never two."

James returned the plan to his pocket, leaned down giving me a nice, soft, friendly kiss. "Victoria, I like the warmth, the simplicity of your home but to translate the feeling into this space. I am impressed." We returned to the car. "Did Johnathan see the rest of your office?"

"No. I don't believe so. He was here a very short time, both times. The first was spent in my office, in the computer. The second just to drop off the gift." We started back to the condo.

"The property listings from the computer in your office, can you access from your library computer?"

"Yes."

"Only your properties?"

"No. Pretty much everything in the State, southern Massachusetts and Connecticut. As real time as it takes another real estate agent to put their listings in. If you want, sometime I'll show you. I'm in at least once a day."

"I would like that."

"James, what are you asking?"

"I have no idea how your business works. If we need to expand a facility, open a new one. If we decide to move somewhere, I tell Johnathan to do it. It is done. Now this is part of your life, it is a part of mine. I should know more of this."

Interesting. "Not many people want to know about it. Kind of like sausage. People love to eat it but they don't want to see it made. I appreciate your interest."

We walked into the condo, through to the living room. James started to add logs to the dying fire. "Victoria." He stood before he was done, turned to look at me. "While I was gone I realized that you probably were not going to run from me because you were frightened. It was a great relief. If you run it will be because you decided to run. That I do something to cause your reaction. Are you still thinking about running?" His hands were on my shoulders.

"You came back with a couple of deadly questions James. The first you may have not even realized you asked. This question, no I haven't thought about running. The first, the reason I didn't realize the extent of the talisman was because I hadn't thought about what Johnathan said. I hadn't thought about it because it leads to you.

"James, when you leave for the day, when you left on your trip, that part of my life went into a box. It was put away. If you decided to leave, wait for another turn of my wheel - another lifetime; the hole you would leave might only be the size of the box. The rest of my life might still function. If I integrate the two, I will be broken beyond repair. When I said it before I wasn't sure - now I know." I hesitated. Debated whether to continue with my question.

"Victoria." I took a very deep breath.

"James, are you seeing in me the woman you loved before? Not who I am now?"

He thought for a minute. Then two. His eyes remained on me. "You Victoria, standing here in this moment, are the result of all of your soul's journeys. Without the lives before I remember us together; without the lives since; you would not be here as you are. Take out one life, the result would be different. The soul I would still love. That soul would still be a part of me, but the person would be different. Victoria, your soul is a part of mine. Truly, standing here, I love who you are also. You surprise me. You attract me. You interest me.

"If the fire had happened to the person in Billy's drawing, she would have demanded my return. You didn't. If I had been Asra-pa; she would have run screaming. If I had joined us in her time; her terror would have demanded my end. We are together now as we are meant to be. I am not going to leave you. Never." James pulled me to him, held me to him for a long time.

I relaxed, allowed myself to think about what he had said. My head debated. Ran through the logic of the situation, its absurdities…then stopped with an inescapable truth. Well James, here goes the ride. You may be the one running away some day. My inescapable truth? I had nothing of true value to lose but him. Geez.

"I'll go to Ledge House with you tomorrow." James released his hold. Gave me a wonderful smile, a drop your socks kiss.

He reached into his pocket. "I should return your plans. You will need them." He turned to light the now dead fire. I sat on the loveseat.

"Was Charon the guy that ran into me at the condo? Touched my arm at the restaurant?" James seemed to think about my question without expression. Then a smile.

"Yes. It was Charon. It was Charon at the auction also." It took me a second to realize that Charon had been the Irishman in the attic. I had to laugh. The guy was good.

"Is Charon still watching me?"

"No. Not when I am here." His answer raised more questions for me on such a minor subject. I dropped it. If I didn't focus on a babysitter, maybe James wouldn't. Subject change.

"Did you see anything odd in the plans? Something that wouldn't work right in three dimensions?" Having another set of eyes looking for errors couldn't hurt.

"What do you mean?" He flipped the match, lit a log, sat at my feet, arm around my leg.

"In my last office there was a woman who had been in this business twenty years before I met her. I couldn't count how many plans she'd reviewed for her Clients in that time. She decided to build her retirement home. Small little house, up the street from here. When she finalized the plans, she brought them into the office, put them on the wall. She asked everyone, there were nine of us, to look at them, see if anything was wrong. No one in that office was a new. We'd all been around the block a few times. The plans stayed up for a week. No one could find anything wrong. She built the house. The weekend after the big move she came in and asked why someone didn't see the bedroom closet door problem.

"Of course we didn't know what she was talking about. Apparently, with her queen size bed in the master bedroom, the major walk-in closet door could not be opened, couldn't even be accessed. The house was sited on the lot so that she couldn't simply expand the bedroom. She ended up moving every wall on that side of the house, all the electrical and plumbing. So I ask again. Did you see anything that didn't look right?" James was trying not to laugh, truly trying. I laughed. "It is a funny story, of course when she held up the plans again I couldn't figure out how we'd missed it. No one could. The closet had been placed in the middle of the only wall a bed could be placed on."

I opened up my plans, slid to the floor. James was still suppressing his laugh.

"Victoria, that is truly a funny story. I will be glad to take another look." Still chuckling. "Did this really happen?"

"No joke James. She was not a happy camper for the three months she had to rent an apartment."

"I truly can not see a problem. I will show it to Johnathan if you would like. I will bring it back tomorrow."

"You know, I'd appreciate that." He returned the plans to his pocket.

"The sun will be rising soon. I would like to make love to you before I leave. Would that be alright with you?"

"Already?" I looked through the windows to the horizon. Didn't see anything. "Yes, very much."

James rose to his knees in front of me, pulled off his sweater, pulled off my sweatshirt; leaned back to his heels focusing on the tattoo on my left breast. Followed it with his fingers from my shoulder, around my nipple, under my breast to it's end. Leaned to me taking my breast into his mouth, sliding his hands around my back, stretching me to the floor. I kissed his head, one hand to his back touching every inch of skin I could reach. The other under his chest to the top to his pants, released the buttons until they were too tight to continue. "James" was all I said. One hand freed from my back, he released himself from the buttons; his pants, my pants gone.

Slight movement. Tongue, mouth to the other breast. His legs inside mine, I was trembling, his heart pounding "God James." He was inside me. This, this instant reaction, never in my experience. Felt him release my breast. He was on his hands, a push to the end of me. He stayed, my legs around him. He lifted me, himself to his knees, then standing, moved to the bedroom.

"Too late." He whispered. My back on the bed; thrusts were urgent, hard, my nails into his back, the cheeks of his ass. I felt him buried in me, pulsing, starting to come. I let myself go, joined him, held him as tight as I could with hands, legs, my body. He flowed into me. Still for a second, started to move out of me, one more thrust. He released again, I came again. He collapsed to my shoulder.

"Dawn." James was gone before his weight leaving me registered.

I lay feeling the end of the orgasm. The talisman shocked my leg. I sat up, ran to the living room expecting to see him on the floor, he wasn't there. I opened the garden door, he wasn't in the yard. I walked to the edge of the cliff, about a hundred feet away. I looked to the rocks. The rays of the sun were brightening the eastern horizon. Nothing on the rocks that I could see, nothing in the water. Would he float?

I thought for a second. Who do I call? Johnathan's gone too. Still, I called his cell, left a message. Hell. Threw my sweats back on, grabbed the keys. Shit, shit, shit.

I looked everywhere I could on the way to Ledge House. Nothing. The gate was locked. I climbed the gate. Realized no shoes. I was barefoot. I must have looked like an idiot, not that anyone saw me. I started running up the driveway to the main house. A small car started down the driveway, pulling beside me. The driver's window came down. A little man asked in very broken English, "Do you need help?"

"Did James get home before the sun?" I was out of breath.

The man's eyes almost popped out of his skull. He said something to me, pulled a cell out of his pocket, urgently spoke to someone in the house,

I guess. The only word I understood him to say was James. He waited a second, then two. He smiled. "Yes, yes, James fine."

"Thank you." I turned, walked back to the gate.

"Wait, Wait." The car pulled to the gate, the small man got out of the car with his key ring. Flipped through all the keys, talking the whole time to himself. He had a suit on. How strange. This early? He unlocked the gate, held it open for me. Yeah, I felt like an idiot. What was I going to do, climb it again? Not in this lifetime. I was surprised I could do it the first time.

"Thank you again. I don't know if I had another climb in me." I smiled at him while I opened the car door.

"You need keys." He said. I didn't have any plans to do this again. I was going to set an alarm for us. No, not again. Although the sex was great this morning, not worth his risk. Funny, each time was better than the time before. Normally, I would be getting bored, usually after the first time I was bored, the anticipation was gone. James, I couldn't get enough of James. I went home, left the sweats on, crashed in the bed.

Chapter 41

My eyes opened at 11:30. I laid in bed thinking about what I had done earlier. I did have to laugh. Poor man, probably thought I was nuts, but he didn't ask questions. That was nice. He hadn't reacted to my question with any bull hockey; that was also nice. Didn't ask who I was, didn't ask why I wanted to know if James was home. Either very smart man or very lax security.

I forced myself out of bed. Made coffee. Sat in the library, flipped on the computer. I wondered if I could get a phone number for the house. Someone in the house that didn't die at first light. A moment's hesitation as I glanced to the empty space on the wall, then remembered. Johnathan was going to take a look at the plans.

I finished my first cup of coffee, was looking at the beach trying to decide whether to make some breakfast when the talisman gave me hard shock, tickled, rolled quickly on my ankle. I could almost feel James's hand. Didn't expect that. Usually James waking was a little buzz, a light tickle. Interesting.

I went to the kitchen to grab some yogurt, moved to the utensil drawer. Out of the corner of my eye I saw James standing in the kitchen window. I glanced at the clock, 12:15. That was big time early. I had to laugh looking at him. Big smile, tips of his fangs showing, huge flashing eyes. He looked, if it were possible, like a little boy on Christmas morning. The only thing missing was the bouncing from one foot to the other. I opened the garden door, James was waiting.

"Early." I kissed him. "You look like a little kid, too funny." I started walking back to the kitchen, was picked up, hugged, spun, put down. I shuddered. Why don't we just stay here?

"You are coming to the house." James was wired. His excitement was odd, but contagious; it started to overrun my anxiety. "Are you ready to go?"

"I haven't even showered. What's the hurry?" I wondered if he was going to crawl out of his skin. He couldn't stand still…very, very odd for him. James tilted his head.

"Do not worry Victoria, it will be fine. Are you afraid to meet my family?"

I smiled. "No….yes. They mean so much to you. You have history with them. If I screw up, say something wrong. I've met 'the family' before James. It never goes well. Do they even know I exist? I'm a stranger walking in with someone they care for." What else could I say? Well, what if I fucked up royally, that I implied. Meeting people didn't bother me, social situations didn't bother me, I usually didn't care. I did now…odd for me. What the hell was going on? Something wasn't right.

"Shower while we talk." He took my hand, urging me to the shower, smiling again, nothing was going to dull his excitement today. Excited? James excited?

He walked into the bathroom with me. I pushed him back into the dressing room. "I'll leave the door open, we can still talk." I did want to take him into the shower, but I wouldn't get the answers I wanted. My attraction to him was ridiculous, getting worse. Right now, since he walked in the patio door, it could be classified as overwhelming. Should I say something like 'What the hell's going on? You're acting weird and I'm getting there.'

"So, to answer your questions." He began. "They know that you are my soul, that I have found you. They laugh at me sometimes, not to my face, but I know. Zara is cooking as we speak. Making a huge supper for later. Zara runs the house. Her two daughters came to clean. Her husband was one of the two men that brought the trough and the wood."

"Do they know what you and Johnathan are?" The shower felt good. Maybe this would calm me down.

"Yes. Everyone on the property does know us all. Her family, grandmother, grandfather, their grandparents going back ten generations, have been with me. She grew up in my family as her daughters did, as her grandchildren are."

"You're kidding me. None have been away?" Talk about servitude.

"Only for school, college, vacations, when they choose to leave. As I think of it, all of the people, all of my human family has been with me for generations. The only outsiders have been mates. Right now that is two. But you will meet everyone while we walk."

I had to let that sink in. The concept screamed questions for another day. "Anything else I should know? Is it alright if I talk to them if they ask a question? Is there anything I shouldn't say, talk about?"

"Victoria, the field is completely open. Talk to them, any topic is fine. It does not...matter. What are you asking me?"

"I don't know. I just don't want to...I guess..." The glass door of the shower slid back, James joined me. "...screw up." His arms were around me. He moved against me. Leaned his weight against my back. Head on my shoulder, another excitement against my ass. My hands were over his as they touched every inch of me.

"Victoria." He whispered. "It is a family. They fight, feelings get hurt, they get angry, throw fits, stomp out of rooms, even throw things. It is a family. Do you think I control the people around me? I do not. Could I? Maybe. I have never tried." I could feel him wanting to enter me, waiting for permission.

"Finish last night, please." I started to turn. His hands stopped me, lifted me against him, slid me down until he was in as far as he could go. I shivered. My feet barely touched the tile. I was lifted, held, allowed to slide, lifted before my feet touched anything. Slow, controlled, wet, saw his spirits surround me.

My skin gave, I slid into him. I could feel what he felt, my God. The tingle at his spine, moving up, down, out into his arms. The contractions of his body, building, building heat, fire releasing. Throbbing. Wave breaking, slowing. Releasing more fire...building again. Pressure again. Breaking again, again.

I was back in my body, back on the tile. Feeling the end of the last orgasm in myself...then he was out of me. I turned, kissed him, held him, his arms around my back, my heart pounding, the water cooled. Freaking amazing experience. "Is that how it feels to you?"

"Some of what I feel, yes. Did you enjoy?" He moved back, looked into my eyes with the red, the light. He was wired. I was getting wired, wanted him again. This was verging on the absurd. Control Victoria.

"Can you truly feel me?"

"Yes. I feel everything your body does. It is thrilling. I do believe you might be clean. If we stay a moment more...I will not be able to...stop myself." I wasn't the only one. He stepped out of the shower. I turned the water off, he handed me a towel. By the time I'd dried, James was dressed, hair damp. "Victoria. I could stay inside of you for an eternity. I am satisfied for a moment, then my desire for you returns. I have never felt this before. Not when we were together before, never. I am not in control of this. This morning I could not leave this place without feeling you again. I tried, but I could not. I do apologize for leaving like that. I did not mean to. Did not think that you would be so concerned that I would not make it home." He laughed. Followed me into the kitchen to grab cell, keys, walked to the alarm. Stopped before I set the code.

"James. Is today different? Since you returned...is it different for you? I believe I feel the same way."

"Yes. I am not sure why." He smiled. "Now. I would like you right now." He reached his hand to my waist. I stepped back. He started to step forward.

"James. Go to the horse while I set the alarm or we will never leave." I laughed. He nodded, moved quickly to the patio door. He didn't know what was going on? I heard the door close. I set the alarm, hurried to the patio door, stepped through, locked it.

"When Cat called the house, Zara found me half dressed in the entry." James was smiling. "I barely made it back. That is the talk in the house today." James mounted.

"Thanks for the humor. By the way, do you float?" His hand reached down for me. I took it, sat in front of him. Felt his body radiating against mine.

"No, we do not. But we do not drown. It matters?"

"James, I believe more than anything, yes." Easier to admit than I thought it would be, good. The need for him was building again. "I've never seen you...so wired. I was good until I saw you at the window. I want you again, yes. I'm also crawling out of my skin."

"There is a great deal of energy around us today. That I feel. I woke feeling this way. We will be fine. Let us go to the house Victoria." Switch flipped, subject change.

Before moving the horse James shimmered easily, hid himself. "There are many people out today, walking, in cars." We started moving. James's tone had changed. He had put his concern away. Withdrawn. Regained control for the outside world. Ok. I would give it my best shot.

In this position James could talk to me with ease while we rode. "Victoria. We will be fine. Our energy together may be something that will adjust. My desire for you, yours for me may be the same energy. I am feeling better, are you?"

Actually, I was. "A bit, yes."

"As long as you are touching me I believe I will be able to control today." He took a quick kiss of my neck. "Please do not worry. My family understands these things." I squeezed his arms. Good point. Now, I did felt better.

The ride was nice. Very nice. People looked at us, rather, the horse. James picked up the reins. It occurred to me that riders are ignored. "People become upset if they do not believe the horse controlled." He lifted the reins so I could see them.

We stopped at every sign, every crossing. He made exaggerated movements looking for cars before we moved. It was a much longer, slower ride to Ledge House. James returned his arms to me as soon as we turned into the dirt road we usually took to the quarry.

The horse stopped in front of the property line. "The property is protected by a spell. When we cross the line you will feel a bit of a buzz when I stop covering. Nothing on the property can hide. Zara insisted. Always insists the spell is in place before she will allow her family in." We moved across the property line. Sure enough I felt James become James again.

"So everyone I see is as they are. No games. No tricks."

"Yes. Zara says it is only fair. Her Mother and Grandmother felt the same way. I must agree. It is good to see who you are talking to. It has served its purpose in other ways. That is why Charon was just outside of the gate when he spoke to the news people. It is also difficult to lie."

"James, what if Miss Katie had taken him up on the offer? If she had wanted to see the animals?" No answer.

We stopped at the barns. The heavy machinery I'd seen across from the barns was gone. Grass was starting to show in the cut earth. The remaining trees had been trimmed, suckers removed. The size of the soon to be meadow had to be at least three acres. The Sanctuary sign was removed, the fence remained. The man who had opened the gate for me stepped out to take the horse. "James, good ride?" Accented, work clothes, older - maybe early 70s, weather-worn face. James smiled.

"Too many people and cars, but nice." I slid to James, to the ground. "Victoria, I would like you to meet Villiam. Villiam this is Victoria." I held my hand out. He took it. "Thank you for your help this morning. I don't think I could have done the gate again." I smiled.

"Lucky I go to church early." He laughed. A good laugh.

"We are just going to walk through the barns, the weathering. All of the horses are free?"

"Yes. Some are wandering, others are at the trees. The birds are also free, not tethered. The sun is so warm today. I can tether them." The more he spoke, the better his English became.

"No Villiam. We will let them enjoy the sun while they can. Victoria will be fine." James held my hand while we walked to the other stalls. I counted six doors. Actually, two individual stalls, the remaining stall took the remainder of the old garage. "The horses seem to prefer to be together so we let them. The individual stalls are for hoof grooming, shoeing if we have to, illness. The exterior doors gave the impression of individuality to anyone looking at them." There were numerous saddles, two bits and reins on the rear wall. Each a little different, in style, size, I assumed use.

"Given the weather during the interview Victoria, the attention of the news crew would have been on the animals, not Charon. Their minds would retain the initial image of Charon. Filming would be of the animals." Now that was an interesting thought. The second or third time James had made the observation. I wondered how many times I'd truly seen what was in front of me and not what I assumed was there.

We walked around to the other side of the old garage, the side whose roof had been extended. The birds, a spectacular, black tipped snow owl, another breed of owl - maybe a large barn owl, some large brown and black hawks with white markings, various breeds and colors of falcons and one buzzard. They all seemed to be a little ragged. "These are my birds, my hunters, my fliers." James moved away from me a few feet. One of the hawks was to his arm in a flash. The owls moved in his direction, a couple of falcons walked to me. The snow owl looked like the one I'd seen move over James's body. I looked at his face. Couldn't see the owl mixed with the other...animals. The wolf was still prominent but the other side ... nothing was prominent.

"They are molting. If you sit Victoria, some may come to you." I did sit. Three came, one falcon, a large hawk and the snow owl. When they started nudging my legs I stopped moving. Didn't want to scare them. I couldn't believe they were so calm, amazing.

"Are they tame? Have you tamed them?" I didn't think these birds could be tamed. James looked at me, the birds around me, smiled a great smile.

"No Victoria. I would never. They are mine, the raptors. You saw some fly. It is wonderful to watch them free." The first statement was said as if

I should understand. I didn't. "They know my spirits. They are attracted, calmed, accepting. An amazing thing." James, for all his years, was still fascinated by the birds. He said something, the ones on his arms flew down; the others moved away. James stood, held his hand to me, helped me up.

We went into the weathering, the space for the birds. James explained which bird liked what area, the different perches, a bath constructed like a little brook with running water, their general care and maintenance. The weathering was slightly warmer than the air outside. I was informed that it takes about five months for one of them to fly as it should after molting begins. He wouldn't be able to fly any of them safely until sometime in the late summer, early fall. Interesting. All of the equipment for flying was in a huge locker in one corner.

We walked to the meadow along the fence on a brick path to the horses. When we stopped, the horses looked up, started wandering in our direction. "The horses needed a field. Do you remember? This was all conglomerate. Too hard and steep for them. Charon worked with the Sanctuary when he designed the space. It worked out well." The horses reached us before James had finished talking. A dark brown and white bumped him quite hard. "I know you are there." He turned to them. Patted noses, rubbed ears and flanks.

The dark brown and white moved to me. Gave a very gentle nudge. I patted his nose, ran my hand down his flank. The others followed him. For me, this was a treat. When everyone had their pats and pets the dark brown and white came back for more, rested his flank against me. "Victoria, he knows your spirits. He likes you. I did not see you around horses. You rode a few times, excited one so that you were nibbled, but that's all. Did I miss something?"

"No. My daughter took me riding, if that's what you'd call it. But no. I've always loved them. You saw the great nibble. I was black and blue for a couple of weeks after that."

James smiled. "You do not understand?" I shook my head. "You ran your hand a little too many times, a little too hard, over his nose." As he talked, his smile grew. "Victoria. How can I say this? The horse reacted like I did. Yesterday in the field when I entered you. A horse's nose is very sensitive." He was having quite a chuckle with this.

It took a second for me to understand what he was saying. "Oh…why didn't anyone tell me? Poor horse." I joined his laughter. I had been on a property tour for the listing of a farm. The whole office had been there. We were standing outside a stall when a big nose had rested on my shoulder. I'd said hi to the horse. He was beautiful and I just started petting his nose. He'd looked like he was enjoying it. All of a sudden he was chewing on my hand and arm.

Even though horses' teeth are pretty flat, the strength in his jaw bruised my hand and arm from little finger almost to my elbow. Very black and blue for a couple of weeks. I had tried to be cool about it saying to others I was just fine. By the time the tour had ended the back of my hand was turning color, my arm was throbbing. Without thinking I gave James a kiss for his explanation, for reminding me of yesterday. I shivered. He took my hand but stepped back. "Careful."

We walked around the path up to the top of a major outcropping. I could easily see the beach standing higher than Hanging Rock. This outcropping looked down on the famous rock. "I didn't realize there was anything this high on the property James. It's wonderful." I turned, taking in all of the views. "My gosh. I can see all the way into Portsmouth. It was almost level with the top of Purgatory Road; the school. I can see over the river to Little Compton Point and beyond." It was quite a view.

"We did not know it was here. Finding it was a surprise. The trees and brush obscured everything. Charon found it when he pulled the geodesic maps. Thought it might be here." We started walking back to the main house. "Enjoying?"

"Yes. This is a treat. You are creating a masterpiece out here. You must be pleased."

"I am. Very much so. Completely unexpected." A Red Tail Fox ran in front of us, up over the outcropping. "I was surprised at all the animals, birds, the variety in the area. Raam is trying to catalog them. Give them a quick look, vaccinate. He does this everywhere he goes. Padma says that before he is done he will have vaccinated every animal on the planet." That was funny.

We were at the house. Had the copper gutters been replaced, polished? The small amount of wood trim been painted? Serous work had been done in such a short time. James held the rear entrance door. "Ready?" No.

"Sure." We walked into the large milk porch, around the corner, into the kitchen. It smelled great. A million pots, people chopping and talking. When we were noticed everything stopped.

"Zara, can you break for a minute?" James was smiling ear to ear.

"Of course, for you any time." The oldest woman wiped her hands on her apron walking to James. "Victoria, I would like you to meet Zara,

Zara this is Victoria. Zara believes she is my Mother." James laughed. Zara slapped him on his shoulder. "Zara, your daughters, please."

"Victoria." Her smile returned. "These are my daughters, Kim and Laurie." Each waved at me, said hi. "And my granddaughters Julia and Lizzy. Girls this is Victoria, Uncle James's friend."

I can't say that I'd ever seen a professional kitchen in full use. "Zara, your kitchen smells wonderful. Do you cook like this every day?"

"No not this big, but every Sunday, yes. One of my rules. Everybody back to work!" Zara went back to cooking. James led me to the billiard room.

The open room behind the library had become the billiard room. A much better location than the rear of the house, against the humid swimming pool. The open, light, pastel room I had last seen had become, in my lexicon, a men's parlor with a billiard table. One corner had a deep, semi-circular Caesar Stone, chrome and glass wet bar that one would stand at, no bar stools. Very retro-modern, clean design. Yes, I loved it. Ten club chairs were grouped in twos near the walls.

The table, currently being used, centered the room. The walls, red mahogany wainscoting and framing were hung with all the implements of billiards. I could smell fresh cigars and pipe tobacco in the room.

Johnathan, in an old Woodstock tee shirt and very worn jeans was leaning against the bar watching two men I did not know, play - play that stopped the minute we entered. All three men straightened.

"Victoria, I am truly glad you could join us today. James, nice to see you vertical." Johnathan was doing everything he could not to laugh. The others did. James shook his head.

"Victoria, I do believe you recognize Johnathan, even though he did dress down today. This," James moved me to a thin, tall redhead, "is Kim's husband Edmond." Edmond walked to me.

"Victoria, pleased to meet you." Good handshake, human blue eyes, he stepped back.

"and this is Charon." He walked to me, held out his hand. I could not believe this was the guy on TV, the guy who had walked into me on the sidewalk. Shit, the guy who had run into me at the condo with Bill. No way. Wild blonde hair, very fair, a touch of pale, about 6'3" or so; eyes a color I'd never seen. Navy blue – not black - with their little strokes of lightening declaring the blue.

"Welcome Victoria. I am glad to meet you, very glad." His voice was lighter than it had sounded. A touch of Russian – yes, Russian was the undertone.

"I am glad to meet you both." I had to force my eyes from Charon to look at Johnathan. "Great room for the guys to hide in." Johnathan relaxed. Now that was a little out of character…or was the other persona out of character?

"You're looking at the wrong guy for the room Victoria. This is James's design, although it does work well. As for a men's club, do you play?" Johnathan knew me well enough to be casual in his talk. So different from the 'out with James's doing business' attitude.

"I do a little. Haven't played in a few years. You guys look like you know what you're doing." If I could find my stick. Generic sticks are a bitch.

"We've always talked about getting a table but were never in a place long enough to go through the trouble. I guess we'll be here for a while." Johnathan glanced at James. "So if we let you come in, you'll play?"

"I'll give it my best shot. Do you play ah…seriously or for fun?"

"Ahhh, Victoria, do we play for money or do we play to pass the time you ask? Well, I guess a little of both." Everyone laughed. "Bring your stick next time, you wouldn't want to use one of ours."

"If I can find it I will." Play began again. James led me across the entry to the Great Room. Fieldstone fireplace laid, not lit. Pieces of the stones had been hollowed out. Each hollowed space held a religious symbol. This is where I stopped.

Interesting, unexpected. Top left, a statue of Christ holding his hands out. Clockwise, next to it but a little lower a sweet jade Buddha reclining in death; a wooden Star of David; the complete OM in beautifully carved ivory; Crescent Moon with Star.

James moved up behind me, put his arms around me. A spark snapped, made me jump. "Each is a religion practiced in the house. Their positions are moved clockwise on the equinox. Everyone brings their own symbol and is free to change the symbol at any time, but cannot touch another's. We have had some interesting discussions as a result of the fireplace. You are free to add if you would like Victoria."

James turned me to the flat screen. "The sound is excellent. Every once in a while we will all end up watching a movie." I was turned again with a tightening hold. "This is where the girls play." A quarter of the west side of the room had a cute little pink plastic fence around it. Inside were all manner of doll houses, art boards, games, stuffed animals, dolls along the wall and two large wicker baskets, each with their name on it. "The toys always end up inside the fence when they are done playing. Another of Zara's rules. The library now."

We walked back across the entry hall his hand at my waist. James knocked on the closed double doors, waited, knocked again. Slowly opened one door a crack. "We are coming in." No response. He fully opened the door, stepped in, looked, turned to me. "Come in. No one is here." I stepped through the doorway. When I did, the noise of the cooking, the billiard game, everything was gone. Quiet, still.

The library was a real reading library. Center table with some newspapers opened, chairs pulled back, a couple of very worn, very large club chairs. One on each side of the large south window. Massive book cases on the east and west walls complete with sliding ladders. The bookcases were packed with books; old, new, leather bound, small, tall, some with dust covers. It was obvious that all had been opened, used, read multiple times.

James moved his arms around me, stepped closer, slid his hands under my sweater, chemise, skin to skin against my back. I shook. Maybe we should have stayed at the condo today. He leaned to my shoulder, started whispering.

"Fiction on the right, non-fiction on the left - subject, author. On the west wall, under the window are children's books." His hands slid under the waist band of my jeans, I shivered again. James straightened. "Are you cold?"

"No, not at all." I gave up my control, arms around his neck pulling him to me. His arms, hands moved freely; from shoulders, to waist. Held my waist. Lifted me up the front of his body. His heart was pounding.

It felt so good, being touched by James. The house, the land, the animals, nothing else mattered but this, here, now. My eyes closed. He moaned, released his control. Shit. A bell rang. I jumped. He startled.

"If we do not go, Zara will look for us." He didn't stop. "We need to go." He still didn't stop. I didn't want to. He lifted my sweater, moved his mouth to my breast, sucked, bit as hard as he could without damage. My hand moved down the front of his pants touching him. "Please Victoria." Whispered. My hand held more of him. The thrill was mine, his, the bell rang again. "Victoria, she will come looking for us. You have to stop. I cannot." His hand was moving down my stomach, the jeans were unzipped.

I took a very big breath, blew it out. He really wasn't going to stop...I didn't want to. I let him go. Removed my hand. Moved his out of my jeans.

Stepped back zipping. James closed his eyes; went still for the first time today. I tried to gather my composure…like that would work.

A knock at the door. James opened his eyes, big smile, very controlled. "Come." He held his hand for me to take. My face must have been screaming red. My first step was a stumble. "Zara, a moment." James looked at me, the blood fading from his eyes, The black remained full of light.

"My legs are shaking. Shit James. How can you do this to me?" No response. I released his hand, walked around the reading table. Better. "Ok. Let's do it." I took his hand again.

We walked slowly to the dining room doors. The table was full, place settings for all. Food everywhere. Open bottles of wine, glasses for those who would partake filled. Two seats empty, head of the table and the seat to the right. Think we were missed? James walked ahead of me, pulled the chair out for me. I did it. I started laughing, couldn't help it. As soon as I did, everyone did, including James. Too smooth. I was just too smooth.

"James, second bell and I will find you." Zara pointed a finger at him. The laughter started again.

"Zara, you would have regretted that." Zara smiled, almost laughed.

"James, after this morning, well, what can I say but thank you for our wonderful family, this wonderful home. To you my dear son we tip our glasses." Everyone who could drink did. Then Zara continued with a small, quiet prayer. When she said 'amen', the food started moving, the talking started to build, dishes clinked. There were three faces I didn't know. Not sitting together. One woman. Indian, eyes with light, very thin, beautiful. Absolutely beautiful. Age, maybe 30, maybe not. I couldn't tell. Padma. Once I found her it was easy to find her husband, Raam. Sitting, his height was implied, but said Northern Indian. I bet at least six foot with broad shoulders. Thinner than he should be.

I looked around the table. The Asra-pa were all very thin. Skin unused. If their eyes didn't give them away, their lack of…what…meat, would. Even Johnathan was gaunt. Five pounds over rib counting thin. I logged the realization away.

James leaned to me. "I will introduce you to Padma, Raam and Cat later." None of the Asra-pa were uncomfortable with the empty place settings. No one around them seemed to even notice. It was obvious they had been together for, probably, more years than I'd been around. This was their 'normal', outside was odd. I had to smile.

Charon sat next to me. Smiled. "It's so good to finally have you here

Victoria. Are you enjoying?" I said I was, complemented him on his performance and we started talking.

James was sitting next to Zara's husband Cat. They were laughing and talking. "You climbed the gate Victoria? Barefoot?" James looked at me. Charon stopped talking.

Johnathan started laughing. I smiled at him. "Yep. I didn't realize I was shoeless until I was at the top. It was faster to keep going."

Johnathan was laughing harder. "You know James, it's probably on one of the cameras. A little after dinner entertainment. Actually, you may be on the entry camera. Is the library covered?" What? Security cameras? Ah, rats.

"No, unfortunately it's not linked in yet. The other two we can pull, easily." Charon's number would come up if he pulls the tapes. Everyone at the table thought it would make fine after dinner entertainment. As I'd told James, first family meetings never went well for me.

The eating and talking continued for at least another hour. The food, half of which I couldn't identify, was four star, five if you include the delight of James's hand on my thigh, moving to my knee, thrumming back to the top of my thigh, rubbing, and playing. James didn't miss a beat of his conversations. I struggled to remember the topics of mine.

When it seemed that everyone had finished eating, James stood. He thanked Zara for the wonderful meal, thanked everyone for their help and love in all things and started to excuse himself, us.

"James." Johnathan was deadpan. "it will take Charon less than five minutes to pull the footage. Stay. I'm told it is quite interesting."

"Victoria and I will be in the library. Let us know when it is set up." James pulled my chair back as I stood.

I stretched to reach his ear. "Protocol, should I help Zara clean up?"

He leaned down to me, "No, Zara never cleans up. It will be done before morning. I believe Charon and Johnathan have the responsibility tonight." That was a bit of a surprise. "You will not help with these things unless I do." He was being too serious when I looked at him. "Victoria." He smiled just a little, shivered. We returned to the library, James latched the door.

"Are you angry?" I had to ask, he was so solemn. James looked at me, eyes brilliant red, only light, no black. Talk about a 'tell' out of the norm.

"No, not angry. Serious." I felt the same. In a blur his jeans were on the floor, mine were unzipped going to my ankles. I stepped out of them.

James held me. Lowered us to the floor. Entered me in one motion, as if we'd never been interrupted. We were both desperate in our movements. Incapable of touching enough, feeling enough. The wave built quickly, higher, longer without breaking. When it rolled over us we were looking down at ourselves engulfed in the sensations.

I closed my eyes, we were back in our bodies. James's nails in my back, my back was hot, getting hotter, fire - then it was gone. In my preprogrammed head I thought I knew what he wanted, what was happening. Knew what the problem was. He wouldn't. Not now. Not here.

We slowly let go of the feeling, let it drain from us. James began to pull himself out of me. The feeling started again. No control. He screamed. I held him to me, pulled him back into me. The heat of my back was fire. We both released as if we never had.

Someone knocked on the door. James stopped, closed his eyes, went completely still. The knocker retreated. His eyes opened. He looked to his hands. Pulled out of me. "Roll over Victoria." I did. Anything to relieve my back. He lifted my sweater, began softly licking the burning sensations. Relief. Instant relief followed his mouth.

"James, what you are doing…it feels so good." I couldn't help it. I stretched my arms and legs as far as they would go, then relaxed. Relaxed for the first time that day.

His head was next to mine. I was kissed. "I understand today. What has been wrong."

"Yes. Do you feel better? Should we go back out?"

"Yes, then upstairs."

"Yes, upstairs." I was starting to feel stoned, no other way to describe it. "I feel like I just had some very good smoke." Did he know what I meant?

"Just a few minutes. We will go upstairs. Can you do this Victoria?" James had lost his excitement, his fidgeting.

I laughed. "I'll definitely give it my best shot. That's all I can promise."

"I can not ask for more. Take my hand." James started laughing as he stood trying to recover his pants. His laugh started me laughing, which kept him laughing. We were both useless. "No. Your house, the little house Victoria."

James let go of me, sat on the floor. His spirits were moving - not just over his body but up to the ceiling; he was lit from the inside, he was beautiful. Completely without control.

I zipped my jeans, went to my knees, held him. My back flashed fire. Then it was gone. James started to slow his laughter, opened his eyes, looked into mine. I was lost. My heart, my soul broken with this? I couldn't think of a better way to go.

"James. Do you know how beautiful you are? How lovely you are to touch. To hold. I could stay this way, never move again and be happy, be satisfied in my heart?" He was looking at me, not moving, just still, just looking. His hand reached to me, pulled me down to his mouth.

"Victoria. Do you love me?"

"Yes, James, I love you." I answered without hesitation, without anxiety, without regret.

"Johnathan will move the others. Would you mind returning to your home. There are too many people here."

"No, I would like that. Will you make a fire?"

James smiled. "For you, yes." He sat up. Closed his eyes, went very still for more than a couple of minutes. His eyes opened. He finished buttoning his pants. "Johnathan will give us a ride, make our regrets to the others."

"Does he know what happened?"

"I showed him. He is worried, wondering if we are well, if we can stay in our bodies." James smiled at me.

I looked at my arms and legs. "I am, aren't I?" There was a fifty-fifty shot I wasn't.

"Yes. You have not seen your back, you have not seen mine since I returned." His smile got a little larger. I'd touched his back, run my hands over it, but seen? No.

"Turn." I lifted his sweater. "What is it? What happened?" Over all of the spirits on his back, running down his arms, under his pants was a bird in such detail I would expect it to fly away. "Do you know?"

"Yes, I know. I was born with it. As the other spirits came to me it faded until the spirit was nothing, a little tremble. I woke in Geneva feeling strong magic, more power. When Johnathan woke, he had a shimmer." There was a knock on the door, James unlocked it, Johnathan stepped in. James walked back to me. "Victoria, please turn around. I will not embarrass you." He lifted my sweater over my back, to my shoulders. The cool air felt good.

"James, what is it? Tell me. Johnathan's looking at it."

"The Phoenix on my back is on your back Victoria, just now. It came to you, down my fingers to you. Look at your belly."

Without even thinking about Johnathan, I lifted the front of my sweater. The roses on my thigh encircle my torso, linking with the tattoo on my breast. I remembered Johnathan.

"Oh." I pulled my sweater down. "Johnathan, sorry, I forgot you were there. James, can we go now?" I needed to go home, put my feet on solid, familiar territory.

The ride home was quiet, at least externally. James kept his hand under my sweater against my back. I kept my eyes closed. I knew James and Johnathan were talking. Johnathan was asking questions, James answering but in my head they were just impressions. "James, it's obvious she's allowed you in, but does she understand what has happened? Truly understand?"

"What James has told me, Yes." I answered. Silence. Startled.

"Victoria, you are listening to us?" James asked. I opened my eyes. He was smiling.

"Impressions, of course then Johnathan started talking." I said.

"No. He did not start talking. You focused."

To that I had nothing to say, no thought. Johnathan dropped us off, handed James something, told James that he was available if needed, left. James went to build the fire. I went to change into my sweats, look in a mirror. Holy Shit. The wings stopped at my wrists, its head at my neck, legs over my ass. The front looked like some tattoo artist had gone mad linking everything together. My left leg was the only unmarked limb I had. James joined me, looking. "And I thought licking my blood had satisfied you. What does this mean James?"

"We are joined." He looked tentative. "Yes, your blood returned my control. Giving the Phoenix to you gave me relief. Yesterday, today it was driving me. I did not know what the obsession was, what was driving me. This is new to me Victoria. The magic last week, the power took me a couple of days to get under control. Then I saw you on the beach. I could not get to you fast enough. This morning, for that I apologize. I woke at ten this morning. Never before that early. I could not wait to be here. To be with you. When you were talking to Johnathan in the billiard room all I could see, all I could feel was us together. Touching. Today has been completely out of control. It seemed that you felt it too. Driven to be with me."

I put on my sweats while he was talking. "The Phoenix coming to me? That was the problem? Since the beach. Every time you touched me yesterday, today it was all over for me. The more I tried to stop it, the more I couldn't." I walked over to him, put my arms under his sweater, let them run to his back, held him. "I'm not freaking out James. Just trying to understand."

"I have never shared a spirit. I did not know it was possible. The Phoenix. The beginning…and the end. Are you sure you are ok?" His hands pulled me tighter against him.

"Yes. I'm sure. Do you mind if I have a drink?"

"No, not at all. Why would you ask such a thing? Tonight I would join you if I could." We walked to the kitchen. I made my drink. Retrieved my emergency cigarettes, started to light, looked at James. "Go ahead. Then please hand it to me." I started laughing, he started laughing.

"Victoria, one of the things I love about you is that you are real. No faking, no lying, no games. You are true to your words when we first spoke." I took a puff, handed it to him. We walked back to the living room.

"Your family is wonderful James. Really. I had as great a time as was possible today." We sat on the floor in front of the fireplace. James returned the cigarette. "I can see why you feel safe with them. They feel incredibly comfortable and safe with you, with all of you. I didn't expect that."

"Whether they like it or not, they are our family now Victoria. Johnathan understands this. Understands what happened in the library. I believe he expected it to happen when the Phoenix reappeared on me, just not this soon. I was not paying attention. First time in many years I have been taken by surprise. No, you took me by surprise. I took steps but did not learn." He gave me a kiss, I kissed him back. "I understood that my drive to find you was my love for you, my desire to be complete with you. But now, I think it is more. Victoria, do you hear me? Are you listening?"

"James, I do. Every word. I need to step back a bit." I looked at the floor. "I need this to age, what has happened, been said. I do need a bit of my reality so I can process events. Does that make sense to you?" I looked at him hard. He had not a clue. "James, look at it." I put my hand on my head. "Go ahead. See that I heard everything you said. I understood every word. But you need to see, feel my response."

"You will allow me in?"

"Yes, because I can't explain it. You need to understand. This is how it works for me. Just do it." If we were going to move forward, this, how I process, come to understandings, make decisions, he needed to know. I have had more fights with significant others when I don't instantly respond to something. Instantly have an opinion about something. I didn't want that with James, not worth the misunderstanding, the perception of indifference.

"Sit in front of me." He pulled me against him in the V. I felt...what?... movement just under my skin, almost like feathers ruffling. "Victoria, did you feel that?"

"Yes. Now my back itches. Thanks."

"No, I did nothing. That was you." He ran his hands under my sweatshirt, flat, rubbing. "Better?"

"Oh, much, thanks. Please James, just look." His arms went around me, held me close. My arms on his holding him to me. We touched as before, then still. I felt the touch inside, all over. He was seeing, looking, feeling how I saw what had just happened. He took his time, no rush. I felt the touch ease, withdraw.

Then, in my ear. "Thank you. Yes, I do see what you mean...how you come to understandings, process implications. Interesting." He relaxed his body again with a little chuckle. "Good idea Victoria."

I laughed. "Rub my back again please. Will this itch go away?"

"Yes. Just settling in." His hands on my back, down my arms inside the sweatshirt sleeves was the most wonderful back scratch ever. "Johnathan gave me a copy of the security footage. Would you like to see it?" He was still rubbing my back.

"I forgot to ask Johnathan about the plans." Something to distract my desire to attack him, one desire satisfied leads to another.

"It is on your desk. He said he could not find a problem."

"He gave you the security tapes. What a riot. You know, without a crowd, it could be fun. I'm game." I did want to see it.

"Good. Bring your drink." James held his arm down to me when he stood.

I did grab my drink, James fed the fire. I went into the bedroom, clicked on the TV, the DVD player, was it on DVD? Hope so, no tape player.

Billy's pen and ink sat against the wall on the floor. I hadn't looked at it since I'd put it there. I sat on the edge of the bed trying to visualize it on one of my walls. The more I looked at it, the more familiar the people were, the setting, the Plains.

It occurred to me that if I was standing there now I could walk to the village. I knew James spent time over the south ridge of the hills; said the ridge captured the magic of the land. I knew James had an open lodge at the bottom of the ridge. I had seen Billy on the east hill watching us.

James hadn't see him. I'd walked part way with him, he was leaving for some time.

James's hand on my shoulder pulled me back to the bedroom. "You know the picture, the place?"

"Yes. You were leaving. I was sad, very sad." I felt it. "I warned you didn't I?" I looked over my shoulder at him.

"You did. Would you like me to take the drawing with me?"

"No, I don't think so, no. I need it here." I looked at the recording still in his hand. "Oh good, DVD. Can you put it in?" I patted his hand, stood. "I'll be right back." I walked out to the living room, then out to the patio.

This is real, everything he said was real. What he was, what he is, the magic, power, the stories, the Wheel, all of it, real. When I hadn't run I knew I was in for a good ride. The ride was here, now, starting in earnest. How do I integrate it into my life? No… it's the other way around…how do the other things integrate into this? Yeah, better. How do I go back into what had been my reality? Then it hit me. I do nothing, let one flow into the other and it will be fine, just fine. I'll do my end, the rest of the world will do its part. I started feeling better, much better.

I walked back into the house. James was laughing. I couldn't help but wonder what the inside of his head was like. He was in both worlds so smoothly, easily, second nature. I returned to the bedroom.

"As funny as billed?" I asked sitting next to him. He looked at me.

"Are you good Victoria?"

"You know, I think I'll be fine." I smiled at him, kissed him. "So… funny?"

He started the recording again. Just the entry hall, a small blur out of one corner of the screen. James dropped dead weight to the marble floor. Shirt in one hand, no movement. I started to snicker.

Blank screen, then picture. James had not moved. Zara came running down the staircase tying her robe. It looked as though she was yelling, not happy. Her daughters came down the stairs; then Edmond. Cat entered the front door. Zara bent to check James. The men talked. Cat answered his phone. The girls talked. Zara walked out of frame, then back in with a blanket. Covered James.

Villiam walked into the screen, started laughing. Zara seemed to be speaking strongly. Villiam was shaking his head. Zara went back up the staircase. Everyone else was still talking. Zara returned with a large blanket and pillow. The men lifted James; there was no resistance to him, no muscle tension. James looked dead.

Zara laid the blanket on the floor with the pillow. The men laid him on it, made sure his head was appropriately on the pillow. Zara made adjustments then wrapped him in the floor blanket, covered him with the other. Zara stood there for a few minutes just looking at James; leaned down, gave him a kiss on the cheek, moved the hair away from his face. She turned, went back up the stairs. Zara was followed by all except Villiam who exited in the direction he had come. Screen went blank.

"James, that was sweet." James was shaking his head with a big smile. The screen filled with a picture angle from a tree looking at the gate and up the driveway to the house. My car stopped less than a foot from the gate. I got out, stood looking at the gate, then to the hood of the car, back to the gate. I slid my butt onto the hood, stood up. I grabbed the gate, held the top of it. Walked my feet up to a cross bar. Gingerly stepped over the gates' points. Other foot on the crossbar. Swung the outside leg over, walked myself down to the ground and started running.

A small car entered from the top of the screen and stopped next to me. I pointed at the house. Put both hands on the roof of the car leaning over to talk; turning my head to the house, back to the inside of the car. I stood straight. Stepped back from the car, waved at the car, started walking back to the gate. I stopped; looked up and down the gate. Villiam got out of the car, flipped through his keys, opened the gate. I said something to him, got in my car and left. By the time the scene ended, James was on his back laughing.

"Now, that's not very nice. I was busting my ass to find you. There you were all cuddled up, little pillow under your head." I was laughing too. It was very funny.

"Villiam told me that Zara wanted to get me into my bed. She kept telling them all to just carry me upstairs, it was not a problem. They kept telling her to pick me up if she thought it was so easy to carry a dead body up a flight of stairs without dropping it. Zara told them that I would get cold on the floor. They kept telling her I was about to get as cold as it was possible to get. She apparently threatened to sleep on the floor with me. The compromise was the blankets and a pillow. You did scare the heck out of Villiam. It is very funny." James pulled me flat on the bed, leaned over me. I was still laughing.

"I have no memory of climbing the hood of my car. No memory of thinking about anything."

"Back rub?" He asked.

"Oh, that would be wonderful." I rolled over, pulled my sweatshirt up to my arms. James pushed it over my head, off my arms. He lay on my back. His heart beating, his clothes gone. His head between my shoulder blades. Just lying there, the itching started to fade. He kissed my back. Ran his hands up my arms stretching them as far up and out as they would go. Laced his fingers into mine. Stretched me a little more. His arms followed mine, over my shoulders. His head now at the bottom of my neck. His chest against my back touching me completely to the sweatpants. His weight followed my body over my butt, his legs on my legs. He stretched again taking me with him.

James lifted his head. "Victoria, the pants have got to go. I can not make it stop itching without real contact." James lifted himself off of me.

"What are you trying to do?" A question of curiosity, not concern.

"Maybe I can settle the spirit so it will not be so uncomfortable for you." My sweats, underwear were gone. He returned to my back, stretching both of us as far as I could go, maybe a little further. James settled himself in almost a flutter. He kissed my shoulders. Gently rubbed his face over the face of the bird; murmured, settled himself again.

The skin on my back responded to his movements, the murmurs. I relaxed into him when I didn't think I could relax anymore. I stretched when I didn't think I could stretch anymore. I felt a full flutter from my wrists to the top of my legs. The discomfort was gone, the relief was tremendous. Finally, I relaxed. James moved to my ear. "Better?"

"Yes, much. Keep going." His hands released mine. He stretched over me to his full length moving so that his head was next to mine, looking at me. I smiled. James kissed me. Moved his hands up my arms, down my sides. He lifted, kissing the back of my neck, down to the small of my back, slid his hands under me. Lifted with one arm, the other sliding between my legs. Touching, feeling everything about me.

A finger slid into me. I gasped. Another, I held my breath, grabbed the sheets. His fingers moving, knowing exactly where to go. My breath released a loud moan.

I pushed back against him. James moaned, tightened his arm around me, he added a third. I gripped his hand as hard as I could. It was there, the orgasm was building. James fed it, he knew it. His fingers moved against the spot. He held me tighter against his chest, sent me over the top contracting my muscles around his fingers. My breath stopped. The wave crashed. I screamed into the bed. His fingers slowed.

I started to relax. His fingers returned to the spot. The wave without building - crashed again.

Both hands lifted me to my knees. James went to his knees behind me. Pulled back, lifted me on to him. My legs were shaking. I tilted forward. He pulled me back, started moving slowly. I looked down my body watching him push into me, pull out slowly, almost completely; hesitate, back into me. I reached down, touched him.

James moaned deeply; pulled me back against his chest. Tightened his hold, trying to tease. My finger followed him into me. He moved faster. Held me so I couldn't move away. Each thrust deeper, longer, heavier than before. I matched him until I felt the last, the deepest, the heat, release.

I sat back against him. He screamed. I spasmed against his arms around my chest. I shifted weight right, left. lifted up until I could feel his end, pushed back. James screamed again. We came again. Fell forward to the bed, stretched again. James stayed in me, started to laugh. "Victoria, I cannot move." I couldn't say anything. I closed my eyes, drifted. No thoughts. Just James, his weight, his heart slowing. Time passed before I felt him move.

"Do you want to stay?" I mumbled. "It's inevitable."

James rolled to the side of the bed. "Are you sure? I will not upset you?"

"No." I opened my eyes to see his face. He was hesitant. I smiled. "Why not?"

"I am going to die Victoria."

"Again I ask, why not?"

"Another blanket?" he asked.

I rolled off the other side of the bed. Went to the dressing room, pulled a blanket off the shelf. Grabbed myself a clean tee. I returned to find James sitting still on the side of the bed. His eyes opened slowly. I handed him the blanket. He wrapped himself. I got back in bed.

"Come on. I'll be fine. We we'll both be fine. The house alarm is set." James slowly laid on his back. I put my arm around his chest, kissed him, started to drift. I felt him shudder with a deep sound. I felt the talisman buzz. James was gone. I was not.

Epilogue

Holy shit! What was I doing?